Maisie's
RECKONING

BY MARY ANN KERR

THINK
WELL
BOOKS

thinkwellbooks.com

Maisie's Reckoning

Published in part by Thinkwell Books, Portland, Oregon.
The views or opinions of the author are not necessarily those
of Thinkwell Books. Learn more at *thinkwellbooks.com*.

Design and cover illustration by Andrew Morgan Kerr
Learn more at andrewmorgankerr.com.

Published and printed in the United States of America
ISBN: 978-0-9984894-5-2
Fiction, Historical, Christian

BOOKS BY MARY ANN KERR

A WOMAN OF ENTITLEMENT SERIES:

Book One
LIBERTY'S INHERITANCE

Book Two
LIBERTY'S LAND

Book Three
LIBERTY'S HERITAGE

CAITLIN'S FIRE

TORY'S FATHER

EDEN'S PORTION

CADY'S LEGACY

ANNE'S WEDDING BARGAIN

MAGGIE'S REDEMPTION

RAPHAELA'S REPRIEVE

ELIDA'S UNVEILING

MAISIE'S RECKONING

DEDICATION

I dedicate this book by blessing the King of the Universe.
Holy, Holy, Holy is the Lord God Almighty,
Who was, Who is, and Who is to come!

I also dedicate this book to Jim and Twyla Vimont
friends who do much to further the kingdom of God.

ACKNOWLEDGMENTS

DEAR READERS, FINISHING THIS BOOK took a long time! I don't know if I'm running out of ideas, and I need to stop writing, or if it's time to begin a different series. I know my fans love the characters in all the Liberty books, as do I.

All my books have no outline to begin with nor do I know from day to day what's going to happen. As I said before, I write by the seat of my pants, which is an actual writing style. I was nearly finished with this story before I knew who the shooter was!

Maisie's Reckoning harks back to my fourth book, *Caitlin's Fire*. It takes place in Santa Rosa, California in Sonoma County. Matthew and Liberty Bannister travel north to Sonoma for a vacation only to find Caitlin's brother-in-law has been shot. Thus begins another story!

I thank Andrew Kerr, my youngest son, who is an awesome and talented graphic designer, for the beautiful cover he has produced. It's an eye-catcher, as always.

I want to thank my fans who enjoy reading my stories and encourage me to keep writing. Too numerous to mention, thank you for your letters, messages, and e-mails.

May God's presence in your lives fill you with incomparable joy and peace. May you let that love flow through you like a conduit to others, that they may see your good works and glorify your Father in heaven.

Love you all!

mak

List of Characters

Gavin Galway & Maisie Galway. . . . . Owners of store and mine
Caitlin Bannister. . . . . Sister of Maisie Galway
Kirk Bannister. . . . . Caitlin's husband
Mrs. Dunstan (Duney). . . . . Bannisters' cook
Mrs. McDuffy.(Duffy) . . . . .Bannisters' housekeeper
Jonathan Bannister . . . . .Kirk and Caitlin's son
Aidan Hart . . . . .Sister of Maisie Galway
Jared Hart . . . . .Aidan's husband
Doc-Dr. Micah Addison . . . . .Doctor for Santa Rosa
Zebidiah Pindar . . . . Miner at Galways'
Lindsey May Pindar . . . . Wife of Zebidiah
Mini Louise Pindar. . . . . .Daughter of Pindars
Saidy, Lettie Lynn,Jedidiah, Micah . . . . .Pindar Children
Sarah Sue, Jemimah, and Baby Jamie. . . . . .Pindar Children
Jonah Whatcom. . . . . .Miner at Galways'
Cynthia Whatcom (Cindy Sue). .Jonah's wife
Paige and Payton McGrath. . . . . .Doc Addison's receptionists
Martha McGrath. . . . . .Mother of Paige and Payton
Abel McGrath. . . . . .deceased husband of Martha
Marie DuBois. . . . . .Doc Addison's cook
Dr. Oliver Sandhurst .Doc Addison's replacement
Marnie Marie Sandhurst . . . . Oliver's daughter
Corine Marie Sandhurst nee Bloomingdale . . . . Deceased wife of Oliver
Deidra Jennings (Deedee). . . . . Oliver's servant
Ezra Walker . . . . Santa Rosa's new sheriff
Ewen Carr . . . . Foreman for McCaully-Bannisters' Ranch
Colton Broderick Danbury. . . . . Friend of Oliver Sandhurst
Jean Danbury . . . . Colton's deceased sister
Roy and Alfred . . . . Stretcher bearers
April and May Lister. . . . . .Residents of Santa Rosa
Lorenzo Brown . . . . .Foreman for Galway's mine
Jasper Clemmons . . . . .Under foreman for Galway's mine
Denny Watson. . . . . Jasper Clemmons servant
Jude . . . . .Small injuries doctor at the mine
Ernest Smith . . . . .Overseer at the mine
Sandoval Peabody (Sandy) . . . . Overseer at the mine

TRANSPARENT

Think about an unpolished stone,
There's much beneath the surface.
We need the Father's loving hand
To guide us toward His purpose.

Whenever we walk by ourselves
We cannot truly see,
What lies beneath the surface
Must come out to make us free.

We conceal the hurts that batter us,
We stuff them deep inside.
We smile and nod and never know
To others we have lied.

Transparent in this walk of life
The experiences that we bear,
We're not to hide them from the world
They're there for us to share.

The things that we experience,
The things that help us grow,
Are meant to for us to give away
Not meant to bring us low.

God polishes every one of us,
His goal to make us shine.
The trials become as blessings
When He says, "Child you are mine."

MAK

PROLOGUE

The gold and the crystal cannot equal it:
and the exchange of it shall not be for jewels of fine gold.

JOB 28:17

IT WAS ONLY THE BEGINNING OF MAY, but the temperature was sizzling. The sun had reached its zenith several hours before but still shone brightly. The heat of it seeped under the door of the shop. Rays filtered their way into the room, peeking through the lacy curtains, spilling across the floor, and glancing off the polished oak. It fingered its way up the side of the counter and onto its smooth marble top.

Gavin Galway was closing up shop. He mopped his forehead with a pristine white handkerchief. He felt sluggish and overly tired, but he'd had a great day selling gems. Business at their other store in San Francisco was booming. A year earlier he, along with his wife, Maisie, had opened an additional store in their own hometown. Opening a store in Santa Rosa had been a nerve-racking adventure, causing much stress. After hours and hours spent getting the store ready and trying to market and build a clientele, Gavin had been relieved that the store was holding its own. It was not yet yielding much gain, but business was beginning to pick up. Gavin was happy that on this day they'd made a whopping profit.

He wiped his forehead and face, muttering to himself. "I never sweat. I don't know why I'm dripping." He rubbed the length of his left arm and shook it because it seemed to tingle and had lately begun to ache like a toothache.

Maisie had left the store a half hour earlier. She was feeling the heat and had left before closing time. She usually stayed until Gavin was ready to leave, but she was expecting their first child, and the hours spent on her feet caused them to swell. By the end of the day she felt worn out.

Gavin, too, was exhausted. He'd felt extremely tired the last few days but hadn't said anything to Maisie, not wanting her to work any extra time to help him. He felt his shoulders sag after she left, and his left arm felt strange as if it was being squeezed. He shook his head as a foggy sense of unreality came over him. He felt uncomfortable and felt sweat running down his chest. "Even in hot temperatures I seldom sweat." He again wiped his face as he glanced up at the regulator clock, wishing he could go home. He was enervated but stayed at the shop, needing to count out the day's profit and have a good look at the new gemstones.

Zebidiah Pindar and Jonah Whatcom, two of Gavin's trustworthy workers at the mine, had brought the stones in before Maisie went home. Gavin had been busy with a customer so had only taken a cursory look at the gems before putting them under the counter.

He always had workers from the mine come in twos when carrying the stones for protection as well as to keep the employees honest.

Gavin pulled the blinds of the large windows on either side of the front door and another small blind that covered the window built into the top of the shop door. Spreading out a black velvet cloth on the marble topped counter, he reached under it for the box of new gems. He poured the new, unpolished gemstones onto it. They didn't sparkle like polished stones, but he was pleased with them, and several were quite large. He held each one up, looking at them through a magnifying glass, before putting them into a soft leather bag. Spinning the dial on the safe, he stopped and carefully positioned the dial on the safe to the correct numbers. Clockwise around to number one, counterclockwise past four and around again to number four, and then clockwise again to three. He pulled open the weighty door, placing the bag onto the top shelf. Slamming the heavy door shut, he spun the dial, folded up the velvet cloth, and placed it back under the counter.

He took the greenbacks out of the till and spread out the money he'd made that day. He felt elated, as it had been their best day yet for sales. Before he counted the entire lot, he stacked the bills on the counter in piles of like denominations.

The bell over the door tinkled, announcing someone entering. He looked up, startled, as he realized Maisie had not locked it when she left.

Total shock spread through him, and he felt his limbs grow heavy with dread, as he saw a bright red kerchief obscuring all but the gunman's eyes. He was shorter than Gavin, and his hat was pulled low over his brow. His hand held a gun, already cocked, pointed straight at him by a steady hand.

"Get your hands in the air! Get them up, I said!" The man waved the gun at the counter. "Give me the money and the gems!"

Gavin held up his hands in a gesture of submission. "Sold out," he said, "but here's the money." He felt the pain in his left arm increase. Dizziness engulfed him, and his breath came out in a short gasp. His heart thumped hard but erratically, and he couldn't hear. He felt a squeezing as if a metal band tightened, circling his chest. Pain radiated out, spreading up into his jaw and down his left arm. It was a vise getting tighter and tighter as the air escaped his lungs and throat, and although he tried to draw in air, none seemed to enter.

The man leveled his gun and said, "I want the raw gems in the safe! Now!" His voice sounded husky, as if he were trying to disguise it.

Gavin shook his head to clear the lightheadedness, but the gunman took it as a negative and aimed for Gavin's heart. Gavin heard the report of the gun as if through a long tunnel. Excruciating pain filled him as he collapsed onto the floor.

CHAPTER 1

Trust in the Lord with all thine heart;
and lean not unto thine own understanding.
In all thy ways acknowledge him,
and he shall direct thy paths.

PROVERBS 3:5-6

CAITLIN HAD BROUGHT A TREAT for her sisters. Her cook, Duney, at the Bannister-McCaully Ranch, had prepared it specially for the McCaully women. Aiden and Caitlin along with Maisie sat at the kitchen table nibbling on the oatmeal-raisin cookies and drinking cold tea. They were sisters, but in years past had not had a close relationship. In the last couple of years, they had become fast friends. The three were talking and reminiscing about past events. A chuckle or giggle would escape someone's lips. Sometimes, the three would laugh until the tears came in remembrance of some of the funny episodes from their childhood.

"Everyone I know says we look alike, but I don't think we do. Just yesterday, Mrs. Barber told me she gets us mixed up and wanted me to tell her which girl I am," Maisie chuckled. "I don't think we look that much alike."

"I get the same comment. I wouldn't mind looking like either of you, but I don't think we look alike either." Aidan thought both her sisters beautiful, not realizing she was just as lovely.

"Well I do," Caitlin said. "If you got rid of the hair color and eye color, we would all look alike."

"I reckon that's a good observation, Caitlin," Maisie agreed. "Me with my black hair and not a bit of red in it and hazel eyes, and you, Aidan, with your black hair awash with red highlights and sapphire blue eyes, and then you, Caitlin with auburn hair and pure gray eyes, it's a wonder anyone thinks we look alike. I think it's because of our bone structure and the way Da made us stand tall with shoulders back that we look alike. We're also about the same height." She munched on a cookie as she perused her sisters' faces.

Paige McGrath, without knocking, walked straight into Maisie's house. "Hello! Is anyone home?" Her voice sounded breathless.

"We're in the kitchen. Come on in," Maisie yelled.

Paige, Dr. Addison's receptionist, ran to the kitchen and said, "Come quick, Maisie! Gavin's been shot. We don't know what all happened, but Doc has him in surgery right now. He was in a bad way when Kirk brought him in."

Maisie blanched at her words and stood too quickly. She was in her fifth month of pregnancy, and a wave of dizziness caused her to grab for the back of her chair. "Let's go!" she exclaimed.

Aidan took Maisie by the arm, the women hurrying out the door, and Paige slammed it shut behind them. They hastened down the walk to the front gate. Caitlin reached it first, and opened it but didn't wait for the others. She was wearing a circumspect split skirt rather than her customary denims and ran for her stallion, Fire. "Maisie!" she called out, "come on! Get up here behind me! You can't go running down the street pregnant!" She climbed onto Fire and held out her hand to help Maisie.

"Fire won't let me, will he?"

"Yes, if I'm on him, he will. Now come on!"

Aidan laced her fingers together, and Maisie stepped into her hand and was hoisted up. Maisie, feeling awkward, stretched to reach around Caitlin's middle, and the two went down the street at a smart clip, arriving in front of Dr. Addison's office before the others.

Paige and Aidan picked up their skirts and ran down the dusty street, not caring that a few people stared.

Maisie entered Dr. Addison's office, but Caitlin waited at the front door, praying under her breath as she stood there. "Lord, I first of all want to thank You that Gavin wasn't killed outright. I pray You would spare him, Father. Maisie's baby needs a daddy, and Gavin is a wonderful husband. I pray that this event will bring Gavin and Maisie to a saving knowledge of You. Being good people isn't enough. They need a personal relationship with You. Please hear my prayer and see fit to heal Gavin. Thank You, Father, for what You will do in their lives. As Your Word says, 'What Satan meant for evil, You can turn to good'. I praise Your name. Amen."

Paige and Aidan arrived, both gasping for breath, and the three of them entered Dr. Addison's office.

Maisie was standing there, wondering if she could go into the room where Dr. Addison was working on her husband. She raised her eyebrows in a questioning look at Paige.

"I think you ought to wait, Maisie. You wouldn't want to distract Dr. Addison while he operates. I can tell you what I know about it."

"Please do," Maisie said, near tears, her voice breaking.

"Your Kirk," she nodded at Caitlin, "was next door from Galway's Gems. He was in the bank and heard the gunshot. He told the clerk he'd be right back and ran outside in time to see someone jump on their horse. He said he was not paying much attention to whoever it was, because when he heard the shot, he knew someone in the gem store probably needed help." Paige swallowed and continued her story.

"He ran into your shop, Maisie, and saw Gavin on the floor. He slung Gavin over his shoulder and carried him all the way here by himself."

"Kirk came into town with me," Caitlin added. "He had several things he needed to do. Luckily, one of them was to go to the bank. His timing couldn't have been better. I'd say it was one of those God's perfect timing things, Aidan, that you and I keep talking about. It's hard to believe he could carry Gavin by himself."

Aidan nodded her agreement, but Maisie said, "If God's timing was so perfect, maybe Gavin wouldn't have been shot." She gasped and put her hand to her mouth. "Oh my goodness! I just remembered! I—I forgot to lock the door! It—it's my fault he was shot." She began to cry.

Maisie, whose father had not tolerated tears, was raised to be stoic in difficult situations, but tears ran down her cheeks which embarrassed her, but she couldn't stop weeping.

Caitlin, put her arm around Maisie and gave a tight squeeze. "I know Da didn't allow us to cry, but he was wrong. Tears are part of our expression of sorrow and sometimes laughter. I know it's no good saying relax, Maisie, but please know we'll help in any way we can."

Maisie nodded as she wiped her eyes and blew her nose. "Thank you. I thank all of you."

"It's not your fault someone has done this evil deed," Aidan said, "but you must know it's also not God's fault that someone shot Gavin either. We have free will, we're not God's puppets."

Caitlin nodded her head. "Remember that fake priest, Father O'Flannagan who shot and killed our ranch hand, Drew? Drew was a Christian. Do you think it was God's fault Drew was killed? No! It wasn't. Man was created to worship and enjoy God forever, but we are a long way from what we were created for, aren't we? I'll stop preaching, but Maisie, please know this. God loves Gavin more than you do. Now I'll shut up."

"I agree with what you said, Cait, completely," Aidan said. "God does love Gavin with a pure and unadulterated love. I'm wondering… where is Kirk now?"

"He went back to the bank. They were closing when Kirk was doing his business, so I don't know if he finished what he went there to do or not." Paige heaved a sigh finished with her story.

"It's possible he went to our new sheriff's office to have a chat," Aidan said. "That seems the most likely thing he'd do."

Paige nodded her agreement but asked, "Can we pray? I know, Maisie, you're not a believer, but the rest of us are. I'd like us to pray for Dr. Addison for wisdom to know what to do and for Gavin to recover."

"That's fine with me," Maisie said.

"Let's pray," Paige said. "Father, You are a God of wondrous miracles. You are compassionate and worthy of our praise. Right now we have a huge request. Your Word says where two or three are gathered together, You are there in the midst of them. You are here, and we ask You to please bring healing to Gavin's body. Please don't let him die. Father, we know there are many wicked people in this world, and You've given us free will to choose to do good or to choose to do evil. We pray whoever committed this crime would be caught, but more, that this person would repent of their sin, and accept Your son as their Savior. Father, we pray

You would calm Maisie. Bless her with peace, and we pray all will be well with this baby. We humbly ask these things in the name of Jesus. Amen."

Maisie looked at the other women and wondered at their aura of peacefulness. She felt her stomach was a tangled mess of anxiety. She felt the baby kick and wondered how much the unborn babe could feel the tension consuming her. She took a deep breath and said, "Thank you, Paige. That was beautiful. Ah…do you have any idea how long Dr. Addison will…ah…"

The door opened to the waiting room, and Kirk strode in sweeping Maisie into his arms. "I'm sorry, Maisie. I don't know how bad he is, but Dr. Addison began working on him right away."

"Do you know what happened?"

"No, I was in the bank and heard a gunshot. I left the money I was to deposit on the counter and ran out the door in time to see someone galloping off down the street. I would have followed, but I thought I'd better check on Gavin first. I'm glad I did."

"I'm glad you did, too." Maisie said.

"Why don't you sit a spell?" Kirk asked. "I'll go get the sheriff while you wait to see what Dr. Addison has to say."

"Listen to me, young lady! We are leaving on that train first thing in the morning. If you're not ready…well then, you'll just have to leave your things behind, but you will be on that train!"

Tears stood out in Marnie's eyes. "I don't want to go Papa! We're leaving Mama in a grave I'll never be able to visit again. I wouldn't mind going if we could take her casket with us."

"I'm sorry sweetheart." He scooped Marnie into his arms and sat down on the edge of her bed, laying his head on the top of hers. " I think you know, as well as I do, that isn't possible."

Marnie wasn't the only one mourning. Dr. Oliver Sandhurst still mourned his wife of eight years. She'd been ill for a very short time before she died, and it had devastated Oliver that he hadn't been able to help her. The funeral had been nearly two years earlier but Corine was still sorely missed by her husband and daughter.

Corine Marie Sandhurst nee Bloomingdale had been his first and only love. They had met at the World's Fair in Philadelphia in 1876. It had been a case of love at first sight. They were married within six months of meeting. Less than a year later, Marnie had been born and a year later a son, who'd died within weeks of his birth. There had been no more children.

Oliver squeezed Marnie in a tight bear hug. At ten years old she had a wisdom beyond her years. *She's like her mother*, he thought.

"As you know, Dr. Addison, in Napa, California, is retiring. He has been a lifelong friend and asked that I come replace him. He was one of my professors at Massachusetts General which is a teaching arm of Harvard. I have long admired Dr. Addison, and we have kept in touch over the years." He exhaled a deep sigh.

"These past two years have been extremely difficult for me, Marnie. Everywhere I go causes me grief, because I think of the things we have done as a family. I am constantly reminded of my deep loss, and I feel my grief will never heal unless I have a change of venue." He sighed again, gave Marnie another squeeze, and set her on her feet. "Now, please get the rest of your things gathered up. Deedee told me you're almost ready."

"I *am* almost ready, Papa. I'm thankful that Deedee is going with us. I couldn't bear it if she wasn't."

"I know, pet. She's been a tower of strength the past couple of years for both of us. She adored your mother, and she's helped me over the most difficult time of my life. In truth, if she hadn't chosen to come with us, I'd probably have turned Dr. Addison down."

"I love you, Papa!" Marnie threw her arms around her father's neck, hugging him tightly. She skipped off to her room to finish packing.

Deidra Jennings, Deedee, to those who were close to her, thought about the trip she would soon be undertaking. All she had ever known was life here in Boston. Her parents had immigrated from Ireland with the last name of Mac Sheoinin. They had changed the last name to Jennings, the anglicized version of Mac Sheoinin. She'd been an only child, and had no relatives living in the United States as far as she knew. Dr. Oliver Sandhurst and his daughter, Marnie, were the closest thing she had to family. Deedee had adored Mrs. Sandhurst and though she'd tried to be a source of comfort for Marnie and her father, neither knew of the nights she lay abed crying for the loss of Corine. Deedee would have gone to the ends of the earth to stay with the Sandhursts.

Oliver headed for the kitchen where he knew he'd find Deedee. He could smell lunch cooking in the oven, but Deedee wasn't in the kitchen. He retraced his steps and gained the top of the stairs taking them two at a time. As he strode down the hall, he saw Deedee coming out of Marnie's room.

"She's all packed, sir."

"Thank you, Deedee. I cannot express my appreciation enough for all you do. If you weren't coming with us, we wouldn't be going at all."

"Pshaw! It's not only my duty, it's my pleasure. You are my family, Dr. Oliver. Marnie is like a granddaughter to me. I should be thanking you that you want to take me with you. When alls said and done, we're about to embark on quite an adventure, and I'm looking forward to it!" Her greenish-hazel eyes sparkled with anticipation.

Oliver's face took on an expression of surprise at her comment.

"Frankly, I never thought of it that way. I've only thought of it in terms of escape. But you're right, it will be quite an adventure, I'm sure."

Matthew Bannister strode to the bedroom. "Are you all packed and ready to go, sweetheart?"

"I think so," Liberty replied. "Since Cady took the twins to San Rafael yesterday, I didn't have much to do except pack for me. I love those two toddlers with all my heart, but they are a lot of work. I'm looking forward to a two whole weeks on holiday with you. And, by the way, I appreciate that you pack your own clothes."

"I am quite capable of packing my own things, but I agree, it will be nice not to have any responsibilities for a couple weeks. We will be getting quite a break. Kirk and Caitlin will most likely be disappointed we didn't bring the little ones with us, but as you know, Susannah's been begging for them to come down to San Rafael. I hope she knows what she's getting into having two toddlers in that mansion of hers."

Liberty strolled over and entwined her arms around Matthew's neck. "Just think, this is going to be like a second honeymoon. Two whole weeks and neither of us will have to lift a finger! Do you think we'll be bored to death?"

Matthew kissed her soundly before he responded. "No, Kirk and Caitlin have a few plans for us. It's the reason we're not taking the buggy. I'm riding Piggypie, and you're on Pookie. I guess we're going to be doing some range riding and sleeping out under the stars."

"Well, thank you for letting me know, Mr. Bannister!" She spoke with a smile in her voice, but she was grateful he'd spoken before they headed out. She pulled some warmer clothing out of the clothespress, bundling them up to fit into her already bulging satchel. The weather was warm, but the nights were still cool.

"I've never in my life slept outside. I will look forward to it. Do you have bedrolls for us?"

"I do." Matthew replied. His eyes darkened with love as he looked at Liberty and grinned. She had on a black split skirt, her long leather boots, a white blouse, open at the neck and tucked into the skirt, with a belt cinched around her incredibly small waist. A holster belt, strapped about her hips, completed her outfit. She was a beautiful, spirited woman, and he thanked the Lord daily, grateful He'd brought Liberty into his life.

Both Liberty and Matthew had been married before—but unhappily. Those marriage partners were now deceased. The two never dreamed marriage could be so fun. They took joy in each other and were careful to keep their relationship clear of any discord. They didn't do everything together. Each had their own tasks and interests, but they shared an intimate relationship with God, keeping Him the center of all they did. Their home was a place of peace and harmony.

"Are you ready?"

Liberty grinned. "Are you?"

He grabbed Liberty and planted a kiss on her soft lips. "I love you!" He held her shoulders, pulling back his head to stare into her incredible green eyes that were full of warmth. He kissed her again and said, "Let's be on our way."

Liberty picked up her heavy satchel, but Matthew took it from her. "I'll carry that."

"Thank you, Matthew. I think one of the reasons I was first attracted to you is because you are a true gentleman. A lot of men are not, but you are. I appreciate you making life easier for me by your thoughtfulness." She pointed to her satchel. "That's an example."

"You are welcome. You inspire me to find ways to please you. You are quite capable on your own, but you allow me those small pleasures of helping you." He spoke lightly, but his deep blue eyes gleamed with love.

CHAPTER II

Be kindly affectioned one to another with brotherly love;
in honour preferring one another.

ROMANS 12:10

"**BEFORE WE SET OUT, I HAVE A** question for you," Liberty said. "It's just something I do and want to know if you do it too."

Matthew looked at her with questioning eyes.

"Where does your mind go when you don't have to think about anything else?"

Matthew's face was thoughtful for a minute. He sat down on the side of the bed as he reflected. He looked up at her and said, "I reckon it gets to worrying and thinking about all that needs doing."

Liberty nodded. "I used to worry overmuch. Now, whenever I start to worry or fret about something, I pull myself up short. I drop my heart into communing with God. There is a sweetness that comes to me instead of the conflict or worry that I used to entertain in my mind. I can do it anywhere at any time. I can't begin to express what it has done for me and my relationship with God." She smiled and continued to talk

"It's a bit like John Oxenham's poem," she quoted:

> 'A little place of mystic grace
> Of sin and self swept bare
> Where I may look into Thy face
> And talk with Thee in prayer.'

"That little poem expresses exactly what I mean," Liberty said.

Matthew swept her into his arms, holding her close. He whispered into her ear. "I love you! Thank you for sharing that with me. I'm going to practice doing that very thing."

Liberty was thankful for a man who understood her and with whom she could bare her soul.

"Thank you Matthew for taking the time to really listen to me. "

"You, madam, are very welcome!" He kissed her soundly and said for the second time, "Let's be on our way, then."

He held the bedroom door open, and Liberty preceded Matthew down the hall and to the kitchen.

She dropped her hat on the table and said, "Well, Conchita, I think we are finally ready." She strode across the tiled floor and took her cook and all around help into her arms. "I hope this gives you a bit of a break too." She gave Conchita's tummy a pat. "Your baby is growing and that takes a lot of your energy. I want you to rest up while we are gone. Give Diego lots of leftovers." She chuckled when Conchita threw back her head and laughed.

"*Sí*, Mees Libby, I weel do eet. I no work much while you ees gone." Her face was creased with a big smile, and Liberty gave her a tight hug.

"I love you, my friend."

"I luff you too, Mees Libby."

Matthew gave Conchita a quick hug and bussed her cheek. "If there's any trouble, don't hesitate to send a telegram up to Sonoma. Kirk, owning McCaully-Bannisters Ranch, is quite well-known in the area now. A telegram would find us." He gave her another hug.

"Eet weel be quiet here with the tweens an' you both gone. We weel be fine. Vaya con Dios."

"Thank you, Conchita. We'll be home in a couple weeks." Liberty blew her a kiss as she headed for the door with Matthew on her heels.

Diego was waiting for them. He and Matthew had saddled the horses and added the bedrolls behind the saddles.

"Did you check the billet strap again?"

"*Sí*, Mees Libby. She ees now ready. I tighten that strap two times. Your horse, she is a steenker!" Diego laughed, his teeth startlingly white in his swarthy face.

Liberty grinned. "I just hope I never forget her blowing herself up when I'm saddling her, or the saddle and I will land on terra firma and Pookie will go dancing off down the road!" She grinned as Matthew hooked her satchel on the pommel and laced his fingers for her to step into.

"Thanks," Libby said as she stepped into his waiting hands. "Take care, Diego, and let us know if something needs our attention. Matthew and I are looking forward to some time off, but if we're needed, please don't hesitate to let us know."

Diego nodded. "We weel be fine. You haf a good time and relax." He looked up at Matthew who was already seated on his beautiful paint. "Tell Kirk hello from Conchita an' me."

"Will do," Matthew replied. He wheeled Piggypie around and Liberty followed suit. The two set off at a steady pace down the lane.

Maisie was fidgeting. "What's taking Doc so long?"

Paige spoke up before Aidan or Caitlin could. "I have a feeling you don't understand the gravity of the situation, Maisie, and I'm not going to mince words. Your husband was in a bad way when Kirk brought him in here. My prayer is that he survives. Frankly, the way he looked, I don't think he will."

Maisie blanched at her words. "I-I knew it was bad, but not that bad." She began to cry softly.

Caitlin glared at Paige, not wanting Maisie upset by her words. She put her arm protectively around her sister.

"Maisie, listen to me. We'll know pretty soon—we'll find out how bad it is just as soon as Doc is finished doing his magic. We all know Dr. Addison to be an excellent doctor, and he'll do everything in his power to save Gavin. He also prays when he's working on someone. The rest is up to the good Lord. There is a delightful peace in knowing that."

"P-peace for you, maybe, b-but not for me." Maisie spoke haltingly through her tears.

Aidan had been sitting quietly, but spoke up. "Yes, you're right, Maisie. Both Caitlin and I have a peace knowing that whatever comes our way is filtered by the hand of the Almighty. We may not like what is happening, but we know we can endure it with the Lord's help. It's not that He wants bad things to happen, but mankind has a freewill. The comfort is, knowing that the Almighty can take what was meant for evil and turn it to good."

The door from Dr. Addison's surgery opened, and the doctor came out with his head bowed. He took a deep breath and being a close friend of the McCaully's, sat down heavily, next to Maisie, his countenance inscrutable. "I did the best I know how to do, Maisie. He—"

"He's not dead! Oh please, Doc, tell me he's not dead!"

"He's not dead, Maisie" Doc Addison put his arm around her slender shoulders. "He's not dead, but he's close, I'm sorry to say. I don't know if he'll survive this. I can't say for sure. It's going to be touch and go. He's a strong man, and that will help. It's his heart that's the problem, Maisie. He's had a heart attack."

"Heart attack!" Maisie exclaimed.

"Have you noticed him being unusually tired?" Doc asked.

"Yes, but I attributed it to opening a new store and all the work that goes into doing that. I didn't know it was his heart. Wouldn't he have had some signs that he was having trouble?"

"I should think so. Left arm ache is a telltale sign. Being extremely tired and…but sometimes it just hits a body without them realizing it's their heart. I can tell you what I think happened. Whoever shot him, was either a bad aim, or they pulled the trigger when Gavin was already on his way down, collapsing from the heart attack. The bullet went right through, under his clavicle, and didn't hit anything vital. It's the heart attack that is the problem. We just don't know enough about the heart to know what to do. It's a double blow to his body. You can go in and see him. He's asleep, but he's going to have to take it exceedingly slow if he even survives this."

Maisie nodded, and spoke tremulously. "Thank you, Dr. Addison. I don't know what we'd do without you!"

"Well, sweetheart, pretty soon, you'll have to do without me. I am retiring. As you know, my mother passed last year. She lived in Vallejo, but we were never close. Kirk and Caitlin have graciously asked me to come live with them, and I have accepted their offer. It will be good to be with as close to family as I've ever had. You girls and your da have been that for me." He squeezed Maisie's shoulders.

"I have contacted a young man, who is a widower," Doc said. "He was one of my prize students when I taught at Massachusetts General

Hospital. His wife passed a couple years ago, and he is looking forward to different surroundings. He said everything he does reminds him of Corine, and he can't seem to move on emotionally. Oliver Sandhurst is his name, and he has a daughter, but I'm not sure how old she is. At any rate, I have asked him to come replace me."

Maisie grabbed his arm. "No one can replace you, Doc. They can try to fill your position, but no one can replace you." She got up and walked slowly toward the surgery, her steps dragging as if she was loath to see her husband in such a debilitated state.

I should have known he was having trouble. He's been so tired lately. I just thought it was all the work of opening a new store. She saw the pallor on his face, and the thought struck her that he looked dead. She stared at the rise and fall of his chest to make sure he was still breathing.

Kirk entered the waiting area of Doc Addison's office with the new sheriff in tow. He nodded at Caitlin and Aidan.

"I know you haven't met our new sheriff," he said. "This is Ezra Walker. Ezra, this is my wife, Caitlin, and her sister, Aidan." He turned to Ezra. "Reckon you know Doc Addison and his assistant, Paige McGrath, don't you?"

"It's a pleasure, ladies." Ezra had removed his hat when he entered the room. He smiled pleasantly at the women before replying. "Yes, Doc and I have met a couple times, and Miss McGrath and I have spoken several times before." He perused her face closely with a slight smile on his lips. "You *are* Miss Paige and not Miss Payton?"

"Yes, it's my day to work. As you know, we take turns. Payton works Monday, Wednesday, and Friday, and I work Tuesday, Thursday and Saturday. Once in a while we trade days, but not very often. We just go by Miss McGrath so no one is confused. Having an identical twin makes life interesting."

"Nice to see you again, Doc...Miss McGrath." His eyes lingered on Paige, wondering why she did not affect him the way her twin, Payton, did.

Aidan glanced at Ezra, but it turned into a stare. *My goodness. What a nice looking man! Wonder if he's married? The way he looked at Paige, I'd say he isn't*, Aidan thought.

Ezra Walker had medium brown hair, greenish-hazel eyes. His face was pleasant to look upon, sporting a small cleft in his chin. He was dressed all in black, but his bolo tie slide was silver as was the trim on his hat. He looked quite smart to Aidan, who dressed in the latest fashion.

"How is Gavin?" Kirk asked. "Is Maisie with him?" he glanced through the open door and nodded his head as he saw the answer to the last part of his question. He repeated the first part. "How's Gavin, Doc?"

"Well, son, he's not only been shot, he suffered a heart attack."

Kirk's eyebrows rose in astonishment. "Gavin had a heart attack as well as being shot? Isn't he too young to have a heart attack?"

"No, he's not too young, and yes, that fact is the most troubling. The bullet went clean through with little damage. I'm not saying it won't be painful, because it will. But the heart…well, we just don't know how much will be affected. I am praying for a full recovery, but only time will tell. He's going to have to be careful for the rest of his life not to overdo."

"I've never heard of anyone so young having a heart attack." Kirk shook his head. "It's hard for me to comprehend."

Doc nodded. "Yes, he is young. I know it's a conundrum, but if he recovers, I have a feeling the heart attack saved his life." Doc Addison went on to explain to the sheriff and Kirk what he believed happened when Gavin was shot.

Caitlin put her hand to her mouth. "Oh my goodness I forgot!"

"What?" Kirk asked.

"I forgot that Matthew and Liberty are arriving today! They are likely at the ranch. Well, it's all right. They will understand, and Matthew will be able to talk to some of the ranch hands. He knows all the ones we had a couple years back. Most of them are still with us." She spoke to Aidan. "I forgot to tell you that we lost Caleb McHaney."

"What? What happened?" Aidan was aghast.

"No, no, I don't mean it that way. I should reword it." She giggled. "It sounded like he'd died, didn't it? No, what I meant was he's left us. He is now a ranch owner. He married Constance Cooper down in Salvador. Her father deeded that huge ranch over to him. I heard Coop wasn't in the best of health and decided he'd marry Bernie, his housekeeper, and travel a bit before settling down."

Aidan smiled. "Reckon Caleb landed on his feet, didn't he? I don't know anyone who deserves a break more. He put up with an awful lot after his father died. I'm glad to hear it." She spoke in an aside to Caitlin barely above a whisper. "When did you ask Doc to come live with you?"

"About two months ago. He came out to have a look at Jonathan, who was running a fever. I was scared to death. Doc spent the night, and we've always been like family to him. He loved Da. I talked it over with Kirk first, of course, and he agreed wholeheartedly."

"Jonny's how old?" Aidan asked.

"He turned a year last month. He looks so much like Kirk even though he's a baby. We plan to have him call Doc, grandpa."

"Tell you a secret, Caitlin, but promise not to tell."

"I promise," Caitlin said, her eyes sparkling.

"I've started a baby! I'm so excited I could burst!"

Caitlin grabbed Aidan's hands. "Oh Danny! I'm so happy for you!"

"Thank you! I just keep pinching myself. I never thought we'd have children. As you well know when Jared first starting working on your ranch he never wanted children." Aidan continued to talk, her words tumbling over each other. "What a changed man he is now he's accepted Jesus as his Savior. Our lives have changed so much. I credit Ewen with a lot of that. He is the best foreman you could ever have, Caitlin. He was wise in making Jared work for the money he took out of Da's desk. That and having Matthew mentor him…I can never stop praising God enough for what He's done in our lives."

Caitlin nodded her head. "Mine too, Danny. Mine too. That night we knelt in the library and prayed, why I will never forget it, and the change I felt in my heart was unlike anything I'd ever experienced. Oh my goodness! We are blessed, aren't we?"

Aidan squeezed Cait's hands. "Yes, Cait, yes we are." Aidan gave Caitlin's hand an extra squeeze. She loved it when Caitlin called her Danny. "What we need to do now is work with subtlety, of course, on Maisie and Gavin."

Caitlin nodded her agreement, but they stopped talking and listened to Kirk answer Sheriff Walker's questions.

"No sir, he didn't seem to sit tall in the saddle, but he may have been hunched down in case someone fired on him. I really didn't pay much attention, because Gavin is my brother-in-law, and I feared he was the one who was shot."

"How did you get him here?" Ezra asked.

"Threw him over my shoulder like a sack of grain. He weighs quite a bit more than a hundred pounds of grain, but I didn't seem to notice. My heart was pumping pretty hard. I just prayed, and somehow I got him over to Doc Addison. That Doc was in his office was a miracle in itself!"

Maisie came back to the waiting room and waited until Kirk was finished talking.

"When do you think he'll wake up?" she asked the doctor.

"I have no idea. The longer he takes to wake up the better, I think. Sometimes the body seems to need time to deal with shock or whatever has assaulted it. I hope he doesn't waken until tomorrow, but not to worry. I'll be sitting up with him tonight."

"No! Maisie's tone brooked no argument. "I'll sit with him. If I need you, I'll come up and get you, but you've had a busy day, and I don't think I'll sleep well tonight anyway. If you have a cot, I can stretch out and sleep next to Gavin. I'd feel a lot better being with him than going home and worrying."

"All right, Maisie Marie Galway. Have it your way. Frankly, I'm bushed. I am quite sure his wound is cleaned out, and barring an infection, that part of him should be fine. As to his heart—we'll just have to take it one day at a time. If he survives this, it's going to be a long recovery." His shoulders sagged with relief at her offer. "You can sleep right there on that davenport. I'll have Marie bring you a pillow and a couple blankets."

Kirk said, "If you need anything don't hesitate to send someone out to get me. I think Caitlin and I need to go home. We have some Bannisters coming to visit." He grinned at the look on the sheriff's face. "My brother is Matthew Bannister, and if you ever need a tracker, he's the best the state of California has to offer. He and his wife, Liberty, are coming up to Sonoma for a couple weeks."

"Thanks for the information," Ezra said. "There's really not much to go on. You didn't happen to notice what kind of horse the shooter was riding, did you?"

Surprise spread across Kirk's features. "I didn't think to say, but yes, I did. It was a beautiful red dun quarter horse."

"There's not many of those, are there?" Ezra asked.

"Actually there are a lot of them. It's a pretty popular breed." Kirk replied. "If I think of anything else, I'll let you know."

"Do that." Sheriff Walker said. "Meanwhile, I'll mosey around looking for owners of red dun quarter horses."

"Good luck with that, sir, but you're going to find there are too many to try to find your shooter." Kirk said.

Caitlin hugged Maisie and said, "I'll be praying for you and Gavin. Don't wear yourself out. He's going to need you to be strong."

Maisie nodded. "I know, I know! I'm a McCaully after all. We know how to be strong, but I think you and Aidan have a bit more inner strength than I do. You've both had some hard times, where I just seem to have skated by. Now, I reckon, it's my turn. I don't think there's a single person on this earth who doesn't run into trouble at one time or another. It just seems that some people have more than their share."

Caitlin gave Aidan a quick hug. "You take care of Maisie, and I'll probably be back into town tomorrow with Liberty."

"I'll look forward to seeing her. I remember the first time I saw her. I was expecting some masculine type woman, and was shocked to see one of the most beautiful women I've ever laid eyes on." Aidan laughed at herself.

Caitlin chuckled. "Yes, she is gorgeous, but she's also one of the sweetest woman you'll ever want to meet."

Kirk took Caitlin's arm and said, "Come on, Katie."

Aidan smiled when she heard Kirk call Caitlin, Katie. It was what their da always called her. *Kirk is perfect for Caitlin.* "See you two later." She took Maisie by the arm and led her back into the room where Gavin lay. "He has a strong constitution, Maisie. Always healthy as a horse. Do you mind if I pray for him?"

"N-no. Of course not."

Aidan reached placing her hand on Gavin's head. "Our Father in heaven, how excellent is Your name. How you love to give good gifts to your children. Right now, I asked for the gift of life for Gavin. Lord, we ask You not to take him before he acknowledges You as Lord and Savior. I pray through this event that both Maisie and Gavin recognize their need of You. Thank You, Almighty God, for the miracle You will give Gavin and Maisie. I now pray as Jesus did, not my will but Thine be done. Amen."

"Thank you," Maisie said. "I don't know how much good that will do, but I thank you for being so thoughtful."

CHAPTER III

Then said they unto him,
Tell us, we pray thee, for whose cause this evil is upon us;
What is thine occupation? and whence comest thou?
what is thy country? and of what people art thou?

JONAH 1:8

AIDAN HUGGED MAISIE. "I LOVE YOU, SWEETIE. I just wish you could have the comfort of laying all your burdens at the feet of Jesus. It's so comforting to me. Please let me know if you need anything. I could spell you during the night if you want me to. You need your rest."

Maisie hugged Aidan back. "No, I'll be fine. I suppose I'll just close the shop for a bit until things settle down."

"I could watch the shop for you, if you tell me how much things cost. I'd be happy to do that for you. It might even be entertaining."

"I'll let you know, Aidan. I'm glad we both live here in Santa Rosa. Caitlin's a good half hour away, so it wouldn't be so easy to call on them if an emergency should arise."

"True, but Jared and I will help in any way we can."

Aidan waited until there was a break in the conversation between the doctor and the sheriff.

"Just wanted to say goodbye, Doc. And Sheriff Walker, it was nice to meet you." She proffered her hand and the sheriff shook it. Doc hugged her.

"Be sure to let me know if you need help with anything. And Maisie, please don't feel you have to do everything alone. I'm here to help."

"I know, Aidan, and I thank you. Reckon I'll see you tomorrow."

The two parted, Aidan headed for her own house and Maisie went to sit with Gavin.

Aidan's da had bought a beautiful large house on the edge of the town of Santa Rosa as a wedding present. He hadn't cared much for Jared, the way he was then, and had put the house in Aidan's name. Recently, she'd had Jared put on the legal papers in case anything should happen to her. She didn't care to have a baby and not have Jared on the paperwork. She arrived home and headed straight for the kitchen.

Doctor Addison was still talking to the sheriff, and Paige had returned to the receptionist's desk and was working on some paperwork she needed to finish before she went home.

"My horse, Blondie, has been put out to pasture. She's too old to be carrying a load like me, but I bought a red dun quarter horse. I can name six people without thinking who have a red dun."

"It's going to be difficult to track the shooter down. I am hoping Mr. Galway can help me with some information when he recovers enough to talk." Ezra shook his head ruefully.

"Are you married, sir?" Doc asked.

Startled, Ezra answered hesitantly. "I was. She passed having our first baby. Still can't comprehend she's gone, although it was over a year ago. The babe died too."

Doc nodded. "It can take a long time to get over that kind of loss. I had many years with my wife, but the loss of her was a devastation I wouldn't want to ever relive." He clapped the younger man on the shoulder. "The pain eases some with time."

Ezra nodded. "I know, sir. It's just I keep thinking she's in the next room and start to say something, and the realization floods over me that she's gone."

"Yes, it was like that for me, too. I'll be praying for you, young man. I have a doctor coming to replace me who needs a life change for the exact same reason."

"When are you retiring?"

"Soon as Oliver Sandhurst gets here and I introduce him to my present cases. I've moved most of my things out of the upstairs and into the suite of rooms Caitlin and Kirk have given me at the Bannister-McCaully Ranch."

"Are they family?" Ezra asked?

"No, not blood family, but the closest thing I've had to a family for years. My mother passed not long ago, but we were never close. She told me once she'd never wanted to have children. I don't have any other relatives that I know of."

"Me either. I know I have my whole life before me, but I have no one I can call family."

"Well, son, maybe I can claim you. Only time will tell."

"What happened to the last sheriff? Your city council was pretty tight-lipped when I asked."

"Well, he ended up dying, but he was a bad one until the very end. On his deathbed, he asked the good Lord to forgive him and became a child of the king just afore he died."

Ezra's eyes lit up. "You're a believer?"

"Certainly am," Doc replied. "Been one most of my life."

Ezra stuck out his hand and said, "Let me shake your hand, brother!" His features lit up like the sun coming out from behind a cloud.

Doc Addison shook his hand and clapped him on the back. "You're going to have your work cut out for you, son, on this case, but I'll be praying for you—that you find your man."

"Thank you. I couldn't ask for more."

"Why don't you go tell my cook I need dinner down here tonight, and you, Maisie, and I will eat together."

"You point me to your house, and I'll be glad to do that," Ezra grinned.

"Just climb those stairs and whistle when you get to the top to warn her you're coming. Marie is my cook. She'll hear you and respond."

The day was waning, but heat from the floorboards seemed to rise up and stifle any desire to work. It was unusually warm for May, and the door stood open as well as the single window situated at the back of the one-roomed house. Flies buzzed around the center of the room, and the newest baby cried fitfully.

Lindsey May Pindar glanced at the baby. "I know punkin, I know. Yer ready ta eat." She stroked his brow, removing sweat that trickled down the side of his face. "Jest you wait yourself, little Jamie, jest you wait a minute. I'll be back in two shakes of a lamb's tail." Despite the heat, she strode out the opened door and through the rickety gate to get a clear view of the road. Their house was situated at the end of a short lane off the main thoroughfare. Anxiously looking down the road, she couldn't see anyone.

"Zebidiah's late comin' home from work—he ain't never late, and that Mini Lou! What's that girl up to now? She's been a long time comin' back from Diebel's General Store." Muttering to herself, she was fully disgusted with everything at the moment. Figuring she was pregnant again, she took a deep sigh. "I'm tired and my last baby hain't six months old. Where in tarnation are those two? I got dinner ready an' neither one of 'em in sight."

She stomped back into the house and tugged at her blouse, pulling it out of her skirt. Scooping up the crying baby, she put him under her blouse as she sat down in the rocker. The baby, quiet at last, gave a shuddering sigh of contentment as well as giving some peace to Lindsey May's ears. She had some time to think.

"Iffin I'm pregnant again, Zeb is gonna hafta help more'n he does. Mini Lou is gettin' ready ta be on her own. I kin see the signs. She has too much to do takin' care of the little ones, and them jest half siblings. I kin see she's not content. For sure thet girl is a hard worker and has a head on her shoulders. I couldn't love her more iffin she were my own bairn. She may be Zeb's first wife's get, but she's my daughter same as the rest. That goes fer Sadie and Lettie Lynn too. That Mini Lou said she ain't plannin' on a man in er' life fer years ta come. She don't want ta be shackled down with a brood of babies. Huh...I never wanted ta be anything but a wife an' mother. I cain't see anything wrong with that. I seen that Mini Lou studien' so hard ta be speakin' like a lady, but not ta be interested in a man jest don't seem right ta me."

She leaned her head back against the rocker and closed her eyes. She felt tired and worn. She'd born Zeb six children in the past eight years, and although the three girls from Zeb's first wife helped immensely,

Lindsey May still worked from before dawn till sunset. When she found time to sit, she was darning socks, patching clothes or knitting something for one of the children. Sadie and Lettie Lynn had taken the younger ones out to cut some wild lilacs that were in bloom down by the creek, and the peaceful quiet enveloped her like a shroud.

She patted little Jamie rubbing his tiny back. He let out a loud burp that made Lindsey May chuckle. "You already makin' sounds like your pa." She tucked him under her blouse again switching sides. "Yer a greedy little thing, ain't you!" she whispered, glad she had plenty of milk. Once again she leaned her head back against the rocker as she slipped back into her musings.

"Wonder if Jonah is home yet. Shore an' I feel right sorry fer thet poor man havin' ta put up with Cindy Sue. I be a knowin' she don't like ta be called Cindy Sue any more, but thet's what I called her in school, an' I'm not about to change now. Cindy Sue with her hifalutin ways wants to be called Cynthia or Mrs. Whatcom. Jonah does the best thet he kin fer her, but that woman — she ain't never satisfied. Nothin's too good fer 'er. Her parents were nice enough. Maybe they doted on 'er too much, since she was the onliest child they ever had. She ain't got any bairns ta keep her attention neither. Wonder why?"

Baby Jamie was finished nursing, and Lindsey May rubbed his back and burped him again.

"Reckon I'd best put you ta bed and finish up makin' dinner." She laid him in the crib bed Zeb had made years ago in the corner of the room.

She'd made a hash of the beef, diced some onions and now, with deft fingers, peeled the already baked potatoes, dicing them up into squares. "Wonder what in the world we'll do fer food when them boys get a bit bigger. Seems now, we have jest enough."

She could hear her children coming up from the creek. Quickly, she dumped the potatoes into the shredded beef and onion mixture, stirring it up and setting a lid on the top, she moved it to a less heated place on the wood stove.

"Well, jest look at you young-uns! My oh my, ain't those lilacs fit fer a queen! Thank you fer takin' the time ta find these. They're right beautiful." She took the armload of lilacs. "I'll jest set these in a milk can. Uhm...don't they smell lovely? You'll go wash up at the pump. Dinner is about ready. Jedidiah, will you please fill this with water?"

"Yes'm, I will," he replied.

"Here, Micah, you hold these until Jed gets this milk can half full of water." She handed the little boy the whole armful of lilacs and grinned to herself as he arched his back and struggled to hold all of them.

"My, what a big boy you are, Micah!"

The rest of the children chattered as they made their way to the pump.

"Put yer can here by the pump, Jed, it'll make it easier to fill up," Lettie Lynn said.

"Naw, but thanks. I'm gonna put th' can in th' trough. It'll fill up in a trice thet way." He proceeded to put the can into the trough as he spoke.

"Oh, you are so smart," Lettie Lynn replied. "That *is* th' fastest."

He marched back to the house carrying the can, as the other children washed up at the pump.

"There's Pa!" Sadie yelled. "Pa's home! Yay! Pa's home!"

The children ran to Zebidiah's old nag to greet their father.

"Pa! We gots ta go down ta the creek an' get lilacs fer ma. She loves 'em!" Micah exclaimed. "An' Lettie Lynn tooked us."

Zebidiah patted him on the head, as he lifted Sarah Sue, one of the younger ones into the crook of his left arm. He tweaked Lettie Lynn on the ear and said, "Thanks for helping yer ma. Where's Mini Lou?"

"She went ta town ta get some flour. She's bin gone a powerful long time."

"I'm sure she'll be back fer dinner." Zebidiah straightened up and rubbed his back for a moment.

"Is yer back still hurtin'?" Jedidiah asked.

"I'm fine, young man," he replied, "Jest fine." He moved slowly as Jemimah, the youngest girl, clung to his leg, riding on his boot. "Let's be gettin' inta the house. I'm sure dinner is ready fer us, an' I'm right hungry!"

Hearing galloping hooves coming down the road, Zeb spun around, and the clinging child plopped on her bottom with a surprised grunt. Jemimah began to wail, and Zeb bellowed at Mini Lou as he sat Sarah Sue down and picked up Jemimah.

"You needn't be ridin' thet horse so fast!"

Mini Lou sawed at the reins of the Pindar's only good horse, bringing it to a sudden halt.

"You'll not be ridin' thet horse any more iffin yer gonna treat it with no respect! You'll be a ruinin' its mouth an' put years on thet poor geldin' afore it's time, ridin' it like thet in this heat!"

"Hello, Pa," the girl said as she slid from the saddle.

"Don't you go helloing me, young lady. I see you ride thet horse like thet again, an' you'll be a walkin' ta town, not ridin'. An' I'll say it agin! Thet ain't no way ta stop a horse. You'll be ruinin' it's mouth!"

"Yes, sir," Mini Lou replied in a meek tone of voice, but there was a spark of temper in her eyes. She led the horse to the barn to curry him down as he was lathered from riding so hard in the heat.

"You kin brush my nag down too, while your at it!" He gave the reins to Micah to take to the barn. "Thank you, Micah." Zeb headed for the house, muttering under his breath. "I hain't be a knowing what's got into thet girl." He repeated his comment to Lindsey May.

"She's growed up, Zeb. I kin see the look in 'er eyes. She's fixin' ta be on 'er own."

"Waal, she hain't be havin a beau. What d'ya mean?"

"I think she's a plannin' on livin' on 'er own. Makin' 'er own way, so ta speak."

"An how's she plannin' ta do thet?"

"Mini Lou's bin lookin' fer work. Miss Caitlin ask me if Mini Lou was wantin' a job. She was askin' iffin Mini Lou was good takin' care of the younguns an' could she be a nanny fer her little boy. Seems Miss Caitlin is lookin' fer a gal ta take care of the little 'un when she's busy. I think it's one reason Mini Lou was a working so hard at gettin' 'er English ta sound like a lady."

Zeb looked as if someone had kicked him in the gut and grumbled. "She's not old enough ta be on 'er own."

"Yes, Zeb, she is. She's the same age as I was when I married you. And asides thet, she's a hard worker and tryin' ta better 'erself. I think we need ta let her go."

"Who's gonna take over 'er chores?"

"We'll portion 'em out. We'll be fine, Zeb. It's time."

Zebidiah's shoulders sagged with sorrow. Mini Lou had secretly been his favorite child. He couldn't imagine her being out of the house.

"Come on, wash up everyone! It's time fer us ta eat," Lindsey May said. "Thanks, Lettie Lynn, fer settin' the table."

"Yer welcome, Ma." Lettie Lynn glanced at her mother, knowing Mini Lou had been shirking her chores lately. She didn't want to say anything negative about Mini Lou. She loved her sister and knew she ached to be out of the house and on her own. Lettie Lynn couldn't understand that at all. She loved her ma and pa and siblings. She didn't mind working from sunup till sundown and more. Knitting something new, or darning clothing, or socks needing repair, took time, but Lettie Lynn was good at it. She knew working hard helped her ma, and she would do anything to alleviate some of the chores for Lindsey May.

She may not be my real ma, but she may as well be. I love her with all my heart. She rounded up the children and led them to the pump outside, helping the youngest to wash her hands.

Mini Lou came out of the barn, her face set in a frown. She stood watching as Lettie Lynn helped the children wash. While they trooped into the house, she washed up slowly, thinking about the direction her life should take.

I can't stand this anymore. We're so poor, and I'm right tired...I mean very tired...of this kind of life. I've seen how others live, and I want that. Pa is not going to be happy that I want out. I want to make my own way and as I see it, working for Miss Caitlin would be the perfect thing for me. I could give ma some of the money I make to help out here. Lettie Lynn is quite capable of taking over my chores. She's been doing that lately anyhow...I mean anyway. I'm going to be a lady, and I don't mind working hard as long as I can see results. I need a change.

She went slowly into the house, not wanting to listen to the racket of so many voices. She needed time to think. She wanted some quiet time for thinking about what needed to be done.

CHAPTER IV

Pray without ceasing.

I THESSALONIANS 5:17

JONAH WHATCOM SLIPPED OFF HIS HORSE and led it into the one stall in the shed. He threw some hay into the manger, undid the buckles on the saddle and carried it to the saw horse, throwing it over the top. He undid the bridle and removed it with care, giving his horse a loving pat on the neck. "I'll be a curryin' you after dinner."

He strode over to the only door of their house and entered.

"Where you bin, Jonah Whatcom? Had dinner on the table over an hour ago, expecting you ta be home! Yers is cold now, and iffin you want it warm, you can warm it up yerself! I'm done fer th' day."

Cynthia Whatcom had become a nag, but Jonah loved her and would do anything for her. He strode across the room and grabbed her, kissing the breath right out of her.

"I love you, Cindy Sue! More'n life itself, I love you!"

"My name is Cynthia, and you'd do well ta remember it!" She snapped at him, but she wound her arms around his neck and pressed herself in close.

Her figure was as sweet as the day Jonah married her, and for all her nagging, she was soft and pliable in his arms.

"I love you, too, Jonah Ray Whatcom! Sorry fer speakin' so sharp. I was that worried something had happened ta you. I think all kinds of horrid things with you workin' in that mine. Sometimes I have nightmares about it!"

She took his plate and set it on the stove to warm up and sashayed over to the cooler to pour a glass of apple juice she'd canned last fall. She knew he was watching her movements and swung her hips more than was necessary.

The Whatcoms had no children, and it was a sorrow to both of them. Cindy Sue had played with a doll until she was past the age when most girls stopped. She'd always dreamed of having a passel of children, but it wasn't to be. She knew her life was easier for not having to care for children, but she wanted a child of her own.

"Me an' Zeb took a bag of nice looking gems inta the store taday. I think Mr. Galway will be that pleased when he looks at 'em." His eyes slid away from Cindy Sue's, and she wondered what he'd been up to, but she didn't say anything, knowing he wasn't finished talking.

"I'm late cause I bin workin' jest a bit extra so's we kin go down ta San Rafael and get us a baby from thet orphanage."

Cindy Sue's eyes widened. "Air you serious? I mean I knowed we talked about it, but kin we really afford ta get one?"

Jonah grinned at her. "I'm thinkin' we kin. Mr. Galway gave some of the of men a bonus, and I'm one of 'em. I gots a bit of cash now, and hit's about time we had us a little one. What with the money we've saved an' me a workin' overtime…an th' bonus and all…well, I'm thinkin' we have enough money ta do jest that!"

Cindy Sue ran across the room and flung her arms around Jonah's neck, kissing him soundly. "You are a treasure ta me, Jonah. I don't deserve you, but yer a good man!"

The train made its inexorable way west. The weather was perfect. It wasn't too hot, but it wasn't too cold either. Sun streamed across the heartland of America, and Oliver, Marnie, and Deedee sat looking at the beautiful scenery. Shadows filtered across the flat plain, changing shape as the puffy clouds blew their way across the heavens, allowing the sun to make patterns on the wide earth.

Oliver sat thinking about his farewell party at the hospital where he'd been putting in some extra hours.

I'm surprised I won't miss one person in Boston. I suppose that's my fault. I've become a bit of a recluse since Corine died. Still, not to miss one person is a bit sad. I'll have to make sure Marnie meets other children and that I don't try to avoid social gatherings. Sure, I had fellow doctors I enjoyed talking to, but not one that I felt a close bond with. On the other hand, it is with real regret that I closed my practice. I get personally attached to my patients, although I've been taught not to.

Poor old Mrs. Connolly. She's lost her husband and now is in a decline herself. Her children are unbelievably selfish—more like vultures just waiting for her to die. What a shock to them when they find she's donated her entire fortune to medical research. She's a smart old gal.

Then, of course, I'm going to miss Jonathan. He was a bright secretary. I'm glad he found another position so quickly.

"Look Papa! Look at the buffalo!" Marnie's voice broke into Oliver's ruminations. "There must be hundreds of them!"

"Oh my!" Deedee said. "It's amazing to see them in real life. I've only seen them in picture books."

Oliver was surprised he hadn't even noticed them, he'd been so caught up in his thoughts. "Majestic looking creatures, aren't they?"

"Look at all the baby ones!"

"Not too long ago," Oliver said, "I read that one of the big disputes between the white man and the Indian is that white men are killing off the bison for sport. The Indian kills it for livelihood. They use almost every part of it for something."

"What could they use from a buffalo besides the meat?" Marnie asked.

"Do you really want me to list it out for you?"

"Yes."

"Let me see. As you know the buffalo meat is for food. They also dry it, before it spoils, so they can eat it later. They use the bones for making knives, quirts, pipes, sleds, arrowheads…oh my the list goes on. The coat of the buffalo provides them with winter robes, tipi liners, tipi covers, tapestries, shirts, quivers, moccasin tops and leggings, dresses, cradles, bridles, bags and more. The hair on the buffalo is used for pillows, medicine balls, ropes, hair pieces, ornaments and that list goes on and on, too. The rawhide is used to make containers, shields, soles for their moccasins, drums, splints, ropes, and saddles. The first stomach of the buffalo is called the rumen which they use to wrap meat, make buckets, basins, and canteens. And lastly the horns of the buffalo are used for many things such as arrow points, cups, holders to carry fire, powder horns, spoons, ladles, headdresses, toys, scoops, combs…my, I'm surprised I remembered so much from that article!"

"You're a great source of information, Papa! It's your job to remember things, isn't it? I can always count on you to have an answer for my questions."

"Not always, sweetheart, but I do my best."

"I had no idea the natives could use so much of the buffalo," Deedee stated in awe of all that could be made from the buffalo.

"Yes, it is pretty amazing. It's a real tragedy so many are being killed off for sport."

Marnie slipped her hand into her papa's. "That *is* sad."

Deedee nodded in agreement, but wanted to change the subject. She pulled open the lid of the silver engraved timepiece hanging around her neck. "I do think it's time for lunch. Let's head to the dining car, shall we?"

Maisie awoke with a stiff neck and for a second, wondered why she felt so uncomfortable. She could sense it was early morning. She rubbed her neck, her eyes still closed but as thoughts began to formulate, she sat up abruptly.

The realization that Gavin had moaned, fully awakened her. He moaned again. Swinging her long legs over the side of the examining table she'd slept on, she padded over to its twin where Gavin lay. He moaned again, but his eyes were closed. She wondered if she should try to waken him. *Perhaps he is already awake. I don't know what to do. I wish Doc Addison was here. Because I insisted on staying with Gavin, he went up to his living quarters to spend the night.*

She stroked Gavin's forehead with a light hand. "Are you awake, sweetheart?" She spoke in a whisper.

He mumbled something, but Maisie couldn't understand him. Gavin seemed to struggle to open his eyes. When he did, his pupils were dilated as if in fear.

"It's all right my darling—it's all right. I am right here with you. You are not to worry. I'm just thankful you are alive. Doc Addison operated on you."

She decided not to mention he'd had a heart attack. She didn't want to upset him. "Do you recall someone coming into the store?" She waited for him to respond, but when he didn't, she continued to smooth his forehead while she talked. "It would probably be the last thing you would remember." She bent down and kissed his mouth.

Gavin seemed to have difficulty swallowing. He looked at her, but he didn't speak.

Glad to see the fear in his eyes was gone, she said. "I love you, my darling. Don't you to worry about anything. I can take care of the shop, and I can get help from my sisters. I want you to just concentrate on getting well."

He blinked as if in affirmation at her words and closed his eyes. In less than a minute his breathing was heavy but steady.

Maisie straightened up and took a deep breath. The room was cool, and she tucked the blanket covering him, up around his neck. Not knowing what to expect for Gavin's recovery, she hoped Dr. Addison would know exactly how to help him. If he didn't, she was going to send for a doctor in San Francisco who specialized in treatment for heart attacks. Maisie knew enough about medicine to understand that physicians, although schooled in all types of medical procedures, were beginning to specialize. She left the room and entered the reception area, her eyes full of tears.

"What in the world am I to do if he doesn't recover?" she murmured. She sat down for a few minutes to think, coming up with the only solution, not knowing Jesus had said almost the same thing nearly two thousand years earlier. "I suppose like Da used to say, I'm not to borrow tomorrow's trouble," she whispered. "Today has enough of its own. All right then, I'll try not to worry." She wiped her eyes, blew her nose, and stood up. Taking another deep breath, she went back to keep vigil over her husband until Doc Addison came to check on him.

Liberty awoke and quietly stretched, not wanting to waken Matthew. She realized she didn't hear his breathing and looked over to see he was already up. She felt his side of the bed, but it was cool. *He's been up for some*

time. She stretched hugely pushing her heels to their farthest extent, curling her toes, and stretching her arms above her head.

She lay gazing around the beautiful bedroom. It was the same one she'd stayed in when Matthew had amnesia and didn't know her.

The room was unique, done in cream, sage green, and brown. The wainscot was painted dark brown topped with wallpaper in stripes of cream, green, and brown. The trim was all cream. A chocolate-colored love seat sat under the windows that faced south

Liberty stretched again. "Lord," she whispered, "I want to lift up Gavin to You. You are the God Who is compassionate, and Your lovingkindness extends throughout generations. You are the God Who heals. I pray for a swift and complete healing for Gavin. More than that, I pray for a spiritual healing for Gavin and Maisie. They are in need of knowing Your infinite love, dear Father. I pray they find it. I pray Maisie isn't bitter and blaming You for what happened yesterday.

"Thank you for a safe trip here, and may Matthew and I be able to help in any way we can. Will You please permeate our thoughts today, that we might be light and salt to whomever we come in contact? May we, in all that is done this day, bring only glory and goodness to Your name. Thank You for the love You shower upon us. I pray these things in the precious name of Jesus, the name that is above all names. Amen."

Liberty stretched once more and swung her legs over the side of the bed, sitting up all in one motion. She sat there for a few minutes thinking. *I suppose I'd better get dressed and see where this day leads. I don't suppose we'll be taking that camping trip. Cait will be wanting to help Maisie, as well she should.*

She stood up and smoothed the bed clothes, making the bed to save Sweeny, or whoever would check on their room, a bit of respite. Liberty looked at the bed with satisfaction and strolled to the commode room to ready herself for the day.

Matthew sat at the huge round oak table in the kitchen. He was drinking coffee and thinking back to when he'd had amnesia. He'd sat in this very chair wondering who in the world he was and where he hailed from. He'd been bashed on the head and left for dead on the main road near Gavin's mine. One of Gavin's miners, Zebidiah Pindar, had taken him home. He'd been unconscious for over a day. When he awoke, he'd been cared for by Dr. Addison, who realized the Pindar household, which was full of children, was not the best place for someone with a head injury, resulting in a raging headache. At that time, the only thing Matthew could recollect was a pair of green eyes. Another hit on the head had returned him to normal. He smiled at the thought. *I've been called hardheaded before, but I am thankful for that second hit on the head. I might still be wondering who I am if I hadn't hit that post in the barn. I have a lot of memories of the few weeks I spent here in Sonoma. The best part was leading Jared to a personal relationship with Jesus Christ…he, in turn led Aidan, and Caitlin to Jesus.*

Kirk sauntered into the kitchen, having been up and giving his foreman, Ewen some directions for the day.

"Morning, brother," he said to Matthew.

"Good morning, Kirk. I sure am sorry for your sister-in-law and for Gavin. Liberty and I don't want to be a nuisance, and if you feel you have to entertain us, please don't." He took a swallow of his coffee and continued. "If we're in the way, we can go home and come back some other time. If, however, we can be of any help, we'd like to stay."

Duney, their cook, handed Kirk a cup of coffee. "Thanks, Duney." He blew over the top of the mug to cool the coffee before taking a sip, eyeing Matthew as he did so. "You are welcome to stay. I don't know exactly what Katie's present plans are. She'll probably have to see how Gavin is doing before we decide. At any rate, you are family and never a nuisance. We'd like you to stay."

"Thanks. We'd like that."

"We'd like what?" Liberty stepped into the kitchen wearing one of her black split skirts and a pristine white blouse with ruching in rows down the front. A wide leather belt was cinched around her tiny waist. She looked feminine but could ride and shoot better than many men.

"We'd like to stay and help out in any way we can," Matthew replied.

"Well, that goes without saying, doesn't it?" She eyed Kirk. "You didn't sleep very well last night did you?"

"No, Caitlin is usually up before me, but she was worried about leaving Maisie. We did a lot of praying during the night and neither of us slept much. She's still in bed, and I hope she's sleeping. I just hope Gavin makes it. That was a double blow having a heart attack and a gun wound. I know Doc Addison is one of the best, and he will continue to do all he can to help Gavin."

"I wish you'd have gotten a good look at the shooter," Matthew said.

"I know, but if I hadn't taken Gavin to Doc Addison as fast as I did, I don't think he'd have made it."

"Frankly, neither do I." Matthew stood and pulled out a chair for Liberty who'd helped herself to a cup of coffee.

She sat down, took a swallow, and looked up at Kirk. Leaning forward, she spoke. "That was Providential—to have you right there in the bank!" she exclaimed. "I think God has plans for Maisie and Gavin to come to know Him. It's their choice, of course, but I sensed a peace fill my heart during the night. I was praying for Gavin, and I have been assured that he will be all right, not necessarily physically, but at least spiritually, he will be all right." She leaned against the chair back and took another swallow of her coffee as she saw surprise fill Kirk's eyes.

"I pray often and intensely. I realized after years of being a Christian that I expected God to come through and do things the way I wanted Him to without much supplication or discernment of what His will was. I wanted speedy answers, but didn't spend much time in prayer to get them. I started studying the life of Paul and then Jesus. Both spent much time in prayer. Can you imagine Jesus spending all night in prayer when He was God's son? You would think He could do anything without praying to God, but He often went by Himself to pray. If He needed to pray that much, how much more do I?"

"Reckon you're right, Libby," Kirk said. "I don't know anyone who feels they pray enough." He sat down and Duney refilled his mug of coffee.

"Continuing that line of thought," Matthew said, "Did you know James, the half brother of Jesus, who wrote the book of James, prayed so much that his knees were like camel's knees, they were so calloused?"

Kirk shook his head. "No, I didn't know that, but I do believe we don't see the power of God nearly as much as we would if we spent more time in prayer and in fasting. When I talk to anyone about their prayer life, no one says they have prayed enough."

Both Matthew and Liberty nodded their agreement.

"Ah! Here comes my girl!" Kirk exclaimed as Caitlin entered the kitchen.

"Good morning, everyone. Sorry I'm a slug-a-bug this morning. I didn't have the best night."

Duney had been listening for her footsteps and had a mug of coffee ready to hand her.

"Thanks, Duney."

"You are welcome, my dear." Duney's eyes searched Caitlin's, seeing the tiredness there.

Liberty stood and gave her sister-in-law a hug, careful not to spill her coffee. "Praying the way Kirk said you two did last night, means you did have a good night, just not a good sleeping night." Liberty hoped her words were an encouragement as she spoke.

Caitlin grinned back. "That is true, isn't it. We all equate a good night with lots of sleep, but it doesn't necessarily have to be sleep."

"Libby also spent time in prayer last night," Kirk said to Caitlin. "She believes Gavin will find fulfillment and peace."

"Thank you for that, Liberty." Caitlin's eyes were shadowed.

"Thank God for that," Liberty replied.

CHAPTER V

And let the beauty of the Lord our God be upon us:
and establish thou the work of our hands upon us;
yea, the work of our hands establish thou it.

PSALM 90:17

ANOTHER DAY DAWNED WITH THE heavens the color of indigo—so blue it could take your breath away except for the fluffs of cotton shading the hills on the horizon. It was going to be hot, as sunbeams already danced off the water in the trough, and a couple birds were preening their wings on its wooden sides after their bath.

Lindsey May Pindar stood at the kitchen window staring out, but her mind wasn't on the glorious day. She was worried. Mini Louise was acting strange, and Lindsey May didn't know what to do about it. The three older girls were Zeb's by another wife who'd died having Lettie Lynn. Lindsey May couldn't love them more had she birthed them herself. She'd married Zeb when she'd just turned seventeen, the same age as Mini Louise was now. Years before, Lindsey May had admired Zebidiah from a distance and knew him to be a hard worker. She'd met him at a special tent meeting. People from all over had come to hear the preacher talk. He and his girls were sitting right in front of her. She'd wondered where his wife was and learned that she had passed away the year before. He was trying to raise his girls on his own and had a woman come in during the day to watch his three little girls. Lindsey May learned all she could about him and proceeded to put herself in his way. He finally took notice and the rest was history. His children had been, and were, a blessing to her.

Lindsey May, a slight wrinkle between her brows, frowned when she thought of Mini Louise. *Somethin's jest not right. It ain't jest about her wantin' ta move out. Somethin's bitin' thet girl and I'd give my dinner away ta know what it is. She's been right cheeky fer the last couple days, but now she's quiet-like. It jest ain't like her ta be disrespectful, an' it ain't like her ta be quiet. She hain't been a doin' her chores much, and Sadie and Lettie Lynn are pickin' up the slack. If Zeb finds out, they'll be a row fer sure. He dotes on thet girl, fer certain, but he won't be a puttin' up with her nonsense, onlies, I don't be a believen' hits nonsense. Lord, I am askin' fer guidance on this. I don't know what's a goin' on with thet girl, but I know thet you know all things. I am askin' fer You to straighten things out. Help me ta know how ta help 'er.*

She jumped as the door opened with a crash. "What in tarnation does that girl think she's about?" thundered Zeb. "Riding off as if the hounds of hell were after 'er!."

"Zeb...don't you be talkin' about hell that way! Don't you know nothin'? The hounds of hell are an omen of death!"

Zeb blanched. "No, honeybug, I didn't know that. I jest heard the sayin' is all. I'll be more careful-like." He wiped his brow. "She went ridin' off down the road with nary a care in 'er head ta tell me where she's a goin'."

Lindsey May wiped her hands on a towel. She strolled over to her husband and wound her arms around his neck, kissing his cheek. "She's a riding over ta McCaully-Bannisters'. She'll be a talkin' ta Miss Caitlin about workin' fer 'er. Miss Caitlin asked 'er ta let 'er know as soon as possible, cause iffen Mini Lou doesn't, she'll be lookin' fer someone else ta come fill the position." Lindsey May sighed, continuing to talk.

"Mini Lou wants it awful bad. I'm hopin' Zeb, that you make this a good experience fer 'er. Don't be a fussin' an' makin' 'er miserable. She's got 'er heart set on it."

Zeb pulled back from the embrace and stared into Lindsey May's eyes. She could see the hurt in their depths.

"I don't be a knowing why she's so all-fired up ta go live someplace else. She has a good home here an' people who love 'er. Why?"

Lindsey May gave Zeb a tight hug before she stepped back to reply. "She's growed up, Zeb, an' we didn't notice. She's a woman, an' she wants ta be makin' 'er own way. She ain't interested in a man or nothing 'ceptin' she wants ta be on 'er own. I don't rightly understand it myself. I never wanted anything else but gettin' married and having a passel of babies. I don't understand it, but I respect it, Zeb. It's what she wants. She got 'er heart set on it, an' nothin' we say will change 'er mind. She's cut from a different piece a cloth, an' that's the way it is."

"I kin see that, but I don't have ta like it."

"No, we don't have to like it, but I don't want 'er feelin' guilty fer somethin', because we made 'er feel that way. Iffin this is what she wants, we have no business makin' it hard fer 'er. She's worked hard ta talk like a lady. She's gonna find life a whole lot different an' I spect she'll get homesick, but once she's out, she'll not be a coming back.

Zeb nodded. "Reckon yer right. We don't have ta like it, but I wouldn't want ta put an extra burden on 'er shoulders neither."

Mini Louise had started down the lane at a fast gallop before she remembered to slow down and take it easy on her pa's horse. *It's not my intention to ruin this horse. I know I have a temper, but I need to get it under control. Lord, I lift my attitudes up to You. You have answered my prayer about me getting a job. I thank You for that. I know You are a God Who cares about me. I pray I will be a delight to You and that You will smooth the way for me to be a nanny for the Bannisters' boy. I know Ma is trying hard to get Pa to understand my desire to leave home. I think I'll go insane iffin—I mean if I have to spend much more time there. I can't stand all the noise. It's never quiet lessen—unless everyone is in bed. I actually love milking the cow now because it's quiet.* She smiled at her prayer. *Lord, thank You for caring about me. Amen.*

She traveled at an easy canter and was surprised that her thoughts had passed the time so quickly. She rode under the gigantic sign across the entrance to McCaully-Bannisters' Ranch. There was a long lane that curved around to the beautiful two-storied house. When she'd rounded the curve, she caught her breath at the beauty of it. *Lord, let me be a blessing to this family.*

She rode past the barn and bunkhouses. Across the length of the left side of the house was a long hitching rail. She tied up and looked around as she stepped toward the house. Everything, although a big outfit, looked neat and tidy. Under the windows of the house were shrubs in full bloom. She didn't know anything about domesticated plants, all her experience was with wildflowers. *I sure have a lot to learn.* Her eyes widened with pleasure at the bountiful colors and blooms.

Mini Louise climbed the steps and crossed to the heavy oak door. She started to knock, but Mrs. McDuffy, the Bannisters' housekeeper opened it as her hand was in forward motion. She grinned at the housekeeper.

"Good morning, I'm Mini Lou, I believe Miss Caitlin is expecting me."

"Oh, dear! We are at sixes and sevens this morning. I suppose you know all about it since your father works at the mine."

Mini Lou's expression of bewilderment indicated to Duffy that the girl had no idea what she was talking about.

"Come in, girl, come on in. The family is gathered in the kitchen. We also have Mr. Kirk's brother and his wife here. Come along now…there's a good girl." Duffy looked over her shoulder to make sure Mini Lou was following. The girl's eyes were enormous, and she looked as if any moment she'd take flight.

Mini Lou swallowed and followed Mrs. McDuffy across the long dining room and into a kitchen that would have swallowed up their one-room house two times over.

Her quick glance around the table found Caitlin, and she kept her eyes fixed there, feeling overwhelmed by the adults sitting at the table.

Caitlin, seeing the girl, rose from her chair with a smile. "I am so sorry! I forgot all about our appointment." She strode over to the girl wearing denim britches that made Mini Lou almost drop her jaw, but instead, a grin spread over the girl's features as she realized she was going to love it here. Her eyes sparkled at Caitlin's words.

"It's all right. I can see you have company."

"Not really company, they are family." She drew the slender shoulders close to her and walked with her to the table. Kirk and Matthew both stood in respect of womanhood, and it embarrassed Mini Lou, as the blood crept up and into her cheeks.

She looked at Matthew who closely resembled Mr. Kirk. Her eyes traveled over to his wife, and she gaped at the loveliness of the woman. Coppery curls cascaded down her back and green eyes looked warmly into Mini Lou's with compassion.

"You know my husband, Kirk. This is his brother, Matthew, and his wife, Liberty Bannister."

Mini Lou held out her hand to shake Matthew's and then Liberty's.

"I am pleased to meet you," she said.

"It is our pleasure," Matthew replied, as he and Kirk sat back down.

"I understand you plan to be a nanny for Jonny," Liberty stated. "It's a very important task to be responsible for a child and be a model for a little one to follow. Jonny is only a year old, but you will be an important factor in his little life. You look quite capable."

"Thank you, ma'am. I have helped to raise quite a passel of children, and I suppose my mother would be the best as a reference for that."

Caitlin was glad for Liberty's words. She gazed at Mini Lou and nodded her head. "Come with me, Mini Lou. We'll go to the nursery." She glanced at the others seated around the table and spoke as she started out of the kitchen. "Please excuse us."

Mini Lou followed on Caitlin's heels, thinking to herself. *My stars, I am going to learn a lot everyday living here! I had no idea taking care of children was all that important. I didn't know I should excuse myself when I leave the room. I'm going to keep my mouth shut and my eyes peeled.*

Mini Lou had never been inside a beautiful house before. Her eyes darted here and there taking in the understated elegance of the dining room they traversed before going up stairs. The railing and balusters of the handrail for the stairs was a work of art in itself. She looked at paintings of Caitlin and her sisters when they were younger as well as an impressive painting of what must be Caitlin's parents. *Miss Caitlin looks like her mother…a lot!* When they reached the top of the stairs, Mini Lou looked down and felt a slight dizziness. She'd never been up this high in her entire life.

Reckon, I mean I suppose, I have a lot to learn. Think, Mini Lou! Put on your thinking cap! I need to think before I speak so I can say things properly. I suppose I have much to learn, and I plan on learnin', I mean learning it! I plan to be a respectable lady with my own means of money. I don't want to be dependent on anyone.

I think I could make my way by sewing and making hats. I seem to have a talent for it. Perhaps I could teach, although then I'd be tied to one place. I don't care to get married and have a passel of children. I want to travel and enjoy life. Maybe...just maybe I may have my own home someday. It's planning and working hard toward a goal I set for myself that will get me there.

She looked around herself with pleasure as she reached the top of the stairs. An ornate oaken bookshelf stood across the hall from the steps filled with books and bibelots in a pleasing arrangement. Above the shelf was a large painting of the McCaully family. She stood looking at the finely dressed family. Her eyes were drawn to Mac McCaully's hands, which looked veined with hard work.

Caitlin waited a minute and then said, "Follow me, Mini Lou."

Mini Lou came to herself with a jerk and followed Caitlin down the hall with a backward glance at the painting. *No matter what it costs me, I will be successful. If it's hard work that gets me to my goal, I will be a success.*

Caitlin glanced at Mini Lou and then did a double take at her eyes. *Goodness, she certainly looks determined about something. Wonder what she's thinking?*

"Here we are. This is the nursery. I was brought up in this nursery as were my sisters. My da made sure we had all the classical books and learning even though we lived on a ranch."

They entered the room, and immediately Mini Lou felt a homeyness and a feeling of contentment flood through her. She strolled over to the bookshelves that cover three walls. They were children's height about three feet tall. Atop the shelves were birds' nests, shells from the beach, a collection of rocks and gemstones as well as a few little paintings. There were numerous things to spark a child's interest.

Mini Lou gazed in awe at the collections and wondered how someone could be so thoughtful as to include all these things in a child's learning.

"It's a beautiful room, ma'am," she said. "I don't think you could look anywhere in this room and not learn something. Your little Jonny is going to love it when he gets a little older. I will love teaching him and caring for him. I want you to know I'll do my best to be the most agreeable nanny I can be." She pulled a book off the shelf and read the title, knowing she was going to be reading the literature before she taught her young pupil. She looked forward to reading and planned to increase her vocabulary and knowledge through books. She didn't know the basic stories most children read. She had access to the Bible at home, but had never had time to really sit down and study it. Now, with a baby taking naps and going to bed early, she'd be able to read to her heart's content.

I'm going to read and read and read!

Caitlin perused the girl and was satisfied she'd made a good choice. It had been at Kirk's suggestion that she find someone to be a nanny for Jonathan. She had started to balk at the idea but realized her love of riding the range would be curtailed if she didn't. Sweeny, her personal maid, had watched him the few times she'd ridden out, but she wasn't much good with babies. Jonathan was always crying when she got back to the house, and Sweeny was in a sweat over trying to get him to stop.

Cait put her finger to her lips, and pushed the door open that led to Jonathan's bedroom.

Mini Lou tiptoed to the crib and smiled down on the sleeping baby. His face was flushed, and long lashes lay on his cheeks. She looked over at Caitlin and nodded and smiled. The room had a single bed in it where Mini Lou thought she would sleep, but Caitlin opened another door to a beautiful nanny's suite her father had put in.

The walls were freshly painted the palest of pink and wall paper covered one wall with pink rosebuds on stems of green. The bed, nightstand, desk and mantel over the small brick fireplace were painted white. Above the mantel was a huge painting of a trellis of climbing roses the same shade as the wallpaper.

Mini Lou stared in wonder at the room and gazed back at the painting. The trellis was white and a brick path spun its way under the roses, curving around to be lost from sight.

"This is beautiful," she breathed. "Why our whole house could just about fit into this room!"

"Well, as long as you live here, it's yours. You also have your own commode room." Caitlin strolled across the room to open a door. The same wallpaper lined all four walls. A freestanding bathtub with brass handles and a black circle with a hole in it puzzled Mini Lou. handles and a black circle with a hole in it puzzled Mini Lou. same wallpaper lined all four walls. A freestanding bathtub with brass handles and a black circle with a hole in it puzzled Mini Lou.

"What's that?" she queried.

Caitlin leaned over and turned on the taps. "We've had water piped into the house. I cannot begin to tell you what a convenience it is!"

Mini Lou covered her mouth with her hand as she gasped. "You mean…oh my goodness!"

Cait smiled at the girl. "It's been a blessing for Sweeny, my maid. She lugged hot water up here for years." She pointed to the toilet. "That is a wonderful invention, too. No more chamber pots!" Cait exclaimed. "It's called a toilet."

"I thought the word toilet meant fixing up your face or getting ready for a party. It's a French word isn't it?"

"Yes, it is. But it also means one of these contraptions, and it can mean getting a person ready for surgery…washing them down, I guess."

Mini Lou's eyes were like saucer plates. "N-no more ch-chamber pots?" She stuttered.

"Nope! See the handle?" Caitlin pushed the handle and down went the contents in the bowl.

"How in the world do people think these up such things?"

"I don't know," Caitlin chuckled, "but when we found out we had a gold mine on the property, I had a lot of upgrades put into the house. It's made things a lot more convenient, and frankly, it saves a lot of time."

"I can see it would. My oh my! Why I've never even heard of such inventions let alone seen them. Wait until I tell Ma about this. She'll probably think I'm funning her!" Her eyes sparkled at the thought.

Going back into the bedroom, Caitlin opened the huge clothespress. "This is for your belongings."

"I don't have much," Mini Lou stated.

"Well, you will. I will need to have you go into town and get Hannah to measure you out for some new clothes. Do you know Ewen Carr?"

Mini Lou shook her head. "No, who is he?"

"He's our foreman and has known me since I was born. He married Hannah a couple years back. I had a house built in the field, left of the barn, so it's pretty private. It's nice that they have a house of their own on the ranch, but Hannah still has her shop in Santa Rosa. Which reminds me…" She patted Mini Lou on the arm. "I'm pretty sure Maisie will keep the gem mine open."

Mini Lou swallowed, a frightened look in her eyes, and croaked out a whisper. "What in the world do you mean? Is Mr. Galway planning to shut it down?"

CHAPTER VI

For we are strangers before thee, and sojourners,
as were all our fathers: our days on the earth
are as a shadow, and there is none abiding.

I CHRONICLES 29:15

CAITLIN, HER EYES FULL OF REMORSE, replied with regret in her voice for the way she had spoken. "I'm sorry, I suppose you don't know. Someone shot Gavin…er…Mr. Galway last night as he was closing up shop for the day."

Mini Lou's eyes widened and she gasped. "Oh my! Oh what a horrible thing to do! Who would commit such a crime?"

"I have no idea. Gavin's a good hardworking man, and I don't know anyone who doesn't like him. He wasn't dead last night, when we left him, but he was close. He also, evidently, suffered a heart attack. Doc thinks it saved his life…that he was collapsing when the gunman shot him, so he missed his heart. I don't even know if he made it through the night. Doc operated on him. I am hoping you can start today, as I want to be with my sister who needs me. And as I said, I don't think they'll close the mine. It would affect too many people."

Mini Lou's eyes brightened. "It certainly would. My pa depends on his job, and he loves Mr. Galway. I'm sure it will be all right if I stay today. I can get my things later. I am willing to help out in any way I can."

"Does your mother think you're returning home this morning after the interview?"

"Yes, but it will be all right. She worries about everything anyway," Mini Lou said with a cheeky smile.

Caitlin grinned at the girl. "Well, no sense letting her worry for nothing. I'll have you go home and collect your things and tell your ma you have a job. Sweeny and my cook can take care of Jonny until you get back unless Liberty stays here, but I have a feeling she'll want to ride into town with me."

Caitlin led the way back down the stairs and said, "Now scoot! I want you back as soon as you can get here. Sweeny just doesn't have the right touch with Jonny, and I think you will. Be sure you ride safely. Oh…I nearly forgot. You'll eat meals with Kirk, Ewen, Hannah and me. I'll see you later."

"Thank you, Miss Caitlin. I hope I do a good job. Please don't hesitate to correct me iffin…" Mini Lou colored up. "I mean if I need correction. Sorry for my mistake, I've been working diligently on trying to speak properly and increase my vocabulary."

"I must say, Mini Lou, you are doing a superb job of learning! Now you need to get going! It's going to be a busy day. Oh, and tell your pa to come get your horse. You'll be riding one of ours, because I know you are short on horseflesh."

"Yes, ma'am!" Mini Lou responded with a huge grin. She closed the front door with a decided click, ran down the steps and out to the hitching rail. Climbing on her horse, she set off at a fast clip, slowing down only when she thought of her pa and his chastisement for riding too fast in the heat.

Miss Caitlin is so nice. I can't wait to get back here. Wait till I tell Ma about the toilet and running water. She probably will think I'm funning her. Pa'll be tickled I won't be needing his horse anymore. She patted the horse's neck as she thought about not riding the mare anymore.

"You're a good horse, Reddy. I will miss you and our fast rides. Pa won't work you to death and you'll probably last longer without me on your back." Mini Lou felt sad that Reddy would no longer be her constant companion. Reddy had carried her, often enough, away from the noise and busyness of her home. "I have a new home now and, of all things, a room to myself!" She spoke aloud to Reddy, as she often did when riding. "I thought I'd be sharing a room with the baby, but my goodness, I will have all the peace and quiet I want. I'll get to read those books Miss Caitlin said she read as a child. Classics, she said. Books that anyone not dirt poor has probably read. New ideas and that new word I leart—learned...innuendoes...that I would miss out on. I plan to learn all my brain can hold. I *will* be a real lady someday!"

Lorenzo Brown stood with his hands on his hips looking out over the crowd of men. As foreman of the mine, his job was to see to it the work was done correctly. One didn't just take a pick axe and hack into the wall of the mine with jewels that could be damaged. Brown also oversaw and listened to and counseled men who cared to share their problems. Sometimes he felt as if he was a priest or a father confessor.

He stood on a long upended washtub. It was his daily platform. Waiting to talk until he had everyone's attention, he surveyed the large group of men. Finally the talking died down, and the shuffling feet were silent. The men looked at him expectantly. They were used to the bossman starting the day with a pep talk or some tidbit of information or a directive that had come down from Mr. Galway. It was a daily occurrence.

"Good morning, men. First off, I will tell you straight out. I don't know if the mine will shut down for a time or not."

The silence was deafening as the men waited with dread in their hearts at the words their boss had just spoken.

"Mr. Galway was closing shop last evening when someone entered the store and shot him in cold blood. He's still alive, but just."

Gasps and comments arose from the crowd, and a voice called out. "Is he gonna live?"

"Doc Addison doesn't know yet. He's not out of the woods. It wasn't just the gunshot wound that was the problem. Evidently, Mr. Galway suffered a heart attack at the same time. Doc thinks it actually saved his life. He was collapsing as the gunman shot him. Mrs. Galway wants to keep the mine open and the store at this point, but we can't be sure it will be so in the future." He cleared his throat.

"If you're of the persuasion, I say you need to be praying for Mr. Galway's recovery. I will keep you informed as I get further details. We'll be working the same area as yesterday. Are there any questions?"

"Yes, sir, there is. Is Mrs. Galway all right?"

"Yes, she's tuckered out, but she'd already left by the time the gunman entered the store. She spent the night next to Mr. Galway, and gave the information to Sandoval Peabody to deliver the message to me. Anymore questions? No? All right, let's get to work."

He hopped down of the washtub, and headed to the mine's office.

Jasper Clemmons, the under foreman, hurried after Brown. "Why didn't you tell me about Galway before you told the workers?" His voice sounded angry as he spat out the words. "I am under foreman and I should know what's going on!"

Lorenzo, who went by Lenny, swung around in surprise. "I've been busy this morning. Furthermore, I don't quite understand your indignation. I've got more to deal with than listening to you gripe about the workers and everything else around here. You need to pull yourself together and start acting like a foreman instead of a discontented child. If you don't enjoy your job, why don't you quit?"

He didn't see the look of consternation on Jasper's face, but turned and continued to walk toward the office, tired of Jasper's petty complaints. There were several men who had real problems at home, a sick wife or child, a lame horse. He enjoyed working with those who had need of his advice and loved the men who worked so hard to provide a living for their families. His biggest pain was Jasper Clemmons. He really did wish the man would quit. *I'd like to see Zebidiah Pindar take his place. He's a good man who cares about others and is not seeking to stab me in the back.*

Doc Addison grimaced. "I plumb forgot I am to meet the train into Sacramento tomorrow. My doctor replacement arrives a little after noon. I suppose with all that's happened I have a good excuse for forgetting, but forgetting things is getting more common than I like." He sat with slumped shoulders talking to Maisie and Aidan.

Aidan stood abruptly. "Jared didn't go out to the ranch today. He's been waiting around to see if there's anything he can do to help. I'll tell him to hop on the train and go on down to Sacramento to meet your party. Who all is coming?"

"Doctor Oliver Sandhurst, his daughter Marnie, and his housekeeper. I've forgotten her name."

Payton McGrath, who was sitting in the receptionist's chair of the waiting room listening to the conversation, spoke lightly. "It's Miss or Mrs. Jennings…Deidra Jennings, I believe."

"That's it! You have it right, Payton. See, I told you my memory is failing!" Doc muttered.

"Everyone has that problem now and again," Maisie said soothingly, "and especially during times of stress."

"Is there anything else I should tell Jared? Let me run home and get him onto the next train to Sacramento. He can spend the night there and bring your group back tomorrow," Aidan said. "Would that be all right with you, Doc?"

"I suppose so," Doc replied. "I told Oliver I'd meet his train, but then he knows how it is with doctors especially if an emergency arises."

Maisie had dark circles under her eyes. She wasn't used to weeping so much nor sleeping on an examining table. "Go, Aidan. That's a good job for Jared. He likes to help everyone in any way he can, and Doc would appreciate it. I'm sure Caitlin will be in to see us today, and we can tell her Jared is skipping another day."

Aidan waved her hand, "Goodbye!" She headed out the door.

"My, what a change the Lord has wrought in Jared Hart's life." Doc shook his head in wonder. "In all my days, I don't think I ever saw a more selfish person than him. The Lord surely brought about a miracle when Jared trusted in Jesus as his Savior. He now has one of the most kind, giving hearts I have ever seen."

Maisie nodded her head in agreement. "I saw the change in him right away. It gave me pause, because at first I thought he was only shamming, but he wasn't. He really has changed."

She stood and stretched. "I feel as if I've aged ten years overnight."

"You need to rest, young lady," Doc Addison admonished. "Expecting a baby tires a woman out, but the added stress of the last, what…fifteen hours or so has taken its toll."

"I know. And it's not going to get any easier for quite some time, is it?" Maisie's lips were drawn tight as if in pain, and she had to stop herself from wringing her hands.

"No, for sure you will have a lot on your plate. I need to caution you, Maisie. He's not out of the woods by any means. I still don't know if he will recover. It's good that you can afford to have someone to help with the store and that you have a couple servants who will be more than willing to help."

Doctor Addison had awakened in the middle of the night. He could hear a dog barking down the street and figured it was the reason. It was still dark, but a path of light filtered itself across the room from a bright moon. He'd had a window built into the ceiling above the bed because he loved looking at the heavens when he went to bed and lay praying or when he couldn't sleep. The curtains were always open at night as was the window so he could gaze out as he lay on his right side in his huge, comfortable bed.

This is my last night in this house. I believe I will be content living with Kirk and Caitlin. It's not that I don't have money. Goodness, my mother left me enough to fill my coffers until I die. She was so disgusted when I left Boston and the prestigious work I was able to do there. She hated the fact that I was a lowly country doctor, but I've loved my job and the people I've been able to help. I've loved every minute of it.

My, but I was so blessed when Kirk and Caitlin asked me if little Jonathan could call me grandpa. I will have the children and grandchildren Evangeline and I always longed for. I love Caitlin and have come to love her husband, Kirk. He's a man of God, and Caitlin couldn't have done better in finding herself a husband.

His thoughts turned into a whispered prayer. "Lord, how grateful I am for Thy provision. I pray, Almighty God, for Gavin. He's not doing the best, and he's not responding the way I hoped he would. My heart goes out to Maisie. I know all Gavin has to do is have another episode with his heart, and he's done for." Doc sighed heavily.

"Dear Almighty God, I also pray for Oliver, his daughter, Marnie, and his housekeeper...uh...yes, his housekeeper, Mrs. Jennings. I pray they arrive safely and will love the West as much as I have come to love it. I pray the transition of my patients to him will be smooth, and I pray Thy hand to guide Oliver in all he puts his hand to. May living here help to erase the pain of the loss of his wife. I know full well that pain, but I also know there are joys here on this earth after the loss if we will open our eyes and see Thy bountiful hand at work." Doc opened his eyes and looked out at the beautiful sky. Light from the moon filtered into his room, and stars, so big you felt you could reach out and touch them, filled the heavens.

"Lord, I'm thankful Jared will meet the train for me. How I praise Thy name for the change in that young man! Thy Holy Spirit has wrought goodness where there was so much evil. I thank Thee for the love I see betwixt Jared and Aidan." A comet streaked across the expanse as he lay looking up to the heavens.

"Almighty God, I ask for Thy favor to be upon the Pindar girl as she becomes nanny for little Jonathan. May Thy hand guide her and grow her to be the woman of God she is meant to be, and may she be a wonderful influence on the boy as he grows close to her."

He rolled over and with a deep sigh fell back asleep.

The train pulled into the station with a trail of black smoke and a great screeching of brakes, metal on metal piercing the ears.

Marnie jumped up and down in excitement, holding her father's hand, as the group of three waited for the train to come to a complete stop. They were about ten people back in the queue from the exit doors, and there was also a string of people behind them waiting to disembark.

"Oh, Papa!" she exclaimed, "we're finally here! Will your Doctor Addison meet up with us? What if his looks have changed since you last saw him and you don't recognize him? What if he doesn't come? What will we do?"

"I've already thought of that contingency, sweetheart. Doctors can hardly arrange the events in their lives, as you well know, because accidents and illnesses trump their plans almost every time. If he does or doesn't show up, we will board the train for Santa Rosa. What *is* important is that we make sure all our belongings are offloaded and put onto the Santa Rosa train. More than that, we can't do. We just have to see how it all works out." He smiled down at his daughter who saw for the first time since her mother's death, a sparkle of excitement in her father's blue eyes.

Deedee was exhausted. She clung to the back of a seat as the train came to a halt, hoping she could stay on her feet. Descending the train, she was thankful for the doctor's solicitous attention. His hand reached for hers, and then he tucked her arm into his to steady her.

"I've traveled by train before, Deedee, and let me tell you, when you start walking across this platform, you will walk like a drunken sailor until you get your land legs." As he spoke, his eyes searched the crowd for his friend and mentor, but he didn't see Doctor Addison anywhere. He didn't allow the disappointment to show on his face.

"Let's head to the rear of this monster and watch the offloading the same as we did in Chicago."

The three started down the long platform, Deedee, thankful for the arm she felt was holding her up, looked around with pleasure, surprised by the flowers overflowing pots and lilacs in full bloom

Marnie evidently felt the same way as she pulled off her shawl. "It's warm here!" she exclaimed. "Look at all those flowers in bloom, Papa. Just think! A little over an hour ago we were traveling in snow!"

Oliver nodded. "Yes, I suppose we're going to find a lot of differences here in the West."

When they got to the rear of the train, a young man approached.

"Hello," he said. "Are you Doctor Sandhurst?"

"Why yes, I am. I'm Oliver Sandhurst and you are?"

"Name's Jared Hart." He stuck out his hand, and Oliver clasp it in a firm grip.

"This is my daughter, Marnie, and my helper and friend, Deidra Jennings." His eyes studied Jared as he spoke. "We're thankful you've come to meet us. It'll help with our getting onto the next train."

Deidra held out her hand, and Jared took it, giving it a gentle shake. Marnie also held out her hand, and he took it tenderly, bowed over it, and gave her a big grin.

"Welcome to California," he said. "I have come in Doc Addison's stead. He has a patient who was shot and suffered a heart attack at the same time. Actually the patient is my brother-in-law. Doc said to welcome you and to say he's sorry he couldn't make it. He is delighted you have come. All is in readiness for your arrival. Doc has moved out of the second floor of his office building and will be living with another set of my in-laws." Jared grinned. "Doc Addison is family to us."

"We thank you for the warm welcome, Mr. Hart. And we," he gestured to Marnie and Deedee, "are very glad to be here and off the train. We enjoyed the trip, but are eager to get settled. Is it very far to Sonoma from here?"

"Not by train. We'll be all settled in before nightfall." Jared, perusing the doctor's face, could see the doctor was exhausted. "Without further ado, let's get your things separated out and onto the Santa Rosa train."

"Thank you for meeting us. It was generous of you."

"You are welcome," Jared replied.

He found a four-wheeled dolly and proceeded to load the things the doctor pulled from the pile the workers had taken from the cargo cars.

CHAPTER VII

Come and hear, all ye that fear God,
and I will declare what he hath done for my soul.

PSALM 66:16

"PARDON ME!" A YOUNG MAN EXCLAIMED as he elbowed Jared aside and reached for one of the bags on the dolly. He pulled it out and stated, "This is mine!"

"No, it's not!" Marnie said in a loud voice. "That bag belongs to me!"

The young man ignored her and started off with the bag, but Jared got in front of him and asked, "What's in the bag, sir?"

"Please step aside!" the young man responded. "I am only retrieving my own bag!"

"And I repeat, what is in the bag, sir?" Jared repeated.

"I have clothes in here, as well as a set of reins, a harness and a saddle-blanket" he answered.

"Miss Sandhurst, what's in the bag?"

Marnie glared at the man who was most likely in his mid-twenties. "I have one doll, some bric-a-brac that belonged to my mother, a Bible that was mother's and it's all wrapped in a bright quilt my mother made for me!" Marnie folded her arms across her chest disgusted and indignant the young man would try to take her bag.

Jared reached for the bag and took it before the man thought to grasp it tighter. The stranger let it go, and Jared sat it down on the platform, unbuckled the clasp, and pulled the bag open. A beautiful array of color was the first thing to meet the eye, and the stranger gasped.

"I am so sorry! Please forgive me! Why this bag looks identical to mine! Please, young lady, do accept my apologies."

"I accept, sir. Let's go look for your bag." Once Marnie was satisfied the man wasn't trying to steal from her, she tried to make him feel better about his mistake. The two began to paw though the immense amount of luggage as many other people were doing. Marnie spotted his bag and pulled it from the pile.

"Here it is, sir. And I can see why you thought mine was yours." The two bags were of the same make and design as well as the same in size.

The man reached into his pocket and pulled out a Liberty dollar.

"Here," he said. "Please accept my apology."

"I already did accept it if you will remember, sir. You don't have to pay me for anything. If we can't help one another we'd be a sorry lot, wouldn't we?"

The young man's eyebrows rose in surprise. "Yes," he said. "You are absolutely correct. But again, I thank you," he said, as he pocketed the dollar.

"You are welcome, sir."

He turned to Jared, thinking Jared was Marnie's father.

"You have done a good job in teaching your child the value of helping others," he said.

Jared laughed. "She's not my daughter, sir, although from what I've just witnessed, I hope my future children will be as nice." He pointed to Oliver who had missed out on the whole episode but was now finished and turned toward the group. Watching him, Jared saw his jaw drop, and he strode over to them.

"Colton Broderick Danbury!" Oliver clapped the young man on the back and then gave him a huge bearhug. "Why, what a coincidence! What in the world are you doing here? And where are you going? How is your sister, Jean, doing? I haven't heard from either of you since I sent her to that specialist in New York."

"I've come west to make a new life for myself. As to where I am going, I have no idea. As you know, I lived with Jean, who was like a mother to me. She passed away a few months back, and I felt at loose ends. She was all I had in the world. Thought I'd come west and see where the wind blows me. "

"Look, Papa. Look at his bag. It looks identical to mine. He thought I was taking his bag."

Oliver glanced at the two bags. "Simple mistake to make when they are the same shape, size, and color," he said easily. "I am so sorry about Jean. I had hopes my diagnosis was wrong and that she'd recover under the ministrations of a specialist." He looked closely into Colton's eyes. "We," he nodded at Marnie and Deedee, "are going north to Santa Rosa. Why don't you join us? It would be nice to have you nearby."

Colton looked surprised by the invitation but didn't take a second to respond. "I'd be happy to. It would be nice to settle down where I know at least one face!"

"You have good taste in bags, too, Mr. Danbury," Marnie said with a cheeky grin on her face. She hooked her arm in his as he picked up his bag. That too, surprised him, but he looked down at her, and his heart melted.

"We'd better get these things on the Santa Rosa train," Jared said as he began pushing the dolly down the platform. He pointed ahead to a much smaller steam engine with a few passenger cars and a few cargo cars. "That's our ride," he said.

The dolly was stacked high with luggage, but it got to their destination without anything falling off.

Marnie and Deedee strolled alongside the dolly, but stopped at the entrance to the passenger car.

"Look over there, Deedee," Marnie said. "Look at those clouds! And look at that! It's a magnificent double rainbow. Makes me think God is giving us an extra promise that we are going to have a new and wonderful life here in the West. I am excited now to get up to Santa Rosa. Mr. Hart seems very nice, doesn't he?"

Deedee, feeling much better about walking, nodded her head. "Yes, he seems quite the gentleman." She led Marnie up the steps and into one of the passenger cars as the men loaded the contents of the dolly into a cargo car.

Deedee sat with a plop as if the air had been poked out of her. Marni sat across from her and looked with concern at her best friend.

"Are you sure you're all right, Deedee?"

"I'm fine, sugar. Just really, really tired is all. I'm not as young as I look, you know!" She laughed at her comment and Marnie joined her.

"No, perhaps your not, but it's true even though you laugh about it. You do look a lot younger than you are. How come you never married?"

"Never could find a man who'd put up with me." She laughed again.

It didn't take long with three men loading the cargo car. Soon finished, they joined Deedee and Marnie.

Jared, Colton and Oliver sat facing each other across the aisle from Deedee and Marnie.

Oliver was curious about the comments Jared had made. He glanced out the window, but his glance turned into a gaze. On his right, the cobalt blue of the sky seemed to kiss the horizon in the distance, but on his left the sky looked dark and ominous as if a storm was brewing. The view right in front of him showed the hills, covered in moss-green grass. It was so beautiful, it made him catch his breath. It reminded him of Corine. Spring had always been her favorite time of the year. His was autumn. But as he looked at wildflowers raising their faces heavenward, and clumps of various colors dotting the hills, he thought to himself, *I just might switch my favorite time of the year to spring. It's gorgeous.*

He smiled at his thoughts as his attention swung back to the conversation between Colton and Jared.

"You think you'd like to try your hand at being a cow puncher?" Jared wondered if the man was serious.

"Yes, I've read about it, and I do know how to rope and ride," Colton replied.

"Do you know the third R?" Jared asked with a smile.

"Excuse me?"

"The third R in being a cowboy. It's rope, ride, and repair fences."

"Frankly, I don't know how to repair fencing. I've read about the barbed wire, and I could learn." Colton was interested.

"Well, now," Jared said, "I might be able to fix you up with a job right away. I work at McCaully-Bannisters' Ranch in Sonoma County. It's a great place to work, and it's only forty minutes or so from Santa Rosa."

"Sounds interesting," Colton said cautiously. He didn't plan to go to some Podunk ranch and be out of touch with real life and society.

Oliver leaned forward listening to the two men talking without entering into the conversation. He eyed Colton closely. *Wonder what happened? Colton and Jean Danbury were as wealthy as anyone I've ever known. Did they lose their money somehow? His clothes are good, but then so are Mr. Hart's. Hmm, this is interesting. I hope he didn't get swindled or spend endless money trying to find a cure for Jean. His house was a showpiece. He should at least have money from the sale of that.*

He sat back and listened while Jared explained that he worked on the McCaully-Bannister Ranch because he wanted to, not because he had to.

"So you're telling me you enjoy the work so much that you go work on a ranch because you want to, but you have enough money not to work? Is that what you're saying?" Colton didn't quite believe Jared.

"Yes, I used to be the most lazy, shiftless, selfish man one could ever hope *not* to meet." Jared chuckled. "Believe me, I had a lot of people who wished to avoid me. I stole money from my sister-in-law's payroll for the ranch hands, desperate to pay off a gambling debt. I didn't know it was the payroll and hoped I could win money back to pay it off before I was found out. I also owed money to just about every business in Santa Rosa on top of that gambling debt. My wife went around paying off my debts, but she didn't know about the gambling debt or I'd have been out on my ear." He took a deep breath and proceeded with his story.

"Ewen Carr is foreman for the McCaully Ranch. Caitlin, at the time, wasn't married to Kirk Bannister. She was sole owner, so it was called McCaully Ranch then. Anyway, Ewen was sitting in my kitchen waiting for me the morning after my heist. He gave me the ultimatum of working off my debt or going to jail for robbery. I worked off my debt and ended up asking Jesus to be my Savior. It has changed everything and all of me. I'm not perfect yet, but I'm working everyday to be more like Christ and to think of others before myself. I was such an unhappy man, and now I have a joy in my soul no one can take away." His eyes were full of light, and the peace on his face was a joy to behold.

"That's quite a story, Mr. Hart," Colton said.

"Just call me Jared, Mr. Danbury. Here in the West, we're not so formal."

"And you have my permission to call me Colton." He held out his hand to shake Jared's. "Thank you for your story. I was fourteen when I asked Jesus to be my Savior. My father had suffered a heart attack. It really scared me into thinking about eternity. My father died a year later, but my sister and I had become Christians."

Jared nodded his head. "It's amazing what a comfort it is, but I know, too, what a change it has wrought in my life. I used to think Aidan, that's my wife, and she's Caitlin's sister, was the answer to making me happy. No one can make another person happy. I've found happiness is found in doing something for someone else. It is a byproduct of service or a byproduct of creativity. If you say, 'I'm going to be happy,' most likely you won't be."

Colton raised his eyebrows at the wisdom that seemed to pour out of Jared's mouth. "I can see the sense of that." He said.

It was quiet for a few minutes, and he sat back to ponder the testimony Jared had just shared with him.

Perhaps I'll go to this ranch and see what happens. It evidently isn't a drudge job, or if it is, this Jared seems to be happy with it. I'll bide my time and see what turns up.

Oliver observing the conversation had finally lagged decided to satisfy his curiosity.

"Mr. Hart—er Jared—sorry, I'm used to a bit more formality. I was wondering about your comment. You said your brother-in-law was shot but Dr. Addison thinks he suffered a heart attack at the same time? Is that what you were saying?"

"Yes, that's what I said. Doc thinks Gavin was in the process of collapsing so the bullet missed his heart. He's in a bad way, and we are praying all will turn out well. Maisie, my wife's sister, is expecting a baby, and this has hit her particularly hard. We know if he recovers that it will be a long process before he's back on his feet. They own a gem mine, and he was closing their Santa Rosa store for the day when a bandit came in and shot him. That's all we know about it. It happened yesterday."

"No wonder Dr. Addison didn't come to meet us!" Oliver stroked his chin, something he often did often when he was thinking. "So, I know this is the wild west, but do you have gunfights and robberies and such? I've read about it, but I thought the West more civilized now."

Jared stared at the doctor, realizing he'd made him think twice about moving here. "We do have the occasional shooting, but we can go several years with no problems or shootings. Your city of Boston has a lot more violence than we ever have in Santa Rosa," he said succinctly.

The freshness of the early morning air was fast turning into another hot day. Not a hint of breeze could be felt, and the heaviness of a coming storm seemed to weigh a body down.

Ezra Walker had ridden around looking for red dun quarter horses. It was clear he'd never noticed how common the breed was. He wondered what he could now do. He sat in the sheriff's office drumming his fingers on the desk talking to himself.

"I have no idea how in the world I'm going to be able to find the person who did this heinous crime. Let's start with those people working at the mine who have dun colored quarter horses. He ticked off on his fingers There's Zebidiah Pindar whose daughter has been riding that horse a lot. There's Jonah Whatcom, Lenny Brown, Jasper Clemmons, and that young man, Ernest Smith and Sandoval Peabody. That's a good start, but what if I missed seeing the one at the mine? Another fact is that there are others in the area who have dun colored quarter horses. Kirk Bannister said there were at least three cowboys at his ranch that he could think of off the top of his head. I reckon trying to find the culprit by a horse breed alone is not going to be enough."

He put his head in his hands and scratched at the back of his head as if it would clear his brain to think how he could find who shot Mr. Galway. *Lord help me find who did this horrible deed.* He lifted his head and said, "I hope Mr. Galway is better this morning. He's such a nice man. Reckon I should concentrate on those men at the mine. I'd bet my bottom dollar every single man working there would know when gemstones are taken to Galway's store." He stood and stretched. "Think I'll mosey on over to Doc Addison's and see how Galway's doing. Wouldn't hurt to see one of those McGrath twins either." He grinned as he strapped on his gun, picked up his hat, and settled it comfortably on his head. As he headed out the door, he said, "Hope it's Payton." He grinned all the way to the doctor's office.

Jonah Whatcom, the sun already warm on his back, was astride his dun-colored horse on his way to work at the mine. He looked around as he loped along, suddenly realizing spring was in full swing. The lilacs and other shrubbery along the road were bursting with color. He didn't know the names of most of them, but they were beautiful. The flatland and hills were a riot of reds, yellows, whites, pinks and lavender.

He took a lusty breath and smiled to himself at his enjoyment of the little things he took for granted every day. The fragrant flowers wafted in the air and made him feel young and exuberant.

Wonder when I can get down ta the San Rafael School of Primary Learnin'? It's got ta be soon now I've told Cindy Sue about my plan. I need to ask for time off work. My but didn't it make her jump for joy! I'd do jest about anything fer thet woman!

The San Rafael School of Primary Learning was an orphanage as well as a primary school.

Wonder what fees a lawyer charges fer drawin' up the papers ta make it all legal-like? Wonder how much the school charges? Maybe we kin get two children with the money I got. Yep...I'm gonna make my woman right proud!

He was surprised to see he'd already arrived at the mine. He tied up in his regular spot and strode over to his tool box. Looking down, a ripple of shock flooded through him. There, for anyone to see was a couple of greenbacks hanging out of the side of the closed lid. Unlatching the lid, he saw a bundle of greenbacks rolled up inside. He looked around, but no one seemed to be watching. He scooped the money up and hurried over to the office. He entered without knocking and was upset that no one was in the room. He dropped the bundle of money onto the desk of Jasper Clemmons as Lenny Brown came strolling into the office from the little storage room in the back.

"What are you doing in here?" He pointed to the money. "Where did that come from?"

"It's money I found in my toolbox." Jonah hoped his boss would believe him. "I just got here and started ta get my things when I saw a couple of greenback hanging out the side of my box. When I opened it, this here bundle was in it. It's not mine, boss. I wisht it was but it ain't."

"Why are you putting it on Jasper's desk?"

Jonah Whatcom shuffled his feet. "Mr. Clemmons told us not ta bother you. Not ever an' not at all...that we are ta come ta him with any and all our suggestions and complaints."

Lenny's eyebrows rose, and his lips thinned into a straight line. "Here, give me that money. I have a feeling it is part of the money taken from Galway's store yesterday. Someone was trying to plant it on you, Jonah. Watch your back, and I'll be watching it for you too."

Jonah's eyes widened as he thought what would have happened if he'd been caught with that money in his toolbox. *I'd lose my job and most likely hang for something I didn't do. I'd be accused of being the robber who shot Mr. Galway yesterday.* Jonah Whatcom was scared.

CHAPTER VIII

When pride cometh, then cometh shame:
but with the lowly is wisdom.
The integrity of the upright shall guide them:
but the perverseness of transgressors shall destroy them.

PROVERBS 11:2-3

LENNY TRIED TO KEEP HIS TEMPER and not let Jonah see how angry he was. *I don't believe Clemmons is a good man. I wonder why Mr. Galway has not discerned it. Maybe because he's not a believer. Although I reckon many a believer can be fooled by a smooth tongue.*

He took a deep breath and spoke softly. "I want you to know that if any of you men have a problem, any problem at all, I am here for you. It's part of my job. You can spread that word around for me, please. Just so you know, Jonah, Jasper and I don't necessarily always see eye-to-eye."

"Yes, sir, most of th' men know that already, sir," Jonah replied. "But you kin be sure I'll be spreadin' th' word around that yer th' boss and want to hear our voices." His eyes were serious as he looked at this man who was so good to the men. "Thank you, sir, fer watching out fer me. I don't be a knowin' who'd do this ta me, but you kin be sure I'll be on th' lookout. I'll also alert those men I trust ta be watchful-like."

Lenny nodded and smiled a little wearily. "Thanks, Jonah." He scooped up the money and put it into a drawer. "I'll take care of this and see it gets back to the Galways."

"Thanks agin', boss." Jonah turned and went out the door, looking around to see if Jasper Clemmons was anywhere near, but he didn't see him. He now had a real bad feeling about the assistant boss.

Lenny sat down, took off his hat, and clasped his hands together on his desk. "Lord, I pray You will help us find who planted this money in Jonah's toolbox. I thank you that Jonah's an honest man and a hard worker. Please keep him safe. The fact that someone planted money in his toolbox alerts me to someone trying to do him harm. Lord, I pray for Gavin Galway. I pray for his healing, he's a good man, but You know the plans You have, and who am I to thwart them? Father, I pray for Jasper Clemmons. He's not a bad man, just a man with a huge anger that won't let him enjoy life. You can change him if he'll let You. Thank you. Amen."

The door slammed open and Jasper entered, his face looking like a thundercloud.

"What's wrong?" Lenny asked.

"Nothing! Nothing's wrong!" he replied shortly, his voice sounding strident. He looked his desk over, picking up papers as if he'd misplaced something. "It's just nothing seems to work out the way I plan it!" He slammed a folder down onto his desk.

"What's not working out?"

"Anything and everything and nothing…just like I said…nothing!"

Maisie pushed open the window and stood, arms folded across herself resting on the bump that was her baby. She looked out from Doctor Addison's surgery at the gathering storm. The day seemed to match her mood. It was overcast, and she could feel the change in the weather. She felt tired, and her eyes burned from lack of sleep. Staring at a sky laden with heavy dark clouds, she could see in the distance lightening streak from sky to ground in a crooked vertical line. She heard the faint boom of thunder, but it was still quite a long way away.

Won't be long and we're going to have a doozie. As she watched, the wind picked up and the rain, starting in a light patter, turned into a deluge.

The babe kicked, and she rubbed her tummy and then patted it in a rhythm she hoped the baby would recognize once it was born. She'd heard some woman talking about doing that at a sewing bee. The woman swore that the same rhythmic patting she used on her tummy while she was pregnant calmed the baby after it was born.

As she stared at the gloom of the day, tears filled her eyes.

What in the world am I going to do? Da would say, 'Just take it one day at a time, and do the best you can. Strange, but I have no idea what Gavin would have me do. Should I keep the store open? I certainly won't close the mine. Too many men depend on the work there for their livelihood. Maybe I'll take Aidan up on her offer. The only thing is, what if the shooter came back and Aidan was all alone? Oh my! I just don't know what to do. She wiped her eyes with impatience and blew her nose. *One thing is certain. I need to stop feeling sorry for myself!*

Maisie, gazing at the storm that was breaking in Santa Rosa, shivered and rubbed her arms at the sudden chill. Closing the window, she stepped over to where Gavin slept. She felt his brow which felt normal to the touch. *What am I going to do, sweetheart? What in the world am I going to do?*

The train ride to Santa Rosa seemed short compared to being on the Union Pacific. At first, Marnie bounced a bit on the cracked and faded leather seat as she listened to the adults and what seemed to her banal conversation. She stopped because the old leather was scratchy and had no give or springs to make it fun. The train halted to load and unload in a town called Vallejo. A couple people got off and several more got on and quickly found their seats as the train began to roll out with no warning. Soon, they were again heading north to Santa Rosa.

Now that the squabble over the bag was over, Marnie watched Mr. Danbury's face as he spoke. *It's strange how I thought him ugly when we were both certain as to who owned the bag, but he's quite handsome. I like his eyes. They look like the ocean when it's stormy. The gray is dark but lights up when he smiles. One thing I don't quite understand is that Mr. Danbury acts like he needs employment, but it doesn't ring true to me. Wonder why that is? Even I can see that his clothes are good, not cheap. He speaks like a gentleman who is educated. Maybe he hit on hard times and lost everything. Or maybe someone swindled him out of his money. He said his sister died. Wonder what she had that she died? Papa said there are all kinds of things that kill people.*

She continued to listen to the adults as she looked at the countryside. *Deedee must be very tired. Usually she's talking a lot, but she's been quiet since the train left Sacramento.*

Fields and hedgerows were a splash of color as the train pulled out, but black clouds pushed their way across the heavens, and Marnie could no longer see the rainbow. The bright fields seemed darker as rain began to sprinkle the huge window with drops that soon turned into a smear of water streaming sideways as the train chugged along.

Wonder what Doctor Addison is like. He must be very old if he is retiring. Papa said he was the best surgeon in Boston at one time. Wonder if there are any children I will be able to play with. Wonder what our house will be like. Papa said we're going to live over his office so he can keep an eye on me. I doubt that will happen. He's always so busy when he has patients. Deedee and I will have to look out for ourselves, I suppose.

Look at that lightening! Bet there's thunder too, only we can't hear it because of the noise of this train. It's a lot smaller than the train we were on, but it sure makes a lot more noise.

It seemed no time at all and they were pulling into Santa Rosa.

Marnie felt her heart pound with excitement and her stomach growl with hunger. She stood too early as the train came to a stop and had to grab onto the seat in front of her to steady herself.

"We're here!" she exclaimed unnecessarily.

Deedee smiled wearily but replied, "Yes, muffin, we are, and none too soon, either!"

They gathered up their satchels and trooped down the aisle to wait in a small line of travelers ready to debark.

As soon as Oliver stepped down, he was grasped in a huge bear hug.

"Welcome, young man! Welcome to Santa Rosa, California!" Doc Addison felt a surge of relief that his replacement seemed to have arrived with no mishaps. He turned to Marnie, holding an umbrella over her.

"Welcome, my dear. You must be Miss Marnie Sandhurst." Doc's eyes were a warm brown and gleamed with pleasure at Marnie.

"Yes, sir, I am. And I'm pleased to make your acquaintance. You must be Doctor Addison. I thought you'd be old, but you're not!" she exclaimed. She made a little curtsy as her cheeks reddened, and she bit her tongue in embarrassment, but Dr. Addison threw back his head and laughed. His teeth even and white in his tanned face.

"I'm old enough, that's certain." He turned to greet Deedee and looked into a pair of greenish eyes. He felt as if his heart turned over. He moved his arm so the umbrella covered her head from the downpour. *Oh my goodness…Oh Lord, did you bring this woman out here for me to fall in love with? Oh Mighty God…look at her! Why I never thought to…Oh, Mighty God!*

"Cat got your tongue?" Deedee questioned the doctor, her incredible eyes looking full of mischief. She proffered her hand, and the doctor took it in a firm clasp. Deidra felt a frisson of something travel up her arm, and she took a closer look at the man.

He didn't release her hand but as she spoke, he nodded in the affirmative. "Yes. Yes, I believe the cat has." He grinned widely, still holding her hand as she blinked at him.

Feeling a warmth climb up her neck and into her cheeks, she tugged her hand away from his.

He released it as he said, "I'm Micah Addison, and you must be Mrs. Deidra Jennings."

Deedee nodded her head, feeling bemused by this man, but she chuckled. "It's *Miss* Deidra Jennings, sir, I'm an old maid." Her face flushed even redder, and she wanted to kick herself for offering that information. "You're the doctor who is retiring. But you don't look shy nor retiring." She chuckled at her words.

Doc laughed. "You are correct. I'm not shy nor retiring. I know what I want, and I go after it with no side distractions. And now, I do welcome you to Santa Rosa, *Miss* Deidra Jennings." Doc grinned even wider at her obvious discomfiture. *Never been married! What are the men of Boston thinking?*

The rest of the party had been chatting together, but all talking ceased with the feeling of something monumental happening between Doc and Deedee.

Deedee felt discombobulated while Doc Addison addressed the sudden interest of the group with aplomb.

"It's my pleasure to take you to my office and your new home, but I haven't yet met you he said to Colton." He had been so caught up with a sudden rush of feeling for Deedee that he'd been oblivious to everything else. He stuck out his hand and said, "As I'm sure you know by now, I'm Doctor Micah Addison."

Colton clasped his hand in a firm grip and replied. "I'm Colton Danbury, a friend of Oliver's for quite a few years. It was with great surprise that the two of us met in Sacramento, and I have decided to accept his invitation to come up here to Santa Rosa. I'll be looking for some work and have come to see if this town is where I'd like to settle down."

Doc scrutinized Danbury's face and although he somehow knew the man wasn't telling him everything, he nodded his approval. "Do you happen to know anything about gemstones?"

"Well, I do know a bit," Colton replied cautiously. "Why do you ask?"

"Let's get your things off this train and I'll explain over dinner, which is being kept hot for us."

Marnie breathed a sigh of relief. She didn't want to complain, but she was ravenous and the thought that she'd soon be eating made her happy.

Jared led the group to the back of the train. Marnie skipped along beside him, thrilled to have finally arrived. She felt grimy and wanted to take a bath. She stopped skipping and took short steps to get back in line with Deedee. She looked curiously at Deedee's face which looked as if she were deep in thought.

"Are you tired, Deedee?"

"Yes, muffin, I am." She stumbled over an uneven brick on the platform and felt a hand under her elbow steadying her. She hadn't realized the doctor was right there beside her. The touch of his hand brought a sudden rush of warmth to her cheeks, but a certain comfort to her heart.

"Thank you, sir," she said.

"My pleasure, madam." Doc could scarcely believe he'd found a woman he wanted to marry. Evangeline had been dead for years, and Micah Addison had been sure there would never be another woman for him. But here, in an instant, he'd fallen totally in love with this woman. He sensed her goodness and that she was a dedicated Christian. It was one of Doc's giftings. He had an incredible God-given ability to discern. He glanced over at Colton Danbury and wondered what his story was. He certainly hadn't been told all of it.

The off loading of baggage took little time. Jared had secured a dolly and was already unloading as the others approached.

Colton grabbed his luggage and smiled at Marnie as he pulled his bag from the load. "I'd better look inside and make sure it's mine!"

Marnie grinned. "I think you'd better!"

"Jared, you are welcome to join us for dinner. I'm sure Marie has cooked enough for a party."

"Thanks for the invite, Doc, but I'll take you up on that another time. I'd like to get home and make sure Aidan is all right as well as prepare for my day tomorrow."

"All right. I thank you for your help. It's much appreciated."

"Any time, doc. All you need do is ask."

Doc nodded his head. "Thanks again, and I'll see you later." He headed his group toward his office.

Before he opened the door, he said, "I still have a patient in the back room where I do surgery. His wife has been sitting with him. Did Jared tell you about him?"

"If you're talking about the man who was shot and suffered a heart attack at the same time, yes, he did." Oliver figured the man would be his patient on the morrow. Today was officially Doctor Addison's last day as doctor of Santa Rosa and the surrounding area. "How is he?"

"Let's discuss that over dinner, shall we? Marie's been waiting for us to show up. Come on upstairs. It's where you'll be living." He opened the door, ushered them in, and led the way up a wide staircase.

Marnie could see where pictures had been removed from the solid wall on her right, going up the stairs. She felt a bit sad that the sweet man was leaving his house. Halfway up was a wide landing, but it was barren. Making the turn, they went up the remaining stairs.

"Marie! We're here!" Doc called out.

A petite woman, who was quite pretty, came into the wide hall with a smile that said welcome. "Hello there and welcome to Santa Rosa! I'm Marie, Doc's all around help. Your dinner is ready, and you can wash up and make your way to the dining room located right there." She pointed across a large living room that still had furniture and lamps but the walls and bookshelves were empty. "How about you women folk follow me and wash up in the kitchen and Doc, you can take the men down the hall to the main lavatory to wash up."

Deedee and Marnie followed the woman into the kitchen. Marnie liked the looks of her. She had a cloud of black curly hair, eyes as blue as the sky, and Marnie thought they must about the same size, the woman wasn't very tall. She stared at Marie who stared right back with a dimpled smile.

"You two can wash right there." She pointed to a large farm sink.

Marnie traipsed over to the kitchen sink and was impressed. Water was piped in and a body could turn on the tap and have water. She kept quiet until Marie spoke to her.

Deedee, too, was quiet. She was introspective, wondering what her feelings were about Dr. Addison.

"So, you've had quite a trip," Marie said. "I'll wager you will both enjoy your beds tonight."

"I'm Deidra Jennings, housekeeper for Mr. Oliver. And yes, I am exhausted. Thank you for having a meal all prepared for us. Frankly, I don't think I could have gotten anything together for us tonight."

"It's been quite a few years now, but I still remember how tired I was after making the trip out west." She handed a bar of soap to Marnie. "Here you are, young lady."

"Thank you." Marnie took the bar of soap and smelled it. "This smells wonderful. What is it?" She smelled it again. "Uhm it smells nice. Sorry, I'm forgetting my manners. I'm Marnie Marie Sandhurst. I like the name Marie, and I'm pleased to make your acquaintance, Marie." She dipped a small curtsy and won Marie's heart.

"You have nice manners, young lady. I'm pleased to make your acquaintance. And the soap comes from a place down south of us in Napa County. Chandler's it's called. They ship goods all over the world, and I can tell you everything they sell is good."

"My but it smells delicious in here," Deedee said.

"Roast beef, mashed potatoes and gravy, early beets and canned corn." Marie said. "And I made the rolls this morning."

"It does smell good!" Marnie said with a grin. "I am so hungry, I could eat a bear!"

"Well, sweetie, in all truth, it's not roast beef, it is roast bear." She laughed at the look on Marnie's face. "Black bear."

Marnie's eyes rounded. "You really do eat it?"

"Yes, we do. It's delicious if prepared correctly. A most discerning palate would be able to tell it's not roast beef, but most folks wouldn't. You wind up with all kinds of food stuffs when a patient can't pay with cash. I may be speaking out of turn, but one nice thing about living here is that it's all paid for. Doc inherited this building from the last doctor who wouldn't take a penny for it. You can be sure Doc Addison won't hear of Dr. Sandhurst paying for any of it."

Marnie grinned, still thinking about eating bear meat. "Don't tell my papa that we're eating bear meat, and see what he says about the roast."

The men joined them and the conversation they were having was about the man downstairs who'd had a heart attack.

"Marie DuBois," Doc said. "This is Dr. Oliver Sandhurst and a friend he met in Sacramento, Colton Danbury. This is the woman who keeps me fed and clothed, Marie DuBois."

Oliver blinked as she proffered her hand to shake his. It took him aback that the hired help was acting like a hostess for Dr. Addison. He looked into eyes as blue as gentians.

She smiled and dimples dipped into her cheeks. She was barely taller than Marnie and seemed fragile until one looked closely. Strength of character exuded from her, and he thought she couldn't live as help for Dr. Addison without his wisdom rubbing off onto her.

"Marie DuBois, I'm pleased to make your acquaintance."

"And I yours, Dr. Sandhurst."

CHAPTER IX

Recompense to no man evil for evil.
Provide things honest in the sight of all men.

ROMANS 12:17

THE SHERIFF ENTERED THE DOCTOR'S office, taking off his hat as he entered. He looked closely at the girl sitting at the desk and was sure it was Paige and not Payton. For some reason, although the two girls were identical, Ezra was attracted to Payton, who had a tiny, nearly invisible, scar over her left eyebrow near the outside corner of her eye. It was one way he could tell this girl was Paige. He never let on that he could tell them apart.

"Good afternoon, Miss McGrath," he said, his voice smooth and pleasant. "How are you today?"

"I'm doing quite well, sir. And how are you today?"

"Fine, thank you." He glanced at the open door to the surgery and saw Mrs. Galway standing at the window. "How is Mr. Galway doing?"

"I guess he woke up once, but Doc says that sleep is the best thing for his body right now. He said the shock to his system from a dual event has to play itself out. It's worrying Mrs. Galway, but I always trust what Doc Addison says."

"I would, too. Thank you." Ezra, strolled over to the doorway of the surgery. He stood, leaning on the jamb wondering if he should make his presence known.

Maisie had heard him talking to Paige, but it hadn't completely registered until she heard his footsteps. She was exhausted and turned away from the window, not really wanting to chat with the sheriff…not wanting to chat with anyone. Liberty and Caitlin had been with her earlier and they had talked extensively. She knew her night of sleeplessness was catching up with her.

"Good afternoon, Mrs. Galway."

"Hello, Sheriff."

"Paige says your husband hasn't responded much. I'm sorry for that. Sorry for you, ma'am. I was hoping he'd be able to help me a bit. I haven't a clue as to who perpetrated this crime upon your husband, except the rider had a dun colored horse. Is there anyone you know who had a grievance against your husband?"

"N-no, Gavin is easy going and has no enemies that I know of."

"Do you know anyone in dire need of money?"

Maisie looked the sheriff squarely in the eyes. "Surely you jest! There are very few people who are not in need of money. We all need it! Most of the men at the mine wouldn't be there if they didn't need money. No, Sheriff Walker, I don't know anyone who would do such a wicked deed with no compunction about killing, maiming, or the suffering involved in it."

Gavin stirred, and Maisie held her breath looking at him along with the sheriff, who hoped he'd come to. When Gavin didn't open his eyes, Maisie's breath came out with a whoosh.

Tears, held back, choked her voice. "I thought he was going to wake up. Why doesn't he?"

"I suppose his body is recovering from the shock. Being shot and suffering a heart attack is no trifling matter. I just wish I could find who did it to him. He's a fine man, Mrs. Galway. I'll leave you now, but please let me know when he comes out of this and is coherent."

"I will, Sheriff Walker. You can be sure I will."

The sheriff spoke to Paige as he exited the door. "Be sure to let me know when Mr. Galway recovers."

"I will, Sheriff."

He closed the door, but could hear voices and laughter wafting down the stairs.

Doc must be having a party. I thought he was moving out to McCaully-Bannister's today. Must have gotten my dates mixed up.

He strode down the boardwalk to his office and opening the door, realized he had company.

"Can I help you?"

"I'm sure you can. Name's Lorenzo Brown. I am the Galways' foreman at the mine. Got here just a few minutes ago and was hoping you hadn't gone home for the day."

"I'm pleased to make your acquaintance, sir. I'm the new sheriff, Ezra Walker, by name." He stuck out his hand to shake the miner's hand which was already extended.

Lenny cleared his throat as he pulled a wad of greenbacks out of his vest and laid them on the sheriff's desk.

Ezra's eyes widened at the amount of money stacked there.

"Where'd you get it?"

"Jonah Whatcom, one of the miners, came to work this morning and found the money in his toolbox. He brought it to the office. Said he'd love to keep it, but it wasn't his."

"An honest man. Many would pocket the money and say nothing." The sheriff rubbed his cheek as he thought of the man who'd turned in the money. "It was a set-up, wasn't it?" he asked.

Lenny stared at the sheriff, his eyes filling with respect. "That's what I think. I believe it was money taken from my boss, Mr. Galway. Whoever did the deed planted the money to take all suspicion off himself, and I don't doubt he kept a large portion of it for himself."

"How many workers have dun colored horses?" The sheriff's question was abrupt and took Lenny by surprise.

"I ride one, myself," he responded. "Let me think. Ahh, besides me, there's Jasper Clemmons, my under foreman, Zebidiah Pindar and Jonah Whatcom, both of whom brought the gems in to the store that day. There's also Ernest Smith, a young man who is fairly new to the mine, there's Sandoval Peabody, and there could be more. Frankly, I haven't paid much attention to who rides what, but I'll be looking tomorrow. What's the significance of a dun colored horse? Is that what the shooter was riding?"

"Yes, Kirk Bannister couldn't identify the rider, but he said the shooter was definitely riding a dun colored horse."

"He's a sharp man. If he says it was a dun colored horse you can know it for the truth."

"Yes, but there seems to be a multitude of people who own that kind of horse. The ones you named at the mine, I'd already come up with. I had no idea until this came up that there were so many." The sheriff sighed. "Reckon I'm going to fast and pray about this one for any real answer."

"Personally, I think that's a great idea, but I also think you should start looking into those men at the mine," Lenny responded. "Find out who else, besides the ones I told you, have dun colored horses. If you can, look into their background. I have my own suspicions, but I can't share them and have you prejudiced because of my words. I could be entirely wrong, but I'll tell you, I'm keeping my eyes peeled for anything out of the ordinary."

"You do that, and I'll be appreciating it more than I can say. Another pair of eyes and ears in my line of work is always appreciated." He eyed Lenny and asked, "What is your background if I may be so bold as to ask?"

"Well, interestingly enough, the name Lorenzo is both from Spain and from Italy. My parents came here from Scotland. Why they named me Lorenzo, I have never found out. By the way, I go by the name Lenny, and you're welcome to call me that. My middle name is William and it was after William the Conquerer. My family settled in Georgia and came west just after the War between the States. I was five years old at the time. We settled in San Francisco. My father was a doctor and we did quite well until he suffered a heart attack. I was just fifteen at the time and became the breadwinner for the family. It was difficult for my father as he didn't care to give up his practice, but he just couldn't keep up the hours. Treating and visiting his patients took too much out of him. He had a little set aside and between that and me working as a clerk for a mercantile store we got by all right. I was an only child, which I hated, until I became the sole source of income for us. My father suffered another major heart attack and passed away when I was sixteen. One day, Mr. Galway offered me a job at his store in San Francisco. I worked there for a couple years before I moved here at his bidding. I have been working at the mine for the past five years. I am not married, except to my work. My mother passed just last year. I am now twenty-six years old, a God-fearing believer, and a hard worker. Is that good enough for my background?" He grinned at the sheriff who couldn't be much older than himself.

Ezra nodded in the affirmative. "Helps to know, and I thank you for sharing." He picked up the wad of bills and said, "Why don't you walk with me over to Doc's office, and we'll give this to its rightful owner."

Lenny's eyes lit up. "I'd like that."

Both men eyed each other realizing this meeting could be monumental...the beginning of a lifelong friendship.

"Let's go!" Ezra said. He held the door open for Lenny, and the two of them headed down the boardwalk.

The day was fast fading. The air had cooled and felt fresh and balmy after the warmth of the day. Lamps were lit inside some of the buildings, and the saloon across the street seemed to splash light into the dusk as a man entered the swinging doors. Several of the businesses obviously had the owners living above their stores. Lacy curtains spilled light in decorative patterns onto the boardwalk, and a lamplighter could be seen nearly finished with his task on Main Street.

Ezra and Lenny were comfortably silent as they made their way down the walk. Coming level with the saloon, raucous laughter punctuated the feeling of peace with harsh sounds

"Nightly occurrence," Ezra said. "It would improve things if we had a few more females in Santa Rosa. Women seem to have a good and calming influence on an otherwise lonely man."

"I could use that influence, myself." Lenny spoke with a wide grin creasing his face.

"I too!" Ezra said. "I've got my eye on a certain woman, and I can only hope she will be amenable to my advances."

"Same here. In fact, I think she's working for Doc today." Lenny looked a bit smug. Ezra took another look at his new friend.

"Which McGrath?" he asked, holding his breath.

"Miss Paige."

Ezra exhaled and said, "Can you tell them apart?"

"Sure can," Lenny said. "Paige has a pockmark next to her ear. She must have scratched when she had the chicken pox."

"Payton has a tiny scar over her left eyebrow near the outside corner of her eye." Ezra beamed at Lenny. "It's barely noticeable, but they look so much alike I kept looking for differences. I have no idea why I'm attracted to Payton and not Paige. Seems as if I don't need any help to know who is who. I just can tell if it's Payton."

"I understand what you're saying. I have the same feeling about Paige," Lenny responded. "It'd be nice if we ended up brothers-in-law, don't you think?" His face wore a grin that wouldn't quit. "Oh, and I think Paige is working today."

"You are correct, but she should be finished by now. And I think I could handle being your brother-in law. You have a presence that is pleasant to be around. I would reckon it's because we're already brothers in Christ." He punched Lenny lightly in the arm. "Paige is probably with Mrs. Galway, who is staying with her husband in the surgery. Doc has been slowly moving his personal belongings to McCaully-Bannisters' and I think he is leaving tonight now his replacement has arrived.'"

"Dr. Addison is quitting his practice?"

"Not quitting, actually. He's retiring."

"Who will be our doctor? We are constantly having Doc look at one of our miners."

"As I said, Doc is moving out to McCaully-Bannisters', and a new doctor should have arrived today to take his place."

"Reckon I never thought of anyone being Santa Rosa's medicine man except Doc Addison."

"I haven't either, but he wants to enjoy life a bit and with someone always needing his attention…well, he's not getting any younger," Ezra responded. "Here we are."

They entered just as Paige was opening the office door.

"Oh! You startled me!" she exclaimed. She saw Lenny behind Ezra and blushed to the roots of her beautiful strawberry blonde hair.

Ah so that's the way it is. Ezra smiled to himself. *Hope Payton feels the same way about me.*

"Evening, Miss McGrath. Sorry we startled you." Ezra's soothing voice calmed Paige, and she stepped back into the office waiting room.

"Can I help you?" she asked Ezra, with a quick glance at Lenny, trying unsuccessfully to squelch her blush.

"Yes, you can." Ezra glanced at Lenny whose eyes were fixed on Paige. "We came to see Mrs. Galway. Is she still here?"

"Yes, of course. Marie brought some dinner down for her, and I was getting ready to go home."

"Evening, Miss McGrath," Lenny said as he removed his hat. "We'll just be a few minutes with Mrs. Galway. It's getting dark, and if you don't mind waiting, I'd like to walk you home."

"I don't mind waiting." She replied promptly and wondered if he could hear the beating of her heart. Her ears felt plugged with the sound of it.

He smiled, nodded, and followed Ezra into the surgery area where they found Mrs. Galway wrapped in a knitted sweater coat, sitting in a deep leather chair next to her husband. Her head was resting on the chair's back, feet on an ottoman, and her eyes were closed. Ezra could see the bruises of tiredness under them.

He spoke softly. "Mrs. Galway?"

Maisie open her eyes, startled, not realizing she'd fallen asleep. She hadn't heard the tread of their feet in a room filled with silence.

"Y-yes? Oh! Hello Sheriff...Mr. Brown...how nice to see you." She struggled to her feet still feeling discombobulated.

"It's nice to see you again, Mrs. Galway," Lenny said. "I'm sorry it's under such sad circumstances."

"We don't mean to bother you, Mrs. Galway, but we're here to return what we feel is most likely yours. Jonah Whatcom found some greenbacks in his tool box this morning when he got to work. He immediately brought it into the office where Lenny was working." Ezra handed Maisie the roll of bills and folded her fingers over them. "This helps me considerably as now I'm quite sure someone at the mine committed this crime."

"Jonah found it in his tool box?" Maisie, who was generally quick to see a point, felt the weight of sleeplessness, and cast about in her mind what this meant.

"Yes, Jonah is as honest as the day is long," Lenny replied. "Your husband was right in his assessment of him to be one of the men bringing the gemstones to the store. Someone planted this money in his box hoping it would cast aspersions on Jonah and thus divert attention from himself. At least that is how I see it."

Maisie nodded her agreement. "Jonah is a good man and wouldn't do anything untoward. On the other hand, I can't think of anyone who'd want to kill Gavin for money. Life is a lot more precious than a few greenbacks." To her horror, hot tears filled her eyes. "I-I'm s-sorry. I must be more tired than I thought."

Ezra drew her into his arms and patted her back as she let herself go and sobbed on his shoulder. She pulled back, and he produced a fresh handkerchief for her. She wiped her eyes and blew her nose.

"Again, I'm sorry."

"No need to apologize, ma'am," Ezra stated. "You have every right to be sorrowful. Now, Lenny and I will make ourselves scarce, and I hope you can rest a bit more. Also, Lenny and I are both believers, and we'll be praying for you, ma'am."

"Thank you. I don't know how much good it will do. Gavin and I have never taken that path, and I although I saw a great change in Aidan and Jared, I…I just don't know. Again, thank you for this." She held out the money and added, "It will be put to good use, and I do hope you find out who did this. It's an uncomfortable feeling, knowing someone wants to harm you. My sister said she'd watch the shop for me, but what if the shooter comes back for more money?" She sighed as she crossed her arms atop her swollen belly. "I just don't know if it's safe."

"I think I can help with that," Lenny interjected. "I can get one of the men at the mine to stay with your sister in the shop if you want to keep it open."

Maisie's smile was not its usual sparkly one, but it warmed Lenny's heart just the same.

"You just get the word to me at the mine," he added, "and I'll have someone come in to help her whenever you're ready."

"Thank you, Lenny. It is much appreciated."

"We're at your service, ma'am," Ezra added. "We are willing to help if you just let us know what you need."

Maisie nodded, and the two left her.

Ezra smiled widely at Paige and said, "Have a nice walk home, Miss McGrath."

Paige's eyes flew to Lenny's face and back at Ezra's. "Thank you, sir." *Goodness! I wish like anything I didn't blush so readily.*

"Good evening," Ezra said, grinning from ear to ear, as he settled his hat on his head and headed out the door.

Lenny stood waiting as Paige said goodnight to Mrs. Galway. She picked up her things and handed them to Lenny.

"You don't mind lugging my satchel, do you?"

"Not at all." He hooked the satchel over his shoulder, and they left the office. Once outside, Paige dared to slipped her hand under Lenny's arm, and the two headed down the boardwalk with no dearth of things to talk about.

Mini Lou lay in the luxurious bed feeling peaceful. She rolled over onto her back and pillowed her head with her arms, staring at the dark ceiling. Hearing the grandfather clock in the hall strike midnight, she wondered why sleep was elusive. She threw off the bed linens and padded to the window. Kneeling on the cool floor, she rested her arms on the sill and gazed at the beautiful scene spread out before her. Fields glistened in the moonlight, and through the opened window she could smell the sweet peas that climbed a fence near the back porch. She was tired but happy. Thinking about the events of the day, her lips curved up and into a sweet smile.

My, but Ma thought I was funning her when I told her about having running water in the house and the flush toilet. She said something like that would sure cut down on a lot of work. She was glad when I told her I didn't need Reddy. I reckon... oops. If I want to be more ladylike I should say, I suppose Pa will be happy that I won't need his horse while I'm here.

Miss Caitlin said she loves to ride and that sometimes we can ride together. She wants to show me their gold mine and introduce me to life on a large ranch.

I'm sure glad I thought to make up a sugar-tit for Jonny. He sure didn't like it much when he woke up and there I was instead of a face he knew. He started to kick up...he started to make a fuss and cry as loud as I've ever heard. I just plopped that sugar-tit into his mouth and what a surprised look he gave me. He snuggled right into my neck and as Miss Caitlin came in, he'd already stopped crying. She smiled at me, and backed out of the room without a word.

Mini Lou stood and stretched and smiled as she crawled back into bed.

I'm going to love it here! Once dinner was over, and my but wasn't it elegant, we sat in the drawing room and had coffee and little tasty cookies. Being waited on sure beats the drudgery of slaving from morning till night. Miss Caitlin and Miss Liberty treated me as if I was an equal to them. I'm going to do my best to work hard and be a real benefit to my new employers. I'm also going to make myself available to Duney. She said her real name was Dunstan, but everyone calls her Duney. She's a marvelous cook, and I'm going to learn how to make some of those wonderful things we ate tonight. Duffy is nice, too, although if I had to choose, I'd rather be a cook than a housekeeper. I have all these plans rattling around in my head, but I will keep my feet on the ground and make myself indispensable.

CHAPTER X

When thou liest down, thou shalt not be afraid:
yea, thou shalt lie down, and thy sleep shall be sweet.

PROVERBS 3:24

MARNIE COULDN'T GET TO SLEEP. Her mind kept jumping to the events of the day. She lay on her back with her head pillowed on her arm.

I was excited to get off that train and then disappointed that Dr. Addison wasn't in Sacramento to meet us. Then to have Mr. Danbury try to take my suitcase! I was so angry, I could have kicked him. Now we're best friends. It's strange how life can change so quickly.

I could almost feel Papa's relief when we got off the train in Santa Rosa, seeing Dr. Addison there to greet us. I like Dr. Addison. I watched him when he met Deedee. He couldn't keep his eyes off her. His wife died a long time ago. Wonder if he's lonely? I'll bet he is. I don't know how Deedee ever stayed single. She's not beautiful but she's attractive. I think some of her inner beauty shows through her eyes. She certainly taught me a lot about Jesus. I was so mad at God when Mama died. I couldn't understand why He didn't answer my prayers and heal Mama. Deedee said He does nothing without a purpose, but He also doesn't view suffering the way we do. Mama was in so much pain that I was glad when she died to escape it, but then I felt guilty for feeling that way. I suppose God understands my feelings better than I do.

I love my Papa, but there are some things I don't talk to him about the way I could with Mama. Oh, I miss her so!

Tears formed in her eyes and she brushed them away, piqued that she couldn't seem to stop crying about her loss.

You'd think by now I'd be finished with crying over something that's never going to change. I love Deedee, but she's not Mama. What I'm thinking is the pain gets less and less, as time goes by, but I miss her so much!

Papa sure likes Mr. Danbury. And I think he's still a bit in awe of Dr. Addison.

Strange that I'm not going to miss anyone in Boston. I had some friends but not anyone I felt particularly close to. Just Mama's grave…that's what I'm going to miss the most.

Marnie yawned and stretched. She started to pray but tiredness overcame her and she didn't finish one sentence before falling asleep.

In bed, Oliver Sandhurst lay on his back but was wide awake. He hadn't noticed the window in the ceiling until he'd gone to bed, but what a spectacular view. *Dr. Addison is sure going to miss this.* Stars shimmered and winked brightly as if they'd been polished by the deluge of late afternoon rain. The moon, because of a haze of cloud surrounding it, shone dimmer than usual. Its light was filtered and cast a halo of rainbow colors about itself. It was gorgeous.

Dinner had been delicious. Oliver smiled to himself as he thought about the roast beef that wasn't. *Marnie laughed and laughed when I declared it to be one of the best roast beef dinners I've ever eaten. Deedee smiled delightedly and asked me if I was sure. It made me wonder if I'd offended her, but I knew better, looking into those greenish eyes full of mischief. Bear…who would ever have believed that was bear meat?* He chuckled into the darkness.

After dinner, Oliver had gone downstairs with Dr. Addison to meet Mrs. Galway and her sleeping husband, but she also was asleep.

Dr. Addison said he wasn't going to say anything in front of Mrs. Galway, but he was worried about her husband. He'd told Oliver he thought Mr. Galway's chances for a full recovery were slim to nothing.

He'd said it wasn't the wound that was the problem, but he thought the heart attack had done massive damage.

Oliver sighed wondering why he'd chosen to become a doctor. *There's so much pain and suffering involved in this profession. I feel sorry for Mrs. Galway. She seems too young to become a widow. Sometimes, I wonder why I ever chose to become a doctor, but then I'm reminded it really wasn't my choice. I felt a definite calling of the Lord. He knows better than I do. I'm thankful, Lord, that Your thoughts are higher than my thoughts and Your ways are higher than my ways. I can always totally depend on You. Grateful, I'm forever grateful.*

Colton Danbury lay abed wondering what he should do. Doc told him about the need for someone to help in the gem store owned by the couple downstairs.

It was good of Oliver to ask me to stay as long as I need. For some reason, I've an inclination that I need to go out to the McCaully-Bannisters' Ranch. I suppose I will search it out and see what's what. I do know some about gemstones, but not enough to know what to price them or the difference between a flawed one and a perfect one. I think I'd rather try my hand at ranching. If I like it, perhaps it'll be what I'll end up doing.

"Lord, I pray You will guide my steps," he whispered. "I know it was by Your almighty hand that I met Dr. Sandhurst in Sacramento. I don't know what lies in store for me, but You do. I trust You to continue to lead me in the way I need to go. May I be ever mindful to follow your direction."

Colton felt hot and got up to pull open the curtains. He pulled the window open to its fullest extent and breathed in the fresh night air. He could see over the buildings, across the street, to grasses bathed in the moonlight and trees, whose leaves glistened. *It's beautiful, Lord. So quiet and peaceful. It's not like noisy Boston where it seems people are up all hours of the night. Thank You, again, for bringing Dr. Sandhurst and I together. I don't feel so lonely tonight as I have been.*

I am a bit sorry that Dr. Addison is giving up his practice, and yet it is evidently the right time. There certainly was some attraction going on between Deedee and the

Doc this evening. Wonder if I'll find the right woman for me. I pray You bring a believing woman into my life, Father. I leave all my affairs into Your capable hands.

He took a couple more deep breaths of the air, fragrant with the smell of lilacs, climbed back into bed, and was asleep before another thought crossed his mind.

*D*r. Micah Addison lay in the bed he always slept in when visiting the McCaullys'. He thought of Mackenzie Macleby McCaully. He'd been a friend as well as his patient before he'd succumbed to the cancer that was eating away at him. He'd been a stern man but with a heart of gold.

Doc had delivered all the girls, and was anguished when Ryanne had died having Caitlin. He'd stood helpless as the life ebbed out of her. Mac had been inconsolable, but he'd done a good job of raising the girls. Mrs. Dunstan and Mrs. McDuffy, Mac's hired help, had both contributed to their upbringing.

Many times, Doc had wondered about Mac. For some reason there seemed to be something he'd never shared about immigrating to the United States. Doc knew whatever it was, Ewen Carr had been a part of it, and it wasn't good. He sighed.

Mac was a good man, and Ewen is also, and yet there's something that niggles in my heart of hearts. Ah well, Ewen certainly picked a wonderful woman to be his wife. Neither of them ever married. Hannah is a sweet woman. It was good of Kirk and Caitlin to build them a house separate from this one so they can enjoy their privacy.

Ah Lord God, what a day for me! I have no doubt You brought Deidra Jennings into my life. It amazed me that she's never been married. Lord, I pray You also planted that seed of attraction into her heart. Help me to be patient and not rush things. I simply know she's the one, and thank You for Your mighty provision. I've never spent the money I got from my mother's estate. I am sure I could set us up quite comfortably. I thank You for being a God Who sees to my needs before I sometimes am aware of that need.

Doc did a lot of praying before he finally succumbed to sleep.

Maisie sat beside Gavin in the dark, and although it was nearly midnight, she couldn't sleep. She felt more exhausted than she'd ever been in her life, but her mind kept jumping from one thing to another.

She bent to put a taper to a single lamp on the stand and straightened up, rubbing her back. She felt achey all over and was tired of the constraints of the room. Opening the door to the reception room she stretched and started walking around and around the room, surprised by her thoughts.

I scarcely remember a time in my life without Gavin. Me da and Gavin's da were great friends. I grew up playing with Gavin, attending school with Gavin and rarely was there a time when he wasn't at our house or I at his. It seemed as natural as breathing that I should marry him. We have been such good friends. I don't know what I'd do without him. Doc says he's not out of the woods by any means.

She went back into the surgery room and sat next to the bed, taking his hand into hers.

It's strange, but Gavin has always been a comfort to me. He's cosseted me and made me feel special, but our relationship has never been a romantic one. I don't even think I believe in love at first site, except Kirk said that's the way it was for him. He was in a stable and took one look at Caitlin and he was a goner. I wonder what that feels like. I think maybe it's safer to just love one of your best friends. Knowing, without a doubt that your choosing someone you know is good. It's been a comfortable marriage. I wonder if having a baby will change that.

She smoothed the hair on Gavin's head and he smiled. She looked closer hoping she hadn't imagined it. She smoothed his forehead again, and he smiled but seemed to struggle to open his eyes.

Maisie, holding her breath, watched as he opened them and looked around. Her breath came out in a whoosh as his eyes locked onto hers, focused and clear.

"Hello, sweetheart. Where are we?"

Tears of relief and exhaustion filled Maisie's eyes as she responded. "We're in Doc's office."

"What's wrong? Are you all right? Is the baby all right?" He moved his hand up and felt the gauze bandage below his left shoulder.

"Oh! Reckon I'm not thinking clearly. It's me, isn't it." He swallowed and closed his eyes.

Maisie sighed, thinking he'd fallen asleep again.

"Can I have some water?"

"Of course!" Maisie stepped over to the sink, relieved Gavin seemed all right. Using the enameled dipper, she filled a glass half full from the bucket sitting on the counter. Thinking as she poured it that it was clear, clean, and delicious. Deep wells filled with water from the Russian River were filtered by rock and sand, and there never seemed to be a shortage of good water for the folks in Santa Rosa.

Maisie returned to Gavin's side and asked, "Can you remember what happened to you?"

"No, I can't seem to clear my head enough to remember. The last I recollect is you leaving the shop." Gavin spoke in a soft voice.

Maisie held Gavin's head, and although he took the glass, his hand trembled, and she kept her grip on the bottom of it.

"I forgot to lock the door when I left. I'm so sorry, Gavin. It's my fault the shooter got inside the shop."

"What happened? A shooter? Was I shot then?"

"Doc said you were shot, but he thinks you had a heart attack, too. Do you remember anyone coming into the shop?"

Gavin wrinkled his brow in thought. "N-no, not really. I vaguely recollect someone coming into the shop, but my head feels as if I'm in a fog. Heart attack? Why I'm too young to have a heart attack." He voice held no strength, but Maisie could hear the wonderment and frustration in it. She knew him so well.

"Evidently, you're not too young. Doc said he's seen it quite often. He asked me what your parents died of, and I told him your father died of a heart attack, and we don't know what happened to your mother."

Gavin swallowed. "I'd like some more water, please."

Maisie complied and asked, "Are you in pain?"

Gavin drank the water, but he seemed to take some time in answering. "Just where I was shot, I reckon. I feel incredibly tired. Hope you don't mind, but I'm going to sleep now."

"No, I don't mind. Get some rest, Gavin. It's what your body needs."

He closed his eyes, as she smoothed back his hair. He seemed to be asleep in seconds, but he opened his eyes again.

"I could have died, Maisie. I could still die if I have a dicky heart. I don't want to die and not know where I'm going." He closed his eyes and said, "I want You, Jesus, to come into my life. I want to be a Christ follower, like Jared. Lord, I saw the change in him and wondered so often about it, but I have done nothing regarding my relationship with You. Please forgive me for living a life that only served me and my needs. I want to know more about You and will ask Jared to mentor me. Thank You for answering my prayer." He closed his eyes, sighed heavily, and fell into a deep sleep, his chest rising and falling evenly.

Maisie looked at her husband in amazement. *I don't know what to think! My goodness! I never thought Gavin would take that step.* Maisie dragged her feet over to the davenport, and was asleep as her head hit the pillow.

Early the next morning, Liberty and Caitlin rode into town. They stopped by Aidan's house which was on the edge of Santa Rosa, one of the first houses before entering town.

Tying up at the hitching rail, Liberty saw Aidan's house for the first time. It was a beautiful structure and Caitlin commented as she saw the pleasure on Liberty's face.

"Me da bought the house for Aidan as a wedding present. Just recently, Aidan put Jared's name on the papers. Da didn't trust Jared, and no one blamed him, but that was before Jared asked Jesus to be Lord of his life. If Matthew hadn't witnessed to him about his own faith, I doubt Jared would be the man he is today. I will never stop being thankful that Matthew shared his faith so openly with Jared."

"Matthew is not ashamed of the gospel, and for that I am thankful." Liberty smiled thinking of the change in Matthew. "I know God certainly changed Matthew. He was full of bitterness and anger before Jesus came into his life. Now, he's a strong believer and a most thoughtful husband."

Caitlin grinned. "Well, some of that must have rubbed off on Kirk. Matthew was a good mentor, although Kirk resented a lot of Matthew's big brother bossiness until he came to know Christ and the depth of Matthew's love for him. I'm thankful they are so close now, and that you are my sister, Liberty!"

The two women smiled at each other. Liberty looked again at the house. "It has a presence about it, doesn't it? It's almost as if it has an awareness that those who live inside are full of joy."

Caitlin nodded her agreement. "It does, but going inside now is sure different from what it was before Jared and Aidan became believers. It had an oppressive air about it, and you could almost sense the unhappiness in it. Now, I agree with you. It seems to be a house full of joy. Let's go in."

Liberty walked slowly, enjoying the beauty of the flowers lining the walk and the shrubs in full bloom conveying upon the house a peaceful charm.

They walked up the steps, Caitlin rapped on the door a couple times, and opened it.

"Anybody home?" she called out.

"We're in the kitchen," Jared responded.

Liberty drew in her breath at the understated elegance of the house. On her right and left were paned French doors both wide open. The right looked like a library and office, the left a formal dining room.

They crossed this and entered the kitchen which was huge but welcoming. Aidan and Jared were both standing when they entered.

"Come on in and have a cup of coffee with us," Jared said. He eyed Caitlin with a rueful smile. "I know I'm late for work, but Kirk knows why. I'm taking a new man out to the ranch to see if he'll fit in with the boys. He's a greenhorn from back east, but says he knows how to rope and ride. We can always use another hand, and this man, Colton Danbury doesn't know what he wants to do. Kirk said we could try him out and see what kind of worker he is."

"I haven't met him, yet," Aidan said, "but I plan to go see Maisie when Jared goes, and the man is staying with the new doctor." She pulled out the chair next to her, and Jared did the same.

Caitlin took the chair beside Jared, and Liberty sat next to Aidan. Their cook, Cassie, placed a cup of coffee in front of the newcomers.

"Thank you," Liberty said as she smiled at Cassie.

"Where are my manners!" Aidan exclaimed as she stood up again. "Liberty, this is our cook and all around help, Cassie Stewart. Cassie, this is Liberty Bannister, Caitlin's sister-in-law."

Liberty stood up and shook Cassie's hand. "I am pleased to meet you, Cassie."

"Pleased ta make your acquaintance, I'm sure," Cassie responded in a surprised voice. Her eyes widened at the respectful greeting Liberty had given her. She smiled widely into Liberty's green eyes.

Aidan sat down again and said, "I suppose you're on your way to see how Gavin is doing. I offered to spell Maisie, but she wouldn't hear of it. I wonder what she's decided to do about the store. Poor thing, she looked exhausted yesterday. I'll go with you when you're finished with your coffee. Would you like a scone?"

"I would," Caitlin responded.

"Yes, please," Liberty said. "I never seem to turn down food."

Cassie placed a platter of warm scones on the table with butter and blackberry jam on the side.

"How do you stay so slim?" Caitlin asked.

"Running around caring for the twins," Liberty replied as she picked up a scone and began buttering it.

"I forgot you had twins. You're a twin yourself, aren't you?" Aidan asked, buttering a scone for herself before smearing jam on it.

"Yes, My brother lives in San Francisco. He's a lawyer and has six children. His wife, Emily is hoping they are finished having babies." She chuckled and added, "Oh, Cait, I forgot to tell you Conchita is expecting a baby!"

"Oh my goodness, she must be thrilled!"

"We all are. The twins are in San Rafael with Cady's grandmother and Cady is looking after them. I'm hoping Conchita will put her feet up and relax while we're away."

"I reckon I'd better go over to Doc's, uh Dr. Sandhurst's where Colton spent the night." Jared said. "Caitlin, You're going to get to meet him before Kirk."

"How old is he, do you think?" Caitlin asked.

"Mid twenties, I'd say. Nice looking chap. I hope he works out all right. Reckon it won't take long to tell."

When Caitlin and Liberty were finished eating, they all headed over to the doctor's office to see how Gavin and Maisie were doing.

CHAPTER XI

Hear my prayer, O God;
give ear to the words of my mouth.

PSALM 54:2

OLIVER **WAS UP EARLY AND DRESSED**, whistling under his breath as he made his way to the kitchen. He could smell bacon and his mouth watered. He was a little surprised that Deedee wasn't in the kitchen, but it pleased him that she was getting some needed rest.

"Good morning, Marie. Thanks for having breakfast ready, but I won't say I'm hungry enough to eat a bear!" He grinned at her and wondered if he could afford to keep her and Deedee as hired help. Doc said some of his patients paid in cash and some brought some of their harvest or produce to pay their bill.

Marie laughed in delight at the comment. "I'm glad you enjoyed eating it, though. Your little girl told me not to tell you it wasn't beef. She's a real sweet girl, and you must be very proud of her."

"Yes, between my wife and Deedee, she seems to have a level head on her shoulders. I can't take much of the credit as I am quite busy with my work, but I keep Sundays a holy day, and Marnie and I spend the entire day together. Unless there's a dire emergency, I don't do any work on Sundays."

"Good for you, sir." She placed a cup of coffee in front of him as he sat down and laid a plate on the table with a muffin, two fried eggs, fried shredded potatoes, and bacon on it.

"This looks delicious!"

"Thank you. Would you mind if I sit down and talk to you for a bit?"

Oliver looked up at her in surprise, but said, "Certainly, I don't mind! Please grab a cup of coffee and have a chair."

Marie had already poured herself a cup, picked it up, and sat gingerly on the edge of the kitchen chair.

"I just want to be up front with you. Since you have Deedee as your hired help, I'm thinking I'm an extra person you don't really need. However, I am willing to stay here and work for only my board and room. I have no expenses to speak of, and my needs are small. I haven't been able to save enough to live on my own, so I wondered if that would be all right with you. Deedee and I can split the work. On the other hand, I could go live with my sister, although it would not be a happy option, but I certainly don't want to be a burden on you."

She blushed becomingly, but it occurred to Oliver she was quite uncomfortable talking to him in this manner.

"I have no idea how much money I will make or what being a country doctor entails. I believe you would be an asset to this house and never a burden. I won't have you working for free, but until I know what I can expect to make as an income, we will play it by ear. Is that all right with you?"

Marie breathed a sigh of relief. "More than all right. Thank you, sir."

"You are welcome, Marie." Oliver thought himself quite fortunate to have her wanting to stay. The meal she had produced the evening before had been delicious, and she was quite pleasant to look at.

Marie got up and went back to the stove, and Oliver finished his breakfast with relish. He picked up his plate and took it to the sink, thanking the woman for a delicious breakfast.

He whistled as he descended the stairs. *The secretary or receptionist isn't here yet. Wonder what time they come in.* He ran back up the steps and poked his head into the kitchen to ask Marie, but he saw she was sitting at the kitchen table, her eyes closed, her hands folded on the table, and her lips moving in a whispered prayer. He went back downstairs thinking warm thoughts about his new hired help.

Jared and Aidan, along with Liberty and Caitlin, reached the doctor's office and heard the little ringing of the bell over the door.

Payton welcomed them. "It will be just a few minutes before Dr. Oliver Sandhurst will be with you. He was down here a little bit ago, but Maisie was still asleep on the sofa in the surgery, so he didn't want to disturb her."

Oliver heard the tinkle of the bell Dr. Addison had installed over the doorway, and bounded down the stairs. He left Marnie and Deedee at the kitchen table with Colton.

"Good morning, Jared," he said.

"Good morning, Dr. Sandhurst. This is my wife, Aidan, my sister-in-law, Caitlin, both of whom are Maisie's sisters, and this is Liberty Bannister, Caitlin's sister-in-law. Ladies, this is Dr. Oliver Sandhurst."

Oliver was bowled over by the beauty of all three ladies, but the one with green eyes was stunning. He simply murmured, "Please to make your acquaintance." He shook hands with each one. "I can see the family resemblance," he said to Aidan and Caitlin. "I haven't talked to your sister this morning. She was sleeping soundly when I went into the surgery room, and I didn't care to disturb her. I haven't yet met her, as she was sleeping last evening."

He walked to the door of the surgery room and peeked in. Beckoning to the group in front of the reception desk, they all trooped into the room.

Maisie was sitting next to Gavin, who was awake.

"Good morning, Mrs. Galway, Mr. Galway, I'm Dr. Oliver Sandhurst. I arrived yesterday, and Dr. Addison has filled me in on exactly what has happened here. It is difficult for me to believe someone would just walk into your store and shoot you, Mr. Galway."

Maisie proffered her hand and looked into deep blue, nearly violet eyes. She drew in a breath at their look of softness.

"I'm pleased to meet you, sir." His hand was cool and smooth, and Maisie withdrew her hand quickly.

Oliver spoke to her. "I will be taking on Dr. Addison's patients."

Gavin started to reach out, but Oliver said, "No—no—Mr. Galway. You don't need to shake my hand, you need to conserve every bit of energy to get well. I am happy to serve you and will do my best to help you feel better."

Gavin smiled his agreement and said, "I feel as if I've been bucked over a fence by a bull and then trampled on."

"It's going to be a slow process to recovery."

"If I fully recover." Gavin smiled, but looked searchingly at Oliver's face. "There is no guarantee of longevity with a dicky heart. I know that. I also know that I now have a personal relationship with Jesus Christ. If I live longer, I plan to serve Him as He is now my king. Maisie hasn't taken that step yet, but standing at death's door and wondering if I'm going to hell because I had the opportunity and never took it…well, I can tell you, I'm thankful for being able to recover long enough to take that step. I've thought about it many times since Jared, Aidan, and Caitlin made their decision, but I've never taken the time to actually ask Jesus Christ to be Lord of my life, and now I have." He smiled into the stunned faces of Jared and Aidan.

Liberty smiled and said, "Welcome, brother Gavin. Do you know the very angels in heaven sang praises when you accepted Jesus?"

"No, I didn't. I don't know much at all. I wasn't raised in a household that acknowledge God." He looked at Jared. "I want you to mentor me. I saw the huge change in you and wondered how long it would last, but I reckon now, I know it will last for all eternity." His voice began to fade and grow softer.

"I think you need to rest now, Mr. Galway." Oliver's lips were pressed together as if he expected an argument.

Gavin closed his eyes obediently. "I know you're right."

"We love you, Gavin," Caitlin said.

"I know it." Gavin said softly, his lips curving upward.

Liberty took Oliver's hand and Caitlin's who grabbed Aidan's, and Jared completed the circle. Maisie stood on the other side of the bed and watched as Oliver began to pray.

"Heavenly Father, how grateful we are for Your wondrous love and care. We thank You for allowing Gavin time to accept Your son as his Savior. We pray together, right now, for his complete healing, whether that be here on earth to do Your will, or in heaven to be eternally with You. We only ask that Your will is done. How grateful we are for the comfort and joy You bring to our hearts. May we be ever mindful to follow Your leading and to be completely obedient to You. Thank You for Gavin's new life in You. Bless him and Maisie we pray. May this baby Maisie is carrying be healthy and strong. May each of us love You and know You more and more each day. We pray in the mighty and peerless name of Jesus. Amen."

By the time he finished, Gavin was breathing deeply.

Liberty squeezed his hand and said, "Thank you for your prayer, Dr. Sandhurst."

"Just Oliver will do," he replied.

"Dr. Oliver, then," she responded.

"You are welcome, Mrs. Bannister."

"Liberty will do," she responded with a grin.

"I can't believe Gavin's gone back to sleep so quickly," Maisie said.

"Please don't worry, Mrs. Galway. His body has gone through a lot, and it's trying to repair itself. It's good he's sleeping," Oliver said.

She looked at him doubtfully.

"Remember when Matthew lost his memory, and he didn't know who he was when he worked for Caitlin on the ranch?" Liberty asked Maisie.

"Yes."

"Well, he was unconscious for two days at the Pindars', and when he finally woke up, he had amnesia. Your Dr. Addison told me the same thing…that Matthew's body received a bad blow and that it takes time to heal. Just trust in what Dr. Oliver says to you. He knows best. And, I would suggest that you go home to sleep. Perhaps you could have Gavin moved on a stretcher to your house. You'd be more comfortable and if there's a problem, you can always send someone to come get Dr. Oliver."

"I can see to having Mr. Galway moved to your house, Mrs. Galway," Oliver said. "You're not getting enough rest here, but you probably would if you were home."

Maisie sighed. "All right, I agree. I am in need of a bath and clean clothes. So maybe later, when he wakes up, we can move him."

"Colton and I could move him before we head out to the ranch." Jared said. "I'll go up and see if he's willing to help."

He ran up the stairs and knocked lightly on the door.

"Come on in, Jared," Marie said.

He grinned at her, she was not only easy on the eyes but also a dedicated Christian.

"Hello, Marie. Is Colton here?"

Colton overheard and left the kitchen to meet Jared. "Good morning, Jared. I'm ready."

"I was wondering if you'd mind helping me with the patient downstairs. Dr. Oliver said we could move him to his own house, but I need help with the stretcher."

"Certainly, let me get my bags, and I'll leave them in the office so I don't have to bother Marie when we get back."

He left to collect his bags, and looked around to make sure he hadn't left anything. He'd already stripped the bed and the linens and pillow case were in a bundle in the middle of it. He strode back to the kitchen, picking up his breakfast plate and cup, he dumped them into the sink of water.

Marie was a bit surprised by the good manners. "Thank you, Colton."

"No—I thank you, Marie for the wonderful dinner last night, a comfortable bed, and a delicious breakfast." He nodded at Deedee and Marnie. "I'll most likely see you later, but it was nice to meet you. Glad we got our bags sorted out, young lady!"

Marnie grinned at him. "I told you it was my bag!"

"You did, and you were right, but you're a cheeky thing, aren't you!"

"I suppose I am, but only with people I like," she replied.

He laughed. "Well, I like you, too!"

Jared was waiting and Marnie watched at the top of the stairs as they went down.

"Mr. Galway is really bad off, isn't he?" she asked Marie.

"Yes, I'm afraid he is, and he's such a nice likable man. Doc wasn't even sure he was going to make it. In truth, he still is not out of the woods. Now that he's going home, it'll be better for Mrs. Galway."

The two linked arms and strolled back to the kitchen.

"Do you think I could have a puppy now that we live here and we're not in a big city?"

Deedee, still sitting at the kitchen table, looked nonplussed, but Marie answered the girl. "I think this involves a discussion best made when your papa is here. As far as I'm concerned, I think it's a wonderful idea."

Jared and Colton, under Oliver's supervision, carried Gavin home. It wasn't far from Oliver's new residence, but Gavin never woke up during the move, which took Oliver a little aback.

"I hope this wasn't a mistake, but I felt Mrs. Galway needs more rest than she's getting."

Jared, out of breath, only grunted a reply.

Colton said nothing. He was not used to carrying such a weight. He just hoped he wouldn't disgrace himself and drop Gavin on his head.

When they got Gavin settled, Oliver spoke in an authoritative tone. "Mrs. Galway, I want you to get some rest. It's not good for you, and it's not good for the baby for you to go without sleep."

Maisie nodded wearily. "I know, Dr. Oliver, I know. I am pretty sure I will sleep well. Aidan said she'd sit up with him, and I'm going to take her up on the offer. It's why I had a bed set up in Gavin's office. I don't wish to disturb him, and I didn't want people to have to carry him upstairs. I am dead on my feet, if you will excuse the term. I know it's morning, but good night everyone."

She trudged slowly up the stairs and down the hall to the bedroom. She stripped down, glad to take the clothes off she'd lived in for the past couple of days. She took a cold sponge bath, donned her nightgown, and climbed into bed. Her stomach felt tight with a contraction that wouldn't let her relax, but she lay on her side, took one of Gavin's pillow, and placed it over the side of her head, hoping to block out any noise. She lay there until the Braxton Hicks contraction let up. She let out a huge sigh and fell instantly asleep.

Oliver said, "I want to thank you for your help. Jared, before you head out to the…" He turned to see the commotion at the door.

"Aidan," Jared said, "thanks for heading over here so quickly. Dr. Oliver doesn't want Gavin left alone. He could wake up and need water, or get agitated with no one here." He gave her a kiss and added, "Colton and I are riding out to McCaully-Bannisters'. See you later, sweetheart."

Aidan blushed. "I'll have dinner ready when you return. Colton, are you going to be staying in one of the bunkhouses, or will you be coming back to town?"

"I suppose, if I get hired, that I'll be staying at the ranch."

Aidan nodded. "Yes, it's best when the crews live together. I grew up there, you understand."

Colton, with a surprised look on his face said, "I suppose I should have put that together with the rest of the information I had, but I didn't."

Aidan smiled. "You do know that Maisie, Caitlin, and I are sisters. Neither Maisie nor I were interested in the ranch, but Caitlin worked from morning till night there for several years before my father died. He made sure Maisie and I had some inheritance, but he left the ranch to Caitlin, and believe me, she deserved it."

"Let's get going," Jared said. "And Colton, I brought you a horse you can use until you can afford to get one of your own."

"Thanks!" Colton said, "That was thoughtful of you. I was planning to rent one."

Oliver looked quizzically at Colton, who saw the raised eyebrow and smiled a little sheepishly, but he didn't say anything more. He followed Jared out the door.

They went back to the doctor's office where Jared had tied up the horses. Jared's horse stamped impatiently.

"I know, boy, I know. We'll soon be on our way."

Colton went inside and collected his luggage. Jared tied one of the cases behind his saddle and helped Colton strap on the bag that matched Marnie's onto his ride.

Jonah Whatcom, seeing Boss Brown's horse tied at the rail, entered the office, expecting Mr. Brown to be there. Instead, Jasper Clemmons was there at his desk.

Jonah, starting to back out the door, said, "Excuse me...sorry, I thought Mr. Brown was here."

"I told you not to bother Mr. Brown, or don't you remember." He took a cigar out of his mouth. "What do you want?" His voice sounded harsh, and his face wore a deep scowl.

"N-nothin', I don't need nothin'." Before Jasper could say anything more, he turned and ran out the door, slamming it shut behind him. He crashed into Lenny, who steadied him.

"Are you all right?" Lenny asked.

"Y-yes, sir. I-I jest went inta ask you iffin I could have a couple days off. Me'n Cindy Sue want ta go ta San Rafael. Mr. Clemmons was in there an' he didn't seem ta be the person ta ask right now."

"Why's that?" Lenny asked sharply.

"Waal...he's not in th' finest mood, sir. I backed out afore he could say anything more, so he's probably plumb angry with me now. He asked what I wanted, and I said I didn't want nothin'. An then I got out."

"Are you afraid of him?"

"Yes...yes. I am. I don't want ta tangle with 'em cuz I know I'd lose, an' I don't want ta lose my job."

"Long as I'm boss here, you're not going to lose your job, Jonah. You're a good and honest man. And yes, you certainly can have the next two days off."

The door of the office opened with a screech of hinges and hit the wall with a bang.

Lenny spoke softly to Jonah, "You go back to work now. I'll talk to you later."

Jonah left, hurrying to the right of the building, wanting to be out of Jasper Clemmons' sight.

Clemmons stepped out of the office and blew a cloud of smoke into the air. "What's going on here?" he asked with asperity. "Nothing, Jasper. Just having a chat with one of our respected workers." Lenny's voice was soothing, but Jasper was having none of it.

"You're not talking about Whatcom are you?" He spat the words out as if they were distasteful.

"Yes, I am. He's a fine and honest man, and I'll be the first to say so." Lenny said in an authoritative tone.

Sandoval Peabody and Ernest Smith, who oversaw the men in the mine, strolled up, and Jasper beckoned them to come into the office with a wave of his hand.

The two men climbed the three treads together, and Lenny followed, gesturing for Ernest and Sandy to go into the office before him.

"Thanks, Boss," Sandy said.

"You're welcome, Sandy." Lenny looked closely at the two men and said a quick prayer. *Lord, if these men are upright, please reveal it to me. If they're not, I'd like to know that, too.*

CHAPTER XII

Thou wilt shew me the path of life:
in thy presence is fulness of joy;
at thy right hand there are pleasures for evermore.

PSALM 16:11

JARED AND COLTON DANBURY RODE at a goodly pace toward the ranch. When they reached the entry to the property, Jared pulled up.

"See that?" He pointed to a huge arched sign over the entry to the Ranch. Burned into the wood was the lettering McCaully-Bannister Ranch and then the sign that was stamped into every McCaully-Bannisters' horse shoe. It was two slant marks with a capital M-B.

"That used to just say McCaully Ranch. You'll get to meet Kirk, who is Caitlin's husband, and his brother Matthew who owns a vineyard down south in Napa. I guess you met Liberty in town, didn't you?"

"No, I didn't. Who is she?"

"Liberty is Matthew's wife."

"Lot of relatives," he commented. "I don't think I'm going to keep them all straight in my mind. This looks like a nice layout," he said, gazing around as they rode up the lane to the house.

"Yes, Kirk and Caitlin work hard to keep it in good shape." Jared decided not to mention the gold mine to him. He thought Colton was a good man, but he didn't know him well enough yet.

They tied their horses to the long hitching rail and Jared led Colton up the walk to the house. He tapped lightly on the doorjamb and pushed at the door that was part way open.

"Anybody here," he called out.

"Yes, I am," Mini Lou answered, as she traversed the hall from the kitchen. She stepped into the beautiful foyer and saw Jared.

"Hello, Jared." She spoke softly, but her wide smile was welcoming.

"Hello, Mini," he replied. Jared had never called Mini Lou anything but Mini since she was a little thing in pigtails. "I'd like you to meet Colton Danbury. Colton, this is Mini Pindar, a nanny for the Bannisters' baby boy, Jonathan. Mini, Colton's hopefully a new hire, and I'd like to speak to Ewen if he's here."

Mini Lou proffered her hand to Colton, who took it immediately with a serious look in his dark gray eyes.

"I am pleased to make your acquaintance, Mr. Danbury," Mini Lou said, but something within her cringed as if he were a threat to her somehow. She snatched her hand back as if it'd been burned. Surreptitiously, she wiped it on the back of her dress as if he had a disease.

"I'm glad to meet you, Miss Pindar."

Colton's look was assessing, and she didn't like it.

"Ewen is in the library. Please follow me." She led them down the hall and tapped on the library door.

"Come in," Ewen said. He stood as he saw Mini Lou usher Jared and another man into the room. Mini closed the door with a decided click, wondering about her angst toward Mr. Danbury.

Colton looked around appreciatively.

The room was beautiful. Walls of a soft salmon color stood in stark contrast from the dark mahogany of the mantel, shelves, and desk. A fire burned low in the grate. Four wingback chairs all sat facing the fire in a semicircle with a low, square table between them and the fire. It was tastefully done, yet cosy, too. His eyes swung back to Ewen, who had come around to the front side of the desk.

Ewen's look was questioning.

"Good morning, Ewen." Jared didn't seem a bit uncomfortable. "I wondered if you might be looking for a new hire. This here's Colton Danbury, and he's looking for work."

Ewen reached out his hand to shake, taking a measuring look with his frosty blue eyes. "Ewen Carr," he said succinctly.

"Nice to meet you, Mr. Carr."

Ewen smiled and said easily, "Can you ride and rope?"

"Yes, sir, I can, but I evidently don't know how to do the third R."

Ewen chuckled. "I see Jared has you cued in. Repairing fence isn't all that hard to learn to do. I'll hire you and see how you work out. Paydays Friday evening, Sunday we only do the bare essentials and rotate who does them, like feeding the horses, milking the cows and so on. Each man works five days a week, and right now, your day off will be Wednesdays and most Sundays. A workday ends around six in the evening at this time of the year. We have three crews of men. Eli, Manny, and John each run a crew of men. I'll put you with Jared on John's crew. Jared can show you the ropes, and report back to me how you are doing. That sound satisfactory to you?"

"Yes, sir, it does. I will be up front and tell you I've never worked on a ranch before, so I may make some mistakes, but I'll try to do my best to learn fast."

"Thank's for your honesty. You're hired." Ewen stuck out his hand to shake on it. He had a feeling Colton was a believer, but he'd withhold judgment on his work ethic until he knew him better.

"Jared, I know you've been in town helping Maisie, so you two can eat lunch here in the kitchen. Lunch in the chow hall is over."

"Thanks, Boss. The morning has gone by pretty fast."

"How's Gavin doing?" Ewen asked.

"He was asleep when we moved him, but he didn't wake up the whole time. He doesn't look too good. One thing that is on the bright side is that he became a believer last night. Asked Jesus to come into his heart all by himself. You could have knocked Maisie over with a feather. She doesn't know what to think."

"Praise God for that!" Ewen exclaimed. "You boys go eat, and then Jared, you can show Colton around. I've got some paperwork to attend to."

"Thank you, Mr. Carr," Colton said.

"Just Ewen will do, son," Ewen replied. "And you are welcome."

The two men headed to the kitchen. Mini Louise was there with Mrs. Dunstan, learning to cook some delicacy.

When Colton came into the room, Mini Lou felt her hackles go up. Her lashes were thick and dark, and she veiled her deep blue eyes with them, not looking at him at all.

"Mrs. Dunstan," Jared said, "is one of the best cooks in the country." He led Colton over to her. "We call her Duney. Duney, please meet our new hired hand, Colton Danbury."

Duney wiped her hands on her apron as Colton held out his hand to shake hers.

Duney and Colton smiled at each other, and Mini Lou glanced at Colton, her eyes sparking with something akin to anger, and her upper lip curled into t sneer. *He's got no manners. He's supposed to wait for Duney to proffer her hand first. Or…uh…maybe I have that wrong since Duney is hired help. Well, whatever, he somehow makes me jumpy, and I don't like it…nope not one bit!*

"This is Mini Louise Pindar," Duney said, not realizing they'd already met.

Mini Louise looked into the grayest eyes she'd ever seen and seemed mesmerized by them.

"Yes," Colton said. "We met a little bit ago. She kindly let us in the front door."

Mini Lou watched his full lips move as he talked and saw a glimpse of teeth, even and white. *What in the world is the matter with me?* Just the feeling she had when encountering his eyes made her angry. She looked down at the pie crust she was rolling out and plopped the rolling pin into the middle of it with a smack.

"Careful, dearie," Duney said. "You must be gentle with the dough or you end up with tough crust."

"Yes, ma'am," she responded meekly, all the while wishing Colton would leave. *I wish he'd leave the room, leave the house, leave the ranch!*

"Ewen said we missed lunch at the chow hall and said we could eat here. Is that all right with you, Duney or are you too busy?" Jared was hungry.

"No, not too busy. As a matter of fact, Mini Lou and I haven't eaten yet. You can sit with us."

Grrr, thought Mini Lou. *Now I'm going to have to be polite to him.*

"Lay a couple more bowls, Mini Lou, while I dish up." She nodded at Jared. "You can take Colton down the hall and let him wash up. We'll be ready in two shakes of a lamb's tail."

Jared led Colton down the hall, and the two of them washed up. As they came back into the kitchen, they could hear Mini Lou talking.

"I'm really not hungry, Duney. I think I'll go check on Jonathan."

"Nonsense, young lady! We don't skip meals around here, and I am quite sure if Jonny starts crying, we're going to hear him just fine from the kitchen, or anywhere else in the house, for that matter."

Mini Lou blushed to the roots of her hair, realizing Jared and Colton had heard the conversation. She didn't look at either one of them when they entered the kitchen. She stood at her chair with her chin well up and her shoulders held back.

Colton smothered a grin as he looked at her.

Jared sensed Mini Lou's irritation but put it down to the vagaries of women and thought nothing more of it.

Duney brought a huge pot of stew and set it on a pot holder. Butter and jam were already in dishes, and she opened the oven, pulling out a batch of rolls. She dumped them into a flat cloth lined basket.

"Smells delicious, Duney," Jared said.

"I second that," Colton said, his eyes focused on the crown of Mini Lou's shining auburn hair, held back by a snood.

"Don't everyone stand. Please sit down," Duney said, as she placed the basket on the table. As she sat down, she queried, "Mini Lou, would you please ask the blessing?"

Mini Lou startled by the request bent her head. "Of course." *Lord, please forgive me for my bad attitude. That man across the table has done nothing that should upset me. Please help me be nice.* "Dear Father," she prayed, "thank You for Your mighty provision and the blessings we have because we are Your children. Help us be ever mindful of Your love and that we are to share that love with others. Thank You for the food and a lovely place to eat it. Thank You for Your provision for us. Amen."

"Amen," the other three echoed.

She looked up, catching Colton's eyes on her, and she smiled at him for the first time. A dimple dipped into the top of her cheek, and her eyes were warmly blue fringed by her thick dark lashes.

He smiled back, and it almost took her breath away. She stared at him, felt the blood come up and into her face and, tearing her gaze away, she looked down at her bowl of stew in confusion. She wondered at the feelings flooding through her. *This man could destroy all the best laid plans for my future. I mustn't let him get too close. Oh my word, he's devastatingly attractive.*

Mini Lou worked hard at getting her thoughts and her blush under control. She tried, secretly, to take a deep breath. *He gives me the fantods!*

Duney felt the undercurrent of something, and her eyes flew to Colton, whose eyes were fastened on Mini Louise. *Ah, well, there goes Miss Caitlin's nanny.* She smiled to herself, not knowing the conflicting emotions raging within Mini Louise's breast.

Jared, unaware of the magnetism between Colton and Mini Louise, spoke easily across the table to Duney.

"Colton and I moved Gavin to his house."

"He's better then?" Duney asked.

"I wouldn't say so, but the new doctor, Dr. Sandhurst, felt it best for Maisie to be in her own bed. I concur with that. She is exhausted."

"So he's not out of the woods yet, is he?"

"Nope, he's not. Where's Doc?"

"He rode into town. I think he's worried about Gavin and wanted to check on him. He's such a dear man. We're going to love having him here at the ranch."

"Yes, and we're going to miss him being Santa Rosa's doctor. Don't get me wrong. Dr. Sandhurst seems to be knowledgable and competent. After all, he was trained by Doc when they lived in Boston."

"You don't say," Duney said. "My, I had no idea they knew each other."

"This stew is delicious, Duney," Colton said.

"Don't thank me, Mini Louise made it. I made the rolls."

"Miss Pindar, your stew is delicious." Colton said.

"Thank you," she replied primly.

"If you come back on your break, you can come in and have some of the strawberry-rhubarb pie. Mini made it, too."

"Sounds good to me," Jared said. He pushed back from the table and stood, Colton following suit.

"All right, Colton, let's get you acquainted with the ranch, and then we need to go to work."

"Now we're talking business." Colton grinned and added, "Thank you Duney and Miss Mini for the delicious lunch. I look forward to some of that pie."

"I second that," Jared said.

The two of them headed out the door.

Jared led Colton through the barn and stables where Colton saw clean and neat stalls for the horses.

He rubbed the noses of several who hung their heads over the stall doors. "Everything looks like it's in shipshape. This place is huge!" he exclaimed. "For such a large outfit, I'm surprised everything looks so clean."

"There are a lot of cowboys working here, and we all need a place to keep our horses. We take turns mucking out the stalls and keeping things looking good. If we weren't riding out today, I'd have us lead our horses in here, but I plan to introduce you to the crews. You'll be working with me on John's crew."

"Sounds good to me. I just hope I don't disgrace myself," he said with a chuckle.

"If you can rope and ride, learning to repair fence won't take you any time at all." Jared led Colton out to the bunkhouse he'd be staying in.

"This's where we sleep," Jared said. "We make our plans for the day, and play cards some evenings. Each crew has their own bunkhouse. John, head of our crew, talks with Jethro who is the crew boss. Fact is, Jethro's my brother, but we don't let that get in the way of work. Over there," he pointed, "is the chow hall. We have a cook, who makes the best rolls in the world. He a right good cook. He goes by the name of Gus, and he's a full-blooded Swede. I'll tell you one thing and that is you don't want to ever cross him. I've known him to do some nasty things to food when a man's made him mad." He grinned at Colton. "I'm saying really nasty."

"I'll be sure to stay on his good side," Colton murmured.

"Believe me, you'll be glad you did. No one tries to mess with Gus. Well, that's about it. I'm going to take you out to meet the other crews, and we'll wind up with ours." He handed Colton a pair of leather work gloves. "You'll need these when we start work on the new fencing."

They set their horses toward the enclosed range which was acres and acres of grassy plain. They rode for nearly twenty minutes before Colton could see men working in the distance. When they arrived, one man looked up questioningly, but the others continued to work.

"This is Manny's crew," Jared said. "Manny, this is a new hire, Colton Danbury. Ewen just put him on the payroll."

Manny tipped his hat. "Pleased to meet you, I'm sure."

Colton nodded his head. "My pleasure, sir."

Manny pointed to each crew member and named them to Colton. "This is Abbot, Hank, and Frank," he said.

As he spoke, each man signaled as their name was said.

Colton merely nodded to each.

"Will you be on our crew?" Manny asked.

"No, I'll be with Jared on John's crew," Colton responded.

"Well, we welcome anyone who's a hard worker and can get along with the other men."

"See you later," Jared said, as he wheeled his horse around.

Colton followed him as he rode at a canter toward the next group.

Eli saw them coming and took off his hat to wipe his brow on his shirt sleeve as he waited for them.

Jared and Colton pulled to a halt, and Jared said, "Eli is boss of this group of men. Eli, please meet our new hire, Colton Danbury."

Colton saw Eli's face seemed to be split into two camps. His face was darkly tanned, but where he'd removed his hat, it was starkly white.

Eli reached up and shook Colton's hand. "Pleased to meet you."

"Thank you. Glad to meet you, Eli."

Eli's crew had stopped working when the two men rode up, and each approached Colton and shook his hand.

"I'm Mosey."

"Name's Jeb."

"I'm Rhys."

"And I'm Duke."

Each went back to work after introducing themselves.

"Welcome, and we're always glad for a new hire." Eli thumped his hat against his leg, removing the dust and settled it back on his head. "See you two later, I reckon," he said. He picked up some wire cutters and started back to work as Jared and Colton rode off. They pulled up at the last group of men working.

"Hey, John!" Jared said, his voice much warmer than previously. "Meet our new hire, Colton Danbury."

Colton stepped out of his stirrups, already a bit sore. He'd not ridden such a distance for many a year. He stuck out his hand to shake John's.

John looked a bit questioning as he slid his glove off and met Colton's hand, which was smooth as a woman's.

"Always pleased to have a new man on my crew," he said.

"Thanks," Colton replied. "Hope I prove to be a help and not a hindrance."

John nodded. *For some reason he reminds me of Drew.* Drew had been almost like a brother to John and had been murdered a couple years back. He shook off the memory, and introduced his crew.

"This is Sneedy. You need to watch out for him, he's liable to steal your hat." John spoke with a grin as Sneedy shook hands with Colton.

"This is Ricardo. He's a fine hombre."

Colton smiled at the swarthy man who had a wide smile on his face.

"You weel be welcomed here, Colt." Ricardo shortened Colton's name, and the shorter name stuck.

CHAPTER XIII

Thou shalt neither vex a stranger,
nor oppress him.

EXODUS 22:21

LENNY, SITTING AT HIS DESK, surveyed some paperwork left to do. *Reckon without sales happening at the store, I'm going to have to lay some men off. I have no idea what Mrs. Galway has planned. I haven't wanted to bother her, but I'm going to need to know how to proceed. Think I'll ride into town and see how things are going with Mr. Galway and have a chat with Ezra. I like that man!*

He straightened the papers on his desk and placed them neatly into the top drawer. Glancing over, he noticed there were no papers on Jasper's desk, but it didn't give him a clue as to whether the man had left for the day or not. He wondered how a body could be so neat in his work and organization, seeming to like it, yet be so hard-nosed with the crew.

Lenny stood and stretched hugely, locked his desk drawer, and settled his hat on his head. Leaving the office, he noticed that all the horses were gone except Zebidiah Pindar's. Pulling his timepiece out, he looked at it and said, "It's later than I thought."

Zeb Pindar's the only one still here. Bet he's glad to not have to ride that old nag he's been using. Mini Lou landed on her feet and no mistake getting to work for an outfit like McCaully-Bannisters. That girl's a hard worker like her pa.

Looking at Zeb's horse, reminded him to think about red dun colored quarter horses. *Pindar has a beautiful red dun colored horse. Reckon Jasper's left for the day. He, too, has a red dun…who else? There's Ernest Smith and Sandy Peabody. I don't think anyone else, working here, has one.*

Lenny went back up the steps to the office door to lock it. Stepping into the stirrup of his own red dun colored horse, he swung his leg over his saddle and wheeled around, heading for town. He'd ridden a couple miles, enjoying the late afternoon sunshine that was warm on his back, when a report sounded, and he tumbled off his horse. His last thought was…*Clemmons!*

Zeb stayed in the mine, making sure everyone was out before he locked up. All the horses were gone…had been for quite some time. He saddled up his horse, glad Mr. Galway had a long wooden storage bin with cubicles built under the hitching rail where each man could store his toolbox and his saddle.

"Well, Reddy, I'm right glad Mini don't need ta ride you anymore. Yer a benison ta me an' I'm right thankful ta the Lord fer you. Glad I won thet bet. I woulda lost a week's pay iffin I lost. Don't know what I was thinking…showing off, mayhap. Lindsey May woulda skinned me alive iffin she'd a knowed I bet that money so's I could win this horse."

He led his horse over to get a drink and headed for home. Riding Reddy, he took it easy, as if he were trying to make up for Mini Lou's hard riding. He squinted his eyes seeing a horse in the distance. It was another dun, but it was riderless. As he approached, he saw the horse nuzzle something in the bushes.

"Thet's th' boss' horse!" he exclaimed. Zeb alighted from Reddy in a flash, and pushed at the shrubbery, seeing Lenny. He turned him over and felt quickly for a pulse in his neck. Seeing the blood flowing freely from his chest, his eyes widened in consternation.

"Hot spit! He's been shot! Who in tarnation would do such a thing?" Zeb undid Lenny's neckerchief and his own, trying to staunch the flow.

He ripped Lenny's shirt and bound the neckerchiefs in place. Zeb, with a strength born of necessity, picked him up and slung him over his horse, grabbed Lenny's horse's reins and, with a decided effort, climbed on behind his boss, trying to hold him up so he wouldn't bleed so much.

He held him with his left arm and took off at a gallop for town. Zeb felt the ride was intolerably long. His arm ached, and his clothes were stained with Lenny's blood. "Lord Almighty, please help Your servant. I cain't feel m'arm, an' I jest pray I kin hold him till I gets ta town. I thank Ye. Amen."

With a deep sigh, Zeb rode into Santa Rosa. He saw Kirk Bannister walking down the boarded walk, and he called out.

"Bannister...hey Bannister! Help!"

Kirk ran to Zeb's horse and grabbed for Lenny. "What happened? You have a cave-in?"

"Naw. I comed across him on my way home. He's been shot."

"Shot! Not another one!"

"Yep. An' he's lost a lot of blood."

Kirk pulled Lenny into his arms and headed for the doctor's office.

Zeb removed his hat and wiped his brow. He climbed down from his horse and tied it and Lenny's horse, feeling more weary than he had for a long time. He walked stiffly up the step to the boardwalk and followed Kirk into the doctor's office.

"Afternoon, Miss McGrath," Kirk said, as he strode with his heavy burden to the surgery room.

"I'm Paige. Who is that?" Her face turned ashen. She knew in her gut who it was.

"It's Lenny," Zeb answered as he entered the door. "He was shot on th' main road, couple miles from th' mine. I seed his horse first. Where's th' doc?"

"I'll get him!" Paige ran out the door and up the stairs. "Dr. Oliver! Dr. Oliver! Lenny Brown's been shot!"

Oliver rose from his dinner, said, "Excuse me," and ran toward the stairs. He brushed past Paige and bounded down the steps.

Deedee and Marnie sat silent for a moment. Marnie sighed. "I didn't know so many people get shot here. I thought it was supposed to be rare."

"We haven't had a shooting that I know of, until Mr. Galway, for nigh unto three years." Marie took Oliver's plate and set it on the stove to keep warm.

"Who got shot three years ago?"

Marie dished up a plate for herself and sat down to join Deedee and Marnie.

"We had a big to-do here a-bouts. We had a gunslinger from Texas who posed as a priest. He along with the sheriff we had then, planned a takeover of the McCaully Ranch. They found out there was gold up in the hills and planned to kill Miss Caitlin for it. That was just before she married Mr. Kirk Bannister." She took a few bites, knowing Marnie was on the edge of her chair wanting to hear more.

"The gunslinger killed one of McCaully's cowboys. Shot him for no reason at all. Then he decided he didn't want to share the gold with the sheriff and shot him when he was on his way to the McCaully Ranch. Ewen Carr, the foreman for McCaully, was riding home from town and saved the sheriff from immediate death, but the sheriff died that night after he confessed his crime and asked Jesus into his heart." She took a few more bites before continuing.

"What happened...tell me, Marie! What happened?" Marnie's eyes were wide open with anticipation of a good story.

"Well, before the cowboy's murder, Mr. Kirk's brother was riding on the road from the mine, and he got bashed over the head by two of the gunslinger's partners. He didn't know who he was when he recovered and ended up working for Miss Caitlin on the ranch. Mr. Kirk and his brother's wife, Miss Liberty were looking for Matthew Bannister. Miss Caitlin met Mr. Kirk...I don't know exactly how, but she saw the resemblance and had them come to the ranch. Mr. Matthew Bannister still didn't know who he was, but he ended up getting his head slammed against a post in the barn. You see, Miss Caitlin has a horse that wouldn't let anyone around it but her. My understanding is that the gunslinger was going to kidnap Miss Caitlin, but he got behind the horse, who kicked out. The gunslinger went flying and hit Mr. Bannister who was right behind him. It turned out all right as the gunslinger went to meet his Maker, and Matthew Bannister remembered who he was." She sighed, and began to eat.

"Sounds like a story people will never forget," Deedee said.

"It sounds like something out of an exciting book. I hope I don't have nightmares!" Marnie exclaimed.

Oliver had run into the surgery as Kirk laid Lenny on the table.

"How did it happen?"

Zeb entered as the question was asked. He removed his hat as he spoke. "I seed his horse first…nudging my boss in the bushes, he was. I seed 'em in th' bushes, an' I tried to stop th' blood. I never heerd a shot, so I reckon he bin in there fer half a hour or so. I don't know when he left work. Is he bad off?"

While Zeb had been talking, Oliver had been cutting Lenny's shirt away from his body. Feeling around the area where he was wounded.

"I don't know yet, but it looks like the bullet went high which is a good thing as long as it didn't hit the collar bone, and it doesn't feel like it did." He rolled Lenny slightly and saw the bullet had exited.

"Why's he unconscious then?" Zeb asked.

"He's lost a copious amount of blood, I'd imagine. His heart is working hard to get more. Looks as if the bullet went clean through. That's a good thing. I won't have to go digging for it." Concentrating on what he was doing, he didn't look up as he spoke to Zeb. "You saved his life."

Blood suffused Zeb's cheeks at the doctor's words. "He's a good man an' the best boss a body could work fer. I'll be a-prayin' thet he'll recover. Now I'd best be headin' home or my missus will take ta' a-worrin'."

Kirk spoke up. "Dr. Oliver, this is Zebidiah Pindar. He works for Gavin Galway. I believe Lenny getting shot is no coincidence. Zeb, this is Doc Addison's replacement. He is a friend of Doc Addison's and was one of his students back in Boston."

Zeb raised his hand in acknowledgment, knowing the doctor's hands were busy staunching the flow of blood.

"Zeb, I'm going to stay here and see if I can help Dr. Oliver. Could you be good enough to stop by the sheriff's office and let him know what happened?"

"Sure, I kin," Zeb replied.

"I'll stay here and help Dr. Oliver," Paige said. She'd been standing by listening, but went to the sink to wash her hands. "Kirk, you can go tell Ezra, uh…the sheriff what's happened." She spoke kindly to Zeb. "You'd better get home, or poor Lindsey May will be worried."

"Thank you, miss. I'll be on my way." He left with Kirk on his heels.

"Tell Lindsey May hello for me," Kirk said. "I think your daughter is going to be the best thing that's happened to us. Jonathan's taken to her, and she's good with him. Thank you for letting her work for us."

"Cain't say I don't miss 'er, but she's been biting at the bit fer some time, wantin' ta get out on 'er own. Thanks fer being 'er boss." He lifted his hat in a farewell and climbed on Reddy, reining the beautiful dun colored horse around to head for home.

Kirk ran down the boardwalk and entered the sheriff's office without knocking. It startled Ezra who was making a list of all the workers at the mine. He was convinced someone who worked there shot Mr. Galway. He stood as he saw Kirk, who didn't mince words.

"Lenny Brown's been shot on the main road a mile or two from the mine."

Ezra spoke in a shocked voice. "Is he dead?"

"No, but he's lost a lot of blood. Zebidiah Pindar found him on his way home and brought him into town. Dr. Oliver says the bullet went clean through, so that's a good thing." As Kirk spoke, Ezra was buckling on his holster.

"Let's go."

The two men strode down the boardwalk, silence between them.

Ezra prayed. *Lord, I pray for a full recovery for Lenny. In the short time I've known him, he has become like a brother. Lord, he loves You, which really does make him my brother. I ask that You please spare his life.*

As they entered the office, Ezra saw Paige helping Dr. Oliver, who had cleaned the wound and was now stitching him up. Her face was a pasty white.

Oliver saw her face and thought she wasn't used to assisting and that the sight of the wound made her faint.

Paige turned to wash her hands and as she dried them, Ezra put his arm around her shoulders and pulled her to his side, to the astonishment of Kirk and Oliver.

"He'll be all right, Paige," he said. "He's a child of the King, and the King will take care of him for you."

Paige turned into his shoulder, starting to cry. "I-I don't know what I'd do if he died. I-I…"

"Shush, sweet Paige, he'll pull through. He's got a strong constitution."

Paige pulled away from Ezra, stared into his green-hazel eyes, and asked, "How did you know I was Paige and not Payton?"

Ezra was taken aback. *Drat it all!* "It's Payton's day off, isn't it?" He said smoothly without missing a beat. "Tis is your day to work." He gazed into warm brown eyes thinking how much she looked like Payton. *Strawberry blonde hair and brown eyes…an unusual combination.*

Paige looked discombobulated. "Yes, you're right, it's Payton's day off," she said aloud.

"Paige, would you please hold this in place while I tape him up?" Oliver asked. He held a thick wad of pristine gauze loaded with an ointment he'd put on the sutures.

"Certainly, sir." Paige moved into place and held the pad while Oliver taped it to Lenny's chest.

"He's not going to like it when that gauze gets removed with all that hair on his chest. Does anyone live with him, or does he live alone?" Oliver asked.

"He lives alone," Paige vouchsafed. "He can stay at our house, and Payton and I can take turns nursing him. Perhaps my mother will help."

Kirk who had watched the interchange, guessed Ezra could tell the two McGraths apart. *I sure can't. They are like two peas in a pod. One thing for sure, Paige is in love with Lenny. I'm glad. He's a good man, and she's a sweet girl.*

"That's a good idea, Paige, but are you sure it'll be all right with your mother?" Kirk asked. He added, "I'm glad you live close by. That way, Dr. Oliver can check on him easily."

"Yes, it is a good idea," Ezra said. "But now the problem is…who is our shooter? I wouldn't be surprised if it was the same person who shot Gavin Galway." Ezra was disgusted that he wasn't any closer to finding out who was going around shooting people connected with the mine.

"Kirk, would you mind showing me where Jasper Clemmons lives? I'd like to ride out and have a talk with him. See if he has any idea who is doing this."

Kirk, who'd been leaning against the wall, with arms crossed, pushed away and said, "You've never met Clemmons, have you?"

"No, why?"

"Nothing I care to share. Reckon you'll know what I mean."

Paige looked meaningful at Kirk. "I know what you mean." She turned away not wanting to say more.

"Right now, before he wakens, I'd like to get Mr. Brown moved to the McGraths' house," Oliver said. "Paige, could you please run home and let them know we're bringing your beau there to recover?"

"Oh! Please don't tell Mama he's my beau! He is, but Mama doesn't approve of males. She doesn't even like them!" She blushed to the roots of her hair, looking scared she'd be found out. "Sorry and I shouldn't say this! But I bet Papa died just to get out of the house!"

"We'll not say a word about it, and we will pray Mr. Brown charms your mama right down to her slippers," Oliver said. "Your secret is safe with us."

"Where's the stretcher?" Ezra asked.

Oliver pointed. "In there."

Kirk opened the door to a long hall-like closet. Both sides were lined with shelves of medical supplies and tools that Doc Addison had collected over the years. There was a strong smell of liniment. He pulled out the stretcher that was closest, as there was more than one. He got the empty stretcher as far as the door and handed it to Ezra, who placed it next to the surgery table. Kirk and Ezra held the stretcher steady, while Oliver and Paige pulled the sheet that was under Lenny. It was a concerted effort, and with little difficulty, they had him on the stretcher and ready to go. Ezra had not stirred at all, and it worried Oliver.

Paige put a hand to her mouth and gasped, "Oh my goodness! I'll run ahead and let Mother know!" She grabbed a few things from her desk and ran out the door, banging it behind her.

Oliver held the door open, and Kirk and Ezra got Lenny through it, trying not to jiggle the stretcher too much.

"You go first, Kirk," Era said. "I know where the McGraths' house is, but the missus knows you and will possibly be more amenable to your face." He chuckled.

"I wouldn't bet on it," Kirk said under his breath.

They carried Lenny as smoothly as they were able, and Paige held the door while they climbed the front steps.

Mrs. McGrath stood right behind Paige, arms crossed over her flat bosom, a frown marking her gray brows.

Ezra had never met her. She looked formidable. She was quite thin with sparce gray hair scraped back into a thin bun. Her mouth was a slash line across her face, and her jaw was set in what looked like disgust.

"And who is this, might I ask?" Dusk had fallen, and she didn't see Kirk until he'd entered the foyer.

"Why, hello there, Mrs. McGrath. How are you this evening?" He smiled, and she smiled back.

"Good evening, Kirk Bannister." She unfolded her arms and started to take hold of his arm.

He hoped she wouldn't pull on it. His grip on the stretcher was loosening, his hand sweaty and tired.

"Where do we take him?"

"We have a room right here on the main floor." Mrs. McGrath lifted her scrawny chin and marched down the hall. She opened a heavy door and ushered Kirk and Ezra in. "Who is he anyway?"

"He's Gavin Galway's right hand man. Someone shot him as he was heading home from work."

"Oh, my! Poor, poor dear! We'll be sure to take good care of him."

Payton saw Ezra as she came down the stairs. Her eyes widened and flew to her mother who was leading the two men to the spare room.

Paige closed the door and seeing Payton, put her forefinger to her lips. She spoke aloud to Payton so her mother could hear.

"Mr. Brown, a man who works for Mr. Galway, has been shot. Dr. Oliver patched him up, but he hasn't recovered. I offered our house because Mr. Bannister said he couldn't go home as he lives alone." She winked at her twin, who nodded.

Someone knocked on the door and Paige, startled, nearly jumped out of her skin. She opened the door.

"Dr. Oliver! Please come in."

"Sorry, but I forgot to give you some instructions."

Mrs. McGrath, who'd already met the doctor, came striding back down the hall. "Who is it?" she called out.

"It's me, Mrs. McGrath," Oliver said. "It's so kind of you to succor this poor man who has been shot. I'm sure you'll have many stars in your crown for your generous hospitality."

"Oh, thank you, Dr. Sandhurst. Why, I imagine any good Christian woman would be happy to help."

"I hope so, but I just dropped by to say that our patient needs lots of liquids, soups and ground up meat to get his strength back up."

"Oh, sir! You can be sure I know all about that. I nursed men during the War Between the States." She spoke proudly, and Oliver was sure to act duly impressed.

"My, then you wouldn't need my expertise nor my advice. Well then, without further ado, I'll take my leave. I know my cook will have kept my dinner for me. Good evening." He doffed his hat and left before Mrs. McGrath could think of anything to say to detain him.

CHAPTER XIV

Judge me, O God, and plead my cause against an ungodly nation:
O deliver me from the deceitful and unjust man.

PSALM 43:1

EZRA DIDN'T CARE TO STAY OVERLONG either. He knew his attraction to Payton would be noticed by her observant mother. He was grateful to Paige for divulging the information that Payton hadn't let her mother know about them seeing each other. He'd had no idea Payton had kept it a secret from her. He'd been surprised Mrs McGrath was unaware of his relationship with her daughter. He wanted to court Payton, but because of Paige's warning, he would bide his time.

Kirk and Ezra lifted Lenny onto the bed and Ezra carried the stretcher into the hallway. Both men had heard Dr. Oliver at the front door.

Kirk and Ezra left the bedroom and headed for the foyer as the door closed behind Oliver.

"Mrs. McGrath," Kirk said. "This is Santa Rosa's new sheriff, Ezra Walker." She eyed the new sheriff with some misgiving.

Ezra completely ignored the twins as he spoke to their mother. He hoped his words would make an impression on her.

"It is my pleasure to meet you, Mrs. McGrath. As your new sheriff, I appreciate the willingness you have expressed to help succor this man. I know him personally, and you couldn't wish for a better patient. He's kind, caring, and considerate. Now, Mr. Bannister and I must take our leave. Again, we thank you for your generosity."

"I second that," Kirk said. "I've known Lenny for a long time. I'm sure you'll be happy to know, Mrs. McGrath, that he is a well-grounded Christian man." He didn't try to shake the woman's hand as she hadn't proffered it, but he smiled his best smile at her.

Ezra strolled toward the door, saying nothing to the two girls.

Kirk was right at his heels, but he turned before leaving and said, "By your leave, madam, we must go. Miss Paige, Miss Payton, thank you for your willingness to help." He settled his hat on his head as he went through the door held open by Ezra, who had put the stretcher down, leaning it against his leg while he waited for Kirk.

Ezra closed the door gently. "Whew!" he said as he pulled his hat off and wiped his brow on his sleeve. He spoke in a low voice. "I hope Lenny won't unknowingly go spilling the beans to Mrs. McGrath. There will be trouble for sure if he does."

"You better not just hope, you'd better pray!" Kirk chuckled. "She is a curmudgeon for sure, but sweet as honey in front of most people. I've heard the way she talks to those girls when she thought no one was around. It's not pretty. She goes through cooks faster than I can unload a gun! Sorry, here I am gossiping. I just want you to understand that you're going to have a tough garden to hoe trying to get on her good side."

"I'm grateful for the warning. I had no idea Payton hadn't told her that I have been seeing her. It came as a distinct shock. I was going to ask Mrs. McGrath if I could court Payton, without telling Payton first. I am not in the habit of skulking around, but if she is as you say, I can understand why Payton hasn't said anything."

"I won't say anymore, except Katie and I will definitely put you on our prayer list."

"You call your wife, Caitlin, Katie?"

"Yes, I have since I met her. I found out later her father had done the same."

"Lucky for you!" Ezra laughed. "Wonder how I'm going to get around Mrs. McGrath's opposition to men."

"Just turn on the charm and be as pleasant as possible. You'll win her over in time, I reckon."

Ezra nodded agreeably. "I hope so."

They climbed on their horses to head out of town.

"Thank you," Ezra added, "for being willing to show me where Jasper Clemmons lives."

It was dark, but the main road was lit by a half moon with enough light to see where they were riding.

"Hope I don't miss the turning. It should be right along here, I think," Kirk said. "Ah, here it is!"

The lane had no ruts like the main road. It was level but with no light. They couldn't see much but knew they were riding on cobbles. Kirk and Ezra pulled up in front of a huge one story clapboard house. Dismounting, they tied their horses, and headed up the walk.

The front door was level to the veranda and partly made of glass. Two door-length windows flanked it, and light spilled out so they could see the veranda quite clearly. Half barrels, on either side of the door, bursting with bright blooms, splashed color over their sides.

Ezra knocked on the mahogany part of the door with a brass knocker for that purpose. They could hear a dog barking within.

Kirk, waiting for someone to answer the door, took a good look at his surroundings. Everything was neat and clean. The veranda spread itself on either side of the front door. Low tables of wicker along with chairs and settees decorated with floral pillows created an inviting place to relax.

Jasper Clemmons opened the door. "What do you want?"

"Good evening, Mr. Clemmons. I am Ezra Walker," he doffed his hat. "I'm Santa Rosa's new sheriff. Do you have a moment to talk?"

"Come on in. Evidently you know who I am." His eyebrows rose when he saw Kirk Bannister behind the sheriff. "Evening, Bannister. I take it this isn't a call for pleasantries is it? Come on in, the two of you."

"Evening, Jasper," Kirk responded as he followed Ezra into the large foyer. He'd never been inside the Clemmons' house and looked around appreciatively, taking in the large room in a glance. It exuded elegance without being obtrusive.

"Please follow me," Jasper said shortly. He led the way to an immense library open to the spacious hall by two extra wide pocket doors, pushed entirely open.

The library was huge and beautiful. Although the house was a single story, the ceiling in the library had been raised to second story height, but the second story floor was about only about five feet wide around the huge room on three sides. Oak railing encircled the second floor's ledge, and an oaken staircase curved up to the bookshelves lining the three walls. Deep leather chairs and end tables seemed to give an invitation to sit and read.

The fourth side of the room was the focal point. It housed a wide stone fireplace from floor to the second floor ceiling. Glassed cases, on either side of the stone, rose upward and contained, what was most likely, collectibles. It was beautiful.

Ezra looked with a sense of peace enveloping him. He loved books, and this room was a dream come true. He breathed deeply and loved the smell. *I smell books, leather, pipe and some kind of essence...perhaps sandalwood? How did he get the money for all this?*

Kirk wasn't a reader, but he could appreciate the beauty of the room's perfect symmetry and style.

Jasper stood with his arms folded across his chest waiting until the men had looked around the room. "Finished?" he asked, his voice sounding harsh.

"I'm sorry," Ezra said. "I was lost in wonder. I think this is, without a doubt, the most beautiful library I've ever had the privilege to behold. It's as if I'm in a dream."

Jasper's face softened, but his voice didn't. "Let's sit over here," he said, as he gestured toward some seating. He led them to deep leather chairs arranged around the gigantic fireplace. Above the mantle was an arresting picture.

Ezra looked at Jasper Clemmons. "Oh my! Is that a Lusieri?" he asked in astonishment.

It was Jasper's turn to look astonished. "You know of him?"

"Yes, Giovanni Battista Lusieri of Naples. I have much admiration for his works. He was a great artist."

For the first time in a long time, Jasper warmed to a man.

"Yes, he was. Please, have a chair." He reached over and pulled a bell pull before he sat down.

In no time there was a tap on the door jamb, and a young man stood in the opened doorway.

"You rang, sir?"

"Yes." He looked at his guests. "Can I offer you something? Coffee, tea or perhaps some Laphroaig?"

"I'll have the Laphroaig," Ezra said.

"You wouldn't by any chance have some of my brother's wine, would you?" Kirk asked.

"Frankly, I do. It's one of the best wines around according to my tongue." Clemmons smiled for the first time since they had arrived.

Kirk almost dropped his jaw. He'd never seen the man unbend enough to smile, and it was a pleasant one.

Clemmons spoke to the young man who was waiting.

"We'll have two whiskies, one glass of Libby, and how about three pieces of cake?"

Ezra nodded in the affirmative as the young man said, "Yes, sir."

"Please sit," Clemmons said. "Now, may I ask what brings you here?"

"Yes, and it's not pretty," Ezra responded. "Mr. Brown was on his way home from the mine and has been shot."

"Shot?" Jasper jumped up and repeated, "Shot! Is he all right?"

"He was lucky. The bullet went clean through his shoulder." Ezra said. Zebidiah Pindar found him a couple miles from the mine on the main road.

"Who would shoot that man? Where's Lenny now? Who's going to take care of him? He lives alone, you understand." He paced up and down in front of the fireplace.

Jasper's man returned with a tray. Three large pieces of yellow cake with thick chocolate frosting made Ezra's mouth water. Denny handed the drinks and cake to the men, and asked, "Will that be all, sir?"

"Yes, thanks, Denny."

Denny bowed slightly and left. He closed the double pocket doors behind him.

"This is delicious," Kirk said. "Thanks."

Ezra nodded his agreement, his mouth full of cake. He swallowed and said, "We don't know yet who shot him, but we're figuring it has to be someone from the mine. He hadn't regained consciousness when the new doctor finished cleaning and stitching him up. He's lost a lot of blood. He's ensconced at the McGraths'. Does that answer all your questions?" He took another mouthful of cake.

"Yes, thank you. Frankly, Lenny and I don't get along much. I'm not an easy man to be around for any length of time, I'll admit that. But Lenny…he's too soft. For the position he's in, he needs to be tougher. He's nice to everyone, even those men who try his patience. I have no forbearance with those types, and it galls me to see him so nice to them."

Kirk looked around while Clemmons was talking. *Wonder how he can afford all this? Reckon that's none of my business, but two men have been shot, and it has to be someone from the mine. If not Clemmons, then who?* His eyes came to rest on Clemmons.

"Who at the mine besides you, Lenny, Whatcom, Smith, and Peabody, ride red dun colored horses?" Ezra asked.

"Well, you just listed the ones I know about. I'm sure there must be more but if there are, I haven't noticed. Why do you ask?"

"The shooter rides a red dun colored horse," Kirk interjected. "I wish I hadn't been so focused on the fact that Gavin might have been shot. All I noticed was the kind of horse the shooter was riding, and that he might be short."

"That could fit a lot of men at the mine. Sorry, I can't help you there. I've heard Mrs. McGrath is a crotchety and ill-tempered. If staying there doesn't work out for Lenny, he's welcome to recover here."

Kirk swallowed down a chuckle at the thought that the pot was calling the kettle black.

"Thank you for the offer. He seemed comfortable enough when we left him, but he hadn't woken up yet. Lenny's in the Lord's hands after all," Kirk said.

"Don't talk about the Lord in this house!" Jasper's voice was jarring in the beautiful setting. He stood, cutting off any further enjoyment of cake or drink. "Now if that is all, I'd like to get back to my dinner."

Kirk's face was puzzled at the veritable change in the man.

Ezra looked ruefully at the whiskey he hadn't tasted. "Thank you for your time, Mr. Clemmons." He stood up and stuck out his hand to Jasper, who hesitated before shaking it. "I think the two of us have much in common. Enjoy your dinner. We'll see our way out."

Kirk and Ezra headed out the door.

"Whew!" Kirk said. "I've never seen him unbend like that nor lose his temper like that!"

Ezra glanced at Kirk and said, "I read a new book published last year. It's called 'The Strange Case of Dr. Jekyll and Mr. Hyde' by Sir Robert Louis Stevenson. Strange is right. It's a book on good and evil in a man. It was rather gruesome, but Jasper Clemmons isn't evil. He's been deeply wounded somehow, and he's blaming God for it."

"How do you know that, Ezra?"

"I had a strong impression from the Almighty that Jasper needs help…real help and besides, I liked him. And just so you know, I don't believe anyone could playact their astonishment the way he reacted to the news that Lenny had been shot."

"No, I have to agree with you there. He was shocked. I watched his eyes, and his pupils dilated at the news. No, for sure he was not acting," Kirk said.

"I sure am glad you didn't laugh when he said Mrs. McGrath is crotchety! I knew what you were thinking." It was dark, and Ezra spoke with a smile in his voice.

Kirk chuckled. "Well, he certainly proved to be a grump at the end there, didn't he?"

Ezra clapped Kirk on the shoulder. "Yes—yes he did. I hope I can help him somehow. Pray for that, won't you? Be careful on the main road. It's late, but we do have a shooter, although I have a feeling all this is connected to the mine somehow."

"Yes, I'll be careful, and I'll tell Katie about Jasper, and we will pray."

Gavin awoke. It was dark, but he could see a partial moon through the opened curtain. It's beam traveled the length of the floor, up and across the bed. He saw Maisie, her face bathed by the light of the moon, sound asleep next to him. He smiled to himself in contentment. *I'm in my own bed, my wife is here, we're going to have a baby, and I feel a peace in my heart I've never known before. What more could a man ask for?*

He stretched carefully, not to awaken Maisie, and felt the pull of the tape on his wound. *Ah...I don't think the bullet did nearly as much damage as my heart. I am so incredibly tired. I feel I could stay in this bed forever.*

His thoughts turned into a prayer. *Lord, how thankful I am that You gave me the extended time to find You as my Savior. How blessed I am and grateful for Your love. I pray Maisie finds You as Savior too. Thank You for the peace that all will work out somehow. I bow in my heart to Your will If You take me home, I pray for Maisie to find You and the peace You bring.* He took a deep breath and fell back asleep.

Kenny awoke and wondered where he was. He started to rise, felt the pain in his shoulder, and lay back. He heard the sound of a match being struck, and a lamp was lit next to his bed. He turned his head and stared in wonder at Paige as she sat down in a chair close to his bed.

"What happened? Where am I?" His voice was low, and Paige answered softly.

"You were shot on the main road, and you're at my house. Zebidiah found you and brought you into town. Dr. Oliver patched you up, and I offered our house for your recovery. I've been curled up on the settee under the window, dosing off and on. I didn't want you to wake up and not have someone here."

"Thank you for that—I appreciate your thoughtfulness." He swallowed. "I have cotton mouth. Could I please have some water to drink?"

"Just a moment, and I'll get some." She opened the door and left the bedroom on bare feet.

Lenny lay still, not wanting to move because of the pain in his shoulder. He felt woozy and didn't realize Paige had returned.

"Are you awake?" she whispered.

"Yes, just resting my eyes." He looked at her, and added, "Looking at you rests my eyes too, I reckon."

His smile wrenched her heart as she knew he was in pain.

"Who is that snoring? he asked. It sounds like a train. I'd think that would keep the whole house awake."

Paige giggled. "It's mother. Payton and I were just talking about how nice it is when mother snores because we know she's not spying on us." Her face turned red at revealing a private matter, but Ezra seemed to not mind.

She smiled at him and slipped her arm under his neck. Lifting his head carefully, she held the cup for him not wanting to cause him more pain.

He felt his heart beat faster at her nearness. Drinking deeply from the cup, he finished, and Paige pulled her arm back. The nearness of him made her heart race. She wondered at the strange feelings he aroused in her. She'd never felt this way about anyone in her life.

"Do you know who did this to you? Do you remember anything?"

"I remember leaving the mine. The only horse left tied up was Zeb's. He's a good man, and I have no doubt he saved my life. If I'd been the last to leave, why, I could have laid there all night. Frankly, I don't think I'd be here. And no, I have no idea who would shoot me."

"Lenny, I'm thankful Zeb found you, and I pray you have a full recovery. As to your being here, I do need to tell you that…ah…well, one thing you need to know is that Mother has no idea I'm seeing you. She doesn't know that Payton is seeing Ezra either. She's not easy to be around, and—and she doesn't like men." She spoke in a rush of words, hoping he was lucid enough to comprehend what she was trying to say to him.

"I understand," he said, as he took her hand in his. "Don't fash yourself, girl. I won't say a word to your mother, and I'll be polite and circumspect in her presence. I wouldn't want to do anything that could jeopardize our relationship or have the potential of her forbidding me to see you."

"How do you know I'm Paige? Maybe I'm Payton."

He smiled. "You just said you and Payton like it when your mother snores." He took a breath that hurt and changed the subject. "You smell wonderful. Is that Paris?"

"How would you know that?"

"Come closer and I'll tell you what scent it is."

"If I were any closer, I'd be…oh!"

He pulled her onto the good side of his chest, holding her head there. "No, you're not Payton. You are definitely Paige."

"But how do you know?"

"I don't understand it myself, but I don't feel about Payton the way I feel about you."

"And what way is that, Mr. Brown?"

He smoothed her hair, "I think you know by now."

"But Mother—"

"Hush, my love, relax. Things have a way of working themselves out. We'll leave it in the Lord's hands."

Paige, feeling drowsy as he stroked her hair, felt treasured and protected in his arms.

CHAPTER XV

Blessed is the man that trusteth in the Lord,
and whose hope the Lord is.

JEREMIAH 17: 7

DR. **MICAH ADDISON AWOKE EARLY.** He lay thinking about Deedee. He couldn't seem to think about much else. *I thank Thee, Almighty God for another day. I thank Thee for bringing Deidra Jennings into my life. What a gift Thou hast given me! What a most wonderful surprise!*

He lay praying for quite some time. He could smell bacon, and swinging his legs over the side of the bed, he stood, stretched, and bent to touch his toes ten times, each time stretching up to his full height, arms up toward the ceiling. It was a regular ritual for him. He stretched hugely again and whistling, made his way into the adjoining bathroom. He broke into a song he'd made up himself. It was a song of praise and thanksgiving, and he belted out the words as he dried his face.

Whispering, he said, "Ready to face another day, Father. I will have some of that bacon I smell Duney making, and enjoy conversing with whomever happens to be in the kitchen. Then, I plan to ride into town and check on Gavin and call on Deedee. I must remember to call her Miss Jennings." He grinned and was feeling so spry, he thought he should try sliding down the bannister, but prudently decided against it.

He strolled into the kitchen and was pleased to see both Bannisters and their spouses as well as Mini Louise Pindar.

"Good morning! Am I a late riser, or are you all early risers?"

"We all got here within the last few minutes," Kirk responded. "Usually Katie and I are already out on the range by now, but I got home late last night, and Katie waited up for me."

"Jonathan had a bad night, and I slept in after he finally settled down," Mini said.

Liberty blushed as Matthew surreptitiously squeezed her knee under the table, and said, "We are on vacation, and normally are up before now, but we're taking it easy."

"Kirk and I were up for quite some time talking," Caitlin vouchsafed. "He has some bad news to share."

All eyes were on Kirk as he began to related the happenings of the evening before.

"Lenny Brown was shot on his way home from the mine."

Mini clapped her hand to her mouth, her eyes widened in fear. "Oh no!" she exclaimed. "Is—is he all right?"

"Barring any infection, he should be. You all can be praying for him though. He's lost a lot of blood and is staying at the McGraths'."

"I wouldn't think that would be a good place for a man to recover," Mini said. "Everyone knows Mrs. McGrath doesn't like men. Are you sure she won't put arsenic in his soup?"

Kirk chuckled. "I think she'll have to behave herself. Lenny is, after all, an important figure, being Gavin's right-hand man."

Matthew sat back, looking thoughtful. "I should think the shooter has to be connected to the mine somehow. Perhaps in the beginning, shooting Gavin was a matter of robbery and getting rich quick. Shooting the foreman of the mine wasn't necessary unless there is a promotion or some kind of raise in pay?"

His sentence ended in a question as he was thinking out loud.

Kirk perused his brother's face as he thought about the evening before. "For sure it's not Jasper Clemmons," he said.

"How can you say that?" Mini asked. "He seems to fit getting the raise in pay *and* the promotion. I don't like that man. He's not nice."

"I can say that because the sheriff and I paid him a visit last night. He wasn't the most welcoming host at first, but Ezra seemed to charm him. He unbent and became warm and welcoming. He even drinks your Liberty wine, Matt." Kirk took a sip of coffee and continued to talk.

"When Ezra related the fact that Lenny had been shot, he was shocked—shocked enough that I saw his pupils dilate. He wasn't shamming. No...our shooter must be someone else. But, I think you're right, Matt. It has to be someone who would benefit from having Lenny out of the way. Who is next after Jasper?"

Mini knew and spoke up. "Both Ernest Smith and Sandoval Peabody are equal in responsibilities. They are not the best of friends but are decent to each other. Either one of them could be promoted to Mr. Clemmons' position if he ended up boss foreman."

"Do either of them ride a red dun colored horse?"

"Both of them do."

"Well, that settles that. Both men are candidates." Kirk's face looked gloomy.

"We can pray it's one of them and not someone else with a grievance against Lenny," Caitlin said.

Liberty nodded her head. "Yes, prayer is sometimes our last resort when it should be our first. Prayer changes things. We can pray the shooter will be so convicted that he confesses, or we can pray that something will give him away."

"Let's pray together right now," Doc said. "I'll start."

They all bowed their heads, and he began to pray. Each person at the table prayed about the situation.

When they were finished, Duney had them serve themselves buffet style.

The conversation became lighter and sparkled with laughter.

Mini looked at everyone at the table. She couldn't believe that life could be so gracious and fun. Nothing she did now seemed to be a drudge. *The worst thing I do is change a diaper. I don't want to ever go back to the life I had growing up. I know after last night and having so much time to think while rocking Jonathan that I'm attracted to Colton Danbury. There's no point in ignoring it. The problem is he doesn't fit into my plans for my future. I need to guard my heart. I could see he was attracted to me, too. At least I think he was. There was something about him that gave me goose bumps. I didn't like it at first, but the more I was around him, the more I liked it. I don't want anyone or anything to get in the way of me being a lady of means. I am going to work hard. Maybe I can earn enough that I can help Pa and Ma…I mean Father and Mother, but I don't want be a drudge for the rest of my life.*

She heard a cry and hurriedly excused herself. "I didn't think he'd wake up for at least another hour," she said with a smile. When she was out of sight, she took the stairs two at a time.

Hearing the swift ascent, Doc smiled. "Reminds me of you Caitlin and Liberty. Remember that blackguard gunslinger posing as a priest? When the word came that he was on his way, you two ran up those stairs exactly the same way. Mini Lou must be a good nanny to hurry so fast."

Liberty laughed. "I certainly remember. In all truth, I was glad for the way it all turned out, because I got my husband back…at least I got a husband who could remember who he was."

Caitlin giggled. "I remember him getting hit on the noggin again." She glanced at Matthew and giggled again. "Brought you back to your senses didn't it?"

"Yes, although it took me a while to get rid of the headaches. I was thankful I got knocked into that barn post. But I was really glad I wasn't behind Fire the way O'Flannagan was. Fire did a real number on him. I kept thinking of the verse, 'And be sure your sin will find you out'."

"Yes," Kirk nodded his head in agreement. "I am thankful that God's ways are higher than my ways. Sometimes bad things happen, but when we're a child of the king, we can be sure God is working His plan for the better good."

Caitlin had been listening to see if Jonathan was going to continue to cry, but it had stopped almost as soon as she heard the door to the nursery close. *I am so thankful for that girl! Jonathan has really taken to her, and she knows how to care for him. I can rest assured knowing my baby is in good hands.*

Breakfast was over. Liberty and Caitlin made plans to go into town and see Maisie, and Kirk was going to show Matthew a new horse he'd bought. After that, the two men were going to ride out to the gold mine.

"You all know Gavin was moved home, don't you?"

Caitlin and Liberty knew, but Doc Addison didn't.

"Thanks for cueing me in, Kirk. I thought he was still at the office." Doc couldn't seem to get Deedee out of his thoughts, and added, "I think I'll ride into town and see if Oliver needs any help. I'll check on Lenny at the McGraths' and see Gavin." *And I'll be sure to see Deedee!*

He rode into town on his red dun colored horse. It was a gelding named Rufous. He smiled as he thought about it. Rufous meant reddish brown in color. He missed old Blondie, but she'd had a good life, and Kirk had put her out to pasture. She was too old to ride anymore and was enjoying the life of ease. He planned to give her some kind of treat once every other day or so. He didn't want her to think he didn't love her anymore.

For some reason, I think I won't be enjoying a life of ease just yet. I wonder if I should look for a place of my own. Deedee isn't the kind of woman who would enjoy living on someone else's generosity. It doesn't bother me because I've felt as if I'm part of the McCaully family. Have been for years. Cait sure couldn't have married a nicer man. Kirk Bannister has been perfect for her.

As for Deedee, I'm quite sure she would like being married to me once she gets used to the idea. I could lose myself in those greenish eyes forever! It's amazing she's never been married. I have plenty of money now my mother's passed. I can't believe she had so much. We always lived so frugally. He smiled at his thoughts. *Maybe that's why she had so much.*

Wonder who shot Gavin? It's bad enough to get shot, but couple that with a heart attack...I don't know. I know he's in Thy hands, Lord.

He continued to think and pray about the events in his life and was surprised to find himself entering Santa Rosa.

He decided to see Oliver first. He didn't want the younger man to think he was trying to undermine his authority. He pulled up in front of his old premises and looked at the front. It looked inviting to him.

I wonder if Oliver will feel the same way I do. I loved living here and helping so many helpless. I thank Thee, Lord, for giving me the ability to doctor people.

He climbed off Rufous, tying him up at the rail, and first entered the office, but Oliver wasn't there.

"Good morning, Payton."

"Good morning, Doc. How's life on the farm?" She smiled albeit a bit tiredly.

She'd awakened early and thought to help Paige. She was glad she'd gone into the room where Lenny was, because she could hear her mother stirring. When she entered the bedroom, she saw Paige sitting in a chair, but her head was on the pillow next to Lenny.

Payton shook her shoulder to awaken her and pointed to the ceiling.

"Oh my goodness! Thanks, Payton! I would have been caught for sure." Paige whispered, straightening her hair. She looked tenderly at Lenny, who was still asleep. She wanted to stroke his cheek but refrained, not wanting to wake him up.

"I need to go to work, but if you need anything, just send Tessa," Payton whispered.

"Thank you." Paige replied. "I'm grateful to have a sister like you! I pray everything works out for the two of us. Just be really careful if Ezra is around. I swear Mother can smell our thoughts!"

"I will," she said softly.

They could hear their mother clumping down the stairs. She always wore wooden shoes when she was in the house. The girls could hear her coming down the hall. It made both of them nervous.

"I need to go to work, so I'll leave you to it," Payton whispered.

The door opened, and Mrs. McGrath stood in the doorway, surveying the scene. She didn't want to wake the man up, as she didn't want to talk to him, so she held her tongue.

When Payton left, with a little wave of her hand to Paige, Mrs. McGrath closed the door and stalked down the hall after Payton.

"You look a sight, girl! Have you eaten yet?"

"No, Mother, but I'm going to be late. I can get something to eat at the office."

Mrs. McGrath grumbled, but she liked her girls working for money. Although they were her own daughters, she charged the girls board and room and wondered if they knew they could stay in several other places in town for cheaper than what she took from them.

"Neither one of them is very smart," she muttered. "I know their every move and most of their thoughts. They take after their father, that's for sure."

Payton arrived early and readied things on her desk for the day. She checked the surgery room to make sure all was in order and heard someone come into the reception room. She hurried out and breathed a sigh. It wasn't anyone needing help.

Doc Addison eyed Payton. He thought she looked a bit frazzled. "Are you all right?"

"Yes, sir, I'm fine but a bit tired. I prayed all night for some requests I have placed before the Lord."

"How's Lenny?"

"I don't know. He wasn't awake when I left the house."

"Where's Dr. Oliver?"

"He was down here, but went back up to finish up breakfast."

"Thanks, Payton, and I'll be praying for those requests of yours. I don't need to know what they are, the good Lord knows. Think I'll go up and have some coffee and a chat with Oliver." He patted Payton's hand and went up the stairs with alacrity.

Knocking on the door, he waited patiently for it to open. His patience was rewarded as Deedee answered it. Surprise marked her face turning to a blush.

"Good morning, Dr. Addison."

"Micah, please call me Micah," he responded.

"I don't know you well enough to call you by your Christian name."

"I've lived in Boston…for years I lived in Boston," Doc said, "and I know how formal relationships can be, living there. However, here in the

West, we don't call people by their last names. May I please call you Deedee and you call me Micah?"

Deedee blushed and said, "If it's what people do here, then I suppose it would be all right." Her green eyes sparkled with life.

Doc stood on the doorstep, mesmerized by her incredible eyes. He blinked and suddenly noticed her blush. He asked, "May I please come in?"

"Sorry, I guess my mind was wandering. Please do come in. Dr. Oliver is at the kitchen table. I suppose you've had breakfast?"

"Yes, I have, but a cup of coffee is always welcome."

"Please, come on in," she repeated. Looking at him from under her lashes, she felt an embarrassment for asking him into the house he'd lived in for years. "I'd imagine it feels strange to be asked into your own house."

"I have relinquished all claim on this house. Frankly, it's never been entirely mine. It came with the job. Right now I'm staying with the Bannisters at the ranch. However, I am contemplating buying a house. Would you like to help me?"

"Me?" Deedee nearly squeaked, taking a step back in surprise. "I don't know anything about buying a house. I wouldn't know where to begin."

"Neither do I, but I figure both of us could bumble along looking for one that suits."

"Suits?" Deedee asked.

Doc Addison simply smiled. "I need to talk to Oliver," he said.

She led him into the kitchen, where Oliver stood out of respect for his old professor.

"Hello, Dr. Addison."

"Good morning, Oliver. Please call me Micah or Doc. It's what I'm used to, and here in Santa Rosa, we're not so formal."

"Thank you for your permission. I'm glad you dropped by. Please, have a chair. Marie, can we have another coffee, please?"

Marie had already poured one for Doc and placed it before him.

"Deedee!" Oliver called. "Deedee where did you go?"

The two men could hear footsteps nearing the kitchen on the wooden floor.

"I'm right here," Deedee replied. "Do you need something?"

"I'd like you to join us for coffee. That way, I'll have another pair of ears to hear some answers from Dr. ah...from Micah. Pull up a chair"

Deedee poured herself a cup of coffee, smiled at Marie, and sat next to Micah.

"First question and it's an important one for me. How often do people shoot people around here? Is my daughter safe living here in Santa Rosa?"

"There are risks for anyone, of course. We haven't had a shooting here for about three years. It does happen, but not often, and usually there's a motive behind it. I feel safer here than I did living in Boston." Doc eyed Oliver hoping he wasn't having second thoughts about moving west.

"My second question is, are you sure I don't owe you anything for this dwelling? I certainly don't wish to take advantage of you. Marie said the house comes with the job. I just want to be clear."

"Yes, the house comes with the job. I never paid a penny for it, and you will not either."

"I have money from the sale of my house in Boston," Oliver said. "I can easily pay for this place."

"No, it's not mine to sell. As I said, it comes with the job."

"All right. Third question, what do you think the chances are of Gavin Galway's recovery?"

Doc took a deep sigh. "Unless the Lord intervenes, I don't give him any chance. His heart doesn't sound strong, his heartbeat is irregular, and who knows how much damage was done. Coupled with the fact that Gavin was shot and his heart has had to work to get more blood..." Doc shook his head. "I don't give him a chance of recovery."

"I concur with that assessment. It's sad, but I don't give him a future either. I feel sorry for his wife. She's been a great support to him. It'd sure be nice if we are wrong."

Doc nodded his head. "Yes, it would be, and for that to happen will be an out and out miracle."

Oliver nodded his head in agreement. "One last question. Have you seen Lenny Brown yet?"

"No, I haven't. I was going to ask your permission to pay him a visit."

"You don't have to ask my permission for anything you care to do or contribute. I'd be happy for you to continue on here as much as you care to."

"Thank you. I've been thinking of finding a house hereabouts or perhaps building one."

"Is that so?" Oliver replied. "My understanding was that you planned to live with the Bannisters."

"Well, frankly that *was* the plan, but now I find I have another interest taking priority."

He turned to Deedee who'd sat quietly throughout the conversation, looking covertly at him. He'd felt her perusal and hoped he'd passed inspection. A blush rose to her cheeks as he eyed her.

CHAPTER XVI

Cease from anger, and forsake wrath:
fret not thyself in any wise to do evil.

PSALM 37: 8

EWEN RODE UP TO JARED AND COLT, who were working to repair a fence that several cows had broken through. He surveyed the area not seeing any cows nearby.

"I'd like you boys to ride up to the house. Miss Caitlin and Miss Liberty have ridden into town. I'm selecting you two to muck out stables today as well as work to repair any damage to spare saddles or harness. You have my permission to start with your break in the kitchen—get some good dessert with coffee. I'm riding out with Sneedy to check on some of the far fencing. Sneedy said it looked as if it'd been cut."

"Thanks, boss," Jared said.

"I agree. Thanks." Colt hoped Mini would be downstairs. He wiped his brow on his sleeve and untied his horse while Ewen continued to talk to Jared.

"Those cows are branded, but the calves aren't. Reckon we'll just have to see. I hope the cows broke through, and it's not someone out to steal calves."

"Sneedy knows what cut wire looks like. Good luck, boss."Colt and Jared stepped into stirrups and rode back to the big house.

"I know I can mind my own business, but I saw the way you looked at Mini Louise the other day. You interested?"

"I don't mind, and yes, yes I am. I am very interested."

"She's a hard worker. Cait said she is making herself indispensable."

"I have a feeling she *is* a hard working girl and has some goals she wants to attain. At this time, men don't figure into her plans, but I hope to change that," Colt said.

"Well, I can wish you good luck. It'll take that and more to change Mini's mind once she's settled on something. I've known her since she was knee high to a grasshopper. Her mother died when the third girl, Lettie Lynn, was born. Lindsey May married Zeb Pindar when she'd just turned seventeen. She raised Zeb's three girls and was more like an older sister than a mother. She's had five or six children of her own besides the three Zeb had when he married her."

"Whew! That's quite a passel! I had one sister, and that was all. I always wondered what it'd be like to have lots of siblings." Colt shook his head in wonder of someone just twenty-five years old having so many children.

"Another amazing thing about Mini," Jared went on to explain, "is that she taught herself proper English. Her folk talk much the same as many of the hired hands, but Mini set her mind to speak properly. She's mastered it fairly well. She's making herself into a real lady."

The two hitched their horses and strolled up the walk. Jared knocked on the door and pushed it open before Duffy answered it.

"Anybody here?" he called out.

Duffy hurried to the door wiping her hands on an apron. "Why, hello there, Jared! Come on in." She glanced at the other man, who was quite handsome and who stuck out his hand to her.

"I'm Colton Danbury," he said. "I don't believe I met you the other day when I got hired by Ewen."

"No, I haven't met you. I do believe I wouldn't forget a face like yours," she laughed.

Colt looked a bit quizzical, as he didn't understand her reply.

Jared saw his confusion and, punching him on the arm, said, "Mrs. McDuffy thinks your face is easy to look at, cowboy!" He grinned as a bit of red climbed into Colt's cheeks.

"Thank you, ma'am."

Jared chuckled and said, "Ewen said we could come in for some coffee and dessert. Is that all right with you?"

"Certainly," she replied. "I have been helping Duney make some rolls for tonight's dinner. Come on into the kitchen."

Colt's heart sank a bit thinking that if Mrs. McDuffy was helping in the kitchen, Mini would most likely be upstairs attending to the baby.

They followed her across the dining room and into the warm kitchen. Colt was pleasantly surprised to see Mini at the huge round table feeding the baby on her lap.

She was startled when she saw him and to cover her discomposure, she shifted the baby to her other knee, all the while staring at the back of Jonathan's head. Blood crept into her cheeks, and she bit her lip to try to stop the blush but to no avail.

Duney heard their approach and greeted them. "Good afternoon, Jared...Colt. Reckon you boys would like a bit of the pie Mini made this morning."

"Yes, ma'am," Colt said as he looked down on Mini's bent head. "Good afternoon, Miss Mini. Your charge looks pretty happy. He's a real little man."

Mini looked up, her cheeks rosy. "Good afternoon, Colt." She glanced at Jared. "Good afternoon, Jared." Looking back at Colt, and staring straight into his dark gray eyes, she felt as if her muscles weakened. She held Jonathan a little tighter. "Yes, he's a happy baby and as sweet as they come."

"Looks as if you know your way around bairns. Bet you'd make a wonderful mother." Colt said, his attitude appreciative.

"I do know my way around babies for goodness sake," her tone caustic. "I've got seven younger siblings and having a baby of my own is the last thing I need...at least not for years to come anyway!"

Colt's eyes widened at her declaration.

Jared laughed and eased the atmosphere in the room. "I don't blame you, Mini. You must be enjoying the peace and quiet here at the ranch. Colt, here, had no idea you came from such a large family until I told him. He had just one sister who recently passed away, and it has been a sore trial for him to lose his only relative."

Mini's eyes flew to Colt's face. "I *am* sorry for your loss. I reckon, I mean—I would think that would be one of the most difficult things that has happened to you. And I really am sorry. I suppose I thought everyone around here knew I'm the eldest of a large family. One works from sunup till sundown tending to the needs of so many children plus all the other things one does to keep a household running. It's never quiet unless everyone is in bed, and sometimes even then it's not quiet. I am thankful to have this place of employment, and yes, Jared, I am enjoying the peaceful quiet of this house."

Colt's eyes gleamed with pleasure at her words. "Thank you, Miss Mini, for your kind words. It's going to take a long time to get over missing her. Jean was older and although she was my sister, she was like a mother to me too. I do miss her."

Mini's smile was genuine. She now felt sorry for this cowboy and somehow protective of his feelings. Her glance at him turned into a gaze as she realized he had feelings like everyone else, and he must be suffering.

Jonathan began to squirm, bringing Mini back to the present and the task at hand. "Sorry, little fellow. Here you go. Open wide."

Jonathan complied and gurgled, spitting ground peas on his front, on the table and on his face. Mini laughed and he gurgled some more as she wiped his face with a cloth.

Everyone in the kitchen laughed at his antics.

Jared pulled out a chair and motioned Colt to sit down. "We'd better eat, because we have some unpleasant work to do, and I'd like to get it over with."

Duney placed a large piece of pie in front each of them.

"Thank you! This looks delicious!" Colt said.

"I second that," Jared said. He took a bite and said, "Um—um...this is scrumptious!"

"And I second that!" Jared exclaimed. "You do know how to make pie, Miss Mini. Thank you!"

"You're welcome," she replied warmly.

Colt looked down at his plate. *I don't want to scare her off, but it's hard to keep what I'm feeling off my face. It's difficult to believe that I'm in love with this strong-minded young woman...hopelessly in love. I came out here to start a new life, and somehow I'm going to convince her to change her mind about me. How...I have no idea, but one thing for sure is that I'll be working here until I can accomplish that feat.*

Colt looked up and saw Mini's eyes on him, and he smiled his devastating smile. It was her turn to stare at her plate.

Doc left Oliver's kitchen whistling to himself as he descended the stairs. He was pleased with what he considered progress with Deedee. He knew he'd stirred her interest, and that she'd looked at him quite often as Oliver asked his questions.

His walked slowed as he approached the McGraths' house. He prayed, thinking about what a termagant Mrs. McGrath was. It was a wonder to him that the twins had turned out so well. He attributed much of that to their father who'd passed away in his office. He'd promised Abel McGrath as he lay dying that he'd watch over his girls. It was one of the reasons he'd hired the pair of them to work in his office.

He walked up the steps and knocked on the door.

It opened and he said, "Good morning, Martha, how are you on this fine spring day?"

"I've been better. Couldn't sleep a wink last night thinking about a strange man lying abed in my house. It's only because of my Christian goodness that I would allow it."

"I understand. I suppose you're remembering the verse about loving your neighbor as yourself."

"He's not my neighbor!" Martha McGrath snapped. Her voice sounded clipped and angry with temper.

Doc's head jerked up at her words, and he stared into her flushed face. "Ah…but he is, Martha. According to the Good Book, he *is* your neighbor."

"And I say to you, he's not my neighbor! I don't rightly know where he lives, but he certainly doesn't live in my neighborhood!"

"I beg to differ, ma'am. You are in error to think he's not your neighbor. Don't you know the story of the Prodigal Son? I suppose a better question is, do you read your Bible?"

"No, I don't have to. I know what it says, and I know my Christian duty. And I don't need you preaching to me, Micah Addison!"

"Well, Martha McGrath, perhaps you better start reading the Good Book. You evidently *don't* know what it says. Now, let me in to visit your patient *and* your neighbor."

"Stop your incessant talk, Micah. You've been yammering ever since you came west. Come on in. I don't know how my girls put up with you for so long. I'm hoping Dr. Oliver will be more amenable."

"Thank you," Doc smiled and added, "for your wonderful Christian hospitality and for caring for your neighbor."

Martha's eyes were slits as she stomped down the hall. She didn't bother to knock, shoving the door open with force. It crashed against the wall so hard it caused a painting to fall off its hook.

Paige scrambled to her feet.

"Mother!" she exclaimed, but in a soft voice. "You gave me a fright!"

Lenny, who'd been asleep was startled awake because of the commotion. He groaned in pain as he started to sit up in bewilderment.

"Well, now," Doc said. "I think that answers my question." He strode to the bed and helped Lenny to settle back down.

"And what question is that, Micah?" Martha asked, her tone loud and sarcastic.

"You are in need of learning to love, Martha. You put on a Christian face, but your heart is hard as a cobble and in need of the love of Christ. I feel sorry for you, ma'am. You have no compassion nor care for anyone except yourself. You don't read your Bible, and you don't have a clue what a personal relationship with the Almighty entails. You are hateful and full of untamed anger."

Martha McGrath's face took on a purple hue. "Get out! You get out of my house right this minute!" she screamed. "Get out!"

"Calm down, calm yourself, Martha, or you'll be having a heart attack. I'll get out when I get someone to transfer Lenny to a place where he will receive loving consideration. I'm sure he has that care from your girls, but as you said, this is your house. I've heard the way you talk to your daughters when you think no one is within hearing. There's no word for it except nasty. You charge them far more than they would pay for a room at the Lister sisters' house. Your entrance into a sickroom has shown me, without a doubt, ma'am, who your really are and where your concern lies. I'll have you know, Martha, that unless you repent, you'll live the rest of your life alone and bitter."

Martha started to rant, but Micah Addison ignored her. He turned to Paige and said, "I will remain here with Ezra while you give Dr. Oliver the message that Ezra needs to be transported to Jasper Clemmons' house immediately."

"Jasper Clemmons' house!" Martha McGrath shouted. "Why that cantankerous imbecile! He's a two-bit miner who doesn't know anything!"

"I had a good talk with Kirk Bannister this morning, who visited Jasper last evening. The man evidently knows a great deal more than you. He's invited Lenny to recover at his house if he wasn't getting the proper care and attention here. I won't leave this man in your care, Martha."

"Well, I never!" Martha exclaimed again.

"That's your trouble, ma'am. You never have," Doc said. "Scoot, Paige. I don't plan to be here all day. I'd like to check on Gavin Galway, and see how he's doing."

Paige, with a scared look at her mother, fled from the room and ran down the hall.

Martha gave a loud hissing sound of disgust and stomped down the hall after her daughter, who hurried out the front door not wanting to be confronted by her mother.

Doc sat down complacently next to the patient, smoothing the frown from Lenny's brow with his forefinger.

"It's all right, Lorenzo Brown. I believe, for your girl and her twin, things are going to get a lot better," he whispered.

"I hope so. Both those girls are scared to death of their mother," Lenny replied. "Would it really be cheaper for them to live elsewhere?"

"Yes, I think anyone letting a room would be cheaper than what the two of them pay their mother, and I know they'd be a lot happier. I'm supposed to watch over them, but I'm afraid being so busy, I lost sight of caring for them the way their father asked me to do." He sighed wondering where the time had gone. "I will look into finding a place for them. Meanwhile, we need you to recover. How are you feeling?"

"I'm doing much better than I was yesterday. What's that you said about Jasper? Did he really ask for me to recover at his place?"

"Yes, Have you ever been there?"

"No, I don't think I even know where he lives."

"According to Kirk Bannister, you will be tenderly cared for. Kirk and Ezra visited him late yesterday. Seems Jasper has quite a showplace. Kirk said Ezra thinks Jasper has been wounded in his soul, mind you. He was pleasant until Kirk brought God into the conversation. I think you recovering there, would be a good influence on Jasper, besides the fact that this house is not one of peace. You need to rest and not worry."

"Thanks, Doc, I leave it all in your hands. I also appreciate your desire to help the twins. Ezra has his eye on Payton and I have my heart set on Paige."

"I know," Doc replied. "I have eyes and ears, you know!" He grinned at the surprised look on Lenny's face.

Paige ran across the street and up to the office. As she entered, Payton looked up startled. "Is something wrong? Is your Lenny all right?"

"Yes, but Doc and Mother had a real set-to. Doc wants Lenny moved to Jasper Clemmons' house immediately."

Relief flooded Payton's being, and she slumped in the chair. "Oh, thank goodness! The way you came in here, I thought something had happened to Lenny. Dr. Oliver is in with a patient, but he should be out in just a few more minutes." Fear flashed in her face again. "Lenny's not alone with Mother, is he? I-I mean, oh Paige, you know how horrible she can be. Why she could put something in his soup to make him sick. Remember how she did that to us that time?"

"Yes, I remember. How could I not? But, Doc knows, and he's sitting with Lenny, so don't fash yourself. He also said you and I could live a lot cheaper if we moved to the Listers' house. What do you think about that? We're old enough to live on our own, and I'd like nothing better than to get out of that house and away from Mother."

"Oh! That would be wonderful. Let's ask Doc to help us. I'd move today if we could."

Oliver came out with a man whose arm was freshly splinted. "Remember, don't take that splint off. Come back in a few weeks and we'll see how you're getting on."

"Yes, sir, I will." He left the office, and Oliver turned to the twins.

"You're both here?"

"Yes," Paige answered. "Doc wants Lenny moved immediately. He's sitting by his bed until you come with someone to help move him."

"Hmm," Oliver said. "He mentioned that when he came by earlier, for coffee. Where do I get someone to help?"

"Just go over to the saloon and pick a couple men who don't look like they're into their cups. It's what Doc always does."

"All right. You can go back home, Paige, and I'll see to it right now."

"All right," she responded.

As Dr. Oliver left to find a couple stretcher bearers, Paige tapped Payton's hand.

"What's the matter, Paige?"

"I'm scared to go home. Mother's eyes were shooting daggers at me as if Doc's comments were coming our of my mouth. Doc really let her have it. I've never heard him speak thus to anyone. Mother's face turned purple and she screamed at him to get out."

Payton gasped. "What started it?"

"Mother slammed open the door and it woke Lenny and he tried to sit up. I don't think he even knew where he was for a second. It made

Doc mad that Mother was so inconsiderate. Oh, Payton! In a way I'm really glad Doc let loose. We can afford to live someplace else and see our beaus without having to sneak around."

Payton nodded her head in agreement. She leaned over and hugged Paige. "I hope we move today!"

"I do too!" Paige exclaimed. "Now, I need to run down and talk to the sheriff. Doc wants him to know we're moving Lenny out to the Clemmons' house. I'll see you later. Love you twin!"

CHAPTER XVII

It is better to dwell in the wilderness,
than with a contentious and an angry woman.

PROVERBS 21:19

DOC **ADDISON SAT AND WAITED UNTIL** Oliver showed up at the McGraths' house. Lenny was sleeping comfortably, so Doc slid into prayer for Martha and her twin girls. He lost track of time and was surprised when Martha tapped and quietly opened the bedroom door. He stood as she entered the room followed by Dr. Oliver and two men he recognized. Martha seemed placid enough until he looked into her eyes. They spit fire at him, so he ignored her. *At least she opened the door in a quiet manner, probably because Oliver is here. It always amazes me how a body can be so out of sorts all the time and stay healthy. I would think the woman would be ill. She's been so mean to those poor girls. It's a tribute to their father that they've turned out so well.*

"Hello Roy. Good to see you, Alfred. Thanks for helping out." Doc reached into his pocket and drew out a couple dollars, handing one to each man. He winked at Oliver and said, "You men need to be gentle. He's got a gunshot wound to the chest, and we wouldn't want it to start bleeding again."

"Thank you," Roy said, pocketing the money.

"We'll be sure to keep him level and try not to bump him on anything," Alfred added.

Doc gently rubbed Lenny's arm, and he awoke slowly. "Hello." His grin looked a bit wan and dark smudges showed beneath his eyes. His chest hurt like the dickens.

"We're going to take you to Jasper's house. I think you'll do better there in a peaceful environment." He looked meaningful at Martha, who glared back at him.

Oliver and Doc took hold of the linen underneath Lenny when Martha spoke harshly.

"You're not taking *my* bed linens with you. They're mine and I don't have the money to buy more. You just take that man and not any of my things!"

Both men dropped the linen underneath Lenny.

Doc looked disgustedly at Martha. "These came from my office, Martha. They are not yours. You are an uncharitable kvetch, Martha."

"I don't know what that means," she replied, but Doc didn't deign to answer.

"Oliver, you take Lenny's feet, and Alfred, you and Roy hold the stretcher close. Martha, you get out of the way! On the count of three we'll lift him. One—two—three!"

The two men lifted in unison and got Lenny onto the stretcher.

Lenny looked pale but gamely said, "Thank you, Mrs. McGrath, for your hospitality in letting me spend the night here." He closed his eyes as a wave of pain pierced his chest. "I have been most comfortable."

Martha smiled, albeit a bit grimly, as she replied, "You are welcome."

Roy and Alfred started out the bedroom door as Doc hurried in front of them down the hall and out to a waiting wagon. It was difficult to get Lenny in smoothly, but Doc had already laid some blankets down for padding. They left the stretcher under Lenny so they didn't have to move him after they arrived at Jasper's.

Doc and Oliver climbed onto their rides and followed the wagon down Main Street and out to Jasper Clemmons' house.

Oliver looked around with interest at the countryside. Flowers dotted the fields and he could hear birds chirping their songs. Bushes blossomed in indescribable colors and the scent was heady. The sun was warm on his head and shoulders, and he lifted his head to see a cobalt sky. A little breeze kissed his face and a calm and peaceful sensation filled his being.

I believe I'm going to love it here. It's going to be a good place for Marnie and me...for our hearts to heal. I think so many areas in Boston held memories that kept the loss of Corine ever before us, and so we couldn't get past the loss. I have hoped this move would help me, and I believe it's already begun a work. I haven't even been here a week, but the thought of Corine is not continually on my mind. Everything here is new to me and interesting. It's taking my mind off myself and off Corine. I'm beginning to feel like a new man and that the chance of future happiness is a real possibility. It's as if I'm like a butterfly coming out of a cocoon in which I've wrapped myself for over a two years. I know I've neglected Marnie and left most all her care in Deedee's hands. I need to buck up and think of her instead of myself.

They hit a rut, and a groan escaped Lenny's lips. It wasn't long before they turned into a long lane that was smooth with cobbles instead of dirt or gravel. Oliver again looked around with interest. The sides of the lane were groomed. Pruned trees, bursting with purple leaves were interspersed with trees of a willowy nature that were a soft, light green. The contrast was lovely. Closer to the house, the trees gave way to shrubs and clumps of flowers rioting with a variety of texture and color. The lane swooped around in a circular drive the inner circle a mass of ferns and grasses. A peacock strutted across the cobbles, the strut turning into a run for cover from the approaching horses. Alfred had slowed when they entered the lane, and he slowed even more as they approached the house.

He drew the wagon to a smooth stop, but before it was completed, Roy hopped down and was already opening the gate to the back of the wagon.

"I'll go and see if there's anyone to let us in," Doc said as he strode to the veranda.

My! This looks mighty nice, Doc thought as he knocked on the wooden part of the door. He could see into the foyer because part of the door was glass. He perused the veranda on either side of him. *Looks like a nice place to relax and have good conversation or read a book.*

The veranda looked tidy and welcoming. Greenery climbed up white columns situated on either side of the entry to the veranda. Flagstone flooring housed wicker and wooden chairs, low tables, a couple settees and a swing. Textured pillows splashed bright colors and created a feeling of homeyness.

He knocked again using the brass lion's head. He could see someone coming to the door, and he stepped back as the door opened.

"Hello, I'm Denny Watson. Can I help you?" He appeared surprised that someone would come to the house.

"Yes, I believe you can. Jasper invited an invalid to stay here and recuperate if the place he was staying wasn't working out. Needless to say, it wasn't working out. Is it all right if we bring him in?"

"Certainly. Would you like to see where he will stay, first?"

"If you think I should," Doc answered. "It doesn't have to be fancy. He just needs a bed and some peace and quiet as well as soups and liquids."

"Well then, get him, and I'll direct you to the room. May I ask the gentleman's name?"

Doc had started to turn away, but he spun back and said, "It' your boss' boss—Lorenzo Brown."

"Bring him in straightaway!" Denny ran to the kitchen while they were loading Lenny onto the stretcher. "Mona! We have a houseguest who's been wounded. It our boss' boss, Lorenzo Brown. He'll need soup and juices and water."

"Sure thing, Denny. I'll start on the soup right now."

Denny arrived back at the front door at the same time that the stretcher did.

"Follow me," he said to Roy and Alfred. He hurried down the hall before them. Oliver felt intrusive, but Doc beckoned him to go ahead and he followed Oliver down the hall.

"You're now Lenny's doctor, Oliver," Doc said in a low voice. "I know you're not used to making house calls, and it takes a bit of getting used to, but I know you're going to do a fine job." He patted Oliver on the back, and they followed the stretcher down the hall.

Oliver glanced into the library and caught his breath. It was so lovely. "'Tis a beautiful manse," he whispered to Doc.

"I know. I've gathered Jasper's wife was nearly as rich as Vanderbilt. Jasper Clemmons does not have to work. He does it because he enjoys it and it takes his mind off his loss."

"He's a widower, too?"

"Yes, it's been a little over a year now."

"Poor soul," Oliver murmured.

"Yes, that's true. It's embittered him." Doc's answer was in an undertone. He wouldn't want to upset Denny.

"Perhaps I could help him somehow."

"Perhaps, but I shouldn't get my hopes up. He is not only mourning, but he's wallowing in it."

"I've done that. I was just thinking on the way here that I feel as if I've been freed from a cocoon. I've neglected Marnie and left much mothering to Deedee, who was most likely deeply mourning herself. I feel ashamed."

"Don't. I still miss my Evangeline. But, truth to tell, your Deedee has caught my eye as well as my thoughts."

Oliver smiled. "I believe I noticed that. I thought something was going on the day we arrived!"

They followed Alfred and Roy into a luxurious room, and saw Denny pulling down the bedcovers to make room for Lenny.

"You might want to put a blanket under him in case he does any more bleeding," Doc advised.

"We have tons of linens, so don't worry yourself about that. My desire is that Mr. Brown be comfortable," Denny said.

"Okay, boys," Doc ordered, "you take his shoulders, Roy, and Al, you take his feet and shift him to the bed."

The men made the transfer as quickly and smoothly as they could.

"Thank you, Alfred. Thank you, Roy. You two have been a real help today, and I'm sure Mr. Brown appreciates it."

"I certainly do. Thank you for taking the time out of your day to help me." Lenny's voice sounded weak.

"You are welcome," Roy said.

"Yes, you *are* welcome, and if you need anymore transfers, just send someone for us. We'll be glad to help." He turned to Doc. "Thanks for thinking of us. Reckon we'll be on our way. Bye now."

They left with Denny leading them down the hall.

Oliver had seen Lenny's face grimace with pain when he was transferred to the bed.

"I hope we haven't been too brutal on you wound," He said. "I know those bumps on the road must have hurt. How are you feeling?"

"I must have lost a lot of blood to be so tired. It honestly doesn't pain me as much as I thought it would," Lenny replied. "It does hurt, but worsens when I'm moved. Reckon I've done a lot of sleeping so I don't feel the pain so much."

"Sleep is the best thing for you," Doc said promptly. "And I know you might prefer the McGraths' for personal reasons, but it will be better for you to be here. Less stress for you and no possibility of offending Martha McGrath."

"I have no doubt you're right, Doc. I hope you find another place for those twins to live. It's a real tragedy their own mother hasn't a bone in her body that cares for another person other than herself." Lenny relaxed and felt his muscles almost melt in the comfort of the bed. The one he'd been lying on at the McGraths' had been hard as an unpadded board.

Doc, again felt a rush of remorse go through him. "I have been negligent in caring for the twins. The reason those girls turned out so well is because of their father. He protected them from their mother as much as he could. I will talk to the Lister sisters before this day is out. Neither of them are married. I heard it was much the same scenario as the twins received from their mother, but the Listers' father was cowed by his wife and didn't stick up for them the way Abel McGrath stuck up for his girls. The Listers are sweet, dear elderly women, who have their quirks, but don't we all. They will adore having the twins stay with them, and they will be glad to help…especially because of the memories they have of their own mother."

While they spoke, Oliver had been checking the bandage on Lenny's chest. Satisfied there was no new bleeding, he stood listening as he observed the room.

A pale mint green colored the walls, and the cornice, trim boards and mantel were of dark mahogany. It looked tasteful and refined. Built-in book shelves, filled with books and bibelots, stretched from floor to ceiling. A large mahogany desk and chair stood in one corner under a large window. In another corner stood a marble pedestal of the same color of green as the walls mixed with white and streaks of a rusty color. Atop the pedestal was a copy of the statue of Michelangelo's David. A couple paintings of famous scenes by world renown painters graced the walls, and French doors opened to a private veranda.

Oliver was amazed at the tastefulness of the room. He wondered if a designer had been brought in, or perhaps Jasper's wife decorated the interior of the house. It never dawned on him that Jasper, himself, had seen to the smallest detail of each room, and all the accouterments in the house had been selected by him.

Denny busied himself, dusting imaginary motes off the mantel and bookshelf as he listened unabashedly to the discussion between Doc and Lenny.

When the conversation finally lagged he spoke to Lenny. "Can I get you some soup, Mr. Brown?"

"I'd think I'd like that, and a cup of coffee, if it's not too much trouble."

"No trouble at all, sir. Your wish is my command."

"Lenny chuckled, "1001 Nights" or "Arabian Nights," correct?"

Denny laughed, "Correct. I have made use of Mr. Clemmons' library. It is a dream come true for a reader such as myself."

"I think I'll like recuperating here," Lenny vouchsafed. "I love to read, but haven't had much time."

"Then you'll enjoy your time here and have many an interesting conversation with my boss. He loves to critique books and discuss them. Now, I'll go get that soup and coffee." He left on silent feet, as the floor was covered with a deep Aubusson carpet.

"Lenny," Doc spoke softly, "be careful talking about God to Jasper. Kirk said he went cold as ice and kicked them out of the house when he spoke about God last evening."

"I'll be careful," Lenny replied. "I wonder why that should set him off if he's as literate as Denny says."

"I am quite sure it happened about the time his wife died. She wasn't healed, and he blamed God."

"Ahh, that makes sense."

Oliver, who'd been listening, spoke. "It's easy to do, unless you have a close relationship with the Lord. One must understand that His ways are higher than our ways, and His thoughts are higher than our thoughts. The truth of the matter is He does nothing that does not have a purpose for good. Yes, it would be easy to turn one's back on God when Satan is whispering in your ear that God doesn't exist—that He doesn't help in times of trouble. He's the great deceiver who loves to get us off track. He wants us to concentrate on our problems instead of concentrating on the One who knows best. By the way, I am speaking from experience."

"Thank you for sharing that," Lenny said. "Perhaps it will help me to understand Jasper. We haven't had the best relationship, and maybe it's because I'm a Christian and do what I know to be pleasing to God. I'll be sure to try to help Jasper all I can." His face reddened as he realized Denny had heard his words.

"I'm delighted to hear you say that," Denny said, as he slid a tray of food onto the desk. He put his hands on his hips and spoke to Lenny as if he were a friend. "Mr. Clemmons is in need of friendship and patience. He is a man of great passion, and his passion was his wife. When she died...well...I'm sorry to say, it changed him. Because of your words, Mr. Brown, I will hope and pray for you to be able to warm Mr. Clemmons' heart in a way that hasn't been seen in quite some time."

"I think only the Lord can do that." Lenny's eyes swept over the men standing in the room. "I am going to challenge each of you to pray for the salvation of Jasper Clemmons. With all of us praying, he won't have a chance to ignore the knocking of the Lord on his heart."

Doc and Oliver helped Lenny to sit up as Denny plumped more pillows behind him. He placed a bed tray over Lenny's legs and set the tray with the soup and coffee on it, adding a piece of carrot cake.

"How is that?" he asked.

"Fine, thank you. This smells delicious." He bowed his head and said a quick prayer. Picking up the spoon, he took a sip of soup and smacked his lips. "This is delicious! Please tell your cook I'm enjoying the soup."

"Her name is Mona," Denny said. "She *is* a very good cook. The last one the Clemmons' had didn't last long. He burned nearly everything. They were happy to find Mona. Everything that comes out of that kitchen is delicious."

Lenny polished off the soup in no time and was soon eating the cake.

"Would you like some cake?" Denny asked Doc and Oliver.

"I would, but I'll pass," Doc replied. "I need to get back to town and see Gavin Galway and have a talk with the Lister sisters."

"I'll pass, too, sorry to say," Oliver said. "I will go with Doc to check on Mr. Galway." He hesitated before adding, "You are sure your boss will be fine having Mr. Brown here?"

"Sure, I'm sure. Mr. Clemmons has a heart of gold once you get to know him. He'll be delighted to have a captive audience." Denny smiled at his words.

CHAPTER XVIII

The Lord gave, and the Lord hath taken away;
blessed be the name of the Lord.

JOB 1:23

SHERIFF EZRA WALKER TOOK A RIDE out to the gem mine. He whistled as he rode and broke into a song he made up as he loped along. "Tis a wondrously fair day! Oh you and I can say…Tis a wondrous day I see, a joy for you and me!" he continued to hum his tune as he cantered onward, enjoying the balmy day.

The sun warmed the air, as a heady fragrance from flowers in bloom seemed to waft his way. He sniffed and could smell several kinds of flowers, but the lilacs made the biggest impact, spewing their heady scent. He could see wildflowers dotting the fields on either side of the road, and the colors were an incredible sight.

"Ahh, it truly *is* a wondrous day. Thank You, Father God, for allowing me to bask in such beauty…splendor You have created for me to enjoy. What a glorious love You must have for us. I give You praise and thanksgiving. I pray You would guide my steps and help me find out who shot Mr. Galway and Lenny Brown. I can do nothing on my own, but You are able to do abundantly more than I can ask or think. Thank You in advance for the miracle You will do in solving this case. You know I have no idea who did these crimes, but You do. I ask for You to give me wisdom in figuring it out from the clues You give me. Amen!"

He arrived at the mine full of determination, knowing God would supply all he needed. He tied up at the hitching post and strode to the office, knocking on the door.

"Enter!" Jasper said, his head down figuring out some expenditures on a sheet of paper. He looked up and, surprised by Ezra's presence, stood up immediately, nearly knocking over his chair in his haste.

"Sorry, I didn't expect anyone except a miner, or I would have answered the door. Before you ask me anything, I need to apologize for my behavior last night. I'm not on best terms with the Almighty, and for Bannister to go off like that, well…I simply couldn't stomach it."

"Apology accepted, except, I really did want a taste of that Laphroaig!" He grinned at Jasper, who grinned right back.

"Please come over this evening, and we'll have a glass, share ideas, and have an enjoyable evening."

"I'd be happy to do that, but before I say yes, I need to let you know you already have a house guest."

Jasper's shocked face caused another grin to spread over Ezra's face.

"I can't keep you in suspense. You invited him last night."

It didn't take Jasper a second to grasp what Ezra meant. "Lenny is at my house? So, Mrs. Martha McGrath's house wasn't the best place for him after all. I told you so! Abel McGrath was the only one who could keep Martha in line. She is not a nice person…not at all. All the town folk know how she's treated those beautiful twins of hers. She's cruel." Jasper shook his head ruefully. "I imagine a lot of people think the same of me. I've been trying to insulate myself against people, but it isn't working. Since my wife died, I haven't wanted to be around people. Too many memories and too many questions for which I have no answers." He sighed deeply and continued to talk. "Lenny is welcome at my place, and I will enjoy the company while he recuperates. Denny will treasure having someone to dote on and fuss over. And, my invitation to you still stands. Perhaps you could come a bit earlier to dinner?"

"I'd enjoy that, thank you!"

New to Santa Rosa, Ezra's eyes gleamed realizing not only would Lenny be a friend, but Jasper Clemmons would also rank high on his list of acquaintances.

"Dinner is at six thirty sharp. If you come a bit earlier, you will be welcome to have an aperitif."

"I'll come early. I'd like to see Lenny before anything else."

"Of course. Perhaps we can have our repast in his room."

"I'd like that." Ezra said. "If we could, Lenny won't feel left out."

"Right. Now, how can I help you?"

"I suppose you have deduced that someone here has to be our shooter." Ezra scratched his nose, something he was wont to do when thinking deeply.

"Yes," Jasper replied. "I think Lenny thought it was me for a while."

"Really?"

"Yes. Jonah Whatcom put money on my desk that he'd found in his tool case. Someone planted it there to throw suspicion on Jonah, but it certainly wasn't me."

"May I ask, how much do you trust Ernest Smith or Sandoval Peabody?" Ezra watched Jasper's face closely.

Jasper's face was a study of conflicting emotions. "I—I don't rightly know now you ask. Both seem to be hard workers. Why would you ask about them?"

"Are they privy to what happens around here?"

"Y-yes, both men are. That's because I keep them informed. They both oversee the men as they are working in the mine. They both know when we are ready to take a shipment of gems to Santa Rosa."

"I'm curious, has either of them complained about any of the men? By that, I mean complaints that would put a worker in a bad light or cast aspersions on their character?"

A look of comprehension filled Jasper's face. "Yes, Sandy...Sandoval Peabody has complained about Jonah several times in the last couple weeks. I thought perhaps, he didn't like Jonah. Do you think that he's been setting Jonah up to take the fall?"

"Frankly speaking, yes—yes I do." Ezra sighed. "Wonder how we can prove it. Is Peabody very tall?"

"No, not really. He's short, but then so is Ernest Smith."

"Smith has made no complaints about anyone?"

Jasper stood staring at the floor, thinking for a full minute.

"No, he hasn't. Not that I can remember. I think I'd remember a complaint. Just a moment."

Jasper went to his desk and pulled open a drawer, drawing out a ledger. He sat down as he thumbed through the pages.

"Here it is," he said. "Come look at this, Ezra."

The entry said Jonah stole some equipment from a storage closet.

Jasper had a fine hand, his writing clear. It related exactly what and when Peabody had made a complaint. Jasper flipped the page and pointed to another entry.

"There it is." He stared at Ezra. The complaint was that Jonah Whatcom was slowing production down by complaining about every order he was given.

"I wrote it down, but I knew when I did it wasn't true. I write down every complaint a man brings to this office. Jonah Whatcom is an honorable man. He irritates me beyond belief sometimes. I told the men not to bother Lenny about anything that I can take care of. It got misinterpreted, and Jonah told Lenny I didn't want any of the men to go to him for anything. It's not what I said, but that's how it looked to Lenny."

"Well, now we have a problem. We need to find some kind of evidence that Peabody is our shooter. What would he have to gain if Lenny was out of the way?"

"I suppose I would become head boss, and Peabody would take my place. So, it would be some prestige as well as a hefty pay raise. Once that was established, I wouldn't give a Liberty dollar that I'd be alive for very long. If he was willing to kill Mr. Galway for money and Lenny to advance himself, he'd stop at nothing until he ran this place."

"My thoughts exactly. And yet, it *is* a supposition. We don't know for sure he's our culprit."

"I'd bet my prize horse it's him!" Jasper exclaimed.

Ezra nodded his agreement, his eyes gleamed. "I'm going to get a few heads together and figure out how we can catch our man."

"You do that. I'd be happy to be part of the discussion." Jasper said.

"You will be. Have no doubt about that." The two men continued to talk, forging a friendship that would last throughout the years.

Liberty rode with Caitlin into Santa Rosa. The two of them enjoyed a good hard ride, so they galloped together both hunkering down over the necks of their horses. As they approached Santa Rosa, they slowed and came to a sedate walk to cool off their horses.

They headed straight for Gavin and Maisie's house and tied up at the long hitching rail.

"That looks like Doc's horse, doesn't it?"

Liberty nodded but was mesmerized by the Galway's two story clapboard house. "Tis lovely," Liberty said.

"It is, and Maisie has done all the decorating, inside and out. I didn't think I'd like a house painted yellow, but the green roof and shutters make it unique and…and I guess I'd say handsome." Caitlin grinned.

"Matthew decorated our house before we met, but I see nothing in it that I don't like or enjoy. I've added some shrubs and flowers and such, but the interior of our house is much the same as when I met him."

"He must be a good decorator."

"Yes, and I'm sure Conchita had some input." She flexed her hands. "I think I really gripped the reins, my hands feel stiff."

"I do that too, sometimes," Caitlin replied. "Well, come on in." Caitlin pushed open the front door and they entered right into the living room.

"This is really different. I like how open and roomy it is!"

"Maisie had most of the walls taken out. She kept the parlor for guests, but this is open. See how the fireplace opens on this side and on the dining room side? Isn't it beautiful?"

"It is!"

The fireplace bricks climbed up to the ceiling. There was storage on the right side for logs. The mantel, trim boards and cornices were painted a stark white. Drapes, at the large windows, were white and all the walls were painted white. French doors opened to an enclosed porch, the flooring all flagstone. All color came from paintings, pillows and carpets. It was lovely and so different that Liberty wished Matthew could see it.

"Halloo! Is anyone here? It's Liberty and me." Caitlin called out to an empty room.

"Welcome! We're in here," Maisie called out. "We've made Gavin's office into a bedroom, since ours is on the second floor."

Doc was sitting complacently beside Gavin, and Maisie sat in a cushioned easy chair.

"Hello, Doc. What are you doing in town and visiting a patient? I thought you had a new doctor taking over the reins," Caitlin stated.

"I do. I'm simply visiting an old friend, as a friend and not a doctor."

"And he's welcome, anytime," Gavin added.

"How are you, Gavin?" Liberty asked. "You were asleep the last time I saw you."

"Truth to tell, I'm not feeling the best. I'm having some real pain in my chest, and it feels as if I've been running. I gasp for breath, and I am weak as a newborn kitten."

"You're going to get better, darling. It just takes time," Maisie said.

Doc looked up to see Liberty's eyes resting on his sad ones.

Liberty nodded her head as if he'd spoken his sorrow to her.

Maisie continued to chatter as if by talking she could reassure herself that Gavin would get well. "Aidan stayed here the first night and gave me a real break. I slept for eleven hours that night. Can you believe it?"

"I can well believe it," Liberty said. "Matthew's first wife ran off with… ah…that's not my story, but she came back to the Rancho, dying of diabetes. I nursed her day and night for nearly a week. When she died, I took a bath and fell into bed. I slept the rest of the day, all that night, and part of the next!" She smiled at Maisie "So, I do understand a bit how tired you were, but I can't imagine being pregnant and staying up all night!"

"Well, when we were first married, Gavin and I would stay up all night just to talk."

Gavin laughed. "That's true. We had so much energy." He laughed again, grabbed his chest, and his eyes widened in consternation. "Doc!" he gasped. "Ohh, the pain! I can't…"

Doc tried to sit Gavin up. Gavin's face paled, his lips turned blue, he exhaled and stopped breathing.

Doc began to pray. "Lord I pray Thou wouldst heal Gavin. Right now, put the breath of life back into him. We pray in the name that is above all names! In the name of Jesus we pray, but not my will but Thine be done!"

Gavin remained still with eyes closed.

"N-no!" Maisie cried. "Why he was getting better! Oh Gavin!" She kissed his lips and threw herself onto his chest, sobbing her heart out.

Doc let her cry for a bit before saying anything. "No, Maisie, he wasn't getting better." Doc spoke to the distraught woman in a soft voice. He let her sob a bit more and then pulled her from Gavin. Turning her into his arms, he patted her back. "I don't know what to say to you other than both Dr. Oliver and I gave him no chance unless he was miraculously healed. Too much damage from the heart attack with the added stress of the gunshot wound. We didn't tell you because we didn't want to add to your worries, sweetie. You've been through a lot this past week." He continued to pat her back as she cried.

Liberty took hold of Maisie's arm and turned her to hold her close. She crooned and rubbed Maisie's back, knowing she must be in shock.

Caitlin whispered, "I'll get her bed ready."

Doc nodded and added, "I'm going to the office to notify Dr. Oliver." He left quickly, knowing he needed to make arrangements to have Gavin cleaned up and spread the word that there would be a wake tonight. He hurried to his old office and spoke to Oliver.

"Oh, my! That was quick. We knew it was coming, but what a shock for his poor wife. I'll head over there and see what I can do to get Mrs. Galway settled in bed."

"Is there anything I can do to help?" Payton asked.

"You can go with me to see the Listers," Doc responded. "I want them to take a good look at you, so they will be amenable to your renting from them. After that, I want you to move into that house today. You can pay your mother what you owe her for the rest of this month, and if you need money for a security at the Listers, I can help you out with that." Doc stood, holding onto his suspenders as he thought of what else needed done. He spoke to Oliver.

"I neglected to tell you that we don't have a mortician here in Santa Rosa. It was part of my duties to prepare the body for the wake and burial. I'll make the arrangements this time. I have four women who do the preparing for me. The Lister sisters work together, and then Daisy and Florence Danbee if the Lister sisters can't do it. I need to talk to the Listers anyway, so I'll take care of the arrangements. I think you'd better go help Maisie. You'll probably have to give her some laudanum to settle her down."

For some reason, Oliver felt hesitant to go, but he responded in the affirmative to Doc.

"Certainly, I'll go over immediately." He left the office and hurried to the Galway house. His step was fast, and it kept pace with his thoughts. His mind raced as he thought about his reaction.

What is the matter with me? I am confused about my feelings. Mrs. Galway is in need of my help, yet I don't wish to be near her. Why?

He plumbed the depths of his feelings. *Why do I feel this way?*

As he strode along, he realized, for the first time, that he was attracted to her…extremely attracted to her. *It isn't her looks, although she is beautiful with her ebony hair and hazel eyes. No, it's something much deeper. Although she isn't a Christian, there is a sweetness about her. It's not helplessness. It's sophistication mixed with a naivety or innocence. I don't know. I just know when I've been around her, I can't stop looking at her. I need to be on my guard. Guard my heart, Heavenly Father, guard my actions, and help me as I minister to Mrs. Galway's needs.*

He arrived at the house and strode up the walk, still praying for help. He tapped on the door, and it opened almost immediately.

"Hello, Mrs. Bannister. I've come to see if I can help Mrs. Galway in some way."

Liberty, with no usual smile on her face, welcomed him. "Come on in, Dr. Oliver. Caitlin is upstairs helping her dress for bed. I hope you can do something for her." Liberty closed the door behind the doctor and said, "Please come this way." She led him up the stairs and down a long hall.

The door stood open, and they could see that Caitlin had gotten her sister into bed.

"I didn't love him enough!" Maisie spoke brokenly to Caitlin. "I loved him, but it was never romantic like you and Kirk! Oh, Cait! Perhaps if I'd loved him more, he wouldn't have died! It's my fault someone got into the store and shot him. I forgot to lock the door."

"Hush, Maisie! You're not thinking clearly. He didn't die of the gunshot wound. He died of a heart attack. He was on the verge of one for days according to Doc. It's not your fault, sweetie. It was simply his time to go. Now, get into that bed and get some rest."

"I'm not an invalid, you know! I'm simply pregnant."

"I do know...believe me, I do. I also know that you've been under a ton of stress, Maisie, and you and that baby need a rest."

"What *am* I going to do about the mine? What shall I do about the store? Gavin took care of nearly everything!"

"Don't fash yourself, Maisie. I am quite sure things will work out. They have a way of doing that. You could get Lenny or Jasper to take care of the store. You are going to be busy taking care of you baby. Now, please get some rest."

She pulled the covers up over Maisie's shoulders as Liberty made their presence known.

"Here's Dr. Oliver come to help you," Liberty said, her voice full of compassion and sorrow for this young woman.

Maisie's eyes flew to the doorway and filled with tears.

Oliver strode over to the bed, and his heart smote him that he'd been unwilling to help this woman in her sorrow.

"I am sorry, Mrs. Galway. So sorry. I know how hard it is to lose a spouse, and my heart aches for you. You do need, however, to take care of yourself and the baby."

Overcome with compassion and forgetting his resolve, he sat on the side of the bed and was going to take her hand, but Maisie sat up, throwing her arms around his neck, she sobbed onto his shoulder.

It took Oliver as well as Liberty and Caitlin by surprise.

He patted her back and was shocked at his feelings for this woman. He drew her a bit closer as if by his nearness he could bring comfort to her.

Maisie clung to him as if he were her lifeline. Guilt mixed with joy at the man's closeness permeated her being. Guilt, because her husband lay dead downstairs. Joy, because this man seemed to bring a feeling within her she'd never before experienced. An incredible feeling of rightness and some other feeling that ran like hot liquid through her veins making her heart beat like a jungle drum. She wondered if he could hear it.

She pulled back and looked him in the eyes. There was warmth and sorrow in his, but Oliver was shocked at the passion he could see in hers. *She must feel it too…it isn't only me!*

CHAPTER XIX

Weeping may endure for a night,
but joy cometh in the morning.

PSALM 30: 5

"**WHAT JUST HAPPENED?**" **CAITLIN** leaned close to Liberty's ear, speaking in a soft whisper. She turned her head slightly to see Liberty's reaction.

With raised eyebrows, Liberty's moss green eyes widened. She leaned in close and whispered back, "I believe we have just witnessed the beginning of a romance." She grinned at Caitlin's astonished face. "Dr. Oliver's a Christian, so this should be interesting. It's amazing how God provides for us before we even ask. Maisie will need someone to help get her through this, and I think Dr. Oliver is it. Let's leave and give them some privacy."

Caitlin pivoted and Liberty followed her out and down the hall.

Once they were out of hearing, Caitlin became voluble. "I can scarcely credit it!" Caitlin exclaimed. "I mean, Gavin is not even cold. I don't mean that it can't happen like this, mind you. It's surprising though, isn't it?"

"Yes, it is, but I don't think there is anything that brings out a man's chivalry or gallantry as much as a beautiful and helpless woman."

"Maisie told me, more than once, she was never romantically in love with Gavin," Caitlin said. "He was more like a very best friend to her than a husband. They grew up together. But this! My goodness...just wait until Aidan hears about this. Oh my!"

Doc Addison could walk fast, and Payton had a hard time keeping up. "I'm concerned about Maisie Galway. She's been burning the candle at both ends and now that Gavin's gone...I don't know how she's going to be able to bear it. We can only pray that she and her baby will be all right. She's in the Lord's hands whether she realizes it or not."

"I can't imagine losing someone when you're not a believer," Payton replied. "When someone dies who's a believer, I feel bad that I won't see them again here on this earth, but I can rejoice that one day I'll see them in heaven. There's much comfort in that knowledge."

"I agree. You have a good head on your shoulders, young lady. I must tell you that I'm very sorry for not keeping a better eye on you and Paige. I humbly apologize. I know I saw one of you every day, but your papa asked me to help you and Payton because of the way your mama treated you. I have been negligent, and I hope this works out. I would like to feel I've done your papa a good service. He was a wonderful man and put up with an awful lot. I think someday research will find that stress can cause many ills. I have believed for a long time that it killed your papa. He had much to bear."

"Apology accepted," Payton said, "although I don't think you have to make it. We've done all right even though Mama is not easy to be around. I always wondered if we'd have been boys, would she have been different, but then I think not. She doesn't like boys or men, or people for that matter."

Doc sighed but continued his line of thought.

"You know your mama is going to be mightily upset about the two of you leaving. She won't have the income you've given her, and she won't have you around to boss. She, most likely, is going to try to woo you to stay put, but who knows what she will do. When you pack up, I want someone there with you. You two *need* someone there. I'll try to stay here in town until you're moved, hopefully later today."

Doc opened the gate to the Listers' yard, and said, "Here we are."

Payton saw a lace curtain tweaked, a glimpse of a face, and the curtain closed immediately. She smiled to herself, wondering what the two ladies would be like. She'd only met them because Doc used the two of them to help him out when someone died. She'd handed them money from Doc to pay for their services, but neither she nor her sister Paige knew them well.

The porch had three steps up and then a wide covered wooden porch with a swing and a few wicker chairs. Knitted and crocheted pillow covers in various designs made a show of color.

Doc knocked on the door. It opened almost immediately.

"Good afternoon, Dr. Addison, please come in."

Payton followed him into the living room, and April Lister stared wondering what the girl was doing there.

Payton felt uncomfortable under such close scrutiny, but she stood her ground.

"Hello, Miss April. How are you doing today?" Doc asked in a soft, pleasant voice.

"I'm fair to middling. May is in the kitchen. Who are you?" She asked Payton, but without waiting for an answer, she continued to talk. "Come on in and have a piece of pie, Dr. Addison. You can come, too, my girl." She spoke in a pleasant voice.

They entered the kitchen and Payton gasped. "Doc! You didn't tell me Miss April and Miss May were twins!"

Doc grinned. "Miss April, Miss May, this is Miss Payton McGrath. She and her sister Miss Paige are looking for a place to live. These girls are twins, and have been brought up very much like the two of you. They have worked for me, for some time now, as secretaries. They trade off days. I know you don't gossip, so I'll tell you straight up, these girls need to move out of their house. Their mother is much like yours was."

May shook water off her hands and wiped them on her apron. She strode across the kitchen floor and grabbed Payton by the shoulders. She peered into her eyes and nodded her head.

"You're a good girl, and you can move in today if you wish. We've plenty of room. You and your sister will have separate bedrooms but you will share a bathroom. We usually charge three dollars and seventy-five cents a person per month, but we'll charge the two of you a total of five dollars."

Payton gasped and started crying. "Paige and I have been paying our mother eight dollars a month and then another fifty cents for use of the kitchen."

May, who was still standing close, drew the girl into her arms and patted her back.

"Why, that's scandalous! It's highway robbery!" exclaimed April. "I do hope you girls realize your worth. It took May and me years before we realized that by our cowering attitudes and self-deprecation, we were still allowing our mother's hateful attitudes to control us. We finally came to the knowledge of God's love for us, and broke the chains that our mother forged."

Payton nodded, knowing what the woman was saying. "I have no doubt that would have happened to us, but our Father protected us as much as he was able. He passed away a couple years ago. I would like to tell you something that our mother doesn't even know. We'd be scared to death to tell her, but I'd like to be able to share with you. Both Paige and I have beaus. Paige's beau is the foreman at the gem mine, Lorenzo Brown. My beau is the new sheriff, Ezra Walker," she grinned at them.

"I have a feeling you will be like mothers for Paige and me. Oh, I can't thank you enough for opening your home to us! We will adore living here, and we'll help you out all we can, too."

Doc broke into the conversation. "I need to talk to you Miss May— Miss April. Then I'll leave, as I have much to do this day. Gavin Galway passed away just a bit ago. He had another heart attack. I was wondering if the two of you would—"

"Oh my! Why we thought he was on the mend! Of course we'll take care of him right now and get him ready for a wake." May said. "Payton, you can move in right now while we're away if you like. Let me show you to your room...please follow me."

"Remember, Payton," Doc warned, "to get someone to go with you when you move your things out. I don't want your mother to be alone with you girls."

"That bad, eh?" April questioned. She turned to Payton. "If you can wait about an hour and a half, May and I would be happy to accompany you to your house."

"That's it then," Doc interrupted. "I'll be on my way. Please spread the word about the wake. Bye now!" He hurried out of the kitchen before the Listers thought to see him to the door.

"My, but he was in a hurry. Come on, girl, follow me and see your room," May beckoned.

She led the way to the front door where a stairway climbed up the ten foot wall. When they topped the stairs, there was a large square room with shelves lining two of the walls with books. Comfortable chairs, blankets, pillows, low tables and several chaise lounge chairs made the room cosy. There were a couple baskets with knitting and crochet threads. A loom stood in the corner, and one end of the room housed a large fireplace.

"This is so inviting," Payton said. "It makes me want to curl up with a good book, or sit and knit."

"Yes, this is our favorite room besides the kitchen," May vouchsafed. She walked the length of the room in long strides. She was tall, her face angular and strong. Payton wondered that she and her sister had not stood up to their mother. *Why in the world would that thought cross my mind when Paige and I haven't stood up to our mother? Well, things are going to be different by the end of this day!*

"Here is one bedroom," May said as she entered the bedroom, the door was standing open to the larger room they'd just traversed.

"Oh! exclaimed Payton, "this is lovely."

The room was rectangular with a bay window on part of the far wall, and French doors leading out to a balcony on the same wall. A wide four poster bed covered with a beautiful quilt looked imposing. Gathered eyelet skirting stretched from the mattress to the oak floor. Oval throw rugs, braided in bright colors matching the quilt, lay on both sides of the bed. The walls were covered with a plain wall paper, but on closer inspection, Payton realized there was a pattern on it. Over the bed was a picture, framing a piece of the quilt that was on the bed. A fireplace was housed on the opposite wall from the bed. A large painting of a field of poppies hung over the mantle, many of the colors matching the quilt. Two plush chairs the same color as the darker poppies looked quite comfortable and made a splash of color against the pale walls.

"You may have your pick of the rooms," May said. "Come along and see the other one." She led Payton out the door and on to the next room.

"Here's the other bedroom for rent," she said.

"Oh my!" Payton didn't know which one she liked best.

The second room was done in yellows and a pale sage green. The room was nearly identical in size and looking out the French doors, Payton realized the balcony was shared by both rooms. This room had pale yellow wallpaper with a tracery of ivy just below the cornice. The quilt on the four poster bed was a patchwork of yellows with a gorgeous ivy leaf weaving along the edges above a green eyelet skirting. Over the mantle hung a huge mirror with a filigree of the green ivy painted around the frame. The plush chairs in this room were yellow with green throw pillows.

"Both rooms are beautiful," whispered Payton, awed by the fact that the rooms were twice the size of her own and done up beautifully. "I'll let Paige pick which one she wants, and then I'll take the other one. It doesn't matter to me."

May nodded her head in understanding. It was exactly what she would have said, allowing April to have her choice first.

"Let me show you the commode room. We just had the new flush toilets put into the house. It is so nice and convenient."

When the tour of the house was completed, May and April told Payton to go back to work and when she was finished for the day and went home, to tell Paige of the move.

"Please don't say anything to your mother until we come to your house. When we are finished at the Galway house we will come and help you move. If you can, without arousing any suspicion, begin packing before we get there."

Payton nodded her agreement. "I cannot begin to thank you both for opening your home to Paige and me. I know we will love living here and enjoy your company."

May acknowledged the compliment. "Thank you, but now April and I must hurry to get Mr. Galway ready. What a sorrow for poor little Maisie!" She clucked her tongue. "So young to be a widow."

Caitlin rode back to McCaully-Bannisters at a gallop not slowing down until she was close to the front of the house. She dismounted and slapped her reins around the hitching post. Giving Fire a pat, she ran up the steps to the wide porch and burst through the door.

Kirk and Ewen were having a late afternoon break, drinking coffee and chewing on some cookies Duney had taken from the oven not twenty minutes before.

Kirk and Matthew along with Ewen stood as Caitlin ran into the room, completely out of breath.

"Gavin's dead," she gasped. "Liberty stayed with Maisie, and I'm going right back, but Kirk, I need you to spread the word that there's a wake tonight." Caitlin stopped to take a deep breath. She looked over at her cook who'd put her hand over her heart.

"Oh the poor bairn! Poor little Maisie!"

"I don't want to make more of this than I should, but I believe Maisie is going to find a good support in the new doctor." She looked at the shocked faces and grinned. "All right, I need to go up and check on Mini Lou and Jonathan, and then I'm going back to help Maisie. She was sobbing her heart out when I left." She looked over at her cook. "Duney, do you think you, Duffy, and Mini, could help rustle up some food for the wake, please?"

"Of course," Duney replied.

Cait turned to leave, but Kirk strode over and grabbed her by the shoulders, planting a kiss on her lips. "You are wonderful, Katie. Matt and I will ride around and notify people we know who are friends and acquaintances of Gavin and Maisie."

"Thank you." Caitlin's face was flushed, but her eyes sparkled love to Kirk. She crossed the room at a fast pace and ran up the stairs.

Mini Lou was exiting the nursery and spoke in a whisper. "Jonathan just fell asleep. I was going down to see if Duney needs any help."

"Mini, Gavin just passed away less than an hour ago. I—"

"Oh, I'm so sorry! I thought he was getting better."

"So did Maisie. There will be a wake tonight, so I wanted to let you know. I've asked Sweeny to keep an eye on Jonathan. I know you'd like to be at the wake. Sweeny can put Jonathan down for the night. Right now, I am hoping you can help Duney make some food to take to Maisie's. I need to get going. My poor sister!" She squeezed Mini's arm and ran back down the stairs almost running into Kirk, who'd started to go up.

"I believe Dr. Oliver is going to help Maisie get over this. She's loved Gavin, but I do believe I saw a spark between the two of them today."

Kirk whistled between his teeth. "That would be just the ticket, don't you think? Maisie is stronger than she looks. She's a McCaully, after all, but I know losing Gavin will hit her hard. Having someone like the new doctor would put new life into her."

Caitlin nodded her agreement. "You should have seen them!" She grinned and added, "Could you ride to the mine first and make sure everyone knows about tonight?" she asked. "Perhaps, Jasper could let the men go home early." She wrapped her arms around Kirk and said, "I love you! See you in a bit."

He planted a kiss on her lips. "I love you, Katie me darlin'!"

"I love you, back!"She strode out the door and ran to her horse.

Kirk and Matt rode for the mine as Caitlin had suggested. Dismounting they tied up alongside many horses already tied to the railing.

"That's Ezra's horse," Kirk said. "Wonder what he's doing here?"

Kirk knocked on the door and a voice called out, "Enter!" He opened the door and saw that Ezra was seated facing the desk where Jasper was seated. Both men stood as Kirk and Matthew entered.

"Hello there, Bannister."

"Which one?" Kirk grinned. "Jasper Clemmons, this is my brother, Matthew Bannister."

"Owner of a winery." Jasper finished the introduction. "I'm pleased to meet you. You're putting out a delicious Merlot, sir," he said as he shook Matthew's hand.

"Nice to meet you, Mr. Clemmons."

"And this is our new sheriff, Ezra Walker," Kirk said, wrapping up the introductions.

Ezra stuck out his hand. "Pleased to meet you Mr. Bannister. I'd have known you were closely related to Kirk even without the introduction," he said.

"It's nice to meet you, Sheriff Walker. I am pleased you are a definite improvement over the last sheriff Santa Rosa had."

"Yes, I've heard quite a few stories about him."

Matthew nodded as Kirk spoke up. "We can't stay, we're here to say that Gavin passed away this afternoon and there'll be a wake tonight at the Galways'."

Jasper looked at Kirk with shocked eyes. "He died? Oh my…I am so sorry!" He turned to Ezra, "We'll put off the dinner until tomorrow. I need to go to the wake. Fact is, I want to go to the wake."

"Of course. I'll be there, too," Ezra replied.

"Jasper, Caitlin was wondering if you would let the men know, and perhaps let them off early so they can get home and get cleaned up. I would imagine most of them will want to be there."

"Of course, and glad for the idea to let them go home early," Jasper said. "I'll see to it right away."

"I'll see you at the wake, Jasper," Ezra said. "Be thinking of how we can set a trap."

"I will, believe me, I will," Jasper grated out.

The four men exited the office building.

Ezra, Kirk and Matthew, mounted up and set off at a gallop.

Jasper stood thinking for a few minutes and headed for the bell pull.

CHAPTER XX

Lo, children are an heritage of the Lord:
and the fruit of the womb is his reward.
As arrows are in the hand of a mighty man;
so are children of the youth.
Happy is the man that hath his quiver full of them

PSALM 127:3-5

JASPER CLEMMONS HEADED FOR THE huge old cast iron bell and pulled the rope. It sounded the call to gather outside the mine. He stood with his hands on his hips still thinking.

If Galway and Brown have been shot, I'm next in the way of someone getting control of the mine.

As he stood waiting for the men to gather he continued his line of thinking.

Having both Ernest and Sandy right here at the mine, and one of them the shooter, makes me a good target. I'm definitely vulnerable. He waited for men to appear before he got up on the upended washtub Lenny used as a platform to talk to the men who would gather there. *I'd like to replace this old washtub with a small platform or something a bit more distinguished for talking to the miners. I need to keep a sharp eye on Sandy and Ernest. I agree with Ezra…it's got to be one or the other. My life isn't worth much if the plan is to take over the mine. I would imagine that would be the reasoning. Why else shoot Gavin and then Lenny? But how in the world do they plan to take control?* His thoughts jerked back to the words he must speak to the crew as men began circling the washtub.

One of the men spoke to Jasper and he leaned over, the better to hear just as a shot rang out. Jasper clutched his arm, a look of incredulity spread over his face. The men still in the mine came running out as others crouched down. Another bullet hit the washtub, and Jasper jumped down, still clutching his arm.

"It's coming from up there on the bluff!" a man bellowed, pointing to the cliff over the mine. Another yelled, gather 'round men! "He's trying to kill Mr. Clemmons!"

Several men drew guns and opened fire on the bluff from where they thought the bullets had come.

A man pulled Jasper's good arm, trying to shield him with his own body from the cliff as other men circled around, trying to protect him. It cut Jasper's heart to the quick for their loyalty and he vowed, right then, that he'd be nicer to the miners.

"There's safety in th' mine!" a man shouted. The men huddled together running for the mine's entrance.

Jasper tried to see if Sandy or Ernest was in the group, but his search was in vain—he couldn't see for the crush of men.

When they got to the mouth of the mine, Jasper was bleeding profusely. A man named Jude, who served the miners with first aid for minor injuries, quickly wrapped Jasper's arm and said, "We need to get you into town. That bullet didn't pass through, and you're bleeding like a stuck pig. Doc will need to dig it out. You're blessed, though. Five inches to the left and you'd be a dead man."

Jasper's face turned pasty at his words, but the man thought it was because he was in shock.

"Doc retired. We have a new doctor. Would you please tell the men there's a wake tonight. Mr. Galway passed away today, and they can go home now and get ready." Jasper's arm felt as if someone had seared him with a hot iron, and he tried not to gasp.

Jude yelled out to the men, relating what Jasper had told him.

"I'm riding into town with Mr. Clemmons first," expressed one man loudly. Several others voiced their assent.

"We kin only hope that blamed shooter is finished fer th' day," remarked another.

"Those of you who have the time, let's head to town—there's safety in numbers," another stated.

Jasper handed a key to Jude. "Would you please lock up for me?"

"Certainly, I'm sorry this is happening. I hope either the sheriff or some of us at the mine can get to the bottom of this," he replied. "Everyone here knows Mr. Galway and Mr. Brown have been shot."

Jasper made a quick decision and said, "Perhaps you could spread the word that it has to be someone right here at the mine who's doing it."

Jude's eyes widened by the revelation, but he nodded. "That makes sense of a senseless deed."

The men climbed on their horses, two of them helping Jasper onto his.

Word spread like wildfire that a wake for Galvin Galway was being held, as well as the fact that men connected with the mine had been shot. Tongues were wagging fast and furious.

Nine of the miners rode with Jasper into town. He felt sick with the undulation of his horse's stride. Sweat poured from his brow and blood stained his shirt. He let it drip, not wanting to take his good hand from the pommel. He leaned forward hoping to stay on his ride as he swayed a bit in the saddle. He could feel a man one either side of him, so close their boots hit his every so often. He was grateful for the compassion and care they were silently expressing.

The ride seemed endless, but at last Jasper saw they were entering Santa Rosa. They pulled up in front of the doctor's office. Jasper started to dismount, but his legs felt like rubber, and one of the men caught him as he began to fall. Jude stepped up and Jasper put his good arm around his shoulder. He and another man helped Jasper up the step to the boardwalk. Another miner held open the door, looking on with sympathy etched in his eyes.

"Be praying for you, boss," he said.

Jasper simply nodded and tried to smile but his face screwed up into a grimace instead. *I need it,* he thought and was surprised he agreed he needed prayer.

The men got him into the office, but no one was there. One man ran up the stairs and knocked on the door.

Marie answered and, after a quick conversation, the man ran back down.

"The new doc hasn't come back from Galways' yet. I'll run over there and get him," he offered.

Jude, who led Jasper toward the surgery, spoke in a curt tone. "Please hurry!" He sat Jasper on the surgery table and helped him to lie down. "I'm going to give you some water, and I want you to drink it. You're losing too much blood. Wonder if they nicked an artery?"

Going to the sink, he filled a dipper and held it while Jasper tried to sit up and drink. Jasper lay back feeling giddy. "I feel like I've had too much to drink, and I'm not talking about water," he said.

Jude grinned. "You will feel worse after the ether, but at least you won't have to endure the digging without it."

"I think I'd rather drink something strong and bear the pain than go under ether. That stuff makes a body sick." He closed his eyes and drifted into unconsciousness, but not before he muttered, "We need to set a trap for Sandoval Peabody."

Jude raised his eyebrows in surprise and whistled under his breath. "Is that who's doing this?" he whispered, but there was no answer from Jasper.

Jude began to pace the room, waiting for the doctor. He heard the office door open and breathed a sigh of relief as Doc Addison entered.

"Hello, Jude. I heard Jasper's in a bad way," he said as he rolled up his sleeves.

"He's lost a lot of blood, Doc," Jude responded. "I'm getting worried. He just passed out a couple minutes ago."

Doc washed his hands with soap and water and then liberally splashed carbolic on them. "Let's see what we can do," he said. He gingerly removed the soaked bandage. "You're right, he's lost a lot of blood. Bet the shooter's angry he didn't finish the job."

"He tried. He shot more than once."

Doc clucked his tongue. "Such evilness! It shouldn't amaze me, but it always does." He examined the wound probing a bit. "I pray it missed the bone."

"Me too," Jude responded. "Jasper's gruff and many times taciturn, but at heart he's a good man."

"I know. He's a very good man. His problem is that God didn't work the way he wanted Him to work." He cleaned the wound with carbolic, and cut the opening bigger, using a probe to locate the bullet. "Ahh, there it is. Yes, so many want healing, finances fixed, relationships mended, or God to tar and feather someone they are angry with, but none of those things are God's bottom line." He inserted Tiemann's Bullet Forceps and carefully extracted the bullet, dropping it onto a piece of gauze. He spread the wound open and poured carbolic into it with a liberal hand.

"What do you mean, God's bottom line?" inquired Jude.

"Well, the way I see it is we all want God to work the way our limited human mind comprehends, and sometimes He does. When He doesn't, we get angry and blame Him. Some get so angry they turn their back on Him. Others, thinking it's not Christian to be angry, suppress it, but it usually comes out in some way."

He threaded a needle with catgut, and before he began to stitch, he soaked the catgut with carbolic. Spreading the wound, he poured more into the exposed flesh, as he continued to talk.

"God's bottom line is justice. Whatever God does is right and just. It doesn't need our approval. If someone dies that we love, we blame God for not intervening, but God has a purpose for everything, and His knowledge is indisputably higher than ours. To go our own way is folly. To follow God's way is freedom. When all is said and done, we are finite...a speck of dust in the greater scheme of things. What is surprising is that God loves us so much, and sent His only son to die for us. He is not some spirit out there distant and removed from humanity. No, He is an intimate God and cares about the smallest detail of our lives."

Doc poked the needle through the flesh and expertly began to sew up the wound.

As he was finishing, Dr. Oliver entered the surgery with bright eyes and flushed face.

"Sorry I missed out here," he gasped. "I ran all the way, but found it difficult to get away from Mrs. Galway. She is distraught." He took a deep breath. "Thank you, Dr. Addison, for stitching him up." He glanced at the piece of gauze and raised his eyebrows. "You extracted a bullet?"

"Yes, our shooter tried for Jasper today," Doc replied. "I can't, for the life of me, figure out the reasoning of the shooter. How in the world does he expect to gain control of the mine?"

Jasper moaned, his eyes opening slowly. "Get on with it, Doc, but I'm not taking any ether. A few shots of whiskey will do me just fine."

Doc, Jude, and Oliver laughed.

"I can give you a few shots if you want," Doc chuckled, "but you were out long enough for me to get that bullet out. Now we need to pray for swift healing and thank the Almighty for sparing your life."

Jasper, tears seeping out his eyes, spoke huskily. "I need to ask Him for forgiveness. I have been so angry at Him for taking my sweet Charity. She was everything to me, and I know that was my problem. All things here are temporal even our loved ones and relationships. God needs to be my everything."

"Amen to that!" Doc declared.

"How are you feeling, Mr. Clemmons?" Oliver asked.

"Like someone skewered me with a hot poker," Jasper replied. "I will go to the wake for a bit, but I'm not staying the whole night. I feel weak as a kitten."

"Frankly, speaking as your doctor for many years, I think you should give the wake a pass. You need to be home and in your own bed. Folks will understand why you're not there."

Jasper swallowed. "Reckon I'd like that more than anything." He closed his eyes as a feeling of helplessness and weakness overwhelmed him.

Oliver, looking closely at Jasper, said, "I don't think he should ride. We'll need to get him onto a flatbed."

Doc nodded his agreement as he put his hand on Jasper's forehead.

Jasper opened his eyes, and Doc smiled at his patient. "Just making sure you haven't passed out again," he said.

Jasper nodded. "No, and you're right, I don't think I could make it home. It's not the wound, it's the loss of blood."

"I'll go over to the saloon and get Roy and Alfred," Doc said. "I also need to get over to the McGraths' and make sure Payton and Paige move out without being verbally beaten down by their mother."

"I'll stay here until we get Jasper loaded, and then I'll leave it up to those two to get him safely home." Oliver looked to Doc for approval.

Doc nodded his agreement. "I'll see you later, at Maisie's," he responded, and headed for the saloon.

"Right." Oliver glanced back at Jasper, who still had his eyes closed.

Jonah and Cindy Sue Whatcom had ridden to San Rafael in their wagon. They returned home with not one, but two children. A pregnant woman, whose husband had passed away a few months earlier, had died in childbirth. She'd left a two year old boy and a newborn baby girl. No relatives had been found, and the sheriff of San Rafael took the little boy and baby to the San Rafael School of Primary Learning. It was not only a school but an orphanage as well.

Jonah and Cindy Sue arrived at a perfect time. The orphanage was not equipped with enough staff to spend a huge amount of time on a newborn baby. The director was at his wit's end to figure out how they were going to accommodate a newborn. Funding was not available to hire a wet nurse or a babysitter.

When the Whatcoms showed up at the door, the director was beside himself with thanksgiving.

"If you will take both children," he said, "we will waive the adoption fee and pay for it, using the orphanage's funds for that purpose."

Cindy Sue swallowed down her ecstatic response and turning to her husband she spoke in a demure tone, as she smoothed down her dress.

"Jonah, do you think we can take two babies instead of one?" She swallowed, her eyes were sparkling in her excitement, but she didn't want to seem too eager in front of the director.

Jonah, seeing her desire and knowing she was filled with excitement but restraining herself, hesitated before giving his answer, just as she hoped he would.

The director said a quick prayer that the couple would take the baby and decided to voice additional benefits.

"We will give you the diapers and baby paraphernalia we have collected over this past week, including the Nestle formula that is popular for women who can't nurse."

"I reckon we'd be happy ta take the two of 'em. I wouldn't want ta be a separatin' a brother from his baby sister. That all right with you, Cindy Sue?"

"I'm thinkin' it'd be right sad ta be a separatin' the two.

The director pulled out a pristine handkerchief and wiped his brow.

"Let's go over right now, and we'll have Mr. Humphries, the orphanage's lawyer draw up the papers. He keeps paperwork ready, so when we have an adoption the papers are all ready to go, except for filling in the blanks. You will fill out the paperwork today, and tomorrow morning when everything is finalized, you need to stop by the lawyer's and get the paperwork. After that, come here with the papers and pick up your children. By the way, the boy's name is Jacob."

"That's a good Christian name fer a boy. Let's go sign them papers," Jonah said.

The director led them to Stern, Hancock, Edwards, Humphries, and Falter's law offices.

It was providential that Elijah Humphries was free. He was a busy man, but an appointment had been cancelled, and he was going over some paperwork.

The director as well as the Whatcoms were shown into his office.

Elijah was organized and hated clutter. The top of his desk was cleared off every afternoon when he was finished working. The paper's he'd been reading were stacked neatly on a tray.

Cindy Sue perused the room slowly, taking in the beautiful decor.

The walls were done in a light cream color, containing certificates, framed in a dark mahogany. Regular books as well as great tomes filled the bookshelves. Comfortable chairs for visitors were dark leather, and Elijah's desk chair, a swivel and tilt model, was oak but stained to match his desk. Dominating the wall behind the desk was a huge seascape of a frigate running before a storm. The office appeared barren, and yet there was a peaceful ambience that filled the room with a feeling of peace and contentment.

The director made the introductions and Elijah, after greeting the couple, gestured to the leather chairs.

"Please be seated." He sat with them instead of behind the desk. "Can you tell me why you'd like to adopt?" he asked.

"We've hain't never had no children, and me and Cindy Sue want children more'n anything. I've saved money ta be able ta pay fer all the folderol that adoption costs. The director is willin' ta waive th' cost iffin we'll take both babies. Ta tell th' truth, we'd a paid ta have both of 'em. It'd be a tragedy ta separate them. We love th' Lord and will raise them ta be Christ followers, that's sure."

"That blesses my heart, Mr. Whatcom. I also heartily agree that it'd be a tragedy to separate siblings. I have the paperwork ready for you to fill out, and tomorrow, you can drop by and pick them up."

Jonah and Cindy Sue filled in the dates, names and all the necessary information entailed in the adoption process.

"Kin we change the middle name of the boy? Jonah's middle name is Ray, and I'd like the boy to be Jacob Ray Whatcom."

"Certainly, and you could change his first name if you wish, and you can name the girl, as she doesn't have a name yet," Elijah replied.

When they were finished, the director had to sign in a few places.

"Tomorrow morning you can pick up the paperwork, and make your way to the orphanage to pick up your children. I'll look forward to handing them over to you," the director said.

They started to say their goodbyes, but Elijah forestalled them.

"Do you mind if I pray first?" he queried.

"Not a-tall," Jonah replied. "This is gonna be a big change fer all of us, and we'd welcome th' good Lord ta be in it."

"Our heavenly Father. How we do love Thee. Thou are the author of family and relationships, and we give praise to Thee for the guidelines Thou hast laid out for us to follow. May Thy word penetrate deeply into Mr. and Mrs. Whatcom's hearts. May they know the peace that passes all understanding because they walk in Thy ways. I pray this new family bonds easily with the glue of Thy love filling every situation. I pray for peace and patience in difficult times, and that love and laughter will fill the rooms of the Whatcoms' house. May Mr. Whatcom be the priest, the spiritual head of his home the way Thou hast designed a man to be. Bless them, Lord, in the name of Jesus I pray. Amen.

"Amen," echoed Jonah.

The director led them out of the law offices.

"I bid you farewell until tomorrow morning."

"Thank you, sir, and we thank you fer all you've done."

"You're welcome," the director said, breathing a sigh of relief that the baby would be gone by tomorrow.

The Whatcoms booked a room at Three Hawks Inn and spent the rest of the day prowling around the small town. They found more Nestle formula and stocked up on a lot of it, thankful they had funds to spend on the children.

When they were snuggled together ready for bed, Jonah took Cindy Sue's hand and began to pray a prayer for guidance, to praise and to give thanksgiving. Both had a difficult time sleeping in a strange bed and with the excitement of the morrow.

Morning dawned with sunny skies. Wisps of cotton, stark white against the cobalt blue background, marched their way across the heavens by a gentle zephyr.

Jonah and Cindy Sue enjoyed a delicious breakfast at the inn. They took their time as they'd awakened early. Breakfast was not yet being served when they entered the dining room, but there was hot coffee, and the two sat and talked at length before they could give their order.

They dawdled over their food, until the lawyer's office was open and then made their way over, excited and a bit scared to be parents. They had lain awake far into the night discussing their new circumstances and both felt the Lord's pleasure.

"Looks ta be a fine day ta begin a family, Cindy Sue. I am feelin' blessed."

"Yes, we are blessed, but I'm blessed the most," Cindy Sue replied. "I have a wonderful husband who has put up with an awful lot. I promise I'll be th' best wife you could ever want, Jonah Ray Whatcom. I hain't plannin' ta do anymore naggin'. Yer a good man and deserve bettern' I bin. I want ta be a mother the children will look up to and not a shrew. I thank you, Jonah, I couldn't be married ta anyone better."

Jonah beamed at her comment and, right there on the boardwalk in front of the law office, he swept her into his arms and gave her a passionate kiss.

Entering the office, Cindy Sue's cheeks were flushed and her eyes bright.

Elijah was waiting for them and the paperwork ready, sitting on the reception counter.

"Congratulations!" The lawyer said to the new parents as he shook their hands. "I sometimes wonder if my wife and I should have done the same years ago. We were childless, but now we have a bevy of girls at the mission, and also have claimed Liberty Bannister, from Napa, as a daughter."

"Any relation ta Kirk Bannister from Santa Rosa?" Jonah inquired.

"Why yes. She is his sister-in-law."

"Small world, hain't it?"

"Sometimes it would seem so," Elijah replied, a twinkle in his bright blue eyes.

Jonah and Cindy Sue left the office and headed to the orphanage. When they entered the edifice, the director was right there to greet them.

"Good morning! What a beautiful day to start a new chapter in your lives. Please, come into my office," he said, as he ushered them into the main office.

Little Jacob sat on a chair swinging his little legs like pistons, sucking his thumb, and looking around for something more interesting to do. As

Cindy Sue entered the room, he hopped down and crossed over to her, slipping his hand into hers.

Surprise and wonder filled Cindy Sue, and she knelt down and pulled the boy to her, giving him a gentle hug. He wrapped his little arms around her neck, and tears filled her eyes at how right his body felt in her arms. She scooped him up, and he snuggled his face into her neck.

"Well, that went smoother than I anticipated," the director said. "The baby girl is there in the bassinet. If you will give me one set of the papers, you are free to go. That wooden drum you passed on your way up the outside steps, is full of the children's things. I wish you luck and pray you will be one happy family."

Jonah handed him one set of papers, keeping the other for himself.

"Thank you, sir, fer yer generosity. We will be the best parents we are able ta be. He picked up the bassinet, and they headed out the door with their two children."

CHAPTER XXI

For the oppression of the poor, for the sighing of the needy,
now will I arise, saith the Lord;
I will set him in safety from him that puffeth at him.

PSALM 12:5

APRIL AND MAY FINISHED THEIR UNSAVORY task and headed back home to clean up. Both women were nervous of what Mrs. McGrath might do, but they were determined to help the twins whose story was so close to their own.

They dressed in their Sunday best and put on their prettiest bonnets. Feeling fortified by looking their best, they strolled over to the McGraths' house.

Taking a deep breath and muttering a quick prayer, May knocked on the door.

Mrs. McGrath answered. "Why hello ladies!" she voiced her surprise. Her words were pleasant, but her eyes were sparking anger.

I'll wager she knows why we're here. April thought as she spoke.

"Good afternoon, Mrs. McGrath. How are you today?"

"Quite well thank you," but she didn't invite them in.

"May we come in?" May asked.

"Oh, my goodness! Where are my manners? Of course, come on in." She led them to the settee, but May and April didn't sit down when she gestured to them to do so.

"We're here to help Payton and Paige to move into our rental rooms." April, her heart pounding with trepidation, spoke evenly with no tremor in her voice.

"I beg your pardon!" Martha McGrath said. It was a statement, not a question, and keeping her voice low, in case the girls should come running, she said, "My girls are not moving in with you."

"Yes, actually, they are. We have rented rooms to your daughters and have come to help them make the move."

"My daughters are not going anywhere!" Martha hissed. "They are *my* girls and they will stay right here where they belong!"

May raised her voice, which was something April had never, in her entire life, heard her do.

"We are taking those girls with us! They are of age and will receive love and care in our home. Something I am quite sure is lacking in this one! We know what kind of woman you are, Martha McGrath. You are the kind that gives Christianity a bad name. We were raised by a woman similar to you, and we know the subtle ways you have hurt those girls of yours. They are good and sweet young ladies with beaus to match that you don't even know about."

Martha McGrath gasped in astonishment and rage.

"Girls their age should never be afraid to share beautiful happenings with their own mother," May continued.

When her voice penetrated the upstairs rooms, both girls had come running down in time to hear most of what May had to say.

Martha saw them and began with a hiss that turned into a scream. "Sneaks! Both of you! Hussies—the both of you!" She picked up a vase from the end table and threw it at them.

Both girls stepped back up the stairs as the vase crashed against the stair railing.

Turning, they ran up the stairs and gathered what they could in their arms, knowing whatever was left for a second trip might not survive till they got back to collect it. Neither girl wanted to stay at the house while the other took their things to the Listers' house.

They lugged as much as they could carry down the stairs and were surprised by April.

"Give those things to us, and go get the rest. If your mother is anything like ours was, there won't be anything for you to return to collect."

"Why you…you—"

"Go ahead and say it," May interrupted. "It won't bother us one whit. Both of us heard the like growing up!"

There was a knock on the front door, and Martha stomped over to answer it. Seeing who it was, she tried to slam it closed on Doc's face, but he stuck his foot in the door.

"This is all your doing you dirty, nasty ole coot!" Martha spoke the scathing comment into his face.

"Yes, yes it is. Your dead husband asked me to take care of your girls, and I have been negligent in not getting them out of here sooner." He glanced at the Listers and announced, "I brought a flatbed. I'll stand right here, and you can load those things onto it."

Paige and Payton came down with loaded arms, and Doc said, "Just take them out to the wagon, and go get anything you'd like to take, we've plenty of room."

Both Paige and Payton's eyes filled with tears at his thoughtfulness. They'd thought they'd lose many of their belongings as soon as they left the house. Both girls ran down the front steps nearly running into their new landlords and dumped their belongings into the wagon.

"I've never met you formally," Paige said, breathlessly, "but I cannot thank you enough for opening your home to us!"

"Oh dear girl, we could not do less!" exclaimed April.

"Go get the rest of your things, and we'll try to get you settled before the wake," May said.

Without another word, the girls ran up the front steps and up the stairs. Both perused their rooms, opening drawers and making sure they had everything. They hugged each other, their eyes now bright with excitement and happiness.

Holding hands, they descended the stairs, where they turned to their mother, who stood, looking balefully at them.

"Good bye, mother," they both said in unison.

"God will get you for this evilness," she replied in a hiss, her arms crossed against her scrawny frame.

The twins strode out the door along with Doc, who closed it gently before bounding down the wide steps. They gratefully left a house full of bitterness and anger to Martha McGrath.

Jonah and Cindy Sue traveled home with Jacob and the baby girl. They crossed the bay on the ferry, and Cindy Sue snuggled the baby close, making sure the breeze didn't touch her.

Jacob sat on Jonah's knee, one thumb in his mouth, and the other hand curled around Jonah's thumb. He'd made no sound, and both new parents figured he couldn't speak.

Jonah ruffled the young boy's auburn curls. "Let's get down and stand by the rail, son," he said. He climbed down, turning to haul the little tyke out of the wagon.

"Bird...bird!" Jacob said, pointing to the sky.

"Well, bless my soul, boy, you can talk!"

Deep blue eyes full of laughter and excitement looked into Jonah's. He jumped into Jonah's arms with no fear he'd be dropped, but it took Jonah unawares, and he had to grab at the boy before he could fall.

"Whoa there, Jacob! You better be a warnin' me afore you jump!"

"Jump!" Jacob repeated.

Jonah held him close and strode over to the rail so the boy could see the waves and the front of the ferry pushing through the water. Wind whipped his curls, and he plopped his thumb back into his mouth, seemingly full of contentment.

After the crossing, the family made their way to Sonoma. Thankfully, the director had furnished them with a couple of already prepared bottles for the baby. It wasn't warm milk, but the baby girl took it with no hesitation.

Jonah pulled over at lunch time, and they enjoyed fried chicken, potato salad, and pickled hardboiled eggs, prepared by the cook of Three Hawks Inn.

Jonah pulled the chicken apart for Jacob. Cindy Sue's arms were tired, and she laid the infant in the bassinet, sitting on the floorboards of the wagon, near her feet. She tenderly tucked the sleeping baby into the covers. Stretching her aching arms, she took a breast of chicken to eat and sat thinking of how different life was going to be.

The luncheon was delicious and satisfying.

Jonah took Jacob into the woods and got him to go potty, taking care of his own needs as well. Cindy Sue trooped into the woods also.

Climbing back onto the wagon they started out at a fast clip, wanting to get home.

"What shall we name the baby?" Cindy Sue asked.

"Dani," Jacob said. "Baby Dani."

"Is yer baby's name Danielle?" Jonah asked.

Jacob nodded his head vigorously. "Baby Dani."

"Well, I like that name. How 'bout you, Cindy Sue? We kin call her Dani, same as Jacob does, but we'll name her Danielle Sue Whatcom iffin it's all right by you!"

"That sounds right good ta me. Then Jacob's middle name is Ray, and Dani's middle name is Sue named after their parents!" She smiled. Jacob looked at her and chuckled.

Doc entered the saloon, looking around for Alfred and Roy.

"I need help again. I'd like you to take Jasper Clemmons home," he said reaching into his pocket for a Liberty dollar.

"What's wrong with him?" Roy asked.

"He was shot in the arm at the mine about an hour ago."

"I don't know if we want to help out this time. What if the person shooting everyone is waiting for us, Doc? What if he wants to take a potshot at us?"

"He won't be. He's home getting gussied up for a wake."

"Who died?" Roy asked. "I didn't know anyone died. We've been in the saloon since luncheon."

"Mr. Galway died," Doc said succinctly.

"Ah, that's too bad. He was a good and upright man. Everyone around here respected him." He thought for a moment, "Reckon our shooter is now a murderer."

Doc glanced at Roy. "I'm not so sure. Yes, his intent was to kill Mr. Galway, but Mr. Galway died of a heart attack."

"That so?" queried Alfred. "I'd think he'd be too young for that."

"No...no he wasn't."

"Well, if you're sure our man, making target practice out of people, isn't going to be gunning for us we'd like to help out."

"Thanks, boys." He handed them a dollar each. "He's over in my old office. Dr. Oliver is there, and he'll help you get set."

Doc hurried over to the Listers' and saw that the wagon was already unloaded. He breathed a sigh of relief as he walked up to the house.

"Hello, Doc," May said, in response to his knock, wiping her hands on her apron.

"I'm so thankful to the both of you for taking in these girls. If they need money for the deposit just let me know. I'd be glad to help out."

"No—no you don't need to do that. As a matter of fact, the girls won't be renting from us."

Doc's eyes widened, his face full of consternation. "You've changed your mind? You don't want the girls?"

May chuckled. "Nothing like that, sir. We've decided to adopt them. We have no one to leave our things to when we pass on, and these two girls will be a boon to us. April and I are attached to them already. They are sweet-natured and polite, and we will love having them live with us."

Doc's face cleared, and he smiled. "You and April are going to have many stars in your crowns! Thank you, thank you for being who you are. You are lovely Christian women, and I know the Almighty loves you and takes pleasure in your generosity of spirit. I will be taking the wagon. Thanks for getting it emptied so quickly. We need to take Mr. Clemmons home. Will you be at the wake?"

"We wouldn't miss it. April's helping the girls get settled, and I'm in the process of making some food to take."

"Well, I won't keep you. I need to get the wagon back to the office. Thanks again, dear sister!"

May watched as he climbed up onto the driver's seat. "God bless you Doctor Addison." She whispered the prayer. "May Thy hand, Lord Almighty, direct his steps and please, as Thy word says, give him the desires of his heart."

Doc turned the wagon around with expertise and drew up in front of the office. He jumped down and went inside.

"Wagon's ready when you are," he said to Roy and Alfred. They were waiting in the reception room for the wagon.

Removing his hat, Doc strode into the surgery room, entering the opened door.

"I've given Mr. Clemmons, with his consent, a bit of laudanum to help with the pain," Oliver said.

Doc nodded. "That should help ease him a bit over those ruts in the road. The wagon's ready, so I'll be heading over to Galways but first, I'd like to talk to Deedee if that's all right with you."

Oliver raised one eyebrow. "Of course," he responded. "And may the Lord bless you," he added.

Doc grinned. "I'll take that gladly, any day!" Making a quick exit, he ran up the stairs and knocked.

"Hello, Dr. Addison," Marnie said. "Please come in. We are having a snack. Marie made cookies, and the three of us are eating them." She stood aside as he entered. "It must feel a bit strange to be a guest in a place you've called home for so many years."

Doc, surprised by the comment said, "Yes...yes it does. You are a perspicacious girl."

"Why, thank you," she grinned. "Let's go to the kitchen."

She led him to the big comfortable room and because of her words, he felt a pang of regret that it was no longer his home.

"Hello, Deedee, hello, Marie." He glanced with a smile at Marie, but his eyes fastened on Deedee.

"Good afternoon, Doc," the two women responded in unison and grinned at each other.

"Pull up a chair," Marie invited.

"Would you like a cup of coffee?" Deedee asked, already rising from her chair to get one for him.

"I'd like nothing better. I've been running around getting things arranged for the wake, and I—"

"Did poor Mr. Galway die?" Marie asked.

"Yes, I'm sorry, I was thinking you'd already heard. Yes, he succumbed to another heart attack."

"Dr. Oliver was worried about that," Deedee said, as she sat a cup of brew in front of Doc.

"Yes, we had talked about it. We knew unless the Lord intervened, that he'd suffered too much damage to the heart to survive long." He took a cookie and munched on it as his eyes held Deedee's. "One precious thing to come out of this was that he repented of his sins and asked Jesus into his heart." He took a sip of coffee. "I know you didn't know him, Deedee, but may I escort you to the wake tonight?"

Deedee, blushing said, "Why, I-I don't know. I think I need to stay here with Marnie."

"No, I'll be here," Marie interjected.

Doc's eyes were warm on Deedee's face. "Please?" he added.

"Then yes, I'd be happy to go with you," Deedee responded. "What time?"

Doc reached into his fob pocket and took out his timepiece.

"Well, it's five now. How about six thirty? That will give me time to ride out to Bannisters and get cleaned up."

"Fine," Deedee replied. "I'll be ready." Her voice was even and sensible, but her greenish eyes were warm and full of excitement, and her heart was beating fast.

"All right then that's settled." He rose from the table and said, "Thank you for the coffee and cookies. I'll be back as soon as I can."

Marnie, Marie and Deedee heard him whistling as he ran lightly down the stairs.

"Deedee, I think he's a wonderful man," Marnie said.

"I *know* he's a wonderful man," Marie added. "And Deedee, he's got his heart set on you."

"I don't know why. I certainly haven't gone out of my way to charm him. I recognize goodness when I see it, and the good Lord has given me an ability to discern character. That man reeks of integrity and goodness. I can't think for the life of me why he should be attracted to me, but I don't deny it's flattering and has made me feel young again. As to my personal feelings about him, I just don't know. Everything is so new and just getting here and all, I don't want to lead him to think I have set my bonnet for him."

"Why not?" Marnie asked. "Are you afraid of him?"

"No! Of course not!"

"Are you attracted to him?"

"Marnie, you little stinker! That's none of your business!"

"Actually, it is. I would be left without you here. On the other hand, I'll have Marie, and if you marry Dr. Addison, I could come visit and stay a few days or if you live really close, I'd be in and out of your house every day!" She grinned at the look on Deedee's face.

"Well, then," Deedee said, another blush rising to her cheeks, "truth to tell, I can't seem to stop thinking about him."

"See…it didn't hurt for you to say that," Marnie said.

"No, it didn't. I just hope I'm not imagining too much. Perhaps he just wants a companion to do things with. What if he just wants me for a casual friend?"

"You don't have to worry about that," Marie said. "I know him as well as anyone, and he's definitely, romantically attracted to you. Have you looked into his eyes? He's bowled over by you!"

"I have trouble looking deeply into his eyes. I start blushing every time I try."

Marie laughed. "Well, I suggest you not worry about the blush and take a really good gander. You'll see exactly what I'm talking about!"

As the Whatcoms' drew up in front of their house, Jonah breathed a sigh of relief.

"I'm plumb tuckered out," he said. "What with all this excitement and not sleepin' much last night, I'm lookin' forward ta a quiet evenin'."

He placed Jacob down and went around to help Cindy Sue alight. As he did so, he tipped his hat lower to shade his eyes as he looked at the road leading to their house.

"Someone's a comin' down th' lane."

Cindy Sue shaded her eyes. "Why it's Zebidiah," she remarked.

Jonah went around to pick up Jacob and stood waiting for Zeb to pull up.

"Glad I caught you home. Congratulations! Looks as if you have a fine boy there!" he said.

"Yep, yer right. He's tailor made fer us! We just got home. If you could see on th' other side of the wagon, there's a bassinet on th' ground. We got ourselves a brother and newborn sister." Jonah spoke proudly. "Why're you here an' not at the mine?"

"There's a wake ta-night fer Mr. Galway. We've had some doin's since you've bin gone. Someone shot Mr. Brown th' day you left, I think it was. I found 'em on th' road on th' way home from work. Got 'em in th' chest, but it looks like he'll be all right. Today, Mr. Clemmons got up on th' tub ta tell us Mr. Galway died and ta go home early and git ready fer the wake. Someone spoke ta him, and he bent over ta hear better. Good thing or he'd be daid. Someone up onta th' cliff there, shot at Clemmons an' got 'em in th' arm. He lost a lot a blood, but we got him inta town safe. Word is someone at th' mine is doing this. Cain't, fer the life of me, figger out why!"

"Lord have mercy! That's a lot ta swallow! That a body kin be that wicked! Someone at th' mine is a doing it? Gracious me! As you said, good thing Mr. Clemmons bent over. That's th' Lord's doin'."

Zeb nodded his agreement. "I believe that, too. Now, I best be goin'. I'll understand iffin yer not there. You must be tired after a long day on th' wagon. The missus an' I'll be a goin', Saidy and Letty Lynn'll be a watchin' our little ones. She's already makin' a cake ta take." He doffed his hat. "G'bye!"

"God speed, Zeb, an' be careful out there!" Jonah yelled after him.

CHAPTER XXII

To every thing there is a season,
and a time to every purpose under the heaven:
A time to be born, and a time to die;
a time to plant,
and a time to pluck up that which is planted;
A time to kill, and a time to heal;
a time to break down, and a time to build up;
A time to weep, and a time to laugh;
a time to mourn, and a time to dance.

ECCLESIATES 3:1-4

CAITLIN UNWOUND FIRE'S REINS, STEPPING into the stirrup. She thought about what she needed done, ticking off on her fingers, each item. *Doc knows and will take care to get Gavin ready. Duney will get some food ready. Oh my goodness! I forgot to change my clothes, and Liberty asked for a clean blouse.* She dismounted and ran up the steps. Entering the house, she sprinted up the stairs and to her room. She heard Kirk come in right behind her.

"What's wrong?" he asked.

"I reckon I'm a bit more upset than I realized. I forgot to change, and Liberty asked me to get her a clean blouse. Could you please ask Matthew to get one while I change?" She slid her heel into a boot pull and got her leather boots off, while she spoke. Undoing the buttons of her denims, she pulled them off and stepped into the commode room, pulling the door shut behind her.

Kirk ran lightly down the stairs and relayed the message to Matthew, who followed him back up.

After a fast sponge bath, Caitlin slipped on a nice split skirt and black blouse, buttoning it up as she kicked her boots into place.

Kirk entered and gave her a quick kiss. "That was fast, and here's Libby's blouse."

"Thank you." She pulled on her boots, strapped on her gun, and ran down the stairs and out the door. As she stepped into the stirrup, she thought she should ride out and let the crew know about Gavin. Settling her hat on her head, she rode at a gallop out to the area where John's crew was working.

She talked to Fire as she rode. "Sure glad I have my thinking cap on! Jared and Aidan don't even know yet that Gavin passed away! Poor Maisie." She rode first to Eli and Manny's crews, letting them know about the wake. Some of them knew Gavin, others did not.

John saw her first, and driving in the last Brinkerhoff wire staple from Diebel's General Store, he waited for her to pull up.

When John stopped working, his crew looked to see what was going on, and they too, saw Caitlin galloping up.

"Hello, John. Fencing looks good. You always make it look so easy." She smiled, but her eyes were clouded over, and John could see it.

"What's going on?" he queried.

"Gavin passed away a few hours ago. There's a wake at Maisie's."

"I thought he was doing better."

"N-no, Doc said he and Dr. Oliver didn't want to worry Maisie, but evidently neither one of them thought he'd last long. He had too much heart damage." Tears filled her eyes. "I just wanted to let you know. All the crews are knocking off work early."

Jared and Colton drew close and heard the comment.

"What's the matter, Caitlin?"

"Bad news, Jared. Gavin passed away today."

He gasped. "Oh, Lord, please be with Maisie! Does Aidan know?"

"No, not yet. Liberty and I rode in today to see if there was anything we could do for Maisie. Gavin laughed about something, lost his breath, and that was it. Liberty is still with Maisie. I need to get going, but I was wondering if you and Colt would saddle up a horse for Mini and let her ride with you into town?"

"Certainly," Colt replied before Jared could. "I'll go get cleaned up. Jared, you go ahead and ride to town so you can tell your wife. I'll ride in with Mini Lou."

Caitlin looked at Colt taking over the planning and nodded her agreement, but her eyes were full of curiosity. *Colt's used to being in control. Very interesting. He's definitely not a drifter. Talks as if he's well educated. Wonder if Dr. Oliver knows his story. Oh, well, it's none of my business.*

"Sounds good to me," Jared said. "Poor Maisie, expecting a baby and now this happens."

"It's a shame, for sure," John said. "We need to pray for her."

"Yes, we do," Caitlin said. "And Colt, Mini is in the kitchen helping Duney. Tell her I said for her to get ready and ride in with you. John, make sure the men riding into Santa Rosa take the food Duney's preparing. Ricardo, could you please see to Jared's tools? He needs to ride into town with me and tell Aidan about Gavin."

"*Sí*, Mees Caitlin, I do eet," Ricardo said. He gave Jared a slap on the back. "You geet going, Jareed!"

"Let's get to it," John said.

The men packed up their tools, and John hung the roll of unused wire around a fence post.

Jared climbed on his horse. "See you later," he said as he reined his horse to follow Caitlin's.

Colton packed up his tools and headed for the bunkhouse where he lived. He washed up and changed into clean clothes. Settling his hat on his head, he led his horse over to the big house and tying up, walked back to the barn to saddle up a horse for Mini. He led the mare to the hitching post, tying her up next to his, and strode to the front door.

It opened before he could knock.

Duffy ushered Colt inside.

"Welcome, Colt. So sad, isn't it? Mr. Galway was such a dear man. He was too young to die, that's certain."

Colt removed his hat and said, "Yes, ma'am it is sad. Miss Caitlin told me to get Mini Lou and escort her into town."

"Oh, please follow me. She's in the kitchen."

Colt followed her with no hesitation. She led him across the dining room, opening a French door to the kitchen.

"Mini Lou," she said, "Colt is here. Miss Caitlin told him to escort you into town. You need to run up and change, dearie."

Mini Lou looked up, staring into Colt's eyes.

"Hello." Wiping her hands on a towel, she said, "I'll try to be quick." She turned around to face Duney, "Who's taking this food into town?" She waved her hand expansively to include all they had been baking.

Duney looked at all the food. "I have no—"

"Miss Caitlin told John to arrange for the men attending the wake to take it in." Colt interjected. "You should have no problem getting it all there." He spoke with authority in his voice, and Mini Lou stared at him.

"Ah, that Miss Caitlin," Duney said with a nod, "she is an amazing organizer. She always thinks about every detail."

Duffy saw Mini Lou gawking at Colt. "You need to scoot, Mini Lou, don't keep the young man waiting!"

"Yes, ma'am," Mini Lou replied, a blush rising into her face, as she realized she was staring. She ran from the room mounting the stairs two at time.

Colt grinned at both women. "I do believe you lit a fire under her, Mrs. McDuffy."

Mrs. McDuffy grinned back. "You can call me Duffy, same as everyone else." She suddenly sobered. "I sure feel sorry for Miss Maisie. What a tragedy for poor Gavin to die so young! None of us suspected he had a weak heart."

"My only sister died just a few months ago. I miss her. We were very close. Dr. Oliver had been treating her and sent us to see a specialist. He was pretty sure she had something wrong with her heart."

"I'm so sorry," Duffy said. "Do you have any brothers?"

"No, there was just the two of us."

Colt and Duffy talked for a few minutes, but Colt heard Mini's light step coming down the stairs and was surprised she could be ready that quickly. She entered the kitchen, and he stared at her transformation.

"You are an efficient young lady," he pronounced. "I don't think I've ever seen someone so quick to change…not even a man!"

She grinned but didn't reply.

He took in the changes and marveled to himself. She had on a dark blue dress that enhanced the color of her eyes. Her hair was braided into a crown around her head, and he wondered how she'd done it so fast. Curly tendrils framed her face. A shawl was looped over her arm for this evening.

She looks fantastic, he thought.

"Let's be on our way then," he said. He held out his arm and without hesitation, she took it, feeling weak at the knees by his nearness.

I suppose this is it, she thought to herself, ruefully, her thoughts turning into a prayer. *I wanted riches, Lord, and a glamorous life. I can't help but think you've brought this cowboy into my life, but more, into my heart. I can't stop thinking about him! He's a believer like me, and I don't care now if I live in a shack. I'm going to do my best to get him to love me. Just holding his arm makes me feel warm and protected. I knew this was going to happen!*

Colton led Mini Lou to her horse.

"You already saddled me up?" she asked. "That was thoughtful. Thank you."

"You are welcome, Miss." He looked askance at her dress. "I forgot you might be wanting a buggy."

"No thank you. Frankly, I love to ride, and if it won't embarrass you, I'll just hike up my dress, and ride with my boots showing."

"Fine by me," he replied with a smile as he laced his fingers to give her a hike up on the horse. He wondered at her affable tone.

She laid her hand lightly on his shoulder, and stepped into his hand. Lifting her up, their eyes were level for a second, and he saw hers were sweet and no longer guarded.

Her eyes are beautiful. Maybe she's decided I'm all right. That would certainly be a step in the right direction.

"Colt, would you mind if we stopped by my parents' house?"

"No, of course not. Is it on the way?"

"Yes, except for going down the lane to the house," she replied.

"Let's go," Colt said.

Mini Lou kicked her horse into a fast gallop.

Colt, startled, grinned and followed.

They sped along the road, past hedgerows and open fields filled with spring flowers.

Mini slowed and Colton followed suit. She turned into a dirt lane lined with trees that arched over the lane. It was gorgeous.

They pulled up to a small house with a short hitching rail, where an old nag of a horse was tied.

Colt looked around. The small barn's roof sagged and was sorely in need of paint as was the house. The trough leaked, and everything looked old and worn but neatly kept. Mini Lou slid from her horse and stood patting and soothing the ole horse that seemed to match it's rundown surroundings.

"Hello there, Dandelion!" She said. "I've missed you."

The single door of the house opened, and children of all ages poured out, followed by a young woman with a baby in her arms.

"Mini Lou! Mini Lou is here!" Shouts and laughter filled their ears.

Colt grinned as he dismounted.

"Hello there to you all!" Mini Lou said. Hugs and kisses were distributed, and Mini Lou picked up Jemimah, settling her on her hip. "Hello, Mother," Mini Lou said, striding over to give her mother a hug. She pulled back and turned to Colt.

"Colt, this is Lindsey May Pindar, my mother. Please meet Colton Danbury, a hired hand at McCaully-Bannisters'."

Lindsey freed a hand and held it out in welcome as she looked deeply into Colt's eyes. "I'm right pleased ta meet you, young man."

"The pleasure is mine," Colt replied as he took her roughened hand in his.

"And these are my brothers and sisters," Mini Lou said. "This is Saidy, Lettie Lynn, Jedidiah, Micah, Sarah Sue, I'm holding Jemimah, and mother has baby Jamie."

Colt went along and shook each hand until he got to Jemimah, who was shy and turned her face into Mini Lou's neck. He patted her back.

"Is Pa home?" Mini Lou asked.

"Not yet. Did y'all want ta be a talkin' ta 'em?"

"No, not really, I just wondered if you'd heard. I think you'd better change your clothes into your Sunday best. Pa will be wanting to go to the wake. Mr. Galway died today, and—"

"He died! Lord, have mercy on Mrs. Galway an' th' family," Lindsey May said. "Yer right, Mini Lou. I'd best be gettin' my Sunday-go-ta-meetin' clothes on. Saidy, you and Letty Lynn will be a watchin' the little one's ta-night. Saidy git a loaf of zucchini bread out of the root cellar, so's I kin take it ta the wake. Oh, an' what a sad day fer Mrs. Galway."

"We're going to go ahead and ride into town. I'll see you later, Ma."

"All right, sweetie, I'll be a gettin' ready so's when yer pa comes home, I'll be rarin' ta go. Nice meetin' you, Mr. Danbury."

"It was nice meeting you, too, Mrs. Pindar and the children."

That comment brought a smile to Lindsey May's lips. She glanced at Mini Lou and was surprised to see the warmth in her eyes toward Mr. Danbury. *Thought she weren't interested in findin' a man. That look sure looks promisin' ta me! Maybe thet girl'll get some sense in 'er yet.* Her glance swung back to Mr. Danbury. *He looks ta be a fine specimen of a man. Ah well, it's in th' Good Lord's hands after all.*

"Thank you, sir. You take good care of my Mini Lou, now, ya hear?"

"Yes, ma'am," he said with a grin.

Mini Louise scowled at her mother, but Lindsey May didn't see it.

"Let's be going, Colton," she said, as she turned her horse to ride out. "Oh!" she exclaimed. "There's Pa now."

Zebidiah rode up to the house, and Mini Lou could see the question in his eyes.

"Miss Cait told us, Pa. I came by to tell mother. And Pa, this is Colton Danbury, a cowboy with McCaully-Bannisters'. He's riding into town to the wake. We'll see you there."

"Nice ta meet you, son," Zeb said. "One thing Miss Caitlin doesn't know is that Jasper Clemmons was shot today, right at th' mine. We got him ta safety an' then rode with 'em inta town. Word is that someone at th' mine is doin' th' shootin' but we haven't figgered out the what-fer yet. I need ta get cleaned up afore we go. Again, it's nice ta meet you, Mr. Danbury."

"Thank you, sir. It's nice to meet you, too. You can just call me Colt or Colton. I'm sorry to hear about the shootings. We're riding in now to the wake. Hope the road is safe."

"Well, now, it seems that all the shootin' is connected ta th' mine. You should be all right."

"Thanks, Pa. See you later." With a wave of her hand, Mini Lou started down the lane.

"Good day," Colt said, and he tipped his hat to Zeb and Lindsey May, kicking his ride into a gallop to catch up with Mini Lou.

He caught up with her, and yelled, "Nothing like riding off into the sunset together, is there!" He grinned as she started to glare at him, but his grin was so infectious that her lips twitched into an answering grin, and she threw back her head and laughed.

They slowed to a canter, and it wasn't long before they were riding into Santa Rosa where they pulled up to a walk. They dismounted, but somehow Mini Lou tripped, and Colt caught her in his arms. He looked into her eyes, and his arms tightened around her.

Mini Lou, startled by tripping, looked into Colt's eyes as he caught her. All doubt gone about loving this man, she lifted her hand and traced the groove in his cheek with her fingertip.

He, surprised by her touch and pliant body, pulled her close and kissed her lips. The kiss was long and passionate, and both pulled back and stared into each others eyes with wonder and astonishment.

Mini Lou could see Colt felt the same way as she did. She stood back from him and bared her heart and soul to him.

"I wasn't planning on someone like you to sweep me off my feet," she said breathlessly. "I wanted to be a lady of means, and not have to work from dawn until bedtime the way I've lived, until living at McCaully-Bannisters'. Somehow, Mr. Danbury, you have inveigled your way into my heart. I love you. I can't stop thinking about you. At first it made me so angry that I got all jittery when you were in the same room with me. It didn't take long before I realized what was happening. I fought against it and lost. And I've thought about this, long and hard. I've prayed about this and fasted, wanting to know God's will for me. Now, sir, I will work from sunup until bed, if I can share my life with you."

Colton, astonished that this woman would be so transparent with him, realized this was exactly what he'd been looking for when he came west. He said a quick prayer of thanksgiving to the Almighty.

"I feel the same way about you, Mini Lou. Since we're here before your parents, can we sit here outside the bank and talk?"

"Certainly. If we sit here, we'll see them when they come into town, and we can join them in going to the Galways."

They tied up their rides and stepped up to the boardwalk to sit on the bench located in front of the bank, which was now closed. Colt took Mini Lou's hand in his. A frisson of love seemed to crawl up his arm, and he sidled even closer to her. He was amazed at the feelings this woman awakened in him. He felt protective of her, yet overwhelmed with a desire to kiss her again. With an effort he tried to gather his thoughts, as she sat beside him.

"You do know Dr. Oliver and I were on the same train, coming west, and met up with each other at the station in Sacramento, don't you?"

"No, I didn't know you even knew him."

"Yes, I've known Dr. Oliver for years. We met by accident, I should say, we met by God's plan at the station. He invited me to come up to Santa Rosa and see if I would like to live here. I thought it would be good to know a familiar face where I ended up settling down. So, I took him up on his offer. He was my sister's doctor. I took her to see him, quite often. After a year or so he advised us to go to a specialist, one whom he recommended, as my sister was getting worse. The specialist confirmed that my sister, Jean, was suffering from heart failure. Dr. Oliver had suspected as much, but hoped he was wrong. She passed away a few months ago."

"Yes, I remember you telling me that, and again, I'm sorry. It'd be horrible to lose a loved one that way."

"Yes, it's not been easy. I miss her. But, there's something else that I haven't shared with anyone since coming west."

Mini Lou stared down to her lap, clenching her free hand under her skirt for fear he might have some dreadful secret. She was loath to hear it.

"Before my sister died, she made a request of me. She wanted me to travel someplace where people didn't know me—"

Mini Lou interrupted. "Goodness, that's a very strange thing to ask of a body."

"Yes, you might think so, but she didn't want me to marry someone who didn't love me but loved my money. You see, I'm not a cowboy. Actually, I'm not employed. I suppose you could say I'm self-employed. I am, and I say this humbly, extremely wealthy. I manage my money and live quite comfortably. You could call me a philanthropist."

"I'm sorry, but I couldn't call you a philanthropist. My vocabulary doesn't extend to knowing what kind of job that is. I have no idea what that word means. What is a philanthropist?"

"In all honesty, being a philanthropist is not a job. I manage my money, investing in different profit making ventures and making more money. I donate vast amounts to charities and to help other peoples' lives to improve without them knowing I did it."

Mini Lou's eyes widened as she stared at Colton. "You're not jesting, are you!" Her jaw dropped, and she swallowed. "My stars..." she sat stunned and then added, "Reckon, I should say, my Lord! I've fallen in love with a man of wealth!"

"And I've fallen in love with a woman who loves me for me!"

He pulled her to himself, and kissed her soundly. Both were shaken with the impact of the kiss. It was a promise given to each other.

"May I please ask your father for permission to marry you?"

"Yes! Yes you may!"

CHAPTER XXIII

The blessing of him that was ready to perish came upon me:
and I caused the widow's heart to sing for joy.

JOB 29:13

DOC **ADDISON, AFTER TALKING WITH DEEDEE,** realized that the sheriff had not been apprised of the latest shooting. He took out his handkerchief and wiped his brow.

"I'm going to be up all night, and I'm tuckered out." He spoke aloud to himself. "There are so many things to think about. I sure hope I don't forget anything," he muttered to himself, as his legs propelled him toward the sheriff's office. The shade on the door window was pulled down and a placard hanging by a string said, 'CLOSED.' He jiggled the knob, but it was locked.

"Drat it all!" He looked up and down the main street, and thought he saw Ezra down by the McGraths' house. "Drat again!" he exclaimed. He started walking, and saw Ezra look his way, so he waved to him, but Ezra evidently didn't see and started up the walk to the McGraths'.

Doc hurried toward the McGrath's house and yelled at Ezra, but he was out of breath, his voice not loud enough to be heard.

Ezra knocked on the McGraths' door, and it opened immediately.

"What do you want? You know that miner isn't here anymore."

"Evening, ma'am," Ezra doffed his hat. "Yes, I do know that. I just came by to ask if you knew Gavin Galway passed away today, and there will be a wake for him tonight."

Her voice was caustic, she said, "Course I know it! You sure you came by for that reason, or are you sniffing after one of my tramps?"

Ezra's pupils dilated in shock at her words, but he schooled his face to a deadpan calm. "Tramps, madam? Are you having trouble with tramps coming to your door?"

Martha McGrath's face turned purple with rage. "You buzzard! You know very well what I mean!" she hissed.

"You're mistaken, madam. I haven't seen any tramps in the area. As sheriff, I walk Main Street up and down several times a day and have never noticed anything untoward."

Doc came up the walk, panting from walking so fast. He heard Ezra's comment, and grinned to himself. "Ezra—Sheriff Walker, I have some important news for you."

Martha glared at Doc but didn't say anything because she was curious, wondering what Doc had to say to the sheriff. Her face fell with disappointment as the sheriff again lifted his hat to her, said, "Good day, madam, I'll be sure to keep a sharp eye out for any tramps," and hurried down the steps.

Full of venom, Martha spun around and slammed the door behind her. Taking three steps toward the kitchen, her rage and malevolence consumed her. Suddenly, her eyes bulged, she grabbed for her chest and fell face forward onto the floor.

Doc and Ezra, completely unaware, chuckled as they shook hands in the middle of the McGraths' walk.

"You sure do a poker-face well. Remind me to never play cards with you," Doc chuckled again.

"Whew, that woman is full of rancor. Wonder what caused her to hate people?" Ezra took out his handkerchief and wiped his forehead.

"I have no idea. Her husband was one of the nicest men I've ever known. I'm thankful the twins took after him. They could have become bitter with all their mother's maliciousness." Doc drew a deep breath, tired from nearly running down the street to waylay Ezra.

"By the way, they have moved in with the Lister sisters. They will pay less for rent and live in comfort instead of constant turmoil. I have found, in my many years of living, a number of people, like Martha, who seem to thrive on chaos. They love stirring things up, spreading horrible rumors, and feeding upon the misery of others. It's a terrible life for those caught up in the storms they create."

"I can't thank you enough for getting Paige and Payton out of that house." Ezra sighed. "There's an awful lot of wickedness in this world, isn't there?"

"Yes, I'm afraid there is. On the other hand, there are many wonderful people in this world, who live day in and day out working to make a living and many times in service to others. The choices we make are crucial. It doesn't matter if you are born in the rudest hut or a beautiful mansion, and it doesn't matter how you were raised, whether you were loved or not, you have the choice to live your life in freedom. You can allow all the bad that went on before to control and consume you for the rest of your life, coloring all your future with real or imagined hurts, or you can choose to live in an enjoyment of each day." He sighed, and it was quiet as they walked along, but Doc wasn't finished.

"I suppose one of the reasons I feel Payton and Paige's pain is because my own mother rejected me. Never was I good enough. Nothing I did could please her. She used to beat the stuffing out of me with a willow switch, and most times I never knew why." He took a deep breath and plunged on. "I remember the day I accepted Jesus Christ as my Savior. I was at church and believe me, we went every time the doors were open. I don't believe anyone had any idea of the way my mother treated me. I was an only child, and my father left us when I was about five. He'd had enough, I suppose. I was twelve the day I accepted the Lord as Savior. It was a revelation to me that anyone could love me, let alone die for me. I woke up the day after and felt cocooned in His love. No longer did I care about the treatment I received from my mother. Sure, it hurt, but I determined she would never again control the inward parts of me. They belonged to God and she couldn't touch me where it really mattered." He glanced at Ezra who had a frown between his brows.

"I didn't mean to upset you. It's just that each of us has the ability, with the Lord's help, of course, to throw off the chains of the past and move on. When we allow little things that are said, hurt us. We are allowing the bad to control our feelings. When Jesus came into my heart, and I let go of what others could do to me and let Jesus fill me up, why I became a different person. It does not matter to me, one whit, what others think of me, or say about me, or do to me. Fact is, I feel sorry for them. What does matters is that I am a child of the King, and I make sure my mouth and actions and thoughts are pleasing to Him."

"That's the only way to live, isn't it" Ezra's eyes glinted with pleasure at Doc's words. "And you didn't upset me, not at all. It's just that my parents doted on me, and it's hard to realize many children are raised by uncaring parents who don't wish to be burdened."

"I'm going to upset you, now, though," Doc said." The reason I hunted you down was because Jasper Clemmons was shot at the mine while he was talking to the men. The miners surrounded him, trying to protect him, and brought him into town. I operated on him and got the bullet out. He's now on his way home, but I needed to let you know."

"This has got to stop!" Ezra declared. "I've had enough!"

"Yes, I agree. We need to set a trap for Sandoval Peabody. At least that's what Jasper muttered to Jude before he passed out."

"I rode out to the mine today, and that's the only person who seems to have a few things against him. He's short, he rides a red dun colored horse, he's made accusations against Jonah Whatcom who, I understand, is as truthful as the day is long. We can't prove anything yet, but we are keeping an eye out for him. He'll probably be at the wake, don't you agree?"

"I should imagine so," replied Doc. He took out his timepiece and whistled through his teeth. "I'm supposed to escort Miss Deidra Jennings to the wake, so I'd better be on my way. Thanks for listening to me. I didn't plan on telling you my life's story." Doc grinned at the younger man with affection in his eyes.

"Thank you, I appreciated it. It will also give me better insight on how to handle a problem, if things come up between Payton and me."

Doc clapped him on the back. "You need to get over to the Listers and escort the twins to the wake. No need to skulk anymore, the Listers know all about you and Lenny. By the way, those sweet women plan to adopt the twins. They have no other relatives, and have fallen hard for the girls. I couldn't be more pleased."

"That *is* good news!" Ezra exclaimed. "I do feel sorry for Mrs. McGrath, though. She is bitter and doesn't have any idea that life was meant for us to do good and to love others. Poor woman."

"Yes, you are right. I had such a set-to with her earlier, that I lost all sympathy for her, but you are absolutely right. She certainly needs our prayers. I'll see you later, sir," Doc said.

"Lord willing, yes, you will." Ezra changed the direction of his steps and headed to the Listers' house.

Doc, rather than riding back to the ranch, entered his old home, but instead of going up the stairs, he quietly entered his old office. He went into the surgery, closed the door, and took off his hat. He slapped it against his leg, removing the dust. Next, he divested himself of his frock coat and shook it vigorously. He got a clothes brush out of a drawer and brushed down his trousers, took a cloth and shined his shoes and then filled a basin with water. Washing his face and hands, he wetted his hair. He sagged his knees to look into a cloudy mirror, barely able to see his reflection, and combed his hair. Straightening his tie, and cuffs, he donned his frock coat and felt ready to present himself to Deedee. He exited the main room, closing the door gently behind him. Whistling happily under his breath, he climbed the stairs with alacrity in anticipation of being in Deedee's presence for the rest of the night.

Jonah Whatcom, although weary from a long day and sleepless night, knew he needed to go to the wake. He'd liked the owner of the mine. Gavin Galway had always been kind to him when he took gems to the store. He wondered what was going to happen with the mine.

"Cindy Sue, I'm gonna help you git the youngins' ta bed, an' then I'm gonna git myself over ta th' wake."

"You do what you think is fittin', but I don't need no help. There's only th' two of 'em, an' both behavin' like angels. Jacob is a little man, an' he kin help me with Dani. She's a good baby, I kin tell. Oh sure they'll be times I'll be at my wits end, but I'm so grateful ta be havin' children. I'll never be able to thank you enough!"

"Pshaw, woman. We were both a hopin' ta have children. I cain't ever tell you how much I love you. You were enough fer me, Cindy Sue. I never needed children ta make me happy, but whatever makes you happy, makes me happy. I love you so much, I hain't got th' words!"

Cindy Sue ran over and kissed him soundly. "Now, you git yerself ready an' go ta that wake. Don't be a worryin' about me."

Jared and Caitlin rode into town and pulled up in front of Maisie's house. Caitlin slid off her horse, looked up at Jared, and smiled. "I'll give you a great tidbit to give Aidan," she said. "Maisie is devastated about losing Gavin. There is no doubt about that, but Liberty and I witnessed a real source of comfort for her. I believe when the time of mourning is over that Dr. Oliver will be Maisie's new husband." She grinned at the shocked look on Jared's face.

"You're not jesting, are you?"

"No, I'm serious." She wrapped Fire's reins around the railing. "Dr. Oliver sat on the edge of the bed and there was a definite attraction between the two. To confirm it, I asked Liberty what just happened, and she said we had witnessed the beginnings of a romance. She went on to say that Maisie was going to need someone to get her through this and that God has provided Dr. Oliver. Yes, I'm serious, but glad for her. I'll tell you what I told Liberty. Maisie told me once, several years ago, that she was never romantically in love with Gavin. She said he was comfortable, and that she didn't believe in all that emotional folderol anyway. She grew up with him, remember. Now, she's feeling the folderol." Caitlin grinned again. "It doesn't mean she didn't love Gavin.

She's going to be mourning the loss of him for sure, but having Dr. Oliver is going to speed up the healing process for her." She smoothed Fire's forelock while she spoke. "I must go inside as I've been gone overlong and need to let Maisie and Liberty know I'm back. I'll see you later. Wish I could see the look on Aidan's face when you tell her!" She unhooked the satchel from the saddle horn that had Liberty's blouse in it.

Jared grinned. "I can't wait! Thanks, Caitlin, for all you do. You're a stabilizing force in the family."

Caitlin's head jerked up in surprise. "Why, thank you, Jared, for your kind words." She turned to go up the walk, and Jared reined his horse and squeezed his knees. His horse immediately started into a trot to the edge of town.

My...my...my! Maisie is going to be all right. Thank you, Lord, for Your provision in our lives. Sometimes we don't see it until much later. Sometimes we never see it, but all the same, I thank You for providing for Maisie. She's not like Caitlin and Aidan. They are strong women, but Maisie is fragile. Again, I give You thanks for the love You lavish upon us. May my sister-in-law come to a saving knowledge of You.

Caitlin ran up the steps and without knocking, entered her sister's house. She heard voices in the kitchen and strode down the hall to the back of the house where the kitchen was located.

Maisie's tearstained face looked at her pathetically. "I really thought he was on the mend. Doc said he didn't want to cause me more stress... oh, you heard what he said. I feel so discombobulated. I loved Gavin very much, don't think I didn't!"

Before Caitlin could even form a reply, Liberty put her arms around Maisie's shoulders.

"Maisie, the whole family knows how you loved Gavin. Gavin was a happy and contented man. You made him that way. What is a real blessing is that Gavin asked Jesus to be his Savior. We know where Gavin is, and I can tell you he is full of joy. I wish you could experience that joy. God is watching over you, Maisie. He doesn't want you to feel alone. Don't you go worrying about what people think. We all love you. You are a special kind of woman, and it would take a blind man not to know that. Let's wipe your tears and then I'm going upstairs to change my blouse. Is that what you're going to wear to the wake?" Liberty, who usually didn't babble, kept up a running monologue, trying to keep Maisie's mind occupied. She and Caitlin both knew Maisie was feeling guilty about her feelings toward Dr. Oliver.

"Goodness, no!" Maisie replied. "I need to run up and change into something black."

"People will be arriving shortly, Maisie," Caitlin said. "So scoot yourself upstairs and get changed."

"Dr. Oliver is a Christian, isn't he?" Maisie asked.

"Yes, he is." Caitlin answered.

Maisie stared at her sister, feeling confused and heartsick. "Maybe he was just being kind to me."

Caitlin rolled her eyes at Liberty, who stifled a giggle. "Perhaps, you're right. Time will tell though, won't it?" Caitlin replied.

Maisie nodded her head, but Liberty, seeing an opportunity, spoke up. "Why would you think that, Maisie? Why would you think Dr. Oliver is a Christian?"

"I reckon it's because, with very few exceptions, those who say they are Christians seem to be the nicest people in Santa Rosa."

"Hmm. I think you should think about that. You know it's not because they are good in and of themselves. It's because they try to live the way God's Word tells them to live. I think I hear a carriage pulling up."

Maisie put her hand to her mouth, but she dragged herself up to the stairs. She felt unbearably tired and wished she could lie down for a spell. The Listers had prepared Gavin's body, and two men had put him in the drawing room for the wake, so all was in readiness.

Maisie went into the bedroom and a flood of tears filled her eyes. She undid the buttons from her shirtwaister and let it drop to the floor, pulled the strings of her petticoat and let it drop, and stepped out of them. She sat down, undid the buttons on her shoes, and in only her chemise climbed into bed with no thought of the wake. She took a deep breath and was fast asleep when her head hit the pillow.

The soft, early evening air felt balmy with the promise of a beautiful day in the offing. No stars had yet made their appearance, but the sun had disappeared over the horizon, and the stillness of twilight wrapped itself around the two people in the wagon.

Zeb and Lindsey May headed toward town, each immersed in their own thoughts. Finally, Lindsey May spoke.

"Who do you think is a shootin' ever one?" she asked.

"Someone who's a wantin' control of th' mine, an' it ain't either of th' bosses, that's certain." He pulled up at Whatcoms' lane and said, "I think I'll ask Jonah ta ride with us. I don't want 'em ridin' alone. That shooter has plans an' there's safety in numbers."

"I'd like ta see th' new babies. I'm glad Cindy Sue will now have somethun ta occupy her time."

Zeb turned into the Whatcoms' lane and headed through the canopy of trees arching over the lane, blocking out the sky. It was beautiful, and both Zeb and Lindsey May looked on with pleasure.

"Sure is pretty, ain't it?"

"Sure is," Zeb replied. "I always did like this lane. Makes me think the garden of Eden maybe looked like this."

CHAPTER XXIV

Let him kiss me with the kisses of his mouth:
for thy love is better than wine.

SONG OF SOLOMON 1:2

ZEBIDIAH AND LINDSEY MAY pulled up in front of the Whatcom's house, as Jonah was stepping into his saddle.

"Hello agin, Jonah." Zeb hailed his friend. "We jest came by ta see if you'd like ta ride along with us. We're a bit worried about what's bin happenin'."

"Shore...I'd be right happy ta do that," he replied. "Come on in an' see our babies," he invited.

Lindsey May hopped down with no help. "I'm happy fer you, Jonah. I know yer Cindy Sue's bin hankerin' ta have children fer some time. I'm grateful ta the Almighty fer providin' them fer you."

"You an' me both!" he said. He led his horse to the barn to unsaddle him, while he and Zeb talked.

Cindy Sue invited Lindsey May inside. An infant was in Cindy Sue's arms, and a sweet looking little boy with a mass of curls on his head stood with one hand holding onto her dress and the other with a thumb plunked into his mouth.

"Oh, Cindy Sue, I'm so happy fer you. What a sweet family you have! The good Lord must be a smiling at you fer providin' a home fer 'em. They'll be right content here with you."

Cindy Sue, a look of surprise on her face turning to pleasure, said, "Come meet Jacob." She squatted down and whispered into his ear.

He released her dress and took his thumb out of his mouth.

"Miss Lindsey May, this here's Jacob Ray Whatcom. Jacob meet my friend, Miss Lindsey May."

Jacob surprised everyone by saying, "Meet you." He smiled sweetly and Lindsey May knew Cindy Sue had a precious little boy to raise.

"You look like a fine young man, Jacob, and I'm right pleased ta meet you." She squatted down and asked him, "Can I look at your baby?"

Jacob's eyes widened, and he nodded in the affirmative, plunking his thumb back into his mouth.

"Is it a boy or a girl?"

"Hit's a girl. Her name is Danielle Sue Whatcom, but we're going to call her Dani, same as Jacob does."

"Well, I'm glad fer you, Cindy Sue. I bin prayin' an' prayin' fer you ta have a baby, an' now here you got two!" She grinned at the surprised look in Cindy Sue's eyes.

"I thank you, my friend," she said humbly. She knew she hadn't been nice to Lindsey May. "I want to apologize fer the way I've treated you in th' past. It wasn't Christian. I bin jealous of you, Lindsey May, fer having so many babies an' me havin' none. Would you please fergive me?"

Lindsey May reached over and squeezed her arm. "I do fergive you, Cindy Sue. I didn't know it was that. Now we kin be best friends."

"I'd cherish that," Cindy Sue said. "Iffin I don't know how ta do something I kin ask you."

Lindsey May nodded, knowing it was part of the apology.

"We best be goin', Lindsey May," Zeb called out.

She stood and so did Cindy Sue. "I'm glad we'll be friends agin," she said.

"Me too," Cindy Sue replied.

Zeb hopped down and helped Lindsey May back into the wagon. With a wave at Cindy Sue, they headed down the lane. It was now dark, but Zeb had lit lamps on either side of the wagon to help them see.

"Reckon I ain't a needin' th' lamps. Look at that moon! It's near bright as th' sun," Zeb said. "Did Cindy Sue tell you about gettin' two bairns 'stead a one?"

"Naw. She is jest so happy. That little tyke is a darlin'. I hain't tole you yet, Zeb, but I'm in th' family way agin."

Zeb nearly ran into the ditch. "Yer expectin' agin?"

"Yep, an' I'm gonna be a needin' more help than I have. Letty Lynn and Saidy have taken over all Mini Lou's chores, an it's jest too much. I'm tired, Zeb. I'm really tired."

Zeb sat quietly for a bit and then said, "Maybe Jedidiah kin take over the milkin' and Micah kin be a collectin' th' eggs an' feedin' th' chickens. Those boys ain't too young ta be a helpin'."

"I never thought about that. But yer right, Zeb. It's time those boys had some chores. Thank you fer the idea."

As they rode into town and down Main Street, they saw Mini Louise with Colton Danbury sitting in front of the bank.

They pulled up and Colton, not wanting to waste time, stepped up to the wagon.

"Hello, sir, madam," he said, as he doffed his hat. "I know this is a bit sudden, but I'd like to ask permission to court Mini Lou with the intent to marry her."

Zeb's eyes grew round and he simply stared at Colton.

"Is my daughter willin' ta marry you?" Lindsey May asked, her heart thumping with joy.

"I am, Ma," Mini Lou said. "I had my mind set on being on my own and making my own way. But, Colt came into my life, and I'm afraid I fell in love with him. I want to marry him."

Zeb swallowed. "You know what yer takin' on, son? Mini Louise ain't no doormat. She's got a mind of 'er own, that's certain. Truth to tell, she ain't always easy ta live with, bein' headstrong."

"I have seen a bit of her temper. And yes, sir, I know she has a mind of her own. It's one of the things that attracted me to her. Do you have any objections?"

"Kin you afford ta be married? She cain't be a livin' in th' bunkhouse, you know. An' I reckon the real question is, are you a Christian?"

"Yes, I am a Christian. Frankly, I wouldn't marry anyone who wasn't. And yes, I do know she can't live in the bunkhouse," he chuckled. "I can afford a house, and I'll explain more about that later. For now, I just would like your approval."

"Yes," Lindsay May said. "Yes, you kin be a marryin' 'er."

Zeb looked at his wife in surprise. "Reckon I agree. Mini Lou knows she's always bin my favorite, an' I know she'll be a hard worker and make you a good home."

"Thank you! I thank both of you!"

Mini Lou slipped her hand into Colt's and grinned at her parents.

"I think Miss Caitlin is going to need a new nanny." She threw back her head and laughed for sheer joy. "I just want you both to know, I appreciate you, I love you, and my dreams have all come true!"

Ezra headed over to the Listers and realized he'd never taken a good look at the house before. It looked a bit like a miniature castle. It was a Queen Anne style house with scalloped lap siding. The house was a light sage green with pristine white trim. A six sided turret jutted out on the left side with a door leading to the large front porch.

He walked up the steps and knocked on a door painted white with four lead paned windows across its top.

"Why hello there, Sheriff Walker! Come on in. We were just getting ready to head over to the Galways'." May smiled warmly as she stepped back to allow him entrance.

Ezra doffed his hat, and May took it, placing it on a high doweled shelf of the oak coat tree.

"Thank you, Miss Lister. I came by to escort you all to Mr. Galway's wake. I hope you will accompany me." Ezra couldn't help but compare the sweet atmosphere of this house to that of the McGraths'.

"Why, thank you, young man! We'd be delighted. We are excited to have the girls here. We know our lives will be bettered just by having them live with us, but more, we hope we can help them in some way."

"I believe you already have, Miss May." Ezra's eyes smiled into hers and she was pleased with his politeness and demeanor.

"Please, have a seat." She pointed to the parlor. "I'll get the girls and April, and we'll be on our way. We've made some food to take, and it will be nice to have a strong young man help us carry it."

May climbed up the stairs as if she were a young girl. Hurrying down the hall, she tapped on both girl's doors.

"One of you has a beau downstairs waiting to take us to the wake. I'll go get April and my shawl, and we'll be on our way. Which one of you is the sheriff's girl?"

"That would be me, and I'm Payton."

"Ah, so Paige is Mr. Brown's girl, am I correct?"

"Yes," Paige blushed. "You need to go downstairs, Payton. I'll get your wrap."

"Yes, girl, shoo! Don't keep that nice young man waiting!"

Payton gave May a hug. "We're going to love living here. You and Miss April are so sweet!" She gave May a peck on the cheek and ran with light steps down the stairs.

Paige grinned at May, who smiled back. "I'll get her shawl." She went into Payton's room and May went down to April's.

They were ready to leave, standing by the front door. Payton slipped her arm into the crook of Ezra's, but he turned to face the Listers.

"Before we leave, and since I heard from Doc that you ladies plan to adopt Paige and Payton, I'd like to ask both of you if I might have the privilege and permission from you to court Payton. It won't be right away, but I wish to marry her."

"Oh my!" April said, putting her hand over her heart. "That is so romantic. What can May or I say, except, of course. We hope the two of you will be happy together."

"I agree. We have heard such good things about you, sheriff. The fact that you are a Christian puts you in good stead with us. As long as the two of you keep the Lord Almighty in the center of your relationship… yes! I don't mean to preach, but I'm excited by this news, and I know I'm rambling!" May said. "Yes, I agree with April. You have our permission."

Payton had tears in her eyes. She and Ezra had talked at length about getting married, but she hadn't wanted him to say anything to her mother. She'd been too afraid, and with good reason.

"I—I don't know what to say. This day started out so horrible, and it's become one of the happiest days of my life, coming here to live and now this! Thank you, Miss April, Miss May!" Payton, overcome with joy, hugged both ladies, kissed her twin, and said, "Let's be on our way!"

Carriages and horses lined both sides of Main Street and some of the side streets as well. Darkness had fallen, but with the moon's brilliance and the stars twinkling brightly, there was no need for lamps. People streamed unerringly up the walk to Maisie Galway's house.

Still warmed from the day's sun, the evening air wrapped the visitors in a feeling of hushed quietness. Friends and neighbors as well as employees of the Galways filled the house and overflowed into the back yard. Tables had been set up, and lamps all around the courtyard had been lit lending a sweet ambience to the area.

Jared and Aidan entered the front door, and Aidan wondered where Maisie was.

She gave Jared a squeeze on his arm, and said, "I'll see you later." Heading for the kitchen, she thought for sure Maisie would be there.

"Hello, Liberty," she said, and gave her a hug. "Hello, Caitlin, where's Maisie?"

"She went up to change, and I haven't seen her since." She leaned closer to Aidan and whispered, "Did Jared tell you?"

"Yes, and I can't wait to see them together!" Aidan whispered back.

"She's feeling guilty about it." Caitlin said.

"Well, she shouldn't. He's going to help her through a really bad patch." Aidan replied.

"I'm so glad we all agree. It'd be horrible if one of us tried to make her stuff her feelings or deny them. I like the new doctor and can see why Doc wanted him here." Caitlin wiped her hands on her apron.

Maisie's cook, Inga, was thankful for the help Liberty and Caitlin had given her. People brought food into the kitchen, and now that the wake had truly started, they no longer tried to keep it warm. A huge dining table seemed to groan with all the weight of the food covering it. Salads were on the sideboard, and a buffet, under the end window held desserts. The buffet's drawers were pulled open for silverware. Stacks of plates rested on two end tables. A credenza, in the front entry, held pots of coffee and jugs of water and juice.

"I'm going up to see what's keeping Maisie," Aidan said.

She returned and Liberty and Caitlin looked at her questioningly.

"She's sound asleep. I mean, out cold!" Aidan exclaimed.

"Let her sleep for a bit," Liberty said. "Poor thing, she needs the rest. Caitlin, why don't you make an announcement that the food is ready, and just let people know Maisie needs a short nap."

Caitlin started to make the announcement, "Friends and relatives, I want to thank you for—"

Ernest Smith and Sandoval Peabody entered the front door. Caitlin stopped talking and waited until it was again quiet. "I want to thank you all for coming this evening. Thank you for the lavish amount of food, and our hope is that you will share anecdotes and reminisce about Gavin and what he meant to you." She took a deep breath and added, "My sister will be down shortly. She's sustained a severe shock today, and with expecting a baby and all, it's taken a lot out of her."

Ezra, Kirk, Jared, and Matthew eyed the newcomers, gauging their reaction. The two men seemed oblivious to the perusal and were greeted by some of the other miners.

Doc sat next to Deedee, but he, too, kept an eye on Ernest Smith and Sandoval Peabody.

Deedee turned to him and looked deeply into his eyes, the way Marie had told her to do. A rosy blush rose to her cheeks, but she couldn't turn away from that pure blue gaze. She now had no doubts as to Micah Addison's intentions.

"Do you mind?" he asked, and he took her hand in his.

"No, but I am a bit discombobulated. I never thought to fall in love. You have bowled me over, sir, and I don't quite know what to think of it all. Me...get married? I never thought it would ever happen!"

"I haven't asked you, yet, miss, but I will. What in the world have the men in Boston been thinking? It's amazing to me you've never been married."

"Marie told me about your Evangeline. She must have been a special woman."

"Yes, she was special. It was a difficult time when I lost her, but you won't be fighting a ghost. The past is past. I have good memories, but nothing that hinders me from starting over with you. I never thought to fall in love again, but there you were on that train platform, and I was a goner for sure." He smiled warmly, and tenderly squeezed her hand.

"I wanted to believe it, but I've never thought about getting married. I've honestly never been attracted to a man. I thought something was the matter with me, but I suppose God was just setting this up for the two of us. I have been so wrapped up in the Sandhursts' and serving them, I haven't had a thought for anything else. On my days off, I spent my time mainly in doing things with Marnie."

Her no nonsense way of talking pleased Doc. His gaze switched back to Ernest Smith and Sandy Peabody.

At Caitlin's announcement to the attendees of the wake, Dr. Oliver decided he needed to check on his patient. He saw Doc engrossed in conversation with Deedee and smiled inwardly. *Lots of love going around.* He went up the stairs unnoticed. Tapping on Maisie's door, he heard no answer, so he opened it gently. He trod silently to the bed, and looked down on Maisie as she slept. She looked enchanting, her coal black hair spread across the pillow, as she lay there breathing evenly. He noticed the bruised look under her eyes and realized how exhausted she must be. He felt a rush of protection and a longing to hold her and make all the bad things go away.

She stirred and opened her eyes. Her hazel eyes widened when she saw Oliver standing beside her bed. She held out her arms, and he sat down and drew her into his.

"Ah, Maisie," he whispered as she laid her head on his shoulder, nestling into his neck. "I don't know how this wonderful thing between us has happened, but there's no denying it. I don't want you feeling guilty over this. It's a beautiful thing, and frankly, I believe God directed my path to Santa Rosa just for this. He knew we needed each other."

"I am so confused, Oliver. I thought Gavin was healing up and going to be all right. Why did God let him die? If Christians were praying for him, why did he have to die? I keep hearing about how loving God is, but that doesn't seem very loving to me."

"That's because our view is from a human perspective. We don't see the eternal plan. I was angry when my Corine died. I needed my wife, and Marnie needed her mother. It took me some time to cling to the verses in Isaiah 55 that God's ways are higher than my ways, and His thoughts are higher than anything I could ever think. Your husband came to a saving knowledge of Jesus as his Savior. I saw the look of peace in his eyes. That is God's gracious plan for us. To be in relationship and worship God...to fellowship with Him...there is nothing higher. When we follow the plan, we are at peace with God and the realization comes that what He does is always right. Gavin is now at total peace and the joy he is experiencing, well, we can't even begin to comprehend it."

Maisie pulled back and looked into Oliver's eyes. "Do you really think so?"

"No, I don't think so, I *know* so!"

Tears started in her eyes, and she whispered, "I loved Gavin, I loved him deeply, but I have never known a romantic, emotional, can't-get-you-out-of-my-head kind of love. I can't help feeling guilty. It is overwhelming that my husband is lying dead downstairs, and I'm in love with his doctor!"

"Hush, Maisie. I know you loved Gavin. He was happy and content in your love. It was special and you had all those years of getting to know one another growing up. Believe me when I say Gavin would want you to be happy. You do know that, don't you? If you died, you wouldn't want Gavin to live all alone and be miserable, would you?"

"N-no, no I wouldn't."

"There, see, you know in your heart. It doesn't matter what other people think or say. What matters is that God knows your heart. He knows you were faithful to Gavin and loved him. I promise, it's going to be all right. We will wait until the mourning period is over, and then I hope you will marry me. I love you, Maisie. I don't know how this happened, but believe me, it's real, and I love you."

Maisie smiled at Oliver through her tears. "I love you, too, Oliver. And frankly, I don't want to wait six months. I'm going into my sixth month of pregnancy, and I'm going to need your help when I have this baby. If Gavin can't be, then I want you to be his father. I think two and a half months will be sufficient in this case."

CHAPTER XXV

The way of the wicked is as darkness:
they know not at what they stumble.

PROVERBS 4:19

OLIVER SLIPPED OUT AND INTO THE HALL while Maisie dressed. She opened the door and turned her back so he could do up the buttons. His fingers, usually nimble, seemed to fumble over the buttons. When he finished, he turned her and kissed her soundly on the mouth.

Flushed with passion, Maisie pointed to a set of back stairs.

"You can go down, over there. It leads to the kitchen. I love you, Oliver!" She kissed him quickly, and went back into her room to put up her hair. She pulled it back into a severe chignon, fastening it with a velvet diamond-studded snood. Smoothing down her dress, she examined her face in the mirror. She pinched her cheeks and nibbled her lips for a bit of color. "That will have to do," she said aloud to herself.

She held the railing as she descended the stairs. When people saw her the talk lessened until it stopped all together. She smiled at them halfway down the steps, and said, "Thank you all for coming. I don't know why we wait for someone to die before we have a huge gathering such as this. Gavin would have loved to see you here. For those of you who don't know, Gavin didn't die from the gunshot, he had a dicky heart that we didn't know about. Several days ago, he accepted Christ as his Savior, and I can tell you, he actually died laughing. We will all miss him, me most of all." Her voice wavered, but she swallowed and continued to talk. "I hope you will share some memory or story about Gavin this evening. May God bless each one of you for being here."

Maisie continued down the steps, and immediately there was a crowd of people around her. No one noticed Oliver slipping into the room from the kitchen, except Liberty, who smiled to herself.

Sandoval Peabody, elbowed his way through to stand beside Maisie. He took her hand, and startled she looked at him with a question in her eyes, as she pulled her hand away.

"It's all right, Miss Maisie," he said, his eyes looking warm on her face. "Everything will be all right. I'll take care of you."

"I'm not Miss Maisie to you, sir," she said coldly, staring at him, but trying to move away. She was not able to for the crush of people around her.

His eyes turned hard and opaque, as if he could block his thoughts from her irritated eyes.

Kirk, who'd been keeping an eagle eye on both Peabody and Smith heard Peabody's comment and Maisie's reply. He'd followed right behind Sandy Peabody as he pushed his way toward Maisie. Kirk moved in front of him and slipped his arm around Maisie, pulling her away from Sandy and drawing her close to his side. He turned to face the shooter.

"Is there a problem here?" he asked. Kirk was tall and towered over Sandy.

"No, no problem at all," Sandy said. "I was simply offering my condolences to Mrs. Galway, is all."

"Yes," Maisie said, "there is a problem. I barely know you Mr. Peabody, and to call me by my Christian name is disrespectful. I have family and protection, and I don't want nor need your help."

"So sorry, madam. It was not my intention to offend you. I offer you my most humble apologies."

Kirk saw an ugly glint in Sandoval Peabody's eyes. *So that's it,* he thought. *He thinks to become Maisie's husband and control the gem mine. Maisie comes with quite a dowry to whomever marries her.*

Kirk's smile, not reaching his eyes, was merely a stretching of the lips, as he looked at the man who shot Gavin. "You heard the woman, she doesn't need nor want your help. The jig's up, Peabody."

With a look at Kirk that was pure hatred, he spoke evenly to Maisie. "Good evening, madam, I reckon I'll be on my way." He left abruptly, putting on his hat before he went out the door.

A buzz started up as several people who'd heard the conversation began to chatter to each other.

Maisie let out a deep breath. She turned to Kirk. "He thinks to court me, doesn't he?"

"Yes, and I'm quite sure he shot Gavin," he whispered into her ear. "We simply need to prove it. Don't you worry about a thing, my dear sister-in-law. We'll set a trap for him."

Maisie nodded. She turned back to people who were offering their condolences. It wasn't long before Oliver came up to her with two plates of food.

"Come, Mrs. Galway," he said, his eyes shining with love for her. "As your doctor, I think you need to sit and have some refreshment."

"Thank you, Dr. Oliver. I find I am quite hungry, as I haven't eaten the entire day."

People parted and were glad for the new doctor who would fill a plate of delectables for his patient.

Maisie sat with Dr. Oliver on one side, and Aidan on her other. Jared was sitting next to Aidan. Kirk filled a plate and strolled over.

"I know this house is packed with people, but I would like to meet with you upstairs after we eat, Jared. Could you please ask Doc? I'll ask Ezra and Matthew. I found out a couple things tonight and we need to figure out a plan of action." He nodded toward Maisie. "It has to do with our shooter."

Jared nodded. "Of course. I'll wait until I see you head upstairs. I saw you talking to Peabody, but I'd like to know what he said."

Kirk nodded. "You will. Let me go tell Matthew and Ezra."

Jared spoke to Aidan. "I think we know for sure who the shooter is. We didn't know between Peabody and Smith. I'll be right back after I go talk to Doc."

He weaved his way across the room saying hello to the people in his path, until he reached Doc, who was holding Deedee's hand.

Jared grinned at the couple. "Evening, Miss Jennings. Nice to see you again. I just dropped by, Doc, to tell you Kirk would like us to meet him upstairs for a few minutes after he finishes eating."

"Certainly. I see Peabody left. Is he our man?"

"Sure looks like it, doesn't it?"

Jared strolled back to talk to Aidan.

"Of all the miners I know," she said, "I'd have guessed Jasper Clemmons was the shooter. He's been such a crab box for the past couple years, but he didn't used to be that way."

He was surprised by her comment.

"Did I tell you he was shot today?"

"No, you did not! Jared, you are positively useless when it comes to keeping me informed!" She punched him in the arm.

"He was shot talking to the men to tell them they could knock off early and go to the wake if they so wished. Jude bandaged him up and got him into town, but Dr. Oliver was busy here, so Doc took out the bullet."

They talked for a while longer, until Jared saw Kirk heading up the staircase with Doc right behind him.

"See you later, sweetheart," he said. He gave her shoulder a squeeze.

Matthew and Ezra had headed toward the kitchen, and Jared realized they would be going up the back stairs.

That's a good plan. Less noticeable. He followed them through the kitchen, but traversing the parlor, he overheard a man comment to another. "Those McCaully girls are all lookers, aren't they?"

Jared grinned to himself. *They sure are! Especially mine!*

Kirk was waiting for them and beckoned them to enter Maisie's sitting room. It was a beautiful room but quite feminine, done in pinks, pale green and white.

There was plenty of seating, two settees, three wingbacks, and a rocking chair all placed around a low-lying table in front of a fireplace that was ready to light.

"Have a chair," Kirk requested. "I need your scintillating minds to come up with some ideas. I know, without a doubt, Peabody is our shooter. He was trying to cosy up to Maisie. I believe he's thinking he can marry her and get control of the mine."

Doc nodded his head. "That seems plausible."

"Don't you think Dr. Oliver should be in on this conversation?" Matthew asked.

Ezra and Doc looked questioningly at Matthew.

"I didn't even think about that," Kirk said, "but he'd be next in line to get shot if any word got out, wouldn't he?" He looked at Matthew with respect in his eyes. "You always have the most observant perspective."

"Well, it makes sense, right?" Matthew looked at the other men.

"I didn't think about that either," Jared said. "I'll run down and get him." Jared got up quickly and closing the door behind him, ran lightly down the stairs.

Some people were still milling all around, but most were now sitting.

It took a couple minutes for Jared to find Oliver. He looked all through the house and finally saw him ensconced in a corner of the back porch on a swing with Maisie, deep in conversation.

"Maisie, would you mind lending me Dr. Oliver for a few minutes. I promise to bring him back to you." He winked at Maisie, who blushed.

"Of course," she replied.

"I'll be back shortly, sweetheart," Oliver whispered. He followed Jared, through the now quiet parlor, into the kitchen.

"What's wrong?" Oliver asked as Jared led him up the stairs.

"Some of us are having a meeting, and we'd like you to be there," Jared replied.

Wonder if they don't want me courting Maisie, Oliver thought. *Why else a meeting up here?* He walked into Maisie's sitting room and saw Matthew

Bannister, Ezra Walker, Kirk Bannister and Doc Addison. When he saw Doc, he breathed an inward sigh of relief.

"Thanks Jared, for getting him," Kirk said.

"I knew if I found Maisie, I'd find Dr. Oliver," Jared chuckled.

The men stood up when Oliver entered the room, and Doc went over to open two large windows. It was too warm.

"Dr. Oliver, please meet my brother, Matthew Bannister," Kirk said. "I know you've met Liberty but I don't believe you've met her husband, my brother. He suggested you should be in on this meeting."

Matthew held out his hand when Kirk introduced him. Oliver followed suit grasping Matthew's in a warm clasp.

Kirk gestured to the rocking chair, "Please sit, Dr. Oliver."

The men sat down when Oliver did. Once Oliver was seated he looked questioningly at the group, feeling relieved this wasn't a meeting to ban him from Maisie. He sat back to listen.

"As I said earlier, we now know for sure, Sandoval Peabody is our shooter." Kirk looked around at each of the men, his face grim.

"Tonight, the gloves came off. Sandy is hoping to marry Maisie and become a man of means. He took her hand and got quite nasty when she pulled her hand away and told him he was disrespectful toward her and that she didn't need any of his help." He grinned at the look on the men's faces. "She's a McCaully, after all's said and done. She does need you, Dr. Oliver...very much. She has a mind of her own, but she is also tenderhearted and vulnerable."

"Maisie made no mention of Mr. Peabody." The shock was evident on Dr. Oliver's face.

"I'm sure she didn't want you to worry. And what she said is true. Caitlin told us about what happened between the two of you today. I'd like to let you know, the family couldn't be happier."

Doc and Ezra looked on with questions they didn't ask.

"All of us feel the Lord directed your steps here for just this purpose. You'll be a comfort to Maisie, and yet, if this information gets out, you'll be a target for Sandy. I don't think he plans on anyone getting in his way."

The light dawned on Doc's face. *What a wonderful couple they will make!*

Ezra was stupefied. *Her husband's not been dead but a few hours, and she's in love with the new doctor? Ah well, who am I to judge. One look at Payton and I was in love.*

Oliver crossed his leg over his knee, looking quite pleased with the outcome of the meeting.

"I don't think he'd come into my office and shoot me, do you?"

"He walked into the gem store and shot Gavin. What do you think?" Kirk asked. "He's attempted murder three times. None of us know when he'll decide to shoot again. I see we have a bright moon although it's not full. He could gun for me on my way home. I certainly made him angry enough."

"I'm sorry, I didn't mean to be flippant," Oliver said. "How do you plan to trap him?"

"That's what this meeting is about. We need to toss some ideas into the hat and see what we come up with," Matthew said. He looked at Kirk and knew what he'd said was correct. *Peabody would take any opportunity to gun down my brother. The man is insane. We'll need to stay together going back to the ranch. We'll stay here until daylight.*

While the men were meeting upstairs, people sitting around were sharing stories about Gavin. Sometimes the comment was serious, about him helping someone out. At other times the conversation was humorous and chuckles or outright laughter ensued. Some people, who didn't plan to stay for the entire night, left and the crowd thinned to more manageable proportions. When the reminiscing started, everyone who'd been outside, came in to listen and share.

Paige sat next to her twin with May and April on either side of them. Paige spoke in a low tone. "I've looked all over, even outside, but I haven't seen hide nor hair of mother, have you?"

"No, I haven't either. Maybe she just wants us to worry about her." Payton replied.

"I thought of that, but you know as well as I do that she never misses a wake. She enjoys them."

Payton nodded. "Perhaps we should go check on her."

"I don't really want to, but you're right."

"We'll be right here, waiting for you to return." April said.

May smiled and asked, "Would you like me to go with you?"

"That's kind of you to ask, but no, it won't take long. We will be back in just a bit," Payton said.

The two girls found their wraps on the coat tree and left.

Maisie wondered what was taking so long upstairs. She felt stifled by the press of people. She went to the kitchen, but several women had everything under control. "I want to thank each of you for your help this evening," Maisie said. "You've made this a special time with all you've done, keeping the table full of food and making coffee. I really appreciate it."

A couple women nodded and said, "You're welcome, Mrs. Galway."

It was even hotter in the parlor where Gavin lay. Maisie crossed the room, and catching Liberty's eye, she fanned herself as she headed for the back door.

Liberty nodded in agreement but continued to sit and listen.

Maisie went out to the back porch to sit on the swing, surprised none of the guests were out there anymore. *I can't believe I've fallen in love. I've never felt like this in my entire life. Everyone seems to support me in this. I know Gavin would want me to be happy. I'm going to miss him.*

She heard the click of the side gate and wondered who would be coming into the back yard. Going around to check, she saw it was Mr. Peabody. It frightened her, and she turned to run, but with her unwieldy body, she stumbled on a rock, falling hard onto the ground.

He picked her up and said, "Hope you're all right, Maisie, my girl."

"I'm not your girl!" she spat.

"You will be…you will be."

She started to scream, "Hel—," but he clapped his hand over her mouth. He undid the neckerchief around his neck and stuffed it into her mouth as she struggled to get out of his arms. He dug his thumb into the side of her neck and she stopped struggling.

"Even pregnant, you're a featherweight," he chuckled as he picked her up carried her toward the gate.

"Did you hear that?" Ezra asked. He ran to the window and pushed it up high, leaning out to see. On the second floor, he could see over the fence. A man was carrying a woman who was kicking her legs in protest.

Ezra yelled, "Halt! In the name of the law, halt!"

Matthew didn't think twice, "Let's go!" He ran down the hall and clattered down the back steps which had an exit to the street. Kirk and Ezra were on his heels followed by Jared, Oliver, and Doc.

Matthew had tied Piggypie down the street to make room closer to the house for guests. He didn't wait to consult anyone, running for his horse, Kirk sprinted after him.

"Who does he have?" Kirk panted.

"Maisie," Matthew replied curtly.

The two brothers didn't wait to join up with Ezra or any of the others, knowing Ezra and Jared had walked to the Galways'. They set off at a gallop.

Ezra came running out of the house and yelled to Jared, "Grab a ride!" He picked a horse that looked like a runner, and climbed on, not waiting for Jared.

Doc and Oliver heard him, and took a horse from the long line of them at the hitching post.

Matthew glanced back and grinned, motioning to Kirk to look. Satisfied they had a posse, they rode at breakneck speed after Peabody's horse. Matthew knew he could take a shot, but if the bullet went through Peabody, it'd hit Maisie.

CHAPTER XXVI

The Lord shall send upon thee cursing, vexation, and rebuke,
in all that thou settest thine hand unto for to do,
until thou be destroyed, and until thou perish quickly;
because of the wickedness of thy doings,
whereby thou hast forsaken me.

DEUTERONOMY 28:20

THE MEN RACED AFTER SANDY PEABODY. He hadn't noticed them yet but must know they were in pursuit. He'd heard Ezra yell at him through the window.

Kirk had taken Caitlin's horse, but the stirrups were up higher than he was used to. He felt like a jockey, but Fire was going full tilt, and Kirk was enjoying the ride. Piggypie streaked down the road right on Fire's tail.

Sandy looked back, and seeing two men gaining one him, raked his horse with his spurs. The horse, viciously spurred, leapt forward, but Kirk and Matthew were still gaining on him.

"I don't need you, you piece of baggage," Sandy sneered, and he pushed Maisie off his horse. With his load lightened, his horse's gait picked up a bit.

Maisie hit the ground and rolled several times, lying still.

Without slowing, Matthew signaled to Kirk he was riding on. Kirk nodded. Both men knew Oliver and Doc would take care of Maisie.

Ezra kept riding, but Jared pulled up and leapt off his horse. He ran to his sister-in-law, kneeling in the road.

Matthew undid the catch on his gun and fired at Sandy. Kirk pulled his gun and did the same.

They saw Sandy turn in the saddle to fire on them, but his aim went wild. Kirk and Matthew fired at the exact same time, and Sandy went flying off his horse. The horse, relieved of its burden, kept running.

The brothers kept their guns drawn as they approached Sandy lying on the side of the road. Seeing no gun in his hand, Matthew holstered his, and knelt to feel Sandy's neck.

"He won't be shooting anyone, anymore." Matthew looked up at Kirk. "He had to be insane to think his plan would work."

"Greed does strange things to a man. What are we going to do with him?" Kirk looked around for Peabody's gun as he spoke.

"I think we'll just leave him here and let Ezra take care of it."

"Ah, here it is." Kirk lifted Sandy's gun. "He has to have a rifle someplace."

"Do you know where he lives?" Matthew asked.

"No, but I'm sure Lenny or Jasper would know."

Ezra reached them, and pulled up. "Looks like you took care of our problem," he said succinctly.

Matthew nodded. "Yes, and now we're going to let you take care of it. Let's head back and see if Maisie's all right."

They rode back down the road at a canter. The moon was bright on the main road, and they could see clearly. Each man was praying Maisie was all right. Being more than five months pregnant, she'd taken a hard fall from a racing horse.

Matthew, Kirk and Ezra pulled up and dismounting, searched the faces of those surrounding Maisie.

Doc and Oliver looked grave.

"How is she?" Kirk asked.

"We don't know. She's unconscious. Can't find any broken bones, but she took an awful blow. Her face is bruised, but we don't see any bleeding. She could be bleeding internally. Jared went back to get a wagon."

Matthew took off his hat and laid a hand on Maisie's head. The others, seeing what he was about, also removed their hats.

"Heavenly Father, how grateful we are for Your mighty provision for us. What an awesome God You are! You are able to do far more that we can even think. We thank You that Your lovingkindness far exceeds what our finite minds can conceive. Right now, we lift Maisie up to You. You know Your will for her. We know Your desire to have a personal relationship with her and to bless her. We agree together to ask You for the complete healing of Maisie. Father heal, in the name of Jesus, anything that might be amiss. We pray for safety and wholeness for the baby she carries. May she have a good delivery and Lord, we pray she doesn't feel she needs to go through the mourning period alone. May You grant her the good sense to marry Dr. Oliver, and not wait. Father, we await the answers You alone can give us. In the precious and peerless name of Jesus, we ask it, Amen."

Oliver looked at Matthew with real respect in his eyes, although Matthew didn't see it for the darkness.

"Thank you, Matthew Bannister. Lord willing, all will be well."

They stood around talking, waiting for the wagon.

Paige and Payton arrived home. On the porch, Paige giggled.

"I know it's home, but I don't know whether to knock or not,"

Payton stifled a laugh. "I think we should just open the door. If we can go in and leave before she sees us, then well and good. I just feel uneasy. I've never known her to miss a wake."

"I know," Paige replied, "me neither. On the other hand, she might not have gone for just this reason. To make us worry."

They decided just to peek in just to see if everything was all right.

Paige pushed the door open on well-oiled hinges and screamed when she saw her mother on the floor. Payton gasped and ran over to her, to feel her mother's neck as she'd seen Doc do numerous times on patients. As she touched Martha, she withdrew her hand as if she'd been stung. Her mother was cold.

"She's gone," Payton said.

"She must have had a heart attack!" Paige mumbled, her hand over her mouth in shock.

"Yes, that's what I'd say, too. We need to get Doc or Dr. Oliver over here. Let's go back to the Galways'. There is nothing to be done here anyway."

The twins, both feeling heavy-hearted at the way they had last seen their mother alive, walked the short distance to the Galways' house.

Both girls walked all through the rooms and couldn't find Doc or Dr. Oliver nor could they find Mrs. Galway. They went back to the parlor.

"Is your mother all right?" May asked, concern etching her eyes as she witnessed the twins' demeanor.

"N-no, Miss May. Sh-she's dead."

April and May both stood in astonishment. "Well, I suppose we should just move ahead of Doc Addison and go prepare her body. Will you want to have a wake for her?"

Payton looked at Paige who shook her head. "No, I don't think she had any real friends, and the people who'd come would come out of duty, not because of their fond memories of her or friendship, but because they are supporting us."

"I don't think you need to prepare her either," Payton added. "We'll just have her put in a box and have her buried in the church yard."

"We will let you two think about it, and you girls can ask your beaus what they think."

Relief flooded over the girls. "Doc will know what we should do. We'll listen to him," Paige said. "Where is he, anyway?"

"Why, I have no idea." April replied. "I saw you looking around. You didn't see him?"

"No, at least not on this floor. Perhaps he's up stairs." Paige's eyes searched the room again. "We went to the kitchen and even outside."

Across the room, Liberty sat with Aidan and Caitlin.

Liberty wondered what the men were doing upstairs, they'd been gone a long time. She spoke in an aside to Aidan and Caitlin.

"That's a long meeting they're having upstairs." She pulled out her grandfather's timepiece from the top of her blouse. "It's nearly two o'clock. Have you seen Maisie? I was wondering if perhaps she went up to lay down again."

"No, the last I saw her, she went out to the back patio."

Liberty nodded, "That's the last I saw her, too. I'm going out to see if she's still there."

"I'll go with you," Caitlin said.

They went out, but didn't see any sign of her. Liberty went around to the side of the house. "Does she usually leave the gate open?"

"No," Caitlin replied, following Liberty to the front yard. She ran lightly down the road and saw that Fire was gone.

"Something must have happened! Fire's gone, and as you know, no one can ride him except Kirk and me."

Liberty nodded, "Pookie is still here, but Piggypie is gone."

Just then, a man in front of the house yelled, "Where's my horse? Someone has stolen my horse!"

Liberty and Caitlin hurried to the front of the house.

"Did you say your horse is missing?" she asked the man.

"Yes! She's gone!"

"Sir, I'm not sure, but I think there's been some kind of an emergency. My horse is gone, and so is my brother-in-law's horse. If you'll come inside for a bit, I have a feeling your horse will be returned to you."

"A body could ask before they take!" he muttered.

"Yes, that's true. Perhaps there wasn't time. Please, come inside for a few minutes. I'm sure it will be straightened out."

Liberty, Caitlin, and the man started up the walk, as Jared and Ezra rode up.

"That's my horse!" the man exclaimed before he saw the sheriff's face. "Uh, oh, good morning, Sheriff Walker, out for a ride are you?"

"Sorry, Sam—this your horse?"

"Yes, I was fixing to go home, but my horse was gone. Gave me a shock and no mistake!"

"I'm sorry. She looked like a runner, and we had an emergency. A man tried to kidnap Mrs. Galway. She's in Doc's surgery right now. We don't know how bad off she is. Your horse rides like the wind. You sure she's not a descendant of Pegasus?"

Sam looked mollified at the sheriff's attempt to appease him. "She's not a mythological horse, but you're right, she's fast."

"Helped us catch our kidnapper. He was also the shooter."

"Who is it?"

"Was…who was it…it was Sandoval Peabody from out at the mine. He's dead."

"Well, I'll be jiggered! I saw him inside, not an hour past!"

Ezra slid off the horse, handing the reins to its owner. "Thank you for the use of your horse, Sam. If you'd like, I can pay for the loan of her. I didn't have time to run down the road to get mine."

"No, it's all right. Sure glad you got our shooter!"

"Well, actually it wasn't me. It was the Bannister brothers that got him. If you'll please excuse me, Doc wanted me to get the McGrath girls and Maisie's sisters over to the doctor's office."

"Of course! Sure hope Mrs. Galway will be all right. Such a sweet lady and so young to be a widow."

Ezra nodded and left the man standing as he strode up the walk.

"I'll go round up Aidan and the twins," Liberty said to Caitlin. "You go ahead to the doctor's office."

"Thanks, Liberty! You are, without a doubt, the sweetest and most thoughtful woman I have ever been around!" She gave Liberty a hug and ran out to the road.

Liberty went inside and saw Ezra, who was talking to the twins. She went over and whispered into Aidan's ear.

Aidan got up, and the two strolled to the kitchen as if there was nothing wrong, but as soon as they reached the back door, they hurried to the doctor's office.

The twins told Ezra about their mother.

He noticed that while telling him neither one had shed a tear. It made his heart ache for them.

"Doc wants you to go to his old office. Maisie was kidnapped and thrown from a racing horse. We don't yet know how bad off she is."

May and April sat listening.

"We will pray Mrs. Galway is all right," May said. "We'll probably head home in just a bit. Both of us have had an exciting day, and we're exhausted."

"Would you please explain to Maisie's cook about her? She's probably wondering where her mistress is." Ezra asked.

"Yes, we'll do that right now," April said.

"Thank you. You two are such a blessing to this community. I don't know what we'd do without you," Ezra said.

April and May beamed. "Thank you for your kind words, Sheriff. "They got up and made their way to the kitchen.

Ezra turned to the group of mourners and announced, "Mrs. Galway was kidnapped a short time ago by our shooter." He heard a few gasps but continued to talk. "He's now dead, but he threw Mrs. Galway from his racing horse, and she is unconscious. As you all know, she's expecting a baby. I need to get back to Doc's office, but I think the wake is over. I would ask those of you who are Christians to turn this wake into a prayer meeting for Mrs. Galway." He took Payton's arm and started for the door.

Jonah Whatcom called out, "Who was th' shooter?"

Ezra turned back realizing many of the men in the room were miners. "It was Sandy Peabody. He hoped to marry Maisie and get control of the mine and her money."

A stunned silence ensued as Ezra led Payton to the door with Paige following close behind.

Liberty and Aidan were a few minutes ahead of Ezra and the twins. Entering the office, they saw Maisie stretched out on the surgery table, and Caitlin standing, white-faced, next to Maisie. She held Maisie's hand and would stroke it tenderly with her fingers. Kirk and Matthew stood back against the sink area, out of the way.

Liberty and Aidan crept quietly into the room. Aidan went to stand by Cait as Liberty made her way to Matthew. He pulled her close to his side and stood with his arm around her.

Oliver was stroking Maisie's forehead, but it was evident that Maisie was still unconscious. A towel was rolled and had been placed under her neck in case there was any injury to the back of her head.

Doc had been listening to Maisie's stomach and breathed a sigh of relief. "I can hear the baby's heartbeat. It sounds regular and strong." He started feeling around Maisie's head to see if there might be any swelling. "I don't feel anything out of the ordinary. That was quite a tumble for anyone, let alone a pregnant woman, but she seems to be all right except for being unconscious."

"Peabody was riding hard and pushed her off his horse as if she were a sack of feed." Kirk's voice was full of disgust. "He was a wicked man with no consideration for anyone except himself."

Ezra, Payton, and Paige, entered the surgery. They stood in the doorway, overhearing the last comment.

"Which one of you shot him?" Ezra asked.

Kirk, with a surprised look on his face, said, "I don't know."

"We both did," Matthew replied, "within two inches of each other. Do you need help picking him up? "

"Sure, Bannister, I could use your help. I just hope we don't get a flurry of complaints about another shooter from people going home from the wake." He grinned. "I'm up for the rest of this night anyway. I'll take your wagon, if you don't mind, Doc, and go collect him."

"I'll go with you, too," Kirk offered.

"Thanks, I'll take you up on that." He turned toward Oliver. "I'll be praying for Maisie. I have a feeling she's going to be all right. Her body has had quite a shock. I'll keep praying until I hear about a good outcome."

"Thank you," Oliver reached out his hand to shake Ezra's. "I hope you're right!"

"See you later," Ezra said.

"Caitlin, would you please tie Queenie up in front of Maisie's house for me?" Kirk asked.

"Of course."

Kirk gave his wife a quick kiss and followed Ezra out the door.

Doc saw the twins hanging back by the doorway. "You two all right?"

"Yes, and no," Payton replied.

"What do you mean?" Doc questioned.

"Our mother evidently died of a heart attack," Paige said. "She wasn't at the wake, and Payton and I have never known her to miss one. We went to check on her, and she was lying about three feet from the front door."

Doc, his eyes full of shock, wondered to himself if she died right after he'd called to Ezra. *She was mad enough, that's certain! Poor woman. Ezra was right, I should have prayed for her when she ranted.* He said aloud, "I'm so sorry. You girls have had a difficult time of it, that's for sure. What do you plan to do?"

"We were thinking of just having her buried and not worry about having a wake, but we wanted to know what you think. Frankly we don't think people would come except those who'd come to support Payton and me."

"That may be true, but I think a wake for her is in order. You might be sorry later that you didn't have one. Your friends are happy to support the two of you. Even if it's small, it's a good idea. You'll want her in a casket though. By tomorrow she's going to…well, you know what I mean."

"Miss April and Miss May said they'd be happy to get her ready. We're just to let them know," Payton said.

Doc sighed. "Such a sad life. Ah, well, we all make our choices, don't we? We live by them and we die by them."

Maisie stirred and all eyes turned to her. She looked as if she were struggling to open her eyes. They slowly opened, and the first face she focused on was Oliver's.

"I saw Gavin," she whispered. She swallowed and spoke aloud. "I saw Gavin, and he was so happy. I've never seen him like that before. He was on his knees worshipping, but his face was all shiny and bright. He told me I needed to come back and live my life for Jesus." She started to sit up, but Oliver held her shoulder back.

"Easy does it, Maisie. You've had quite a tumble."

"I know, but I'm fine. I know I'm fine!" She went right into a prayer. "Lord Jesus, please take control of my life. I want to have a personal relationship with You. Please forgive my many sins. Right now, I can't think of any, except the sin of neglecting to follow You. I am sure I'll think of lots of things later, but Lord I will learn and be the best Christ-follower I can be. Amen."

EPILOGUE

Who shall separate us from the love of Christ?
shall tribulation, or distress, or persecution, or famine,
or nakedness, or peril, or sword?
Nay, in all these things we are more than
conquerors through him that loved us.

ROMANS 8:35

SEVERAL WEEKS HAD PASSED AND JASPER Clemmons was having a big party. He'd invited the workers from the mine and their spouses. He'd asked Dr. Oliver to bring his cook, and Deedee and Marnie. When he heard about Dr. Oliver's friend, Colton Danbury, he'd included him and Mini Lou in the invitation. Doc Addison was invited as well as Kirk and Caitlin. He'd requested them to bring their cook, Duney, to help out. Kirk's brother and his wife, Liberty were invited, and the couple planned a four day trip back up to Sonoma just to attend the event.

Jasper had heard all about April and May Lister and their sweetness, and he'd included them as well. Mrs. Galway, although she didn't know it, was going to be honored.

Jasper walked from room to room making sure all was in readiness. He opened the front door and checked the welcoming veranda. The flagstone was on a level to the house. Light spilled into the foyer as he opened the door. Pots, on either side of the door, full of bright colors, splashed their scent into the warm air. Jasper deadheaded a couple blooms. The veranda was spread out on either side of the front door. Low wicker tables with glass tops, wicker chairs and settees decorated with floral pillows looked like an inviting place for good conversation. He tweaked a pillow and looked up to see his first guests arriving.

He shaded his eyes and saw it was Dr. Oliver and his retinue.

Jasper strolled down the cobble walk to greet his first guests. His quick glance took in Oliver and a woman who must be Deedee in the front with two girls in the back of the carriage.

Hmm. I was hoping the doctor would bring his cook to help out in the kitchen. He stepped up to the wagon and said, "Welcome, welcome!" He held out his hand to Deedee. "You must be Deedee," he said. "Thank you for coming."

"I'm happy to meet you, sir. And thank you for the invitation."

"I'd lift you down, ma'am, but I still recovering from a wound."

"Yes, I have certainly heard about it, and I'm sorry you had to go through the pain."

He helped her down and turned to help one of the girls in the back. His eyes widened as he realized his mistake. This was a full grown woman, just a very petite full grown woman.

He stood, almost mesmerized by her gentian blue, almost violet eyes, fringed by smokey lashes.

"I'm Marie Fournier, Dr. Oliver's cook," she said and held out her hand.

"And I am Jasper Clemmons, at your service," he responded. "The name is apropos to your profession, is it not?" Jasper added, smiling.

Marie grinned back. "You know your French, sir?"

"I know enough to know Fournier means baker." He held out his hand to her, helping her to step down. The top of her head was level with his shoulder. He felt a sudden desire to protect her. He swallowed and turned to Marnie.

"And you must be Miss Marnie," he said.

"Yes, that's me," she responded, ignoring his hand, she jumped down, curtsied, and said, "Thank you for inviting me to your party, Mr. Clemmons. I adore parties."

He laughed in response. Turning to Oliver, he said, "You can unhitch your horse and take her to the stable. Barney will take her from there. And welcome!"

The party was in full swing. Conversation sparkled. Ezra and Jasper were cementing a friendship that would last their lifetimes.

Lenny was surprised at the change in Jasper, but he knew he shouldn't be. *God works miracles every day*, he thought. *We just need to be aware and not look on with blinded eyes.* He sat holding Paige's hand.

"When is the wedding?" Liberty asked.

Paige looked up at Lenny who answered. "We have planned a double wedding in six weeks time." He looked over at Maisie, "Unless you'd like to make that a triple. We'd be happy to have you join us."

Maisie blushed a rosy color filling her cheeks.

Oliver thought he'd like nothing better, but wanted Maisie to make the decision when she was ready.

Doc said, "What about us? Can we join you?"

Deedee punched him in the arm. "You're not making all the decisions for us, Micah!" She laughed at his expression and added, "What about it? Can we also get married along with you two?"

April and May clapped their hands in joy and Paige said, "Of course you can! Anyone else who'd like to be married in six weeks, please let us know!"

Mini Lou spoke up. "Colton and I'd love to be married along with you all. I suppose I'll be giving my notice to you, Miss Caitlin!"

There was laughter and happiness all around.

Colton laughed and said, "One look at Mini Lou and I was smitten." He looked at everyone in the room. "I'll be giving my notice to Kirk. I'm not a cowboy, but I promised my sister I'd find a wife who loved me for me and not for my money." His glance swept across the room, falling on Oliver. "I know you have looked at me with questions you were too polite to ask. So now I'll be straight up. I decided to break with everything back east and come out here to find a wife. I found Mini Lou and that was it. It took a bit to convince her, but she loves me for me. I am having a house built for us, as we will be permanent residents of Santa Rosa. I cannot thank all of you enough. Mr. and Mrs. Pindar, I am thankful for your permission to marry your daughter."

"You're welcome, son. We're right surprised, but glad Mini Lou will be happy married ta you."

Jasper found numerous reasons for going to the kitchen. That he was attracted to Marie was unmistakeable to anyone who saw him in the kitchen. Marie felt the impact of his attentions and seemed to blossom under it.

He went back to the parlor where most of his guests had gathered. He picked up a silver knife and tapped it against a crystal glass.

"At this time, we'd like Mrs. Maisie Galway to stand."

Maisie, with surprise spreading across her face, stood up, wondering what was going on.

"Mrs. Galway, we are pleased to present you the keys to the new county museum to be opened within the year. It will be called the Gavin Galway Museum and will show the history of the area as well as include a tour of the gem mine. We feel it's the least we can do to remember a great man, who cared much for others." Jasper handed her the keys amid the clapping and congratulations.

With tears in her eyes, she said, "I can't thank you enough. I know this has been a trying time for us, but what a wonderful way to remember Gavin and all he did for our community. He accepted Christ as his Savior before he died, and I will say, he died laughing. I have found a personal relationship with Jesus Christ because of the tragedy, and there is nothing better in life."

Jasper hugged Maisie, and said, "Amen to that!"

Books can be purchased on Amazon

Website: maryannkerr .com (signed copy)

Inklings Bookshop, Yakima, WA

Or by writing me at:

Mary Ann Kerr

10502 Estes Road

Yakima, WA

(I will sign the book, and charge a flat 8% tax, unless it's out of state.

Out of state copies are tax free. So each book is 16.20 with tax; the cost of shipping priority mail is $6.49) (Media rate is ($3.49 for one book)

My public e-mail is: hello @ maryann kerr .com (delete spaces) if you care to order a book.

You may message me on Facebook page: Mary Ann Kerr (comments are welcome!)

When readers take the time to write or e-mail me their experience reading my stories, I sometimes put their comments on my blog if they don't mind.

Liberty's Inheritance	(sale price. . . . .$14.99)
Liberty's Land	(sale price. . . . .$14.99)
Liberty's Heritage	(sale price. . . . .$14.99)
Caitlin's Fire	(sale price. . . . .$14.99)
Tory's Father	(full price. . . . . $14.99)
Eden's Portion	(full price. . . . . $14.99)
Cady's Legacy	(full price. . . . . $14.99)
Anne's Wedding Bargain	(full price. . . . . $14.99)
Raphaela's Reprieve	(full price. . . . . $14.99)
Elida's Unveiling	(full price. . . . . $14.99)

If you enjoy the story, please make a comment on Amazon!

Books by Peter A. Kerr (my author son)

Adam Meets Eve (nonfiction)—$10.00 + 5.65 shipping and handling

The Ark of Time (science fiction)—$12.00 + $5.65 shipping and handling

Book by Andrew Kerr (my author son and my cover and design guy)

Ants on Pirate Pond (children's black-and-white chapter book with darling illustrations)—12.95 + $5.65 shipping and handling